A Novel

Nicole French

Raglan Press

This is a work of fiction. Names, characters, organizations, places, events, and incidents are either products of the author's imagination or rendered fictitiously. Any resemblance to real people or events is purely coincidental.

Dedication

To the women in my family, the baddest chicks I know.

Prologue

She's everywhere.

My sheets. My skin. My clothes.

My feet hit the ground as I wind my way around the Charles River. Two-and-a-half miles up. Two-and-a-half down. I plod down the beaten dirt path that runs by the river's edge. I arrive when the water is still smooth, when the crew teams are just starting their morning workouts with early sun gleaming off their oars. I pad up to the Harvard campus and back down to MIT, running away from her face as much as I'm running toward it. Because she's everywhere to me. I can't escape her. And the fucked-up thing is, I don't want to.

It's springtime in Boston, almost summer. The trees and plants in the Commons are in full bloom, a mosaic of color, green, pink, yellow, white, smack in the middle of a city that's mostly brick and stone. This city of mine, a city I love, a city that's as gritty and ugly as it is beautiful. I thought for a long time Boston was my heart, more than any person ever could be. But that was until I met her.

My body clock is off. I used to wake up every day at 5:30, like a machine. Now I wake earlier and earlier to catch the sunrise, just to see that blend of red, yellow, and orange as it peeks over the jagged city skyline. Scarlet. Mustard. Burnt Sienna. Crimson. Goldenrod. Butterscotch. Too many to name, but all the same plethora of colors as her hair. It's like my body yearns for her as much as my soul does.

Every day I get up to see that color, no alarm clock, nothing. The same way I did to watch her sleep all those times. She never knew I did that, never knew I'd lay beside her for hours just watching her face, memorizing the maze of freckles across those high cheekbones, the fringe of long auburn lashes that tremble when she dreams, the bee-stung lips that blow kisses in her sleep. Waiting for the moment when she would wake, aching for when I could see her eyes, the color of ripe kiwis, gleaming with everything I'd ever hoped for.

Adoration.

Admiration.

Lust.

Love.

I never knew I was such a fool until now. Not until I managed to fuck up the best thing that ever happened to me.

Now my life is back to normal. As normal as it can be with half my heart, the heart I never knew I had, torn out of my chest. But still I wake, just as the sun seeps through the blinds. And I can only lay in my bed heartsick for so long. So I run to catch the dawn and then continue with my regimen, with the schedule that keeps me in line. Barely.

5:30 AM: Work out with my trainer.

7:30 AM: Breakfast and review the early Tokyo returns.

8:00 AM until 10:00 PM: Meetings. Lunch meetings. Staff meetings. Board meetings. Coffee meetings. Dinner meetings. All. Day. Long.

10:00 PM: Home. Watch the fire. Try not to think of her.

Fail fucking miserably.

The lab used to provide a distraction, but now all I can see is her, stretched out on my work bench, her heart-shaped mouth rounded into that "O" of total pleasure only we can make together. I found a strand of her hair on the table, bronze and bright against the dark wood, the color of the evening sun as it sinks below the horizon.

I tore the fuckin' place apart.

I'd give it all up for her. This house. This life. This business. This firm. And she doesn't know it yet, but that's exactly what I'm going to do. Whatever it takes. Whatever she needs.

But for now, I wait. Because if there's one thing I know about my girl—no, my *woman*. My perfect, beautiful, brilliant, stubborn, sometimes unreasonable, hot-tempered woman—it's that she can't be forced.

So I'll wait, forever if I have to. Because that's what you do when you belong to someone, body and soul.

And I do, Red. I do.

~

Chapter 1

I woke up with a smile on my face, something that hadn't happened in a while. The familiar room was airy and bright. Thin rays of sunshine streamed through the bay windows that looked over the Public Garden. It was hard to beat the Commons in full bloom: the vivid green of the grass and willow trees was set off by the brilliant patches of color. The soft pink of late cherry blossoms. The thrill of irises and rose bushes lining the paths. This morning in particular, everything seemed to gleam, like the old Technicolor movies that Bubbe, my grandmother, loved so much.

I grinned lazily into the warm, white sheets and inhaled. Nothing smelled better. That light scent of fabric softener combined with something infinitely less definable, a delectable blend of mint, almonds, and something else that only smelled like one thing. I inhaled again.

How could I have ever thought of leaving this behind? Of leaving him?

The door to the bedroom burst open with a clap, startling me from my reverie. I sat up, holding the soft cotton sheets to my bare chest as Brandon eased backward into the room, carrying a tray of food. My head cocked appreciatively. Even in just a pair of worn flannel pajama pants, the man seriously had an ass that wouldn't quit. It helped that he wasn't wearing anything on top. Nothing but a broad-shouldered expanse of tanned muscle that tapered to his trim waist.

He kicked the door closed, humming a song under his breath. When he turned around, I found myself on receiving end of his full six feet, four inches of glory. Wide pectoral muscles smattered with a dusting of dark blond hair. Biceps that would have threatened the sleeves of a T-shirt had he been wearing one. A well-defined six-pack that stacked evenly down to the V-shaped muscles at his hips. An athlete's body that was lean and toned, not bulky. Perfect.

But none of it compared to his smile, that thousand-watt smile that lit up every room he entered and sky-blue eyes that seemed to shine brightest when he was looking at me. He made the sun seem dim in comparison. Even on a day like this.

My heart fluttered. It literally fluttered. What had I ever done to deserve someone like this? How could I ever have thought of throwing him away like some piece of garbage? The thought made me feel sick, so I shook my head and smiled back at him.

"Hey, beautiful, you're awake," he said warmly as he walked the tray over to the bed.

I pushed myself up and stacked a few of the massive down pillows behind my back. "I just woke up. I slept like a rock."

"Good," Brandon said with another sweet grin that revealed the dimples in his ruddy cheeks.

He set the tray on the nightstand and then perched over me on his knees so he could give me a long, lingering kiss.

"And good morning," he murmured against my mouth.

I smiled again, my nose wrinkling against his. God, I loved this man. I couldn't love anyone or anything more.

"Good morning to you," I murmured against his soft, full lips. There was that scent again, in the flesh.

Brandon moved to sit beside me on the bed. He picked up the tray of food and set it between us, and I peered over all the accoutrements, not even trying to contain my obvious enthusiasm.

"And what do we have here?" I asked eagerly.

"I might have had Anna run over to Mike's for some pastries," he said, pointing to the plate stacked with flaky, buttery goodies. "But I cut up the melon and scrambled the eggs myself. You impressed, Red?"

I grinned. Brandon wasn't exactly a cook. I was honestly surprised he knew how to do anything more than boil water.

"You're going to make me fat," I said blissfully as I reached for a chocolate-filled *sfogliatelle*.

"Good," Brandon said with a satisfied grin. "More of you to love, right?"

I rolled my eyes at the corny line, but took a massive bite anyway. Who was I kidding? I loved it.

The merry expression on Brandon's face quickly turned almost predatory as he followed the movement of my mouth, zeroing in on my lips as my tongue slipped out to snag a stray bit of chocolate. I finished swallowing, but couldn't take another bite. With deft hands, Brandon plucked the pastry out of my fingers and set it back on the tray, which he then put back on the side table.

When he turned back to me, I was a statue. He reached up to tuck a few morning-tousled strands of my red hair behind my ear.

"Do you know..." he said as he leaned in slightly.

"Do I know what?" I asked as he ran his nose up and down my neck.

I dropped the sheet from my bare breasts, instead wrapping my arms instinctively around his warm shoulders. My nipples just grazed the hard planes of his chest, and I shivered at the feeling. I had no shame with this man. I was his, body and soul. He knew it, and I knew it. But even so, he also knew how much I loved to hear him say it out loud.

"You are..." he trailed off again as his mouth found the edge of my shoulder and he began to feather his lips along my collarbone.

"I'm what?" I murmured as I leaned back, opening myself up to his eyes and his kisses.

I laid fully back into the pillows, allowing him to cage me under his big, warm body. I moaned under the delectable feel of his stubble along my clavicle, the soft flick of his tongue at the base of my neck, the wet press of his mouth between my breasts. But he knew what I wanted to hear. It was another game we liked to play. And I wasn't going to be distracted.

"Brandon," I said even as I clutched at his thick mane of gold, wavy and curling at the base of his neck. "Brandon, I'm what?"

With a groan, he pulled away from his ministrations and pushed up onto his forearms to hover over me, blue eyes kind, clouded with desire, and glazed with sudden vulnerability.

"You're...everything to me, Skylar."

His voice was thick, and the Boston accent, which he normally kept well-hidden except for moments of extreme emotion, was obvious in the way the "r" all but disappeared as he spoke. I could hardly breathe, but my heart thumped loudly between us.

Brandon leaned down to touch his nose to mine.

"Everything," he whispered. "I love you."

And there it was: everything I wanted to hear, everything I wanted to know. My entire body relaxed at the sound of those three perfect words. Our lips met around them, echoing with our bodies what we'd just proclaimed. God, he tasted so incredibly good. Like butter pastry and sugar and something else that made me just want to...

Vomit?

My stomach lurched. A split-second later, I was shoving him off me with sudden violence. Away. I just needed him away.

"Skylar?"

His voice was frantic as I sprinted off the bed, too concerned with making it to his pristine en suite bathroom to bother with grabbing a sheet to cover myself. Fuck, the last thing I needed to do was lose my breakfast all over Brandon's spotless white sheets. My feet seemed to thunder across the plush carpet, and my body lurched again.

"Skylar?" Brandon called behind me, but his voice seemed far away.

"Skylar?"

~

I sat up suddenly in my childhood bed, a thin sheen of sweat across my forehead as an increasingly familiar wave of nausea rode through me. The motion sent a series of creaks through the old spring mattress that echoed through the darkened room. Shit. I'd woken up too fast again.

A small bag of Saltine crackers sat on the worn table next to my bed, along with a dish of ginger cookies. I grabbed for them, but it was no use. The nausea was already here, and once it was here, there was really nothing to do but ride it out and try my hardest not to lose whatever was left in my stomach. If there was anything to lose after a night of waking up like this every few hours.

Just the thought of it caused another wave to roll through my aching belly as I laid back down on my pillow and silently willed the feeling away. I was only maybe six or seven weeks pregnant, but I was already thoroughly sick of it—pun absolutely intended. Pregnancy glow, my ass. My breasts ached, I was exhausted *all* the time, and in the last week I had actually lost weight from vomiting so much.

In hushed tones from Chicago, Jane, my best friend and former roommate, had told me I probably had something called *hyperemesis gravidarum*, which was a fancy Latin term for sick as a motherfucking dog. This was according to her cousin, the anonymous OBGYN whom I was about ready to fly to Chicago to punch in the face. Seriously, that chick never had anything but bad news for me.

It was funny how your entire life could change in the space of a few hours. Only a week ago, I had watched those two lines turned pink, and two hours later, the first waves of nausea began. I had ridden the four hours from Boston to New York in the backseat of my grandmother's station wagon, my things jammed into the trunk and onto the roof, Dad and Bubbe up front bickering while I tried my hardest to focus on something, anything, that would keep me from throwing up all over Bubbe's macramé seat covers.

Too bad the only thing that worked was a pair of blue eyes I'd had to say goodbye to. Turns out grief beats hormones if I'm willing to substitute one pain for another.

We had arrived at my childhood home in Brooklyn late that night, and I had immediately dropped my duffel bags on the floor and sprinted for the downstairs toilet. I'd somehow managed to unload my things from the car, but since then, I'd been camped out in my small attic room, making periodic runs for the bathroom.

When my symptoms persisted, I had told my dad and Bubbe that I had come down with mono after working so hard to finish law school. Dad, ever in a perpetual daze these days after losing most of the use of his left hand (including his ability to play the piano) in a brawl with a debt collector and his thugs, had nodded and told me to rest up and feel better.

Bubbe was a bit harder to fool. A Ziploc bag of Saltines appeared on my nightstand the next morning, and ginger cookies the day after. To her credit, however, she was waiting for me to say something. That was Bubbe for you: someone who preferred to suspect more than actually know. She hadn't even asked what had happened with Brandon since seeing him at my graduation.

Brandon. God.

My stomach heaved again, this time with sadness. Why did I have to be one of those people who carried every emotion I had in my gut? Just like every other time I remembered the way I had willfully and forcefully shoved the love of my life *out* of said life, my eyes welled up and a giant sob choked my throat. I swallowed it back and shut my eyes again, willing the pain away.

It didn't work.

But Brandon was still in the middle of a very contentious divorce. And then he had made arrangements, behind my back and against my express wishes, to give money to my father's loan shark—the small-time gangster who was also responsible for Dad's smashed hand and a bevy of other injuries that had landed him in the hospital last March. I had known there was no way I could make it work with someone who would keep such secrets from me. I had had enough of those kinds of secrets because of my father, and I couldn't be with someone I couldn't trust.

But that didn't mean every cell in my body wasn't absolutely pining for Brandon Sterling.

The sob in my throat rose and fell as I gasped heavily. Go away, go away, go away. With silent mantras, I willed away the memory of his strong, knife-edged jaw line, his unruly, gold-streaked waves, his tender blue expression and bright smile. I willed away the look on his face when he'd said goodbye, the memory of our last fight, the feel of the last time he'd kissed me. I pushed it all down into the back of my heart where I couldn't feel it anymore.

Except, of course, in the pit of my stomach.

The air felt heavier than it should in mid-May. New York had been having a warm spat for the last week and it seemed like all the heat in the house had risen into my room overnight. A drop of sweat ran down my brow, slid down my cheek, and landed on the top of my collarbone, bare under the strap of my camisole. The feel of it caused my stomach to heave again, this time more violently.

"Just get it over with, Crosby," I muttered as I reached down for the plastic basin next to the bed.

Once I emptied my stomach, both of food and painful emotions, I'd feel better, at least for a little while. It would give me enough energy to go to my doctor's appointment, where I'd find out just exactly how far gone I was. Then I'd finally have to face just what was happening to my life.

~

"Well, you're definitely pregnant, hon. As if the constant yakking hadn't already clued you in on that one, am I right?"

The doctor's voice was annoyingly chipper. I sat sullenly atop the paper-covered vinyl table, shivering in a flimsy hospital gown. When she took a seat on her stool, Dr. Brown's face dropped at my glowering face. She was a lot more cheerful than I'd expected the staff at a free clinic to be, but I was also her first patient of the day.

"I take it that's not good news," she said more sedately.

"Not really," I said, keeping my hands clasped on my lap and willing both the nausea and the welling tears to subside.

Neither obeyed. It was like pregnancy caused everything to come out of me, emotionally and otherwise. I had literally no power to censor anymore. Whereas I had always had a hard time keeping emotions off my glass face, now they seemed to run rampant through every other part of me as well.

I closed my eyes against the tidal wave of grief. I was tired. So, so tired.

"Oh, dear," Dr. Brown said, and immediately scooted over and grasped my clenched fists. "I'm sorry."

She had the good sense to wait a moment while I calmed down. I had to give her credit for her bedside manner. I probably wasn't the only one who walked through her doors with an unexpected pregnancy.

"It's not that..." I trailed off, choking up more. I didn't have to say anything; I knew that. Still, I felt the need to justify my confusion to this woman. "I...the father, he's just not around..."

"Of course, of course," soothed the doctor.

She gave me another squeeze on the hand before scooting back to the small sink to get me a tissue. I took it gratefully and dabbed at my eyes until finally the tears subsided. With a small sniff, I looked to her.

"Thanks," I said. "I'm...well, you can see I'm a mess right now. And I'm supposed to be studying for the bar exam, and I have to start my new job in two months. And the guy, he's...gone. There's...no one else."

It wasn't completely true, but I couldn't ask my seventy-six-year-old grandmother and my father, a newly recovering addict with a maimed hand, to help me bring up an infant while I left to work the eighty-hour weeks of a new associate. They had enough to deal with just getting their shit together. Theirs was no world in which to bring a new baby, and my life certainly couldn't handle it.

It was a thought that just about killed me. It was easier to push away the image of what that baby might look like, but only because I didn't know what it would look like. I hadn't even permitted myself to think about whether it would be a boy or a girl, whether he would be blond or if she would have my red hair. Whether he would have his father's bright blue eyes, or whether she might have my slanted green. Would the baby be ruddy or fair? Tall or dainty?

Because thoughts like that inevitably led to imagining the life that baby might have had, one where Brandon would hold it close, the tiny body so small that he could cradle its head in the center of his broad palm. He would coo, shelter it with his big shoulders, shelter us both...

I choked down a sob and pressed my face into my hands.

"You really don't need to justify your emotions, honey," the doctor said, offering a kind hand on my shoulder while I got myself under control. "Not to me or anyone. Now, have you decided what you want to do?"

I hiccupped back the remaining sobs, somehow managing to keep my emotions in check. The tears were still threatening to fall, but I looked away from the doctor's kind face and focused on the gray steel trellis from the construction outside the office. I needed to remember where I was. Not in a kind, loving relationship with a man I desperately loved, but a single, jobless, daughter of a disabled garbage collector, the previous mistress of a man who couldn't really be mine. More than one future depended on my choice here today. I needed to take care of the people who were already in the world first.

"I have," I whispered. My voice sounded weak and insubstantial. "I want to...but I can't have this baby right now."

Dr. Brown waited a moment before nodding.

"Are you sure about that?" she asked gently.

Was I? Blue eyes—or were they green?—bloomed inside my mind. I shook them away.

Unable to look at the doctor directly, I just clutched at the edge of my hospital gown and nodded shakily. "Yes. I think so."

Smoothing a professional yet kind expression over her plain features, the doctor nodded and stood up. "All right. Let's talk about all of your options. Then you can decide."

I nodded again. "Okay," I whispered. "Okay."

~

When I returned to the house, a reminder card was in my purse for my appointment on Thursday. The doctor and I had gone over all my possibilities, and she suggested I wait until our appointment on Thursday to make my final decision.

The thought of it hurt my chest. Everything hurt about this situation. There was literally nothing good about it. If you had asked me two months ago what I would have done in the event of an accidental pregnancy with Brandon, I would have been terrified, but I probably would have wanted to keep it. Those were the days with Brandon that seemed so easy, when our rhythm, even one that involved fighting and fucking, always involved making up again. They were the days where even our fights had a rhythm to them, complemented by the ease of the rest of the time we spent together.

But that was before my family's life exploded with my father's latest gambling addiction.

That was before Brandon got wrapped up with the mobster who had nearly killed my dad for his debts.

That was before he lied to me about it.

That was before I knew he had a wife.

That was before he had all but called me a whore just for wanting out of a shitty situation.

How could I possibly bring a baby into this mess? What kind of care could I or anyone else be expected to give it? What kind of care would it get from its parents, two people who had functionally been raised by people other than their parents, two people who would both be working eighty-hour-weeks, two people who didn't even speak to one another anymore?

What kind of life would that be?

I was met by the blare of the TV and Bubbe's sharp voice chattering on the phone in the kitchen. The old brown Victorian house seemed to sag a little under the hotter-than-usual May weather, and the sun shining through the front window was producing a greenhouse effect indoors that made the smell of dried potpourri and stale coffee stronger than usual. My stomach lurched again, but there was nothing to lose. I held onto the door, waited for the feeling to subside, then entered.

I dropped my keys on the small entry table with a loud clink.

"It's at three o'clock, Erica," Bubbe instructed as she turned from the kitchen table to glance at me. "Yes, in the temple basement. It's Rachel's turn to bring the knishes, so you might want to bring something else, if you know what I mean."

My grandmother, ever the imposing presence in her five-feet of glory, waved a hand out to catch my attention as I was walking toward the stairs.

"Hold on, Rachel," she said before putting her palm over the telephone receiver. "What did the doctor say, *bubbela?*" she asked me. "Did you tell her how sick you've been? Did she test you for cancer?"

I rolled my eyes and braced myself against the doorway as another wave of nausea rolled through me. Like the last, this one thankfully just kept going.

"Bubbe, I told you, it's just mono. She did some bloodwork to be sure, and I have to go back on Thursday for the results."

I hated lying to my grandmother, who could read my transparent face better than most, but I had to hope that the misery I felt superseded any other tells.

Bubbe squinted for a moment, the movement causing her stiff dome of hair to move slightly, all at once. She looked me up and down, as if trying to determine the credibility of my story. But that was the thing about my grandmother. She wasn't buying what I was selling, but she was willing to wait until I was ready to tell her the truth. Or not.

"All right," she said with a short nod, then turned back to her friend on the phone.

I pushed off the doorframe and wandered into the living room to sit next to my dad on the couch. Even though I needed to be studying for the bar, I wasn't going to be able to do that until I was sure I wouldn't vomit all over the test materials. And I wouldn't be able to take anything for the nausea until I had decided whether or not to take the other pill that would bring it all to a halt.

Dad's eyes were trained completely on the TV while he held the remote with his right hand. His left hand, the one that had been crushed by a couple of thugs looking for him to pay a bad debt, still bore the dark, ugly scars from his most recent surgery to repair the extensive damage to the nerves. It was wrapped with a soft splint while it healed.

He had been at home on disability for the last two months and likely had at least three or more until he would be clear to go back to work at the sanitation department. It was pretty hard to lift garbage cans when you didn't have use of one of your hands.

His injury also prevented him from pursuing his main love: playing piano with his jazz quartet. As far as I could tell, he spent the majority of his time sitting right where he was in his favorite spot on the old plaid couch, watching the morning news, sports, and then flipping to old reruns of classic TV shows in the afternoons.

Right now, he was watching *The Today Show*. His piano, the gorgeous Mason and Hamlin upright that was usually covered with sheet music and Dad's scratched-out compositions, stood against the wall behind us, gathering dust.

"Hey, kiddo," my dad said distantly. "Feeling better today?"

Fantastic. Just trying to decide which painful, life-altering path to take.

"A little," I said. "Did you do your physical therapy this morning?"

"What? Oh, yeah, sure I did."

Dad's eyes didn't move once from the TV, where some pop star was gyrating her way across an outdoor stage. I glanced over at the small shelf where Bubbe kept the daily mail. The rubber exercise ball that Dad was supposed to use to strengthen his muscles and break down scar tissue was also gathering dust. The sheet of exercises his physical therapist had given him had been used as a coaster many times over, and currently had three different coffee mugs clustered over it.

I looked back at my dad, but before I could say anything, another wave of nausea hit me, and this one wasn't going away.

"I'll be back," I choked out before sprinting out of the room and down to the hallway bathroom.

Dad didn't move an inch.

As soon as my knees hit the cold black and white tiles of the bathroom floor, the sweat started to build on my forehead. The nausea didn't fade until I had heaved for about a minute, losing the last remnants of the ginger cookies. I laid my cheek on the fuzzy pink seat cover on the toilet and sighed. The room smelled strongly of Lysol and the scented candle Bubbe kept on the top of the toilet bowl.

I took a deep breath. Then another. I wasn't going to vomit anymore, but the nausea wasn't subsiding completely. There was only one thing left to do, and I really didn't want to do it because I knew I'd still feel shitty, even if in a different way, by the end.

"Fuck it," I muttered to myself as the nausea rose again.

I closed my eyes and let my mind wander where it really wanted to go: back to that bright, warm room that smelled like almonds and sunshine, where a pair of strong arms held me tightly and blue eyes gazed into the depths of my crushed soul. Where my heart (and stomach) felt light again.

It was just for a minute, I told myself even as I fell deeper into my daydream. But that was the problem. It was never just a minute with Brandon Sterling, even in my dreams.

~

Chapter 2

The pills were small and white. On Thursday morning at eleven, Dr. Brown gave me the mifepristone, misoprostol, and a prescription for both Zofran, an anti-nausea med, and Percocet, for the pain that would probably start later that day. The first pill was inserted, along with an IUD, by the doctor while I lay on the paper-covered bench, my bare legs in stirrups under the fluorescent lights. I stared up at the ceiling and counted the beige tiles to keep myself from crying.

It didn't work.

On the way home, I stopped at a Duane Reade and picked up an industrial-sized carton of maxi pads, per Dr. Brown's advice. It was a gorgeous spring day: New York in the full green of late spring and early summer. Birds chirped from all the trees planted on my sidewalk, drowning the everyday drone of cars on the busy streets. The air was balmy enough that most people walking around wore shorts. White, puffy clouds punctuated the sunshine, and every so often, a stray butterfly would wisp through the air.

Everything about it made me feel sick.

Still nauseous from the craze of hormones surging through me, I stumbled into my grandmother's house, ignoring Bubbe's questions about how the doctor's appointment had gone and whether they had given me something for the nausea. I pulled myself up the stairs, and lay in bed, waiting for the hours to tick by while cramps slowly built in my belly.

That afternoon, while Bubbe was out with her mah-jongg group and Dad had gone down to the club to meet with his band, I inserted the second pill. An hour later, the bleeding started. Contractions came and went, and I stumbled back and forth between the bathroom and my room throughout the day, hazy from the Percocet, clutching my belly every time the muscles pulled together.

Twelve hours later, it was done.

~

"How are you feeling?"

I stretched out on my bed, holding my cell phone to my ear while I stared at the ceiling. I watched as a lazy cobweb twisted limply in the dank, airless space.

"Fine," I said. My voice was groggy, like I hadn't used it in several days.

"Maybe I should rephrase," Jane said. "*What* are you feeling?"

Wrapped in an old terrycloth robe that I'd had since high school, I shrugged, even though she couldn't see me. It wasn't a question I wanted to answer, because thinking about what I had done just made me hurt in a completely different way that the Percocet couldn't cure.

"Nothing, really. I just feel...numb. And really tired."

"Is the cramping better now?"

I turned so I was curled on my side. The clock on my bedside table now read ten a.m. Jane, knowing what was going on, had stayed up with me through the day and into the night, picking up every time I needed to cry, needed to yell, needed to whimper, or just needed to be silent with someone else there.

"Yeah, it's pretty much done now," I mumbled. "I...I could tell when it happened."

Jane was silent. We both knew what I meant. She had been calling every hour since I'd gotten home from the clinic, worried that I didn't have the support system recommended for going through the procedure by myself. At first, I'd fought it, but no one ever tells you that an abortion is going to be painful enough that you'll want to have someone there to help. No one tells you how much it might hurt, inside and out.

"Does your grandmother know?" she asked again.

I sighed. "I don't know. Maybe."

That was the truth. I had tried to hide as much of the evidence as I could, and I had told Bubbe and my dad that the mono was acting up again. But the ginger cookies stopped appearing next to my bed, and Bubbe had been giving me awfully sad looks when she came upstairs to check on me.

"What about...you know who? Are you going to let him know what happened?"

I rolled my face into my pillow. There was that ache again, not in my belly, but in my heart. It wasn't the first time she'd brought up his name in the last twelve hours without actually saying it. At one point, when the pain was at its worst, I had cried into the phone that this was all his fault, that I missed him, that he should be here, but I'd expressly forbidden Jane to contact him at all. I didn't want him to know about this, ever.

"It's probably for the best," Jane said when I didn't respond. "You don't need any more stress."

"Yeah."

It was all relative. Just a different kind of stress.

"Did you see the *Forbes* profile I sent?"

I groaned. "Jane! I'm trying *not* to think about Brandon!"

I had, in fact, seen the magazine cover while I was waiting in line at the pharmacy. A full-page spread of Brandon's patented, thousand-watt smile had been kind of hard to miss. Luckily, I had been much too sick to do anything more than glare at it with equal parts longing and hatred. Extreme nausea will do that to you.

"I'm sorry, I'm sorry," Jane said. "I just wondered if you had read the article. He sort of mentions you."

I flipped over onto my side. "What?"

"I'm sending it again."

With energy I hadn't felt in several days, I swiped my laptop off the ground and flipped it open on the mattress. I pulled up my email and opened the link that Jane had sent.

It was a puff piece, a typical rags-to-riches story that highlighted Brandon's many accomplishments in the financial and legal world. Most of the Q&A-style article consisted of fairly generic questions about his secrets to success, daily habits, things like that.

"Go to the fifth question," Jane directed me.

I scanned further down the page and started reading.

Forbes:	Biggest regret?
[There is a long silence. Sterling rubs a hand over his face.]	
Sterling:	Can I plead the fifth?
Forbes:	Not if you want the interview to end.
[Sterling laughs].	
Sterling:	All right, all right. Well, to be honest, my biggest regret happened just recently. I lost someone special because I kept some really

important things to myself that I shouldn't have. It's easy in this business--either of my businesses, really--to get caught up in secrets. We do it all the time, whether it's maintaining attorney-client confidentiality or protecting our clients' investments. But that instinct, one that's served me really well in my professional life, cost me everything. You can't live your personal life like you run your businesses. I learned that the hard way.

[Sterling sighs and rubs his face again. He looks out the window of his office for several minutes.]

Sterling: There isn't a second I don't miss her.

I continued scanning the rest of the article while Jane waited patiently on the end of the line for me to finish. I closed my laptop, then sank back into my pillows and sighed.

"He could have been talking about his wife," I said finally, although the thought pained me.

"Sky."

"Well, he could have. The magazine certainly thought he was, if you read the rest of the profile."

"Skylar," Jane repeated sharply. "You know that wasn't about Ms. Priss. The man just announced to the entire world that he is pining for you."

I pressed the heel of one hand into my forehead, trying to drive that bronzed, razor-edged face out of my mind again. Blue eyes, like pools of water that seemed to seep into every part of me. He was like a bad penny, always turning up. A gorgeous, charismatic, heart-melting penny.

"I can't, Jane," I said finally. "I need to move on. He's not good for me or my family."

Jane sighed through the speaker. "Fine, fine. Have you signed the papers for the DA's office?"

I blinked up at the ceiling and groaned. "I haven't."

"Seriously? Why?"

I rolled over onto my side and stared at the clock radio. Under that was the sheaf of new hire paperwork that I was supposed to bring to the D.A.'s office as soon as I could. The clock numbers were red and seemed to glare at me.

"Because I'm not sure it's the right choice," I replied lamely. Because it's in the wrong city.

"Why's that?"

Jane's voice was sharp, reflecting the frustration I rightfully deserved for shirking on yet another job opportunity so late in the game. We had just graduated from the best law school in the world less than two weeks ago. Most of the people we knew had secured jobs long before. While I'd had several offers, there was always part of me that kept holding out for something more. What that something was...I didn't know.

"Well...I was looking over my contract again," I said while I fingered the edges of my faded floral sheet. "It's not exactly going to pay off my dad's debts very quickly. Or, you know, at all. The job at Kiefer Knightly pays about three times as much, plus a signing bonus."

"Yeah, but you said no to that already, didn't you?"

I squirmed uneasily. I had said no to a job at a big firm offered to me by my mentor, but I had done it in a rage. I had done it after discovering that not only had the love of my life been lying to me about being married, but he had also decided to go behind my back to deal with a local mobster after he had promised me he would stay out of it. Though it made our lives temporarily easier, Brandon's actions had the unintended effect of making my family even more of a target now that Victor Messina knew we had access to money.

So I had fled Boston, unable to stand my ground against a man I could never seem to say no to. I had taken a job five blocks from my family's house, telling myself I was doing it to protect my dad and keep him safe, even though the best thing I could do for him would be to make more money and try to convince my family that New York was not a safe place for them anymore. I'd taken the job in cowardice.

"I think I made a mistake," was all I said to Jane.

"Sellout."

Jane was studying for the bar in Chicago with the assumption that she would be working at the State's Attorney's office. It was a great gig, but public service didn't pay much in Chicago either. She had every right to her indignation.

"Have you talked about it with Zola?" she asked, changing the subject. "He was yummy. And the way he lobbied for you to work there, methinks he likes more than your resume."

I sighed again and closed my eyes. I tried to imagine the handsome face of the young attorney who had recruited me for the job at the Brooklyn DA's office, but still all I could see was a pair of blue eyes and an unruly mop of blond. I squeezed my eyelids shut and focused harder.

"Maybe I need to make a trip up there. Help you break the bad news to Mr. Tall, Dark, and Fuck-Me-Silly, huh?"

I rolled my eyes despite the fact that Jane couldn't see me.

"Maybe you should," I said lamely. "Even though you literally just left." My comeback game was incredibly weak.

"You never know..." she teased, but I could barely hear her anymore.

My eyelids drooped. I was exhausted, maybe more than I had ever been in my life. As if on call, Brandon's kind, concerned face appeared. I was too tired to fight it anyway. Too tired to fight that warm feeling I had when I imagined I hadn't pushed him away, when I imagined that I could still fall asleep in his arms.

"Janey?" I yawned into the phone.

"Yeah, babe?"

"Thanks for calling. I love you."

"I love you too, Sky. I'm glad you're okay."

"Thanks."

I yawned again. The nausea—all of it—was actually gone. I was looking forward to a real night of sleep. And, if I was being honest, the dreams of a certain set of big shoulders that usually came with them.

"Go to sleep, Sky. You sound like you need it. I'll talk to you tomorrow."

I was already snoring.

~

I slept for another day, thanks to the last of the Percocet. I woke up the next morning to an unfamiliar woman's voice, high-pitched and muffled, filtering from the floor below my room. I pulled my head out from under my covers after a distinct squeal echoed up the stairs, followed by flirty protestations in one of the thickest Brooklyn accents I'd ever heard. That was saying something, considering I was a local.

"Danny! You are so bad! Eeee, that pinches!"

My dad's voice, normally mild and gentle, crooned in response. "You know you like it, Katie."

I slapped my blankets down and sat up, suddenly very, very awake. Katie?

Two months ago, Bubbe had informed me that my dad, a man who dated about as frequently as he visited country clubs (which was to say, pretty much never), was seeing a local girl name Katie Corleone. Less than a month later, he was back at the track, getting himself into the mess that put him in the hospital. I didn't have any hard proof that Katie Corleone was the one who got him back in the scene, and just because Corleone was an Italian name didn't mean she was wrapped up with the mob. But at the same time, the woman he'd supposedly been dating had basically vanished while he'd been recovering from his injuries.

Who the hell was this Katie, and why was my dad pinching *any* part of her just a few steps from where I was sleeping?

Another loud squeal and a bunch of giggles erupted from under my door. I huffed, tossed my covers aside, and made a big deal of stomping around my attic room until the squeals stopped. I threw on my robe and walked down the rickety stairs to the hallway, where the door to Dad's room was shut and more indeterminate noises were coming out.

With a glare at the door, I continued to the bathroom, and then downstairs to where Bubbe was busy wiping the kitchen counters. She was color-coordinated as always in a light blue summer shirt and matching slacks, her hair set in its helmet-like, tight gray curls. I collapsed in one of the dining chairs with a loud huff. Bubbe turned around with a jerk.

"Oh, Skylar!" she cried with mock placement of her hand to her heart. "You scared me, sneaking in here like that."

I leaned onto the table and buried my head in my hands. My body didn't ache so much anymore, but I still felt groggy from the Percocet.

"Is there any hot water?" I asked through my fingers as my hair fell over my face.

"I can make some. What do you want, tea?"

21

Another loud peal of laughter echoed down the stairs. I groaned and nodded as Bubbe bustled about the kitchen, uncharacteristically accommodating.

"Are you feeling better, *bubbela*? After your...mono?"

I peered suspiciously at my grandmother, who stood with her back to me as she put some hot water on to boil. I'd have bet ten thousand dollars she knew I didn't have mono, but Bubbe was the queen of "don't ask, don't tell." It was the game she had also played with my sex life. And, apparently, her son's.

"Who's the broad up in Dad's room?" I changed the subject, leaning back in my chair and pushing my hair out of my face. I needed a shower, but I really didn't want to go upstairs and listen to my dad getting busy.

"Broad? Oh, you mean Katie." Bubbe turned around to grab a mug from the cabinet. She glanced at me and frowned. "Skylar, why do you have to sit like that? No woman should be sitting around with her legs spread like a man on the subway."

I couldn't help but smile as I continued to slouch further in my chair, but nevertheless crossed one ankle over the other. If Bubbe was back to correcting things like my posture, I knew she wasn't so worried about me anymore.

"Katie. Yeah, I heard her *name*," I said. I traced a finger over the orange hexagonal patterns of the tablecloth, something Bubbe had probably owned since the late sixties. "I was asking who she is. And why she's making inappropriate noises under my bedroom door."

"Oh, Skylar, she's doing nothing of the sort!" Bubbe protested a little too loudly. She pulled the milk from the refrigerator with a flourish, then turned to face me, one small hand perched on her hip. "Katie Corleone is...your father's...friend. She's been coming around a bit for the last several months. I told you about her; I know I did."

"Maybe," I mumbled petulantly, but I remembered just fine. "You think that's the best idea when he's still in therapy? Addicts are supposed to be on the wagon for a year before they get into new relationships."

Bubbe gave a shrug that just about broke my heart. "She seems to make him happy."

"Does she."

"She does. And God knows my Danny could use some of that these days."

I watched Bubbe as she continued fixing my tea, but she didn't say anything more. Before I could reply, two pairs of footsteps came tromping down the stairs. My dad and a woman I assumed was Katie Corleone stepped into the kitchen. Bubbe waved a distant hand in their direction, but stayed focused on my tea.

I, on the other hand, gawked.

Katie Corleone didn't look like a person; she looked like a cartoon character. She was tall, a lot taller than my dad, mostly due to her five-inch, red platform heels and the beehive of black hair piled on her head. Her bright pink lipstick shone against overly tanned skin. She couldn't have been more than thirty, but her skin made her look older. She wore massive green hoops from her ears, extremely tight boot-cut jeans, and a shirt that had rhinestones glued in the shape of a cat's face across the front.

"Well, hello there!" she exclaimed as she pranced into the kitchen, heels tapping loudly against the linoleum floor. She held out a hand with long, fake nails. "You must be Skylar, honey. I'm Katie. Your dad has told me so much about you, and ain't you just as gorgeous as he said!"

Jesus. The woman sounded like Fran Drescher. Stunned, I allowed her to shake my hand vigorously. When I got it back, my fingers smelled faintly of artificial strawberries.

"Heya, Pips!" Dad said from behind Katie.

Both of his hands, good and bad, rested familiarly on her hips. He had to peek around her shoulder since he couldn't see over the mass of hair. He was still in his bathrobe—I still hadn't seen him wear anything else in the house since I'd come home—but he had a goofy smile on his face that could only be caused by one thing.

Gross.

"Listen, baby, I gotta scoot," Katie said, turning to my dad. "But I'll see you tonight at Nick's, and then we can have some real fun, all right, handsome?"

With wide eyes, I looked to Bubbe, who was watching Katie and my dad with a hand over her mouth to cover a scowl. When Katie finished kissing her slurpy goodbyes, Bubbe turned abruptly to grab my tea, which she set in front of me with a slosh.

"Thanks," I murmured, although she clearly wasn't listening.

"I'm just going to walk Katie out," Dad said with a sheepish grin.

"Bye, Skylar! Bye, Mrs. Crosby!" Katie called before the heavy front door slammed shut behind her and Dad.

I turned to Bubbe. "What. Was. That?"

Bubbe rubbed her fingers across her very tired expression. "That," she sighed, "was Katie."

I didn't say anything, just waited. Bubbe checked out the front window and then took a seat at the table.

"She's been coming here a lot over the last few weeks," she said. "Inviting herself over for dinner. Charming your dad into taking her out, even though he's got no money to take her anywhere, poor schmuck." She sighed. "I'd say something, but sweetheart, it's the only time I ever see him smile, and that's the truth. Or do anything besides sit in that chair and watch the TV."

"You don't think it's kind of suspect? That this Italian chick who disappeared right when he was beaten up reappears just when he's starting to get better?"

Bubbe shrugged, and I hated her sad indifference. The last few months hadn't been easy for her—she'd had to sacrifice a lot forcing Dad to attend all of his different therapy appointments, sometimes against his will. My grandmother's stubbornness was a force of its own, but its limits had certainly been tested.

We sat for a minute, letting the situation sink in. The front door opened, and Dad reentered, whistling a little tune that faded the closer he got to the TV. But instead of the din of some old rerun, we heard the telltale scrape of the piano bench legs against the floor and the creaky lift and clunk of the fallboard.

Bubbe and I froze, staring at each other, almost too afraid to move.

The tones of the piano started to float through the air, one tentative note at a time. They were treble notes, bright and cheery, played slowly, up and down a diachronic scale. All with his right hand, obviously, since the left was still lame.

Silently, Bubbe and I both craned our necks to watch. The ends of Dad's old plaid bathrobe hung off the bench like tuxedo tails while he hunched over the keys, listening to each one, note by note.

Next to me, Bubbe choked on a sob. I glanced over and started, shocked to see a single tear run down her cheek. She had gained a few new wrinkles over the past few months. The sound of the high notes must have been her breaking point.

Dad played up and down the treble keys, dipping into the occasional riff or a familiar chord progression. But then there was a clear bass note: an attempt to use his left hand, the one that had regained little of its dexterity. The hand was still often wrapped up, but no longer in a cast. Covered with a crisscrossing of ugly, still-red scars, it was thin and pale compared to his left. Bubbe and I listened as Dad attempted a chord, pressing only three fingers together onto the keys. He yanked his hand back with an audible gasp of pain.

Bubbe gasped with him. I clenched the table so hard my knuckles turned white. We listened again as the piano was shut loudly and Dad shuffled back to the couch. The TV turned on, and the spell was broken.

"His last physical therapy session is next week," Bubbe muttered. "After that, he'll be over his limit for maximum coverage. He still needs more, though."

She didn't have to mention the fact that his therapy for a gambling addiction was something we had to pay out of pocket. It had already killed most of my savings. There was a clinic that ran a free outpatient program out of Columbia, but the waitlist was over a year long.

I stood up from the table. It killed me to admit it, but there was only one way I could help the situation, and it wasn't by staying in New York.

"Where are you going?" Bubbe asked. Her eyes were now dry, but a crumpled tissue sat on the table.

The opening riffs of *Full House* jangled through the house. It was a show that, when I was growing up, my dad had always hated. Now he was watching syrupy junk on rerun or making googly eyes with Borough Barbie. I didn't want to leave him, but I wouldn't be able to help the way he needed on a district attorney's salary.

"I have to make a phone call," I said, and went to my room.

~

Chapter 3

A thin drizzle of sweat fell down my forehead and landed on one of the thin pages of my study guide. My eraser, hard at work, tore through the material. I shrieked in frustration.

"Goddamn it!"

I hurled the pencil across my room, which had been feeling smaller by the hour. As if on cue, a knock sounded at the door.

"*Bubbela?* Everything all right in there?"

I swung around in my chair just as Bubbe entered. Her nose wrinkled immediately. It was clear why. The room was a mess.

"Skylar, I love you, but you're a pig," she announced as she looked around the space.

Clothes were strewn everywhere. Several sets of dishes were stacked on my desk and the bedside table. The late spring heat of the house had risen into the room and given it an unmistakable dankness that was likely worse for someone who hadn't cooped herself up there for the last almost-two weeks.

Five days after taking the pills, my body was starting to feel normal again. Now it was just like the tail end of a bad menstrual cycle. Most signs of pregnancy were gone: only some slight fatigue remained as my body recovered. Aside from the pain in my chest that throbbed every time I thought of Brandon and what I had done, I was feeling more like myself than ever. Subsequently, my brain was back to working a mile a minute. I threw myself into test prep to avoid thinking about anything else.

I looked sullenly around the room, feeling petulant. "It's fine. And it's just me up here, so who cares?"

"Who cares?" Bubbe asked. "Well, I care! I'll care very much when you start your new fancy job and abandon your father and me to an attic full of roaches and mice. Bad enough you're leaving us again in the first place."

After hearing that I had begged back the job in Boston, Bubbe hadn't stopped guilting me every second she could. She understood the financial reasons, but she had obviously been looking forward to my help with Dad.

It didn't help that I still felt so ambivalent. It had taken a humiliating phone call with Kieran Beckford, partner at Kiefer Knightly and my former mentor, to get the job back in the first place. Kieran also happened to be Brandon's best childhood friend, so despite my desire to stop thinking about him, there was always the sinking awareness that I might possibly run into him at the firm.

Kieran, after all, was his divorce attorney.

On top of that, I'd had to disappoint the Brooklyn D.A.'s office to break the news of my defection, which I'd followed up with yet another phone call to Matthew Zola, who'd stuck his neck out for me in the first place.

"I get it," he kept saying, though it didn't make me feel better about burning the bridge.

He was so, so nice. Why couldn't I be interested in *him* instead? Why couldn't I fall for a stand-up guy who wasn't married, involved with gangsters, and hiding things from me?

Zola had made me promise to meet him for a beer before leaving New York. After I said I would, I had hung up and stared at myself in my bedroom mirror for a very, very long time.

"Get up, Skylar," Bubbe ordered. "You're leaving in a few days, and I want to take you for a graduation present. No granddaughter of mine is going to start her new job at a fancy firm looking like a secondhand ragamuffin."

I looked around my room. I had a lot to do before moving back up to Boston, including finding a new place to live.

"Fine," I mutter through gritted teeth, but set my pencil down and picked a shirt off the floor. It was time to stop being the madwoman in the attic.

~

It wasn't until she'd steered her old station wagon into Manhattan and parked in front of Barney's that I realized just how fancy an excursion Bubbe had planned.

"Bubbe," I said after we had gotten out of the car. "No. We can't afford anything here. Come on, let's just go to Century downtown."

"Listen to me, young lady." Bubbe turned her small form to face me with a hand perched on her hip. "You've let your...loss...and broken heart shatter all over our house. I see you're terrified of leaving your father.

27

But, Skylar, it's because of you that he's going to be okay. It's because of you and what you did—no, no," she said as I opened my mouth to protest, "—I know you didn't pay most of that money, but I know you paid some, and I also know that it's because of you that handsome *goy* paid the rest."

"*I'll* be paying the rest," I insisted vehemently. "It was just a loan!"

"Oh, for goodness' sake, Skylar. I don't know how I raised a girl so afraid of money, but here we are!"

I just glowered at the sidewalk, suddenly fascinated by cracks in the pavement.

"People don't do those sorts of things when they don't care, *bubbela*," Bubbe said, reaching up to pat at her hair, which amazingly, wasn't moving at all despite the breeze flowing down Seventh Avenue. "Now, it's because of you and whatever you did to make that boy care about you that I'm not going to lose my house at seventy-seven. And it's because of you that your father will continue to get the care he needs to beat this...problem."

"You were never going to lose your house, Bubbe," I mumbled. "I would never let that happen."

"Skylar, that's what I'm trying to say. I know this about you. I haven't been very appreciative the last few days, because God knows I'll be grieving your absence, but I know that you're taking this job to make sure your father and I are safe and cared for."

It was the closest she had come to giving me her blessing.

Bubbe tipped up her glasses. "And don't you worry about your father. I'll keep him away from the track if it takes every breath in my body."

"But—"

"No." Bubbe held up a single finger to my lips, forcing my silence. "My granddaughter is taking care of us, so I'm going to take care of her. And no one is going to stop me. Not even her."

There really wasn't anything else I could say to that.

"I've been saving for three years for this, *bubbela*," Bubbe said with glee as she looked up at the elaborate store windows. "Don't you worry. We'll be going to Century too. But I want to have some real fun first. I always wanted to go into a store like this and actually buy something!" She pointed at a Max Mara window display, a disdainful mannequin wearing a chic monochromatic spring suit. "You'd look fabulous in that one. White is your color."

I let her link her small arm with mine as we examined the window display together. "White is asking for a stain," I said. "Let's find something more practical. And less expensive."

For that I received a brief slap on the shoulder.

"You're going to be mucking it up with all of those fancy lawyers," Bubbe argued as she tugged me toward the store.

"Bubbe, I already was mucking it up with the lawyers," I said. "What do you think I was doing with all of those internships and stuff?"

"Yes, but now you *are* one of the lawyers," she said, pulling even harder.

Her sharp look softened when she saw the worry on my face.

"No one is going to say my granddaughter doesn't fit in with them," she said firmly, and I could see that this wasn't just for me after all. So I relented, and let my grandmother drag me inside to look at the pretty clothes.

~

It took most of the afternoon to find four different suits that were stylish enough for Bubbe but cheap enough that I'd let her pay for them. I was right; Barney's had been a terrible idea. Almost everything there reminded me of Brandon. The smell of the leather in the shoe department, the brief whiffs of cologne, and the feel of the sumptuous fabrics—all of it spoke of the luxury in his life, into which I'd fallen and enjoyed so briefly.

At one point, when we were walking through the scents department, I caught a whiff of almond, the same subtle scent that was in the shampoo or whatever hair product Brandon used to tame his thick blond waves. I had to grip the edge of the counter for a moment before I could follow Bubbe into toward women's suiting.

After we found one upscale suit at Bloomingdales and three more at a discount store, I finally convinced Bubbe that I had enough separates to last me for a while at my new job. We loaded the bags into the trunk of her station wagon, and she drove back to Brooklyn, leaving me to run a few more errands before heading home myself.

The truth was, I wasn't terribly eager to go home. It hadn't felt like the home I remembered, which was strange, considering New York, and specifically Brooklyn, *always* felt like home to me. But between Dad's behavior and the ache in my heart, I just felt listless. Drifting.

In need of a distraction.

After talking a walk up to Lincoln Center, the perfect solution dawned on me. I was maybe a fifteen-minute walk from the best distraction in the world: The Metropolitan Museum of Art.

When I arrived at the massive, columned building, I walked up the iconic steps practically two at a time. The Met was a place I went as a broody teenager when I wanted to escape, especially when my mother, a mercurial artist herself, would come around. Ironically, it worked as a perfect foil to her neurotic, unaccountable mannerisms. Stolid and eternal, the masterworks within were the exact opposite of the harsh, modernist art she made.

For me, the only thing that was more meditative was the symphony, and even that had some painful memories, considering the last performance I'd seen was with Brandon on Valentine's Day. It was the first time I'd really let my guard down with him. And after I'd told him the ugly stories of my past, he'd responded with the simple response that was balm to my soul: *I'm all in.*

Ouch. That memory really hurt.

I wandered through the Impressionist gallery, thinking the hazy aesthetic would fit my mood. *The Waterlilies* never got old. It was the middle of the day on a Friday, so the museum wasn't terribly crowded, and I was able to find a seat on one of the small viewing benches.

"I always feel like Monet is so overrated."

The voice of a woman behind me rang out loudly across the room. I rolled my eyes, but didn't bother to look at her.

"I mean, look at it. How hard is it to blob paint all over a canvas like that?"

In front of me, a few other patrons frowned at the speaker, who sounded like the kind of Park Avenue princess who came to the Met more to pad her cultural resume than out of actual appreciation. She sounded moronic. It was a classic for a reason.

"I don't know. I like it. I think it's a classic for a reason," a deep voice echoed my thoughts.

Every muscle in my body tensed. I froze, willing myself *not* to turn around for fear of being seen. My hair, normally a bright orange beacon, was fortuitously tied up under my dad's old Mets cap. Much less noticeable. I could only hope he hadn't memorized my body the same way I'd memorized his.

"Do you mind if we check out the next gallery?" asked the woman. "I'd prefer to look at the Renaissance works instead."

There was a pause. He wasn't looking at me, was he? And what the hell was he doing in New York? Was that even him at all? My skin prickled with that sixth sense, but I didn't dare turn around. I couldn't.

"Sure," said the man's voice. Was it his? How could I not know?

Their steps and her voice trailed off as they left the room. It wasn't until they were exactly twenty-five steps away (I counted the clicks of the woman's heels) that I turned around, just in time to see a dark-haired couple disappear around the corner, the man's hand proprietarily resting at the woman's back.

I turned back around and pressed my forehead into my hands. Great, just great. I couldn't get that face out of my head, and now I was hearing his voice when others spoke. Next, I'd start pedaling conspiracy theories to anyone who would listen.

The thought had barely zipped through my head when suddenly I had the strangest feeling that I *was*, in fact, being watched. I couldn't have told you why, but the hairs on the back of my neck stood up, and goose bumps ran down my arms. I twisted around quickly, hoping to catch whoever was spying in action. But, of course, I was the only one in the room, and all the doorways were open.

I was alone. And apparently going crazy.

I pulled knees up under my chin and stared at the *Waterlilies* again, entranced and simultaneously unable to focus as my mind spiraled out of control. Then I pulled out my phone and called the first person I could think of. Jane didn't answer. So, I took her advice and called someone else. Matthew Zola picked up right away.

~

It was half past six by the time I got back to Brooklyn, slightly sweaty from the long train ride. I was meeting Zola at a small, crowded gastro pub in Park Slope, the kind that had been remade with live edge wood and industrial lighting to appeal to the hipster crowds that had taken over that side of Prospect Park.

Zola was sitting at the end of the long, hand-varnished bar top, sipping on a pint of beer. Clearly just getting off work, his suit jacket was laid on the seat next to him, and his tie was loosened around an unbuttoned collar. He perked up as he saw me weaving through the crowd, and I regretfully noticed again how handsome he was. Too bad I wasn't the slightest bit interested.

"Hey there," he greeted me with a kiss to the cheek. "Thanks for coming out."

"Thanks for the invite."

We were slightly awkward, considering we'd really only spoken a few times before. But even if I wasn't interested in him romantically, there was something about Zola that seemed really friendly, like he was another kindred spirit. It was just a hunch.

"No problem" he said. "Can I get you a drink?"

"A scotch on the rocks," I started to say before trailing off.

I had been drinking scotch for years, but now my drink of choice reminded me too much of Brandon, who also enjoyed it. Great. Now I couldn't even drink without thinking of him.

"Actually, just a glass of red wine," I said lamely as I took my seat at the bar.

Zola signaled to the bartender and ordered while I arranged my purse on the bar top. What was I doing here?

"So, I wanted to say, I get why you had to turn the job down. It seems like it was a hard decision to make."

I nodded, although I didn't really want to talk about it. "Thanks. Yeah, I just...I need the money. My dad's treatments aren't cheap."

Zola nodded, knowingly. Considering the guy saw his fair share of junkies working for the D.A.'s office, he knew what that looked like. He had also seen firsthand what kind of injuries Dad had suffered.

"My old man had a gambling problem too," he offered. "You're doing the right thing. The only thing that can help him is real treatment, if he'll take it."

"He better," I said, even with a sinking feeling in my stomach.

"Yeah, about that," Zola said. "We're still building the case against Messina. I can't talk about it, but...well, we're getting more support, but we could still really use your family's testimony."

I sighed and shook my head. "I'm sorry, but you know the answer to that."

"Skylar, the D.A.'s office can keep your family safe. We can place your dad and grandmother into protective custody. Maybe even near you."

I tipped my head. "Come on. Like that wouldn't be the first place Messina would look for a rat: his only daughter. Besides, I told you already: they won't budge."

Zola shrugged, the easy movement attractive across his chest. He really was a good-looking guy: tallish, but not too tall, slim but with decent shoulders, and a handsome, honest face. His dark eyes twinkled.

"Had to give it another try," he said with a wink as he took a drink of his beer.

"Will you let me know what happens?" I asked.

He shook his head. "You know I can't discuss a case with you, but when it goes to court, I'll let you know. Shouldn't be too long now."

"Good," I said darkly. "I hope you lock that fucker up for the rest of his life."

"With any luck," Zola confirmed. He looked at me curiously. "Hey, are you all right? You seem...angry. More than usual."

I released the death grip I had around my whiskey glass and placed my hands flat on the bar. "Sorry. Things have been...a little intense."

I turned to look at him. His dark eyes were kind, watchful. They flickered briefly down to my lips, then back up. Oh. So it was like that.

"I, um, have a confession of my own to make, Skylar," Zola said as he turned his beer bottle around and around on the bar top.

I perked an eyebrow. "Oh?"

He shrugged boyishly. "Yeah. Well. I think you know I didn't push you for that job just because I thought you were smart."

My brow raised a little higher. "No?"

"I mean, I wouldn't have given your resume to my boss if it didn't pass muster," Zola admitted. "But...I did want to see you again. You know, because I thought you were kind of cute too."

I opened and closed my mouth several times before he peeked at me with an amused grin.

"Surprised?" he asked.

I worried my jaw, but found that I wasn't. Not really. So instead, I shrugged.

"I don't know," I said. "Maybe. Maybe not."

Zola watched me carefully, appearing to weigh something in his mind. "Can I..." he started, "...can I try something real quick?"

His eyes zeroed in on my lips again, and this time didn't flicker away. I tipped my head to the side. He *was* pretty damn handsome. Maybe this would serve as the kind of distraction I needed.

"All right," I consented.

Zola smiled, the kind of smile that would make most girls light up inside. He leaned in and pressed a soft kiss on my lips.

Nope. Nothing.

When he backed away, there was quite a different look in his eyes: one of regret.

"Well...that didn't go how I planned," he said with a wry smile.

I couldn't help but smile back. "It's really not your fault."

"It's not you, it's me? Do I have that right?"

I chuckled, even though disappointment dropped in my stomach like a bag of bricks. This just wasn't going to get any better, was it?

"I guess. But it's true. I'm just...going through some stuff right now. Not really available, if you know what I mean."

Zola squinted at me for a moment, then nodded regretfully.

"Well," he said, "I hope he knows what he's got."

I didn't say anything. There was nothing to say that wasn't going to make me start crying, especially since I still had a healthy dose of excess hormones running through me. The thought made my entire body tense.

"Friends, then?" Zola asked.

I looked up, this time genuinely surprised. "Really?"

Zola shrugged and smiled again. "I still think you're great, and it would be fun to get a beer every now and then when you're in town. As friends, of course. All the lawyers I know are dicks, so it's nice to have someone I actually like to talk shop with. Work for you?"

I nodded.

I reached in to give him a hug, and he tucked me close. There was nothing romantic about it. And it didn't feel strange at all. But it also made me feel even more acutely what I was currently missing in my life.

After finishing our beers and chatting about my upcoming job, we went outside.

"You let me know if you need anything," Zola said with another friendly hug. His hands lingered slightly around my waist, but otherwise there was nothing romantic about it.

"Thanks," I said as I adjusted the brim of my Mets cap. "Let me know if you're in Boston ever."

"I go up there every now and then," he said with a nod. "I'll see you, Skylar."

He got in his cab and left while I stood on the corner, thinking about what I wanted to do next.

I hated being this girl. I never *wanted* to be this girl. It was why I'd really only had one other relationship before Brandon, and why, when that crashed and burned, I avoided getting personal with anyone. And now that Brandon had broken down my walls and my heart in the process, here I was. Pathetic. Pining. Missing. Empty.

"Fuck that," I said out loud, startling a middle-aged woman walking her dog.

She walked faster. I stepped out to the curb and raised my hand for a cab home. It was time to pack up my stuff and get back to Boston. Distraction tactics weren't working this time, but that didn't mean they wouldn't the next. I just needed more extreme measures to get over Brandon Sterling.

~

Chapter 4

The apartment was ridiculously small—even smaller than the college-issued one I had shared with Jane through law school. The living room was basically a brick box, with two exposed-brick walls jumbled with windows that looked down onto Margaret Street and an adjacent alley, and two others, painted a deep red, that led into the two bedrooms. There was a kitchenette in one corner and a bathroom in the other. No table for eating, just a couch that faced away from the kitchenette toward a large screen that had been mounted on one of the brick walls.

There was nothing about the place that felt like home. Fitting, I thought as I walked inside.

Eric Stallsmith, my classmate from Harvard and now roommate, dropped my big duffel inside the front door and started to point around, giving the pretense of a tour.

"Kitchen, closet, my room, bathroom, your room. That's about it." He turned to me and grinned. "It's a mousetrap, but we've got loans to pay off, am I right?"

I gave a wry smile. "It's fine. I'm just glad to have a place to live."

Finding an apartment in Boston was a nightmare at the best of times. The fact that a good friend just happened to have a reasonably priced room in a decent part of town the very weekend I needed a place to live was like capturing a unicorn. It didn't matter that the apartment was maybe six hundred square feet total. With the hours I'd soon be putting in, I'd hardly be there anyway.

When I had told Jane where I'd be living for the foreseeable future, she had squawked so loudly into the phone that I thought she might have damaged my eardrum.

"Eric?" she cried. "You can't! You'll fail the bar. He'll leave his shit everywhere! He will keep you up at all hours of the night with his humping!"

Okay yes, Eric was a bit of a ladies' man. But our relationship had always been more sibling-like, as we were both from New York. So who said he couldn't clean the kitchen like anyone else? After I reminded her that I already knew what it was like to live with a sexually active roommate—her—Jane muttered a warning about catching hepatitis in the bathroom and hung up.

As it happened, Eric was really good at cleaning everything. Much, much better than me.

He turned back to face our small surroundings. "So, I've got two rules. Pick up your shit, and no fucking on the couch."

We looked around the living room. It was immaculate. Eric's "shit" was absolutely nowhere to be seen, and the floors, kitchen, and windows all gleamed where the last rays of sunlight shone into the otherwise dark space.

"Fine by me, but can you actually follow that last rule?" I asked with a raised eyebrow.

Eric shrugged, the action stretching the cotton of his T-shirt over his lithe shoulders. "Sure. I don't usually like to bring them back here anyway. They get too attached, want to stay for breakfast." He smirked. "Too much for a piece of ass."

I scowled at Eric's casual misogyny. Maybe Jane was right; living with him was going to be like living with a frat boy. A really clean frat boy who also had a fetish for gourmet coffee, but a frat boy nonetheless.

"Also, rent includes the split cost of a cleaning lady," he added.

Okay, so maybe not as clean as I thought.

"Please tell me you didn't hire Ana," I joked.

Ana was Brandon's housekeeper and Eric's sometime-booty call. She was the reason I had even met Brandon in the first place, when I had followed Eric back to her apartment during a blizzard. Her apartment, it turned out, was in the servant's quarters in Brandon's enormous house.

Eric snorted. "Come on. Give me some credit. Plus, we wouldn't be able to afford her. With what Sterling pays her, I think you and I are in the wrong profession."

He must have seen the sadness that swept over me at the mention of Brandon. It was impossible not to think of him now that I was back in Boston. Everything in this town reminded me of him, of us. My need for distraction had never been higher. Luckily, I'd come to the right place.

Eric clapped an arm awkwardly around my shoulder. "Don't worry, Cros," he said with a friendly squeeze. "We'll make you forget him. I'm the expert in that department."

He hefted my bag over his shoulder again and walked me toward the door on the left, right next to the bathroom.

"Don't worry. Most of the time I'm not even here to use it," Eric said as he caught my disgusted look at sleeping right next to where I'd have to hear him pee.

"Gross," I said, although I wasn't referring to the bathroom.

Eric tossed my things into a small bedroom that was empty except for an old futon mattress on the floor and a desk lamp beside it. I softened. All of my things had fit in the back of my rental car, and I was going to have to find some time to purchase actual furniture. But Eric had taken the time to find me something to sleep on and given me a lamp to read by. It looked like the bedroom of a Soviet-era spy, but I felt warm. A little bit cared for.

"Thanks, bro," I said, nudging my shoulder into his.

Eric just slung an arm back around my neck and squeezed briefly before letting go. "Yeah, well, you needed somewhere to sleep, didn't you? I'm not so much of an asshole that I would make you sleep on the wood floor. Or my couch, come to think of it."

He stepped away to let me adjust to the new space alone. Eric wasn't going to be the kind of roommate who got into my business, and I was just fine with that. I turned to look at the dispiritingly white walls, the sad mattress on the floor. I was glad for the space, but as I stood there alone, the room felt less like a refuge and more like a trap.

Nope. Wasn't going to do it. I grabbed my purse and headed out, desperate for another change of pace.

~

"Don't worry. You're still my number one, Janey," I said on the phone while I absently walked through a consignment furniture shop in Allston. I had decided that the best remedy for my melancholia was to make my room into a place I actually liked.

Jane huffed. She had opted to spend the summer renting a room in her cousin's apartment in Chicago, much to her parents' chagrin. She wouldn't be able to afford her own place on an ASA salary anytime soon, but she'd also insisted there was no way she was going to live with her parents while she saved her money. Her cousin's place in ritzy Lincoln Park was the next best thing.

"This is bullshit," she griped. "I should fuck it and move back there. Chi-town is driving me bonkers. It is already so damn hot here, Sky, and my mom has been to the apartment four times in the last week. How is a girl supposed to leave for no-strings sex with her mom bringing over Ziploc bags of bulgogi at all hours of the night? And now I've been replaced with Eric the whoremaster? Ugh."

"You love your mom, Janey. Are you really complaining that she's bringing you homemade food?"

I checked out a mid-century bureau. It was nice, but not big enough for most of my clothes.

"No, I'm complaining about the fact that you are living with a human petri dish."

"I love how, when you're making these claims, you conveniently forget that month during first year where you and Eric never left your bedroom," I said, going to check out another dresser.

"Oh, I'd never forget that, babe. That's how I *know* just how gross that boy is."

Jane had never divulged completely what had gone down between her and Eric (although in fairness, I had only known her for about two months at that point). All I knew was what I'd seen: that he'd stumbled in with her after a party during first semester, and for the next few weeks they basically forced me to spend fourteen hours a day at the library if I didn't want to listen to their animal habits.

Then I'd arrived one night to find Jane curled up on the couch with a bottle of wine. It became our first drinking/bitch-about-men session. I had had a boyfriend, Patrick, at the time, a Wall Street asshole and all around terrible human being. We had commiserated, and a bond was forged over cheap wine and bitterness. But from then on, she'd also never had anything else pleasant to say about Eric, who mysteriously seemed to treat her only with distant kindness.

Come to think of it, that in and of itself was a bit odd, considering how easy it was for Eric to forget the women he slept with, or at least treat them like they didn't exist.

"You'll probably need to Scotchgard your sheets," Jane was saying. "Speaking of, do you have a bed yet?"

I grinned into a gaudy, gold-framed mirror on the wall. "Yes! I found a great deal on this gorgeous teak frame, and I ordered a mattress too.

I'm kind of excited about it. Every other bed I've owned has either been university-issued or balanced on rolling wheels."

"Good for you, Sky. You deserve a fresh start. And a hot man to help you christen the thing. Speaking of which, any other hallucinogenic episodes?"

I huffed. Jane had been asking me about the encounter at the Met every day since it had happened.

"I think it's time for a fresh start," was all I said.

"Amen to that, sister," Jane replied. "So, what's on the agenda this weekend? Please tell me you're not just going to hole up with your books. No one normal has even started studying for the bar yet, and you need to get out, friend. Before the grind begins."

I sat down on an orange plaid couch that was probably designed sometime around 1975. "Eric did suggest that we go to this club tonight."

"*Eric* did? I see, you're going to a herpes den. Wear a dental dam, my love."

"Jane, give it a rest, will you?" I was not looking forward to hearing STD jokes for the entire time I lived with Eric. "He's my roommate, and he *is* my friend too."

"Sorry," Jane mumbled. "I guess that settles it, then. I'm just going to have to fly out the next chance I get. Because there's no way I'm letting that walking dildo be the only person who ever gets to take you out."

"Yeah, but you *will* have to study by then," I pointed out, even though I was secretly thrilled with the idea. Even though it had been less than two weeks since Jane and I last seen each other, that was a very long time after living together for three years.

"I can study in Boston too," Jane insisted. "Probably better than here. No mother busting in with food every ten seconds."

"Won't that be expensive?"

"Frequent flyer miles, baby. Credit cards can accomplish amazing things."

~

I returned to the apartment feeling like a pirate with a major score of booty. I was loaded with several bags full of throw pillows, a bedding set, and equipment to paint my room a deep cerulean blue. I had ended up choosing a desk and a nightstand that would go well with the dark-wood aesthetic of my bedframe, and all of the large furniture would be arriving the next day.

I set the bags on the floor of my room and surveyed the space. They said blue was a calming color, right? At least, the sales associate at Home Depot did. I wasn't too sure.

Even so, I spent the rest of the afternoon painting. By the time I was finished, the combination of white trim and the deep blue color made me feel as if I were in the middle of a dream. I smiled. This wouldn't be a terrible place to spend the next several months at all.

"Wow," said Eric when he arrived back from the gym and popped in to take a look at my progress. "Looking good in here."

"Thanks," I replied with a smile as I started cleaning up the rollers. "It's going to come together, I think."

Despite the fumes and the aches in my arms from holding the rollers and brushes for so long, it felt really good to accomplish something. Actually, I hadn't felt this good in weeks.

We were interrupted by a knock at the door and a loud thump. Eric answered, and a few seconds later, he called for me.

"What is it?" I asked as I popped my head out of my bedroom, but no reply was necessary.

"Jeez, Crosby," Eric said bemusedly. "You really did go shopping today. But don't you need a bed more than this?"

He nodded his head at the two block-shaped delivery men who bookended a small upright piano.

I stared at it. "I didn't order this."

The courier in front pulled out a clipboard. "You Skylar Ellen Crosby?"

I crossed my arms. "Yes."

"Then this is for you. Sign here. Where do you want it?"

I accepted the clipboard and scanned the paper, looking for some sign of who had sent the elaborate present. There was no name on the paper, but I had a sinking feeling I knew. I hadn't heard from Brandon in several weeks. No flowers, no letters, all attempts to get me back had stopped. And now...a piano? How did he even know where I lived?

The delivery guy coughed, covering his mouth with a meaty hand. "So, where do you want it?"

I glanced at Eric, who was looking at the piano with a skeptical expression. "We, um...Crosby, it's kind of a small apartment, you know?"

The piano was small too, an Essex upright that would, no doubt, sound like a dream. I sighed. There really was no room for it in our tiny living room. And yet...I didn't quite have the heart to send it away.

"You can put it in my room," I said, gesturing behind me. "Far wall. Next to the closet."

With a grunt, the deliverymen rolled the piano into my room while I signed the sheet. Eric leaned against the wall, watching curiously.

"Another mea culpa?" he asked.

I hadn't told him much about what had happened with Sterling, but he obviously knew it had not ended well. Likely, I guessed, via Jane.

I shrugged. "Might be. I don't know why, though."

I would be lying if I said a part of me wasn't a little flattered. Happy to know Brandon was thinking about me, even if I told him not to.

"Ma'am?"

I turned around to where the deliverymen exited my bedroom. One of them held out another envelope.

"We were told to deliver that as well," he said.

I murmured my thanks and gave them each a twenty, wondering what the letter held. Brandon's letters always had a way of undoing me. It was scary, actually, how much I wanted it to be just one more beg for mercy, ending, as they all had: "Do you love me yet, Red? I love you always. Brandon."

I sat down on the couch while Eric loitered awkwardly, finally deciding to make some coffee. Taking care of women clearly wasn't Eric's forte, but it was nice of him to hang around. I pulled my knees up on the couch and opened the letter.

It was the last thing I expected.

Skylar,

Happy graduation, darling. I couldn't be prouder. A little something to remind you to have fun every now and then once you're off to the real world. Everyone needs to be an artist sometimes.

Bisous,

Janette

Well, that explained how he knew the address: he didn't. Janette Jadot née Chambers—otherwise known as my mostly absent mother—was one of the few people who received address updates from me each time I moved.

It didn't escape me that she called her own daughter "darling" and named herself Janette in the same letter. Nor did the reference to being an artist completely evade the irony of the fact that she left me and my father to do just that. Several times. I could never quite figure out if my mother was masterfully Machiavellian or just tone-deaf.

I shoved the note into my jeans pocket and walked back into my bedroom. The addition of the piano in the corner completed the weird, non-sequitur look with the futon mattress, the desk lamp, my suitcases, and the bright blue walls that suddenly looked like Brandon's exact eye color.

The piano was truly lovely—shining mahogany that would no doubt have fantastic sound. It was an incredibly generous gift, but in no way made up for the fact that my mother had largely been absent from my life since I was twelve. I hadn't actually heard from her specifically in over three years. This was more than just a gift. It was a ten-thousand-dollar announcement. But for what?

"So it's from him?" Eric wandered into my room, coffee cup in hand.

I shook my head and rubbed the sides of my arms as if I were cold. "No, my mother. I really don't know why."

Eric watched me carefully, eyebrows raised as he took a long drink. He was a good-looking guy—I could see how his combination of sardonic charm and slight indifference made certain women come at his beck and call. Fortunately, it did nothing for me, or that sinking feeling of regret. For the fifteenth day in a row, I hadn't heard anything from the tall blond man I actually did have feelings for. And that, of course, was all my fault.

Instinctually, my hand crunched the note in my hand. I held it up, and only then noticed that Janette had scribbled an addendum on the back of the letter.

P.S. All of us will be in Boston next month. We'd love to see you, and I want desperately for you to meet your brother and sister.

See you in a few weeks.

xJ

"Right, then," I said abruptly, and strode out to throw the crumpled paper into the kitchen garbage bin. "I'm going to change, and then I want to go get really good and drunk."

Eric, still standing in my doorway, smiled slyly and gave me a mock salute with his mug. "Your wish is my command."

~

"Nope."

Eric sat on the couch, flipping through channels on the TV that took up most of the space on the brick wall. He wasn't even looking at me when I walked out of the bathroom, still putting on a pair of silver hoop earrings, but his resounding "Nope" could be heard across the room. Probably through the entire building.

I looked down at my outfit. This was the third one that had been vetoed. The first, a knee-length gray dress, had been deemed "Amish", and the second, a pair of loose, stone-washed jeans and a gray flannel shirt, was nixed as "farmer clothes." Now I was wearing a pair of tight black jeans, a fitted black sweater, and my favorite black ankle boots that Jane called my "shit-kickers." I had tied my hair back to let my earrings dangle freely. It wasn't the most revealing thing I owned, but I thought I looked good and a little bit edgy. It fit my shitty mood.

"Christ, you're worse than Jane, do you know that?" I snapped.

"Great minds think alike."

"No, really. What's wrong with this? Nothing is oversized, and I left *three* buttons undone."

Eric looked down at his outfit as if that would explain his response. His fitted gray pants and tight black shirt were a far cry from the jeans and T-shirts he had worn most as a student, but also vastly different from the conservative suits he maintained at the office. His light blond hair was messy in that way that actually required a lot of product, and the V-neck of his T-shirt revealed a small silver cross on a leather cord.

Jane would have cackled and probably asked him where the boy band auditions were happening.

"You look like you're going to a Swedish disco," I said. "I do not see your point."

Eric shrugged and finished off the bottle of beer he was holding. He had, I had realized, an amazing ability to let almost anything and everything roll off his back. The boy was immovable.

"Well, my ancestors did emigrate from Amsterdam," he said. "So, close enough. Look, it's stylish, it's simple, it's easy to take off—" at that I grimaced, not wanting to imagine my roommate naked —"and I look hot, which is the main objective. You, though..."

Eric tipped the bottle at me and cocked his head in a way that was not positive.

"I'm a prude just because I don't want to dress like a two-dollar hooker after sunset?" I demanded with my arms flung out to the side.

Eric snorted. "You said you wanted me to take you out. Well, where we're going, I'm not going to get laid if I look like I'm chaperoning my baby sister on her way to a slam poetry contest, and you're going to be sitting at the bar all night counting coasters. But hey, it's your choice, Crosby."

"I do not look like your baby sister!" I yowled, even as I stamped my foot like a toddler.

Eric came to stand next to me so that we were both looking through the bathroom door into the mirror over the sink. He didn't say anything, just let our joint reflection speak for itself. He looked savvy and hot, a spitting image of Alexander Skarsgård. He had that Nordic roughness in his messy hair and slight stubble, combined with his Upper East Side polish, that would draw girls to him like flies. I, on the other hand, looked like...a beat poet. On her way to an Amish festival. As much as I hated to admit it, Eric was right: I'd probably stick out at a night club.

"You said you wanted something different, Crosby," Eric reminded me with a jocular nudge to my shoulder.

"Goddamn it," I muttered, even as Eric grinned in victory. "Okay, you win. Give me ten more minutes, and I'll be ready to go."

"Take twenty," he said as he headed back to the couch. "And fix your makeup too."

~

Chapter 5

Eric and I ended up at a club in Chinatown, the kind of place off Beacon Street where college kids went to feel more grown up and where investment bankers went to get laid. I just wanted to get lost. Even from the street I could smell the booze, and loud bass lines practically vibrated through the asphalt. It was still relatively early on a Friday night, but the place was already packed with people.

"You clean up pretty good, Crosby," Eric said for the third time, taking in my dress with appreciation.

I pretended to kick at him.

"I feel like Club Barbie," I said. "And stop leering at me like that. It's gross."

Eric made a face. "I didn't mean it like that; you're like my sister."

"Exactly."

The truth was, I was actually relieved that Eric made me change. The club was basically a sardine tin, and, considering it was already a warm night, the short black mini dress I wore had the dual benefits of being cute and cool. I had kept the silver chains, the hoops, and my silver-tipped boots and had put my unruly red waves into a high ponytail to keep them off my neck.

"Well?" Eric asked loudly over the music as he held his hand out like a tour guide. "What do you think?"

I looked around the club. It was basically just an old brick factory building that had been converted into a night club. Exposed brick walls provided insulation for the bass lines that traveled through the floorboards and into my bones. The dark red lighting created a hedonistic air that was only augmented by the young, lithe bodies filling the space from top to bottom. They writhed to the music, chattered over the bass lines, and cast eyes across dark spaces before sneaking off together to darker corners. It was basically sex incarnate.

"I think I've wandered into an alternate universe," I mumbled. This had never been my scene, and yet here I was, by request.

We were surrounded by investment wonks and other urban professionals just off from work, all enjoying drinks and listening to 1990s throwbacks. A DJ "spun" on his computer from the far corner of the club, which was done up like *A Night at the Roxbury* with silvery-blue velvet lounges and a long chrome bar swarming with lines of people. The familiar drum beat of "Poison", that old Bel Biv Devoe song, shouted over the loudspeakers, and the entire club erupted.

It was clear that this wasn't just a spot where colleagues came to kick back. This was a place where people went to meet other people. New people. The old-school music set a sexy, carefree vibe that seemed to be lulling all of the patrons together, like the beginning of some kind of hedonistic ritual. The orgy wasn't happening yet, but you had the feeling it would eventually.

It seemed like a decent enough place to forget everything that had been happening in my life lately. I needed a distraction, and that was the order of the day.

I followed Eric to the bar and stood beside him while he waved down a bartender and ordered our drinks: a whiskey soda for me and a beer for him.

"So how does this work?" I called out over the loud music and the clamor of voices around us. "I've never been a dude's wingman before. Won't these girls think you're with me?"

Eric snorted and took a sip of his beer. "No one comes here with their boyfriends. If they do, they're just setting themselves up for a more intense chase. Look, Cros, all you need to do is stand there. You see something you like, just make eye contact, and he'll come to you."

"And you?"

Eric gave me a particularly sharkish smile that gave his otherwise unintimidating face a rakish appeal. "Oh, that's easy. First I pretend they don't exist. Then I pretend they're the only thing I see."

I scowled. "You make these girls think you're in love with them so you can trick them into sex?"

"Please. No one ever says anything about love." Eric looked down at me sharply. "You're not going to start butting in on my sex life, are you? I left my nosy family in New York for a reason."

I held my hands up in mock surrender. "Hey, it's not my business. These girls want to get involved with your slutty ass, that's their issue. You're not going to ask me to shut up when I have my own opinions, are you?"

Eric chuckled and threw an arm around my shoulder. "Never dream of it, sis."

He looked around the room. A leggy brunette was making eyes at him from the other end of the bar. She was wedged between at least two other men trying to buy her drinks, but obviously was interested in my "date." Eric clearly knew what he was talking about.

"Target identified?" I asked.

Eric glanced at the brunette with a look that made me feel like *I* had been undressed just by proximity. She flushed clearly, even in the dim lights of the club. The guy next to her was talking, but she didn't respond as Eric then looked around at everything besides her.

"Looks that way." Eric pushed off the bar, beer in hand. "You going to be okay?" he asked kindly. "I can hang for a bit. There are a lot of fish in this particular sea."

I shifted back and forth on the balls of my feet. "Hey, I came here to get lost for, not to cramp your style. I'll be fine."

Eric gave me the signature grin that probably got him more tail than most men in Boston.

"All right. I'll keep an eye out. Give me a wave if you need a rescue."

I rolled my eyes. "Go chase some tail, Casanova. And make sure you wear a rubber."

Eric left, and I hopped up onto one of the stools, content to sip on my drink and people-watch with my back to the bar. This kind of place was so out of my element, filled as it was with half-dressed women (although I wasn't currently much more covered up) and men who tracked them like birds of prey. Everyone in here wore a kind of mask: a mask of skin, a mask of makeup and hair products, a mask of shiny fabric and rapacious glances. Everyone was here to be someone they weren't in their everyday lives.

"Can I get you another drink?"

I had to physically stop my eyes from rolling. That line was tired. Everything about this place seemed tired, and I had been here less than fifteen minutes. But I didn't want to go home, where I'd probably just flop on my futon and go to sleep. I wanted to be something besides tired. I wanted to stop feeling like shit.

"Sure," I replied, turning to the speaker.

His name was Marco, and he was a broker at Prudential. With olive skin and dark, slicked hair, he was only a little bit on the short side with a barrel-chested body that filled out his white Oxford shirt and navy pants quite nicely. With a hand at the small of my back like he owned me, he waved a hand at the bartender and sidled close, which was easy considering there were still people teeming for drinks on either side of us. I crossed my legs and turned to face the bar. Marco followed the movement of my legs hungrily.

"The bartender's a friend of mine from college," he assured me. "You in school?"

I shook my head. "Just graduated."

"Hey! Congratulations on entering the real world!" he replied jovially. "Now you have to let me buy you a drink. What school?"

I paused. There are certain kinds of men who can't handle women who are potentially smarter than them. I'd met them before, and when they found out I attended Harvard or had graduated summa cum laude from NYU, they were usually very uncomfortable, which meant they ignored me or made everything a competition of wits. Marco might have been one of those men, or he might not have been. I wasn't really interested in finding out.

"UMB," I stated over the blare of Salt N' Pepa, giving him the acronym for the Boston campus of the University of Massachusetts that mostly attracted locals.

Marco humored me with a smile that was at once condescending and thrilled. "That's great! I graduated from Amherst five years ago!"

I nodded and smiled back, hating the way my cheeks felt like they were about to crack. Come on, Crosby, this isn't you, I thought. But then I shook my head. "Me" wasn't working these days. So *this* would be fine for tonight.

"Let me guess," Marco was saying as the bartender came over. "You like vodka cranberries."

I was about to tell him I preferred whiskey, but then I stopped. Across the bar, Eric was leaning conspicuously close to a girl, a different one from brunette he'd seen before. She had a very pink drink in her hand and smiled when she caught me looking, like a cat who had just caught its prey. Eric looked up.

"You okay?" he mouthed.

50

I nodded and turned back to Marco. Why not have a different drink, the kind of drink that "girls who just want to have *fun*" would have?

"Vodka cranberry sounds great!" I said, trying to invest as much lightness into my voice as I could.

As fake as I felt, it seemed to work. Marco grinned again and ordered the drinks. I took a small sip. Holy shit, that was sweet!

"Something wrong with your drink?" he asked. "I know my friend makes them kind of strong."

This was strong? It tasted like cough syrup! "No, no, I'm fine. Just...haven't had one of these in a while."

Marco leered, probably thinking I didn't drink much and was thus an easy target. I smiled back and tossed down the rest of the syrupy sweet cocktail as quickly as I could.

"Damn," Marco said as he watched. "I guess you got used to it."

"I guess I did," I said, feeling lightheaded. I waved at the bartender. "Another round, please!"

I winked at Marco. It felt unnatural and strange, but he winked back.

"Next one's on me," I said.

Three vodka cranberries and two kamikaze shots later, and I didn't have to fake the winking or laughing anymore. With the pounding music and the roar of people, the world felt exactly as I wanted it: hazy, joyful. Distracting.

"Come on!"

I tugged Marco, who was getting just as sloshed as I was, off his barstool and toward the dance floor. He'd been moving progressively closer to me with every drink, and was more than eager for the physical contact. Grabbing his beer, he followed me eagerly until we were surrounded by people thrashing in the small space in front of the DJ booth.

The crowd had become even more raucous than before as the DJ put on more well-known hits. Ties had come off, skirts were hiked to the point of being indecent, and a lot of grinding was going on.

Marco pulled me close and bent to nuzzle my neck. The feeling made me jump—it was the same place where someone else used to do that, drive me crazy when he kissed me right there, under my jaw, with incredibly soft lips, not a scratchy goatee.

"You're so fucking sexy," Marco crooned into my ear. "Your ass is incredible."

His lips found my earlobe, but before he could do anything else, I pulled back. It reminded me too much of someone else, someone who could do that much, much better.

"So are you," I pronounced, ignoring the way my lips felt bloated around the words.

The vodka was seriously kicking in. I pulled Marco down to kiss me properly. He immediately sought entry in that sloppy way drunk people do. His tongue swiped around my mouth while his roving hands found my ass and squeezed. I tried not to feel repulsed. It wasn't hard. I didn't feel much at all.

Come on. Feel something. Feel anything.

But there was nothing but disgust with myself. My heart sank. Everything in my body sank. It was just no use. Every time he kissed me, I couldn't help but think about the person who used to kiss me like he meant it, used to make me feel every tremor of his touch from the tips of my hair down to my toes.

After a few moments, I put two hands on Marco's sturdy chest and pushed him off me.

"I have to go to the bathroom," I said, figuring at least I shouldn't outright tell an unfamiliar drunk male that he's just not doing it for me.

Marco nodded, his eyes glazed with alcohol and lust. "Sure, sure. I'll be out here."

I stumbled through the crowd and found my way to the congested bathroom at the end of a long hallway where, from the looks of it, several couple were looking for indecent exposure charges. It was hard not to look at the man with his hands clear up his date's skirt, at the couple in the back who were both half out of their shirts. It was harder still not to be jealous.

Once I was in the stall, I whipped out my phone. I knew it was a bad idea. I was drunk. I was being a cliché. And yet I swiped through my contacts anyway, telling myself I just wanted to look at his face, see that bashful, dimple-bearing smile he'd had when I'd snapped a photo of him in bed one bright morning. My heart turned over, and almost as if moving of their own accord, my thumbs tapped out a text to Brandon.

Me: Everything is wrong I miss you. Too much.

My thumb hovered over the send button. No. I shouldn't send it. I sighed. Of course you shouldn't send it, you fool.

Someone slammed into the door to my stall with a loud bang and a rattle of the latch. Startled, I dropped my phone on the floor.

"You idiot, someone is in there!"

A hysterical cackle followed the intrusion, and I focused on breathing as I picked up my phone. But the screen was now different. Now there was a glowing return message.

Brandon: Where are you?

I stared in horrified shock. Startled by the intrusion, I must have accidentally pressed send. Shit. Shit, shit, shit! I started typing out another message to mitigate the first. Say it was a friend. Say it was a joke. Come up with anything but how you actually feel. But once again, the door was slammed into, and this time it flew open as several girls toppled into the stall around me.

"Oh my God, I'm so sorry!" one of them yelped while the others laughed. They were all at least as drunk as I was, wearing heels that were twice as high, skirts that were half the length of mine. I just did my best to untangle myself from their jumbled, cackling mess, then washed my hands and escaped back into the club. There was no reason I needed to answer that message anyway. It was just looking for trouble, and not the kind I wanted.

On the dance floor, Marco was already prowling for a new partner. Someone put a hand around his neck, and I bit my lip, trying to stop tears from welling up. What was wrong with me? I didn't even care about this loser, and yet I was spitting jealous at seeing him kiss another girl.

I turned on one heel and weaved my way through the crowd, past a corner where Eric was getting very familiar with yet another girl, and ignored the several catcalls I received on my way out of the club.

"Lookin' good tonight, Red," jeered one guy as I neared the club entrance.

Without even thinking about it, I whirled around and shoved a hand on his sternum to slam him into the brick wall.

"Shut it," I said through gritted teeth, more calmly than I felt.

The world seemed a whir. All I could feel was anger and sadness— a very bad combination.

Outside, I welcomed a breath of fresh air, even clogged as it was by the pack of cigarette-smokers huddled just down the block. I placed a hand on the side of the building and heaved breaths. In and out. In and out. Outside, the world still spun, but at least I could breathe. A wave of nausea rose in my belly, and this time it didn't go away.

"Oh, God," I muttered, leaning into the cold bricks. And then I lost my dinner and most of my drinks against the crumbling mortar. What a fucking mess.

So concentrated was I on making the world stand still again that I hardly noticed the massive black sedan that pulled up in front of the club. I sucked in air and vaguely registered a clean, familiar, almond-laced scent wrapped around me as I threw up again. And again. A hand steadied my ribs, and another held back my hair.

When I was finally finished, I pulled a tissue out of my purse and blotted my mouth, breathing heavily against the wall as the hands left me. I took another deep breath and turned around.

Brandon stood next to the open back door of his Mercedes. He looked like he had rolled out of bed and grabbed the first things he could find: worn, light-blue jeans, a blue T-shirt that was creased like he'd been sleeping in it, and a pair of running shoes that were only half-laced. His shirt hugged the contours of his chest and the lean, defined muscles in his arms. His wavy hair, gleaming gold at the ends, stuck out from under his favorite frayed Red Sox hat, and the street light above caught a glimmer of stubble lining the sharp edges of his jaw. Those piercing blue eyes that haunted my dreams nightly shined even in the dark, but were slightly puffy, like he had just woken up.

It had been just over two weeks since I'd seen him last, on the same day I'd graduated, when we'd fought and kissed and eventually said goodbye on the banks of the Charles River. On that day he'd worn a suit, the kind that made him look like his billions. Tonight, in the same basic uniform of half the men in Boston, he looked even better.

"H-hi," I said weakly, barely able to wonder what he was doing here or how he knew to come. My head throbbed. My stomach roiled again, but there was nothing in it to come up.

Brandon tipped his head to the side and sighed. He rubbed a hand over the bill of his cap, causing his shirt to ride up and reveal the hard lines of his abdomen. I drooled.

"Get in, Red," he said gruffly.

And, God help me, I did.

~

Chapter 6

We rode in silence, the clean, luxurious interior of the car a refuge from the filth of the street. David, Brandon's kindly, middle-aged driver, gave me a wink through the rearview mirror. At least someone was happy to see me.

Brandon, on the other hand, was a statue in his seat, his eyes mostly shaded by the curve of his baseball cap. Even so, his stare was basically a sledgehammer. I turned toward my tinted window, taking solace in the soft leather seats and the cool glass against my cheek. We were sitting maybe a few feet from each other, but it might as well have been miles.

The nausea was gone, slowly being replaced by fatigue and a mounting awareness that the person I had been dreaming about for the last several weeks was sitting next to me in his expensive Mercedes. And, if his expression was any indication, mostly likely hated my guts.

Oh, God.

Conscious of the way his eyes followed my ever movement, I popped a few of the Listerine squares I kept in my purse. We were going to have to talk, and I needed to get the nasty taste out of my mouth. Then I finally turned to him, taking a deep breath as I met the full force of his piercing blue eyes. Brandon didn't move, just watched me with an expression one might have when encountering a wounded animal that might scratch them. Was there loathing there? I couldn't tell.

"What-what are you doing here?" I asked. My voice was scratchy after having to yell so much in the club. Losing my dinner hadn't helped either.

Brandon finally blinked, then shook his head and rubbed a hand over his face. I knew that move. His patented "I don't want to answer that question" move. The move he made when his thoughts were too much for even him to handle. It tipped the edge of his frayed bill up above his hairline, revealing his face in full. Even puffy-eyed and weary, he was still the most beautiful person I'd ever met.

Instead of responding directly, Brandon pulled out his phone and swiped to a photo, which he then held out for me to view. Apparently, instead of texting him in response, I'd ended up taking a picture. A picture of a toppled mass of women, two of whom had their underwear on full display. I was slammed against a wall behind them, my eyes half-shut and basically looking like I was trapped in some kind of demented orgy. Okay, so it didn't look good.

I glanced up, still suspicious. "Doesn't explain how you knew I was here."

Brandon grunted impatiently, then zoomed in on the top right-hand corner of the picture, where I could see the top of an ad the club had placed inside the bathroom stall door. It read: "Events at Solstice Nightclub in June."

"Huh." I sat back in my seat, shrinking myself into the corner. "We got Sherlock Holmes over here."

Brandon still didn't say anything, just put his phone back in his pocket. He gripped at his knees, clenching at the fabric. I glared at him, suddenly tired of the silent treatment. No one had asked him to come here, and definitely not to treat me like a piece of furniture.

"So, I'm in the car with you. You going to tell me where we are going?" I asked.

He gave me a dark, blue look. "I don't know. *You* texted me."

I frowned. "I never asked you to pick me up."

"I don't know *what* you were asking me to do with those texts. But I'm here, up in the middle of the damn night, and you clearly needed someone to stop you from, I don't know, dying in the street. So, where to, *Miss Crosby*?"

The venom in his voice was so strange; I hated that he was calling me by my last name, just like he had when I was still just an intern at his law firm, only six months ago. I glared back.

"David, could you please drop me off at Sheafe and Margaret Street?" I asked the driver without breaking eye contact with Brandon.

Brandon frowned. "Where is that?"

"Where I live!" I snapped, now preoccupying myself with searching for something—anything—in my purse.

Unfortunately, my clutch was small, so sorting through it was not a good distraction. But I didn't want to look at him, didn't want to feel those beautiful blue eyes boring into me with such vitriol. It hurt too much.

"Where you *live*? What happened to the New York job?"

I ground my teeth, still avoiding his face. His hand was now resting on the back of the car seats, only a few inches from my shoulder. It was physically painful to be this close to him and not touch. I could smell his scent, almonds and soap and sleep, and it was so much more vivid than in my imagination. My thighs clenched.

"I had to take one here," I said finally. "I've got debts to pay and a father to put through some very expensive therapy. A public service job just wasn't going to cut it, so here I am again."

Brandon processed the information while his gaze flew around the car and his hand massaged the leather seat.

"What debt?" he finally asked as he pulled his hands back into his lap. "I paid everything off to Messina. All of it."

"Oh, *I know*," I bit out quietly, chucking my clutch onto the seat between us. "I know all about your so-called 'generosity' to that low-life motherfucker. Set him up for life, didn't you?"

"Oh, so now I'm a jerk?" Brandon looked up to the ceiling of the car as if in pain and groaned. "Perfect. Here we fuckin' are again."

"I don't know. Maybe." Apparently, the alcohol hadn't completely worn off yet. My mouth was shooting off like a teenager's, and I couldn't seem to stop it.

"Jesus Christ, Skylar, I can't keep up with you! Did you call me just so you could berate me again for being a nice guy?"

Brandon yanked off his cap and threw it across the car into the front passenger seat. David picked it up and handed it calmly back over his shoulder to his boss. The car didn't swerve an inch.

"Keep up?" I asked. "I haven't exactly been jerking you around here. Okay, I sent one dumb, drunken text by mistake. Those girls literally fell on me, and my thumb pressed send. No one asked you to get in your Batmobile to save me!"

"You don't get to make me out to be the bad guy here, Skylar!" Brandon erupted. He pulled his hat between his hands so hard I thought it might split apart. "You wanted out, I got the message, and I let you go, didn't I? Even though the breakup made absolutely no fuckin' sense! And there has been no word from you until tonight. None!"

His South Boston accent, which tended to appear only when he was upset or emotional, was now out in full force. I tensed against it, even though at the same time it turned me on. I had been seeking that feeling all night, and was only finding it here. With him. While we were fighting.

How fucked up was I?

"That's because it hurts too much, Brandon!" I yelled back, not even caring that David was sitting in the front seat.

A quick glance revealed that he had thoughtfully put in headphones. I kicked ineffectually at the bottom of the seat in front of me, not caring that it made me look even more like a child. Brandon watched for a few beats, then hurled his baseball cap onto the floor of the car.

"FUCK!" he shouted. "Goddamn it!"

We stared at, bristling under the streetlights that flashed through the windows. Then, before I knew it, we were falling toward each other. I was scrambling across the seat and grabbing at the collar of his shirt; his long arms were yanking me into his lap.

We attacked, desperate to get closer, to consume one another right there in the back of the car. My fingers clawed at the muscles under his thin T-shirt; his own hands were just as savage, clutching desperately at my waist, back, ass, any place he could use to pull me so that I was straddling his lap. Soon my dress was hiked up nearly to my waist, and Brandon growled again as one hand found bare skin and squeezed hard enough that I'd probably have bruises in the morning. Another grabbed my ponytail and pulled. I moaned aloud against his lips. The pain felt good. It was exactly what I needed.

"What the fuck do you want?" he snarled in between angry, forceful kisses. "Is this what you want?" He wrapped my ponytail in his fist and pulled again, even harder this time.

I didn't say anything, just kissed him back, biting at his lips while both of us groaned, desperate to get closer, desperate to get beyond the thin layers of clothing. I slid my hands under the hem of his shirt, wanting to feel his smooth, ribbed muscles. My fingernails dug in, and Brandon groaned. He kneaded my ass and thighs forcefully and ground his obvious desire through the meager material that separated us.

Then the car pulled to a stop. We broke apart, breathing heavily, and caught in a mutual stare as our chests heaved. Brandon's hand tightened on my thigh, but the other dropped from my hair. I loosened my death-grip on his collar. My gaze dropped to his lips, now swollen and reddened. No doubt mine looked much the same.

David cleared his throat. Oh fuck, I thought as a flush immediately covered my body. What the fuck was I doing? I slid off Brandon and hastily tugged my skirt back into place. Ducking my head (I couldn't even think of looking at David), I quickly clambered out to the sidewalk in front of my small brick building. The street, one of the quieter in the North End, was deserted, although sounds of merriment still filtered through the brick corridors leading to Hanover Street.

Willing myself not to turn around, I dug clumsily through my purse for my keys. When I looked up, another car door slammed shut. David pulled the car away, leaving Brandon in the middle of the deserted street, hands fisted at his sides.

His brow was a bit sweaty, as if he'd been exerting himself, and his hair, which had already started to grow out a little since I'd last seen him, stuck out in several directions. He had a slightly crazed look in his eyes, which I had a feeling was mirrored in my own.

"Wha–what are you doing?" I asked as he approached, shoulders moving with the grace and intention of a predatory cat.

The glare of the street lamp caught the ends of his hair, lighting them up like a halo, although the single-minded expression on his face was anything but angelic.

"Which one is your house key?" Brandon demanded as he plucked my keychain out of my hands.

"What the fuck? Let me do it!"

I snatched the keys back from him and fumbled to the correct one, dropping the set twice before finding it. Before Brandon could argue back, I had unlocked the door and charged into the small building, a six-foot-four lion on my heels.

I took the steps of the walk-up two at a time, Brandon hot on my tail. It felt like a race, but no one was having fun. The urgency between us in the car was back, building with every step we took. All I could think about was having his hands on me again, having his lips on me. But I was angry too. Angry that he made me feel this way. Angry that I couldn't stop myself. Angry that we had done everything we had to each other, and angry that things couldn't go back to the way they used to be.

Full of that animal anger, I kept going past the third floor, where my apartment was. I didn't want him to see that space I'd worked so hard on all day—that space that had nothing but a futon and piano sitting in it, but which I'd inadvertently painted the exact color of his eyes. I didn't want his pity. I just wanted to fuck him and be done with it so I could get him out of my system and move on.

We charged straight to the top of the six-stories and out the heavy fire door to the rooftop. It wasn't exactly the posh roof of his massive townhouse—just a concrete slab bordered by a creaky metal railing. A few rusted lounge chairs that some of my neighbors had apparently donated to the building were clustered in one corner. Two taller brick buildings shot up on either side of us, eclipsing the roof in their shadows.

"What are we doing here?"

Brandon's deep voice echoed across the roof. The heavy metal door banged closed behind us, and I turned around to look at him. His eyes drifted down my body, resting briefly on my bare legs—what had once been his favorite part of my anatomy. I was suddenly very aware of just how much skin I was showing. I normally wore this dress like a tunic over leggings; the hem barely reached the bottom of my ass.

"What do you think we're here for?" I retorted, not feeling the slightest bit gracious.

His hungry blue gaze snapped up to meet mine, sending another shock of yearning through my center. His eyes flashed so much they practically sparked. I still felt furious. Furious and full to the brim of naked lust.

He didn't answer. I stared. He stared. All of the pain and torment of the past few months was bubbling to the surface. The intense desire. The yearning.

In my still-drunken haze, there was only one thing I wanted. Now it was my turn to stalk him. So I did, and surprisingly, he backed up, all the way to the thin black railing at the perimeter of the roof.

"Skylar, I want to talk," Brandon said, though his eyes continued to drift over my body, down to my bare thighs and back up to where the silver chains fell into the cleavage he couldn't help but see with his height advantage.

I ran my hands under his T-shirt, eager to feel the warmth of his skin again, the edges of the defined muscles that dipped into his waistband. He grunted heartily at my touch; already I could feel the length of him straining through his jeans. He wanted the same thing I did.

"I don't believe you," I said as I slipped my hands lower and started to undo the buttons of his jeans. I spread the fabric apart and pulled at the waistband of his boxer briefs, the ones that didn't exactly hide just how badly he wanted me. "I don't think that's what you're here for. And it's definitely not what I'm here for."

"Skylar—shit!" he yelped at the sudden contact of my hand closing over him. His hands, stretched out over the rickety black railing, gripped the thin metal edge tight enough to turn his knuckles white. "Baby—"

"I am *not* your baby," I interrupted, even as I ran my nose up and down the straining muscles of his neck. God, he smelled so good. I wove my fingers into the thick hair at the base of his neck and dragged him down to me. He met me heartily, attacking me with a ferocity that neither one of us anticipated.

"Fuck," Brandon gasped into my mouth. "Fuck, that feels so good."

He groaned as if in pain when I pulled my hand back out of his jeans. I shoved his jeans and boxer briefs over his hips, over the perfect lines of his ass and the v-shaped muscles of his abdomen. I knelt down, oblivious to the cold concrete or the fact that any of the neighbors in the taller building could see us clearly if they liked. I only had one thing on my mind.

"What are you doing? I said I wanted to talk," Brandon said, even as the obvious lust caused his voice to crack, eyes wild as he watched my descent.

"Fine, you talk. I'll listen." I took him between my lips, effectively gagging him despite being the one with a full mouth.

His hands immediately found their way into my hair, subtly urging me on.

"Skylar—fuck!" His words choked in his throat as I continued my work. "I...you know...oh my...*shit!*"

His breathing became more and more erratic until at last, his hands tightened in my hair and he started to rock slightly with the rhythm I had set. It didn't take long. One, two, three more times, and his entire body tensed. Brandon swore profusely, and I finished him off. Slowly. And savored every. Single. bit.

When I pulled back, Brandon was leaning completely against the railing to support his sagging weight, his face looking up to the dark night sky. His broad chest rose and fell dramatically as he worked to catch his breath. Every muscle of his legs was on display and fully tensed, the bright moonlight above us drawing shadows around their long, lean lines.

I reached to where my purse lay discarded on the concrete and stood up. All vestiges of my lust were fading fast, even though I hadn't come anywhere near completion myself. I still wanted him—God, I wanted him more than anything—but I couldn't, and not only because I wouldn't be medically cleared to do that for another two or three weeks. I couldn't because while this aching I felt, the knowledge that we just couldn't work anymore, had abated as I lost myself in him and made him lose himself in me, it had only gotten worse after.

I suddenly felt tired. Discarded. Ashamed. And heartbroken all over again.

I felt the remnants of gravel still sticking to my kneecaps and the uncomfortable binding of this stupidly tight dress. I felt the taste of him in my mouth, and the feel of him against my fingers. The unrelenting throb of wanting him still coursed through my entire body, but my skin felt so fragile, like I was made of impossibly thin glass.

I felt like I was going to break. So before Brandon even had a chance to pull his pants up, I fled.

"Skylar!" his voice rang out just before the heavy door slammed shut behind me. Before he could open it again, I had raced down the three flights of stairs and into my apartment.

True to his word, Eric was out for the rest of the night, undoubtedly having found what he wanted in the arms of one of the women who seemed more than ready to take him home. Our spare apartment, with its unadorned walls and ascetic vibe, mild fumes of paint still wafting from my room, was a cold, lonely refuge.

On the other side of the door, Brandon's heavy steps echoed up and down the stairs of the building. A few shouts of my name bounced off the stone floors and plaster walls. But after one of my neighbors threatened to call the police, even Brandon wasn't stupid enough to bang on anymore doors.

After thirty minutes, the footsteps faded away. I sank from my place against the door down to the hard wood floor. I buried my head in my knees and sobbed.

~

Chapter 7

My phone had been silent all day. No messages. Nothing.

Unready to process the events of last night with anyone, not even Jane, I had thrown myself into doing whatever I could to put the haze of last night firmly out of my head. The first thing I did when I woke up was to join a gym, and I spent the rest of the morning in the pool, swimming away my hangover and my shame. When my furniture was delivered that afternoon, I unpacked my clothes, color-coded my closet, and set up my belongings. I covered the piano with a throw blanket until I could decide what to do with it, but everything else (my new bed, a desk I had found at a different consignment shop, and the matching bureau and nightstand I'd found on craigslist) eventually found their homes against my new blue walls.

Still, it took me several hours and several recruitments of my irritable, hungover roommate to move around the furniture until I was halfway satisfied with its placement. Nothing seemed right; everything seemed out of place no matter where I put it.

By the end of the day, while my insides still felt like they had the strength of a blade of grass in a windstorm, I felt like I had done everything I could to stabilize everything I could. I was due in my new offices tomorrow morning to sign my new hire paperwork. I couldn't afford to be a basket case on the job.

Just before going to sleep, I steamed one of my new outfits from Bubbe and hung it on the closet door before taking one of Eric's sleeping pills. I couldn't afford to stay awake with my thoughts, staring up at a ceiling that would undoubtedly reflect a certain thousand-watt smile and pair of dimples. I had a big day in the morning at my new job, and I wasn't going to fuck that up.

~

"Great suit."

Kieran looked the same as always, dressed in a minimalist black suit and shiny black loafers. Her dark shoulder-length hair was pulled back into a severe ponytail, and her face was unadorned except for a slash of red lipstick. Her eyes, sharp and unflinching, flashed as I stood up from my seat outside the HR offices.

I looked down. Out of all of the pieces that Bubbe had insisted on, this one was my favorite: a dusky, light-olive silk from Calvin Klein that was perfect for spring. The color made my green eyes glow, and it fit me like a glove. The jacket was collarless and set off against a crisp white blouse, while the matching pants tapered at the ankles above a pair of whiskey-colored pumps. I'd pulled my hair into a no-nonsense bun and foregone contacts in favor of my tortoise-shell glasses. I looked professional and chic. It was oddly satisfying.

"Thanks," I said with a confident smile, although I was incredibly nervous.

I had just finished signing the paperwork needed to start officially working at Kiefer Knightly, but this was the first time I was facing Kieran. Having served as my mentor at a family law clinic last semester and being instrumental in getting me this position in the first place, she was someone whose opinion mattered to me very much. Did she know what had happened with Brandon and me? Two months ago? Two weeks ago? Or even two nights ago?

As Kieran led me back through the firm, again I mentally thanked Bubbe for the wardrobe updates. This was a law firm, so no one was too flashy or avant-garde, but the attorneys at Kiefer Knightly clearly made some money and dressed like it too.

Kiefer Knightly took up two floors of a large office building near Copley Square, just a stone's throw away from the bustling downtown area of Boston's business district and three blocks from Brandon's firm, Sterling Grove. It was a full-service firm that did a lot of business in family law, my intended specialty and something that Sterling Grove barely touched, which was likely why Brandon wasn't using in-house attorneys to handle his divorce. That, and I suspected that Kieran was the only person he trusted with the intimate details of his marriage.

Kieran steered us past the main reception area down a hallway lined with offices on one side and a long conference room on the other. All of the walls were glass, although I noticed that some of them looked like they were covered in a thick layer of fog.

"All of the walls in the office are equipped with privacy glass," Kieran said, tapping a fingernail against one of the frosted walls we passed. "But FYI, the partners prefer associates to keep their offices transparent when they are not with clients. Makes it easier for Big Brother to watch, right?"

Kieran wasn't one to wink, but she gave me a wry smile to let me know she thought the practice was ridiculous. I followed her down to the end of the hall, where she turned right into a small office on the interior side. She held out a hand.

"Your office. Hey, at least you get windows, right?"

I smirked at the joke. Like every other office, all the walls were windows, but every one of them looked out to another office. It was basically just a glass cube.

I shrugged and set my briefcase down on the empty desk. "I can't complain. It's a job. Really, Kieran, thank you so much for helping me here and for showing me around. I know it wasn't easy."

"It'll be worth it," she said. "The button for the windows is on the far side of the desk. Even though we'd like you to focus on passing the bar before you really start work, we had the paralegals make you and the other new associates copies of the files for a case that's going to trial soon. There will be an associates' meeting about it today, so you should stick around for that. It's in the main conference room at eleven. In the meantime, Chris in HR will be here in a few to get you registered for your bar exam class."

I nodded and sat down behind the desk, eager to get started. Kieran looked at me for a moment, then nodded back.

"Right then," she said. "Well, welcome."

Without a word, she disappeared down the corridor of glass, a feat I would have thought impossible considering most of the walls were transparent. But that was Kieran, I supposed. No muss, no fuss.

I turned to my computer and started to click through the log in instructions. It was nice to have something to do, things to do that would distract me. It was nice to feel productive.

"Excuse me, Ann-Marie told me that Kieran was—oh!"

A familiar deep voice froze my hands over the keyboard. No. This wasn't happening. Not on my first day and not in a building with transparent walls through which everyone could see my equally transparent features. Fuck. How had Kieran said to frost the walls?

"Skylar?"

Goddamn it. The real problem was that someone like him was bound to attract attention, if he hadn't already. And I couldn't look down at the plastic keys forever.

"Skylar?" he said again.

This time he left the "r" off the end of my name, and that familiar tell just about killed me.

I looked up to find Brandon leaning confidently in the slim doorframe, dressed in a beautifully fitted gray suit and pale pink shirt. It was a far sight from the wrinkled T-shirt and baseball cap he'd worn on Saturday, with his blond curls styled elegantly and face cleanly shaved. He looked like a model, not a brilliant business and legal mind. Basically, he had no business being seen by any woman who hadn't been lobotomized. Me, in particular.

Behind him, I caught more than one female associate glancing over their desks with hooded, yet covetous looks, most of them aimed somewhat lower than his back.

I sighed and forced myself to stare at my empty email inbox. "What are you doing here?"

He frowned and pushed off the doorframe to enter the room. "I was looking for Kieran. What are *you* doing here?"

I looked around at my desk, feigning confusion. "I work here."

Brandon blinked. "What?"

I tapped my fingernails on the Cherrywood desktop, focusing on my breathing. I really didn't want to blush in front of my colleagues, although I could already feel it coming. Come on, Crosby, think of things that don't get you excited. Dad's old bathrobe. Tort law. Yanni.

I looked up again to find Brandon glaring at me, and all my efforts were completely wasted.

"What?" I affected innocence. "Yes. I told you I had to take a job in Boston. I can't pay you back otherwise, nor can I pay for my dad's continued treatment."

"You can't pay me back..."

The words trailed off under his breath as Brandon shook his head. Brandon wasn't given to blushes like I was, but I knew his other tells, one of which was the hand currently tugging at his nicely combed hair. Well, what used to be nicely combed.

He exhaled, long and deep, then looked back at me with eyes like fire. Electric blue fire. Without saying anything else, he marched into the small room while the door swung closed behind him. He continued around my desk and leaned over me, forcing me to sit far back in my chair while I gripped the arms of the desk chair.

"What are you doing?" I hissed, trying to keep my face still despite the fact that it was now likely a brighter pink than his shirt.

I tried not to observe how amazing he smelled that close, but failed miserably. A few of the associates were watching through the glass walls with open curiosity. I was mortified and turned on all at once.

Brandon still said nothing, just reached around me and pressed the button Kieran had pointed out on the side of my desk. He clearly knew his way around these offices. Immediately all of the walls and the door turned icy white, and more importantly, opaque.

He stood up, leaving me still gripping my chair arms for dear life and breathing much harder than I wanted to be.

"We're really supposed to leave the walls clear unless we're with clients," I whispered, to which I received another withering scowl.

"I am a client," Brandon said as he pulled off his jacket and practically hurled it, along with his briefcase, on one of the chairs in front of my desk.

His chest heaved. I watched warily as he loosened his tie and unbuttoned the top button of his collar. What did he think he was doing?

"You're a client," I repeated, half-mesmerized by his actions as he stalked toward me again. "What, are you getting *another* divorce today?"

Another glare. This time I didn't look away.

"Well, you're not *my* client," I continued, more boldly than I really felt.

"No," Brandon growled, "I'm not."

Before I could say anything else, I was bodily yanked out of my seat and into a kiss so searing that I felt it in my toenails. My body reacted instinctively, hands grabbing at his mussed waves while his tongue twisted unforgivingly around mine. We both grunted and wrenched at each other, echoing the same urgency from the back of his car, except it was nine in the morning and sober. I felt everything that much more acutely.

Finally, during a quick breath, I remembered exactly where I was and pushed him away.

"Fuck!" Brandon yelped, hopping around like he had been burned.

"Shh!" I pointed to the blocked windows. "They can hear you!"

I hastily fixed the back of my blouse, which had become untucked under my jacket. My hair had completely fallen out of its pins, and my glasses were now somewhere on the floor.

"These walls are soundproofed," Brandon said darkly as he handed me the thick frames. "Kiefer Knightly takes confidentiality very seriously, maybe even more than Sterling Grove. So I can say or do pretty much whatever the FUCK I want, as loud as I want."

I shoved my glasses back into place and scowled at him. He scowled back. We seethed like spitting cats for at least a minute before I broke first and looked away, suddenly preoccupied with re-twisting my hair into its bun.

"You should leave it down."

"You should just leave," I snapped. "This is completely inappropriate. I really have to–"

"Where did you go the other night?" Brandon interrupted sharply while he re-buttoned his collar. "I looked up, and you were booking it out of there. You literally left me with my pants down."

"I had things to do," I said lamely.

I sat back down in my chair and scooted so my navel was pressed tight against the desk. I braced my feet against the wood. I had no intention of being manhandled again for another impromptu kiss—if you could even call that mauling a kiss. Whatever, you liked it.

"Things to do?" Brandon squatted in front of my desk so we were eye to eye. "So that's how it's going to be? Just give me a BJ on your roof and run away? No excuses, no apologies? Nothing?"

I didn't say anything, just watched the moving screensaver on my computer screen as I bit back tears. This wasn't fair. It really wasn't.

"When were you going to tell me you worked here, Skylar?" Brandon asked, this time a bit more softly. But only a bit.

"I don't know," I said sullenly, still unable to look at him. "Maybe I wasn't."

"Did you think I wasn't going to find out?"

"I don't know."

Brandon blew a long, thin stream of air through his teeth. "You're acting like a child."

Finally, I looked up. "Says the man who just barged into my office and grabbed me."

He stood up then and came back around my desk.

"Oh, no you don't," I said, scooting my chair away, which did effectively nothing as Brandon rolled me back out to face him.

He pulled me out of the chair again.

"Hey! I didn't want to get up!"

"I need you to talk to me like an adult!"

"No!" I pushed him away. "Stop grabbing at me! Jesus, didn't anyone ever teach you about consent?"

"Stop it!" Brandon growled, holding both of my wrists in vise-grips and pinning them to my sides. "Will you just fucking stop? Calm down!"

Even though he had said the glass was soundproofed, it was the thought that people could still possibly hear us that finally made me quiet. My arms went limp, and Brandon dropped them. I wanted to skewer him.

"You can't do this," I gritted through my teeth as I skittered around him, out of his considerable reach.

He glared at the chairs that now stood between us, but stayed where he was.

"This is my place of work," I continued in a low, even voice that belied my rage. "You can't just bang around in here like a caveman."

"I'm this firm's most important client," Brandon retorted. "They wouldn't care if I took you ten different ways on top of that desk."

"Yes, but they certainly would care if *I* did, you arrogant twat!" Now my own smothered Brooklyn accent was coming out. "This is *my* career, *my* reputation we're talking about, Brandon! You don't have to worry about yours because it's already made!"

We silenced, caught in another interminable standoff. This time I won when his shoulders eventually drooped in acknowledgement. Brandon blew out a long sigh, covered his face with his hands, and groaned, loud and long, through his fingers.

"All right," he said finally. "I'll leave. On one condition."

"What's that?" I asked. I probably would have agreed to tap dance down Commonwealth Avenue if it meant getting him out of my office.

"You come to dinner with me tonight. And stay. And talk. The whole time. I deserve at least that from you. I deserve answers, Skylar."

Honestly, I would have preferred the tap dancing. "I don't have time for that tonight. I start a bar prep class tomorrow, and I have to catch up on what I've missed being here today."

"Tonight," Brandon repeated. "Otherwise..."

"Stop bullying me!" I spat, slapping a hand onto the leather edge of the chair in front of me. "I don't know if you forgot what it's like to be a new associate, but I don't have time for this shit! I can't afford to fuck up this job, Brandon!"

For a third time, we were caught in a faceoff, fingertips white with the tension as we gripped at the chair and the desk. But I wasn't going to break first this time. No way.

"Fine," Brandon finally relented, with at least enough courtesy to look a little contrite.

Ha, I thought. Two out of three.

He stood up, adjusted his tie and straightened his collar once more. "What about this weekend?"

I didn't say anything, just shot him a dirty look. I wasn't ready to roll over and play nice.

He sighed. "Goddamn it, Skylar, please?"

I exhaled slowly. "Fine. Friday, I guess. What time?"

"Seven-thirty. I'll pick you up."

"No, I'll meet you there," I said.

I didn't want him to know my actual apartment number, even though it was probably only a matter of time until he charmed the information out of HR. That stupid smile got him just about anything he wanted.

Brandon rolled his eyes, but nodded in faux-acquiescence. "Whatever you say, Red."

I flinched at the casual nickname. As common as it was, he had always used it with fondness and so I had come to love it. A few unexpected tears welled up, and I looked down at my empty chair, blinking them away.

"I'll have Margie text you the reservation."

"Fine."

Brandon picked up his briefcase and jacket off the other chair. He walked around me in a conspicuously wide circle to leave, then stopped in the doorway. Chewing on his lip, he looked dangerously like he wanted to tackle me all over again.

"Friday. Seven-thirty," he said, pointing a finger like Uncle Sam. "You promised."

And then he turned abruptly and disappeared down the hall. Somehow, I made it back to my desk, where I collapsed in my chair and buried my face in my hands. So much for a clean start.

~

Chapter 8

Tuesday morning, Eric and I both woke up around five a.m., blearily greeting each other in the kitchenette as the sun was just starting to peek through the blinds.

"Morning," Eric said as he rubbed a pale hand over his half-asleep face.

He turned to the counter to begin his daily regime of coffee. In a kitchen that was otherwise quite bare, Eric had the full setup: a special countertop kettle that heated water to the exact temperature that was supposedly ideal for making coffee, a glass pour-over device that looked more fitting to a nineteenth century laboratory than a twenty-first century kitchen, and a selection of local coffee beans that had all been roasted within the week.

"Morning," I said as I set my very regular kettle on the stove to boil the old-fashioned way. I rummaged around a cupboard and pulled out my favorite travel mug and a box of cheap Irish Breakfast tea.

We had both turned in early the night before, after Eric had come home from a date of some sort (if you could even call his rendezvous dates. I had yet to hear a single one referred to by name). He wore a pair of jogging pants and a white T-shirt: comfortable, casual wear for the several hours we would be spending at a test prep facility. I had pulled on something equally lazy: my favorite old jeans and a T-shirt that said "I'll be Bach" across the front. Eric looked at it and snorted. Yeah, okay, so I was a music nerd.

"I hate this," I griped for the fifth time in the last twenty-four hours.

Eric, too tired to formulate a full sentence, just grunted in agreement.

We were both up at the crack of dawn because Sterling Grove, Eric's new firm (which also happened to belong to Brandon), and Kiefer Knightly paid for their new associates to attend the same bar prep class. This was Eric's second day on this schedule; I had missed our morning class yesterday to go to Kiefer Knightly.

It was supposedly the best prep program in Massachusetts, and its attendees had an over ninety-percent pass rate. The bad news was, it was in Andover, a town about twenty-five miles north of Boston. That would have been a half-hour commute by car, but, like most recent students who lived within Boston city limits, neither Eric nor I had a car. That meant that we were looking at an hour commute each way, not including wait and walk time, for a class that started right at eight a.m. each morning.

Like zombies, we moved around the kitchen in tandem, sipping on our caffeinated beverages while we packed snacks and cleaned up. Then we grabbed our book bags, threadbare from three years of hard use at Harvard, and left to be students for the last time.

~

The test prep center was in an unassuming office park about a mile from the Andover train station. We arrived about fifteen minutes before class, with Eric in a dark mood after realizing just how hot it was going to be schlepping between the station and the classroom every day in the heat of summer.

"This is bullshit," he said again as he wiped the sweat off his brow. Like me, Eric turned bright red when he exerted himself. "I look like I just ran a marathon. I'm going to have to bring a change of clothes every day on top of all the other crap."

I look on with amusement. But he also had a point—in another month, Boston would feel like a sauna pretty much any time of day, and this walk was going to get seriously uncomfortable.

We walked into the thankfully air-conditioned building and up the stairs to where our assigned classroom was. It was a relatively big class, with somewhere around fifty other recent law grads clustered in groups around large gray desks.

"Hey, Skylar!"

I looked to my left to see another friendly face, one that made my stomach drop. Jared Rounsaville was a classmate of Eric's and mine at Harvard. He was a nice, polite, WASPish-looking guy, with straight, light brown hair and brown eyes that crinkled a little at the corners when he smiled. He was starting a job at his grandfather's tax firm this year, although considering that his father was a sitting Congressman, it was also likely that he was planning a future in politics as well.

He was also someone I'd dated briefly and promptly blown off when I'd met Brandon. Running into Jared and his family at the symphony with Brandon at my side last February hadn't been my proudest moment, and I'd gone out of my way to avoid him on campus until we'd graduated.

"Hi, Jared," I said, leaning to accept a quick hug and kiss on the cheek.

Eric watched the two of us with curious, raised brows, but his face quickly dropped into a neutral expression when Jared turned to slap his hand.

"How's it going, man?" Jared asked. "Are you guys..." He looked knowingly between me and Eric.

"No. *No*," I said emphatically when I realized what Jared was suggesting.

Eric's widened and he shook his head effusively. "Um, *no*. Just roommates."

Jared nodded, although he looked between us as if he was trying to figure out whether or not we were lying. Eric and I were basically making twin faces of disgust, so Jared relaxed.

"Huh," he said. "Well, that's wild, you two as roommates. You're at Sterling Grove, aren't you, man?" he asked Eric, who nodded. Jared turned to me. "Are you working there now too, Skylar?"

His big brown eyes blinked innocently, but we both knew it was a loaded question. If I had taken a job at Sterling Grove, the real question would be whether I had been hired by my boyfriend.

I cleared my throat. "Um, no. I took a job at Kiefer Knightly."

"Oh, cool. They handled my sister's divorce," Jared said. "Your boyfriend must have been disappointed though."

And...there it was. Eric shifted uncomfortably and stared at the generic gray carpet, but I was grateful he hadn't bailed.

"Um, well," I tripped over the words and crammed the bottom of my T-shirt inside my fist. "We're, um...I'm not seeing anyone right now."

Every word of the sentence stabbed me in the heart. But if Jared was happy, to his credit, he didn't show it.

"Oh," he said sympathetically. He reached out and patted me on the shoulder. "Hey, I'm sorry to hear that. You two seemed to really be into each other that night at the symphony. I almost didn't even blame the guy for stealing you away."

Eric cleared his throat and looked around the room, but to his credit, he still didn't leave. I had to give it to him: however poorly he tended to treat his romantic interests, Eric was a decent friend.

"Yeah, well," I said in a low voice. I just wanted to stop talking about this. "Things change."

Jared opened his mouth to say something else when the instructor of the class entered the room. Everyone took their seats, and Eric and I grabbed one of the tables together. Jared took another next to ours, and pulled out the assigned book and a notebook. He smiled kindly when he caught me looking at him, but otherwise said nothing more for the rest of the class.

~

Four mind-numbing hours later, we filed down the stairs and out of the building with several hours' worth of homework and studying for tomorrow.

"I can't believe this," Eric groused as we started the long walk back to the train station. "This is more homework than I had in any of my courses last semester."

The sun was high in the sky by this point, and it was warm, even for early June.

"No one gets that much homework anyway during third year, so it's not really a fair comparison," I pointed out, earning a withering glance from Eric.

"First year, then," he said. "More than Torts. Top that, Counselor."

I chuckled. Eric was fun to rile up. It was a lot of homework, but that was to be expected. Studying for the bar exam was arguably the most critical step to becoming a lawyer. If we didn't pass, we were out of a job and for many, hundreds of thousands of dollars in debt. This was a make-or-break kind of thing, and I intended to take it seriously.

"You'll get through it," I said. "I'll help."

A blue BMW compact pulled up beside us. The passenger window rolled down, revealing Jared smiling in the front seat.

"Hey, there, sports fans," he greeted us as he revved the engine. "Need a lift back to town?"

"Absolutely," Eric said, and we piled in.

I sat in the back while the boys sat up front, but as he drove, Jared would glance at me every so often through the rearview mirror.

"How're you doing back there, Skylar?" he asked. "I'm not making you carsick, am I?"

I shook my head. "No, I'm good, but thanks for asking. I didn't know you had a car."

"Oh, definitely. I wouldn't live without one. Otherwise you're stuck in the city, you know?"

I couldn't see Eric's face, but his back straightened considerably. A city boy through and through, Eric hadn't even gotten his license until just last year so he could drive with some girl out to Cape Cod for the weekend. Having similarly grown up in New York, I hadn't gotten mine until college, but had barely used it.

Jared pulled onto the freeway and I sat back in my seat to enjoy the drive. It was a really nice day; I was wishing I didn't have to spend the majority of it holed up studying.

"What do you think, Skylar?"

Jared winked broadly through the rearview mirror.

"Um, sorry," I stuttered. "What? I was lost in my thoughts."

"I'll say. I asked you three times what you thought of the upcoming local elections. Who are your favorite candidates?"

I blinked. "Oh. Yeah, honestly, I haven't really been following local politics. I don't even know who the candidates are."

Jared chuckled. "You and most people. That's okay, I can educate you."

I gave a weak smile. Jared and I had pretty opposite politics. His family was all old-money Libertarians, and from what little I knew of them, his father was the most conservative of them all. Mine, on the other hand, was a crazy amalgam of blue-collar New Yorkers who tended to vote Democrat if they voted at all.

"You all right back there?" Jared interrupted me again. "You seem pretty in your own world today."

His face was so frank and open that I couldn't help but smile back, genuinely this time. "Yeah," I said, "I'm good."

"Are you guys planning to take the train every day for the next two months?" Jared asked.

"*Yes*," Eric replied with obvious loathing. "I don't know why there are no decent classes actually in Boston. It's not like there aren't about four hundred J.D.s graduating every year here."

"How long does it take you to get to the prep center?"

"What do you think, Cros?" Eric asked, turning back at me. "Was it an hour or an hour and a half today?"

"Including getting to North Station and wait times for the train? Probably closer to two."

Eric turned back into his seat, shaking his head. "Bullshit," he muttered.

"Well, hey, if you guys need a ride..." Jared offered.

He glanced at me again in the mirror and raised an eyebrow. I smiled again, even though a part of me felt a little uncomfortable accepting his offer, considering our awkward past. I didn't like to feel indebted to anyone, and I knew that Jared wasn't really the type just to offer handouts, nice as he might seem.

"Absolutely!" Eric rushed in before I could say no. "Dude, you are a lifesaver. Seriously. We got gas money if you'll drive."

"Don't you live in Cambridge, though?" I asked, ignoring the glare I got from Eric over the seat back. "That's basically twenty minutes out of your way."

Jared grinned. "It's no problem," he said. "I get up early. Plus, company will make the commute more enjoyable."

"Well, there you have it," Eric said definitively. "Right, Crosby?"

"Sounds good," I murmured, not sure what else to say. Apparently, everything was settled.

"Sounds *good*," Jared echoed, and continued on to Boston.

~

I spent the rest of the afternoon mostly as I'd planned, lounging on my bed with my study materials and a cup of tea until I developed a kink in my neck that couldn't be rolled out. Time for a swim. I gathered up my things and grabbed my gym bag, eager to take a break.

Two hours later, I walked out of the gym and straight into Jared.

"Hey!" he said loudly, seemingly as taken aback by my presence as I was with him. "What's going on, stranger? I must be a lucky guy, running into you twice in one day."

I hoisted my bag over my shoulder and shifted uncomfortably in my flip-flops, which squeaked loudly under my still-wet feet. "Yeah, I guess. What are you doing in this neighborhood?"

Jared pointed his thumb over his shoulder. "My mom's got a thing for Mike's. She sent me into town to pick up dessert before I head to Newton for family dinner."

I followed his gesture toward the *pasticceria*. It was a famous spot, but also a place that held special memories for me, considering the number of times I'd been there with Brandon. I hadn't been there since moving to the neighborhood last week, and I probably wouldn't go for the foreseeable future.

It wasn't hard to imagine a dinner with Jared's family. I had only seen them in passing at various student events over the years, but everyone knew who his father was, a paunchy, bland-looking politician whose wife was clearly the source of Jared's good looks. I could see them all perfectly, surrounding a doily-covered colonial table, eating roasted chicken and mashed potatoes off pastel-colored china. They would look like a J. Crew ad while they tucked into their Italian cheesecake, which would probably be the most exotic thing at the table.

Don't be a bitch, Crosby.

"So, where are you coming from?" Jared looked over my casual leggings and the damp hair tied in a messy bun. "I'm going to guess the gym."

I nodded. "Yeah. Pool." I didn't know what else to say. The gym had worked out my muscles, but not my bad mood.

"So hey, I wanted to say again: I'm really sorry about you and Sterling."

My stomach clenched at the name. I had been trying not to think about him all afternoon, or the fact that I would have to see him again in three more days. Today had been a start in the process of moving forward with my life, hard as it was. I wasn't being destructive, but productive. The awkward conversations with Jared felt like the wrong direction.

"Thanks," I mumbled down at the pavement. "And hey, I'm sorry too. About, you know..."

"Blowing me off?"

I looked up prepared to see a frown, but Jared was grinning.

"Hey, it's okay," he said as he reached out to pinch my shoulder lightly. "It was only one date. You met someone else. It happens."

"Yeah," I said quietly. "And look how that turned out."

"Hey." Jared reached a tentative hand out and tipped my chin up to look at him.

The gesture made me feel like a child. His face was open and friendly, but his finger lingered on my jaw for just few beats more than it should have. It wasn't until it dropped that I relaxed.

"Friends?" he asked.

I smiled. "Sure. Friends."

"Good," he said. "Because I'm going to need some study partners until we take this friggin' test."

~

Later that night, I was video-chatting with Jane before turning in for bed. Although she was an hour earlier than me, you wouldn't know it by the way she was dressed, completely decked out for a night out.

"Aww, there's the adorably sweet studded face I remember!" I teased, earning a grouchy glare through the screen.

"I have to dress even more punk now than I used to," Jane said as she adjusted some of the spikes she had painstakingly arranged in her short black hair, which no longer sported any of its bright-colored stripes. "The ASA makes me come into work to do clerical stuff in the afternoons, so I have to look all boring and professional."

"You're like hipster-punk Korean Superman," I told her. "You rip off your suit, and underneath is a graphic tee with Nancy and Sid."

Jane grinned and fixed her thick-framed glasses. She prided herself on her collection of quirky frames, which I guessed she also had to eschew for a more sensible work persona.

"So please tell me you're not going to give Jared a second chance?" she said, changing the subject. "We're talking Jared Rounsaville here. Human equivalent of white bread. Mild cheddar cheese. Unsalted potatoes. Not to mention his family basically makes a living out of robbing the poor to feed the rich."

I smirked. "I think you're just hungry."

"Not *that* hungry."

I shook my head and laid down on my pillow, positioning the computer so that it faced me. "Well, you don't have to worry about any funny business. It's just...I was surprised by how nice he was. I didn't exactly treat him that well after we went out. It's refreshing, you know? To see someone without a grudge."

"Hmmm. Is someone experiencing a bit of self-reflection?"

I made a face. "Maybe."

For all her snark, Jane's sympathy emanated through the screen. "Well, in your defense, it is a bit different. You didn't exactly insult Jared; you just never went out with him again. Brandon lied to your face and hid the fact that he was married."

I scowled and pressed my face into my pillow. "Don't remind me."

"'Fraid I have to, chickie. You made me promise. You need to figure out what you're going to say come Friday. Has he texted you since?"

I sat back up. "No." I fought and failed to keep the disappointment out of my voice. "Just a confirmation email from his assistant."

"Where are you meeting? His place?"

My scowl deepened. "No." Again, it was technically what I wanted, since I knew that I probably wouldn't be able to stand my ground in such an intimate environment. "She made a reservation at The Martin."

"Ooh, chichi," Jane said. "That place is seriously swanky."

"It's where he takes important clients," I muttered with no little resentment. I was being treated like one of Brandon's many business engagements, and I didn't like it. Not one little bit.

"It's probably his way of keeping his distance, Sky. Just like you asked."

"He kissed me in the middle of my workplace, Jane. That's not keeping his distance."

"Well, considering what you did on the roof, I'm not sure he was completely out of line on that one."

"Whose side are you on here?"

I harrumphed, and Jane chuckled as she stood up. Through the computer screen, she twirled, modeling an outfit that matched the T-shirt with black skinny jeans, combat boots, and wide studded belt.

"I have to get going, babe," she said. "Got my own fish to catch tonight."

"I don't know how you do it," I replied. "It's a Tuesday night. Don't you have class tomorrow too?"

Jane shrugged. "Everyone needs to let off steam. You swim. I Tinder. But don't worry, Mom, I'll be back before midnight. And no drinking on school nights."

I smiled. "Have fun and be safe. Miss you, Janey."

"Miss you too, Sky. And don't worry. Knowing Old Moneybags, you'll have him in the palm of your hand if you wear a skirt."

I laughed and said my goodbyes. But the pit in my stomach grew a little bit deeper. The problem with having Brandon under my spell was that I couldn't do it without falling under his.

~

Chapter 9

On Friday, I found myself standing outside of The Martin, one of the nicest restaurants in Boston. Built on top of a dock overlooking Boston Harbor, it was the kind of place that had complimentary valet parking and a carpeted sidewalk leading to a pair of big brass doors. The waiters all dressed like the penguins in *Mary Poppins,* and the staff included not one but *three* sommeliers.

Through the glass panes in the doors, twinkled chandeliers hung from high-beamed ceilings, and the prismatic light seemed to reflect off the equally bright array of restaurant patrons. This was the kind of place where the wealthy went to show off their goods while they wined and dined their peers, other equally wealthy customers. Senators and congressional representatives ate here, right along with college presidents and CEOs. Old money mixed with new, all of it in the interest of making more.

So what was I doing here?

A doorman ushered me inside, and I held my breath until I was all the way across the threshold. I had known it would be like this: formal and slightly overwhelming. There had been complete radio silence from Brandon all week, but I had received two more polite phone calls from his assistant, Margie, on Wednesday and Thursday to confirm the date. We were playing a telephonic game of Owl, and neither of us had blinked first.

So, I had dressed for battle, the kind that required the tiny diamond studs in my ears and the expensive silver bracelet Brandon had given me, easily the nicest thing I owned. I had dressed simply in good fabric and clean lines: a floaty, black silk dress that tied at my waist but flashed a bit of leg when I walked and my favorite black Manolo Blahnik pumps that had taken me six months to save for. My bright red hair was pinned up, with just a few tendrils having escaped en route to the restaurant. After lining my eyes with black and taking extra effort to use the oxblood lipstick I only wore on special occasions, I had thought I'd looked good when I'd left the apartment. Eric's begrudging praise had only made me feel more confident.

But standing in this restaurant, surrounded by men in three-thousand-dollar suits and women with jewelry that flashed from across the room, I felt very, very plain.

"Can I help you?"

A maître d' dressed in an all-black suit looked at me lazily from his desk. His glance took in my appearance, resting a moment at my neck, which, unlike the rest of his female customers', was completely bare.

"Um, yes," I said, stumbling slightly as I approached. I had arrived early, hoping to have time to find my bearings before dealing with Brandon. "Reservation under Sterling."

The maître d's eyes opened wide at the name; whether in surprise or recognition, I couldn't tell.

"Of course, miss," he said, now obedient and eager to please. "Your party has been waiting for you."

Shit. Apparently Brandon had had the same idea.

The maître 'd hustled around, eager to escort me to a table in the back of the crowded restaurant. Somewhat reluctantly, I followed him. Were the restaurant patrons actually glancing at me, wondering what I was doing there? Or was I imagining it? I desperately hoped for the latter.

Brandon sat at a table in the far corner like a king presiding over his court. It was clearly the best spot in the place, a table for two slightly secluded in a small alcove away from the masses of people all chattering over their dinners. He was clearly still recognized, however. As I approached, several nearby customers watched from over their plates of steak and lobster, leaning over to whisper once they knew where I was headed. This time I was certain I wasn't imagining the curious looks.

Brandon sat with his back to the corner, watching intently as I approached. It really wasn't fair, I thought, that the man looked progressively better every time I saw him. He wore a sapphire-blue suit and cognac-colored oxfords that would have looked a bit gaudy on anyone else, but somehow just looked sophisticated on Brandon. A crisp white shirt only emphasized his tanned, chiseled features, shaved but for a light five o'clock shadow. His hair, always a bit unruly, was now combed back into soft waves that framed his face like a golden corona. His blue eyes somehow managed to flash, even in the dim lighting of the restaurant.

He stood as I reached the table. Yeah, that suit looked even better when I got the full body view.

"Skylar," he said as he looked at me with poorly masked appreciation. "You look...great."

I looked down at my simple outfit, then back up. "It's just a black dress."

A broad hand clasped my waist as Brandon leaned in to kiss my cheek. My knees buckled, but he held me up. The rasp of his stubble sent goosebumps up and down my arms, and the familiar scent of almonds, soap, and Brandon made my heart thump. It really wasn't fair the way he could do that.

"You'd stop traffic in a trash bag," he said as he leaned away and, to my irritating regret, dropped his hand. "Shall we?"

I accepted the seat the maître 'd pulled out for me, unaccountably nervous with the formality. I knew that years in a very wealthy, corporate world would have trained him well when it came to social niceties, but this wasn't the Brandon I really knew. The Brandon I knew was happier with pizza than *ossobuco*. The Brandon I knew preferred jeans to a three-piece suit. The Brandon I knew was just a local boy from South Boston, not this pristine man buried in pomp and circumstance.

Had that all just been an act? The thought was saddening.

Brandon retook his seat with a boyish grin that revealed his dimples, and I couldn't help but smile back. But this was weird. It was weird being this close to one another, this unsure of what to say.

"I—ah—" Brandon cleared his throat awkwardly. "Thanks for coming tonight."

I cocked my head. "Well, you didn't really give me a choice, did you?"

He smiled sheepishly. "Yeah, about that. I'm sorry. I just...I really wasn't expecting to see you in that office. And after what had happened the night before, I was still kind of upset."

"Yeah," I said. "Well. It's kind of your thing."

"What's my thing?"

"The railroading." I shrugged, opening up my menu. Everything was written in French.

Brandon's forehead crinkled in confusion. "What?"

"You heard me," I said more calmly than I felt. Good. Focus on what makes you angry. "I give you a limit, and you blatantly disrespect it. Do what you want, and force me along for the ride. It's not...well, we're not seeing each other anymore, but if we were, it would have become a problem. A big one."

Brandon cocked his head as he listened. "I railroad?"

I nodded. "Mm-hmm. Pretty much anytime I do something you don't like."

Brandon scrunched his lips together and tapped a few big fingers on the table. "Well, shit," he said finally. "Then I guess you're not going to like this."

He pulled an envelope from his inner jacket pocket and pushed it across the table. Inside I found a check for the exact same amount that had previously been the balance of my trust, plus the extra cost of liquidating it. It was everything I had sent to begin repaying Brandon's original payment to Victor Messina, the man who had beaten my father within an inch of his life.

"You have got to be kidding." I promptly tore up the check and tossed it into the center of the table. "There is no way you thought I was going to accept that."

Brandon shrugged, but made no move to retrieve the shreds of paper. "True. Which is why I had it deposited into your bank account instead." Before I could open my mouth to ask the obvious question, Brandon shook his head, like I should already know. "HR keeps the files of all of its employees, former and current. I can look up your account information anytime I want."

I gestured angrily at the torn-up check and envelope. "This is exactly what I was talking about. You make these executive decisions about my life even after I explicitly state a desire otherwise. Insane gifts I don't want. Going behind my back to fix problems I never asked you to get involved with in the first place. Keeping shit from me I should have known about from the beginning."

"I accepted your inability to take gifts a while ago, Red, but I'm not taking this one back," Brandon said firmly, but with a sense of humor I found infuriating. It was almost like he was enjoying this, like it was some kind of negotiation. "No matter what you say, I care about you, I care about your family, and I'm probably the only thing stopping those shitheads from showing up while you're gone and taking your dad right back to the track."

"*Right,*" I spat. "Now they're just sending their lackeys to do it instead. Stupid bimbos with giant hair to seduce my dad back to the tables. Seriously, what did you think they were going to do when they realized they could use the guppy to catch the whale?"

I stopped, realizing what had just come out of my mouth. My eyes blinked open, wide with sudden recognition. Corleone. In high school, I had known her younger brother, a kid who used to run errands...for the Messinas. Of course. It wasn't until I uttered the words that I realized just why I didn't like my dad's new "friend." It was so obvious.

Brandon eyes were as wide as oceans, and the tiny crease between his eyebrows became more pronounced as he processed my comment. I pressed my face into my hands. I needed to talk to my dad.

"Excuse me," Brandon said abruptly.

He scooted back from the table, and wove his way quickly out of the restaurant. I sat there for a few moments, then pulled out my phone and dialed my dad's number. It went straight to voicemail; he was probably either at the club listening to his band play without him or out with Katie. Quickly I dialed the house line, which also went to the message machine. Bubbe must have been at some temple event tonight too. Damn. Lastly, I called Bubbe's cell, which also went to voicemail.

"Bubbe," I practically barked as quietly as I could manage. "I need to talk to you about Katie. Call me when you can."

"Can I get you something to drink, miss?"

A waiter stood in front of me, hand clasped neatly behind his back while I put my phone away.

"Sure," I said. Might as well. "A glass of your house red, please."

The waiter scurried off just as Brandon returned, oblivious to the way most of the eyes in the restaurant, especially the female ones, followed him with overt interest. I let out a breath I hadn't known I'd been holding. At least he had come back.

"Sorry about that," he said curtly as he retook his seat. "I had to take care of something."

"Something related to Victor Messina?"

I hadn't meant it to come out as a snarl, but it did anyway. In response, all I got was a hard look.

Without breaking eye contact, Brandon held a hand up with the obvious awareness that the entire restaurant knew who he was and would cater to his every need. Our waiter appeared almost instantaneously. I snorted.

"What can I get for you, Mr. Sterling?"

"I'll have another twenty-year Michter's, neat. And my friend here will have your best scotch with a splash of water."

"I already ordered wine," I cut in saltily.

Brandon pressed his lips together in a thin line and looked at the waiter, who visibly quaked.

"Where is it?" Brandon demanded.

"It's-it's on its way, sir. Here in a moment with yours too. Right away, sir."

The waiter skittered away like a scared mouse.

I turned to Brandon. "That was kind of mean. Poor guy is just doing his job. It's not really fair of you to pull out the scary billionaire voice."

"I don't really feel like a nice guy tonight," Brandon replied evenly. "So."

"So."

"You have anything to say?"

I frowned. "About what? You demanded this stupid dinner."

Brandon exhaled strongly through his nose. "You're impossible, you know that?"

"Takes one to know one."

"Skylar, I swear to God—" he started just as the waiter reappeared with both of our drinks.

Saved by alcohol, Brandon grabbed his glass and put down half of it in one gulp. Without asking, he reached over and took a sip of my wine.

"Hey!" I protested, but was once again ignored.

"What is this swill?" Brandon asked, wrinkling his nose. He turned to the waiter and gave him back my glass. "Bring her a glass of the eight-two Margaux."

"Sir, we don't typically serve that wine by the glass—"

"A bottle, then," Brandon cut in. "And another scotch for me."

I just watched the waiter leave with the glass of wine that, in my opinion, hadn't been bad. Brandon didn't even have the decency to look halfway contrite

"Railroading," I said pointedly.

"Whatever," Brandon replied. "It's on me."

I didn't know if he meant the wine or the mess we were in.

"That's a very nice drink to be shooting like cheap tequila," I observed after watching him put down another gulp.

"I can afford it," Brandon retorted and tipped back the rest. "And God knows I'm going to need it for this conversation. So, now that we've established your unwillingness to accept anything from me at all, you want to tell me what the hell the other night was about? And *don't* say no. You contacted me, Red."

I opened and closed my mouth several times. I wasn't going to get out of talking about this. But there were things that had happened in the last several weeks I also didn't want Brandon to know, and I was absolutely terrible at hiding things, especially from someone who could read me as well as he could.

Brandon sighed again. His expression slowly turned from irritable to sympathetic and resigned. "All right. Why don't we just start with this: what were you doing at that club?"

"The same thing everyone was doing there. Getting drunk. Hooking up. You know."

The look on his face told me that he did know, and that he wasn't pleased to hear it.

"Is that what you came here to do?" he asked. "Brag about your random hookups? You ice me out months ago, and the first time I hear from you is at two a.m. when you're shitfaced at a nightclub, puking on the side of the road. Come on, Skylar, that's not you!"

"Maybe it is," I said petulantly. "If that's what it takes, then..."

"What it takes to do what?" Brandon demanded. "To do what, Skylar?"

"To forget you!" I exploded.

My hands landed on the table with a thump hard enough to make the silverware shake. I sucked in a long breath. I wouldn't cry. I wouldn't. Where was my wine?

"Yeah. Well. I'm familiar with the feeling," Brandon said sadly. "Did it work?"

I bit my lip again, this time hard enough to hurt. "I think you know the answer."

Brandon watched me for a moment. He glanced down at my wrist, where I was wearing the bracelet he had given me before my graduation. I hadn't been able to take it off.

"I'm glad you kept that, at least," he said quietly, as he reached out to touch the metal.

I followed his fingers. His hand was so much darker than mine, a ruddy bronze against my fair, freckled skin.

"It's...special," I said quietly.

"So were we. At least I thought so."

We were quiet until the waiter returned with my wine and prepared to take our orders.

"Red?" Brandon asked.

There was that nickname again. Its casual use made my stomach flip in a way that was all too familiar.

"I haven't looked at the menu," I said lamely. "Can you order for me?"

Maybe it was just that I actually was going to let him do something for me, but Brandon's stern features softened a bit more. I could feel my own resolve weakening too.

"She'll have the scallops," he said with a short smile. "And the beet salad to start. I'll have the steak, rare."

The waiter nodded and left us alone once more. The restaurant was a busy din, but I couldn't hear anything. I took another long sip of wine. I had to admit, it was much, much better than what I'd originally ordered.

"Red?" Brandon interrupted my distraction. "Skylar."

I set my glass down. "Yeah?"

"I miss you too."

The simple admission was enough to undo me. Almost immediately tears welled up, so I drank again, remembering Bubbe's advice that you can't cry when you're drinking something. Considering how this night was already going, I was going to have to switch to water soon.

"I still don't really understand," Brandon continued. "Was it just because of the divorce? I mean, I get it...it's a lot to take, and I should have told you about Miranda from the start. But after that night at your place, I thought things were going to be okay."

I shook my head, toying with my napkin. "It was...ugh...what I saw in your papers. The trust you set up. For...him."

Brandon blinked, his eyebrows furrowing adorably in confusion. "For him...oh." He looked up with sudden clarity. "Oh! For Messina, you mean?"

I nodded.

He ran a hand back through his hair, disturbing its neat coif. "Skylar, I—"

"This is what I mean about the railroading. You promised me you would stay out of it," I said bitterly, all of the anger I had felt bubbling up again. "You *promised*. And then you went behind my back and did it anyway. Like I said, it wasn't ever going to make them go away. They know they've found a gold mine now."

Brandon looked on sadly. "I was just trying to help. I'd rather be the target than your family. Keeping it from you wasn't my goal."

"Yeah, but now they're even more of a target!" I cried, viciously swiping at the tears threatening to spill down my cheeks. "They're targets *because* you're a target! And because I have to pay them back—"

"You *don't* have to pay them back, Skylar," Brandon interrupted. "No matter what happens between you and me, you don't *ever* have to worry about that."

"Well, I still have to pay you," I countered.

"Why? You know I would never accept it."

"If I didn't," I insisted, "I wouldn't have taken this job at Kiefer Knightly. I would be able to stay in New York and take care of my family."

"Is that what you want?"

Brandon leaned over and grabbed my hand. I couldn't pull away, locked as I was by his earnest blue gaze.

"Because I can make that happen," he continued. "I can get you a job at whatever firm you want. I would do anything for you, Red, if I knew it would make you happy."

He squeezed my fingers. It felt like he was squeezing my heart. A few more tears fell, and reflexively, I squeezed back. I hated this.

I considered the option. I could let him help in this way. I could take a fancy job in New York, where I could stay close to my dad and keep him out of trouble. Take the New York bar exam instead of the Boston one.

But the truth was, I hadn't only taken the job in Boston just to pay Brandon back or to afford my dad's treatment. These were the excuses I'd used to ignore the real reason: that deep down, I was terrified I'd never see Brandon again.

"Do you want to leave Boston, Skylar?" Brandon asked. His eyes, having lost all their fieriness, were wide and searching.

"No," I whispered. The dam broke. Tears flowed freely down my cheeks, and I couldn't stop them. "I miss you so much. Everything hurts. I see you everywhere, even places you're not. And then, when I had to–_"

I cut myself off before I admitted my worst secret. I pulled my hand from Brandon's grasp and covered my face, wishing more than anything I were not in the middle of a crowded restaurant full of curious onlookers.

When I dropped my hands, I was surprised to find that Brandon had left his seat and was squatting next to my chair. He pulled my head down to his broad shoulder and let me cry into the sleek lines of his suit jacket as he hushed me softly. I clutched his lapels, inhaling the sweet, familiar scent of him, desperate to be close. It felt so good. And yet, it hurt so, so much.

"Shh," Brandon crooned in my ear. "I got you."

God, I was such a basket case. The doctor had told me it would take a while for my hormones to settle down; clearly, she was right. Brandon, to his credit, acted like there was nothing strange about holding me while I bawled in the middle of one of the ritziest restaurants in New England.

"I'm here," he murmured again, gently stroking my back. "It'll be okay, I promise."

When I finally got control of myself, I pushed reluctantly from his chest and sat up, dabbing at my eyes. With one hand balanced on the back of my chair and the other on the table, Brandon had me effectively caged with his warmth. He flashed a slightly toned-down version of his signature thousand-watt smile, but one that was meant just for me. It was a little bit sad, a little bit hopeful, and a little bit something special. My heart melted even more.

He pushed a loose strand of hair behind my ear. His hand lingered, and instinctually I pushed my cheek into his palm. Tenderly, his thumb stroked my skin

"Skylar, I swear to God," Brandon said, his voice cracking slightly. "I *never* meant to hurt you. Do you believe that?"

Slowly, I nodded.

"I...I can't do anything about the mistakes I've made," he continued. "But...I would do anything—*anything*—to make you happy. Do you believe that?"

He leaned in and pressed his forehead lightly against mine. I closed my eyes again and took in his clean scent. Then I nodded once more.

"I love you, Skylar. Do you believe that?"

I opened my eyes. Brandon was perfectly still; only the rise and fall of his chest betrayed his calm.

"Do you love me yet, Red?"

Another tear fell down my cheek. Those words, which had been at the bottom of every mea culpa letter he'd sent, tugged at my heart more than anything.

"I do," I whispered. "I'm so angry at you. At myself. But I don't want to fight it anymore, Brandon, because I do love you, so, so much. I never stopped."

Brandon closed his eyes this time as he exhaled. When he opened them again, his eyes were alight.

"Thank fucking God," he breathed before he closed his mouth over mine in a kiss that seared every cell in my body.

My arms wrapped instinctually around his neck, pulling him closer. I no longer cared that we were the center of attention in a room that had gone suspiciously quiet. I just wanted close again. I wanted to be where I belonged.

A loud throat-clearing interrupted our reunion all too quickly.

"Um, sir?"

We started apart and looked to where the waiter stood awkwardly, holding our plates of food.

"Your dinner, sir," he mumbled, clearly wishing he were literally anywhere else.

I giggled, swiping again with my napkin at the tear stains that had likely ruined my makeup. Brandon shook his head sheepishly as he stood up.

"I think we'll take it to go," he said with a wry smile. "Charge it to my account, and have it sent up front, will you?"

The waiter nodded, his nervous face darting back and forth between Brandon and me before he left to box up our food. I finished dabbing my face with the napkin, while Brandon watched with a kind, yet guarded expression.

"Sorry," he said. "Do you, ah, want to continue this elsewhere?"

I glanced around the restaurant. People were no longer even trying to hide the fact that they were staring at us.

"Yeah," I admitted. "I definitely think that would be best."

~

We left the restaurant with a veritable picnic basket in hand, as the staff had been kind enough to box up our food and even what remained of the bottle of wine I'd barely drunk, all packed neatly into a silver paper bag.

"That's good stuff," Brandon said when I'd expressed my surprise at the wine-to-go. "You don't want to waste it."

It wasn't until much later that I discovered it was a five-hundred-dollar bottle. Waste not, want not, I suppose.

David pulled up in the Mercedes, but instead of leading us to it, Brandon turned to me with a somewhat shameful expression.

"This is embarrassing," he admitted. "But I have to ask you to take a different car."

I bit my lip. Apparently, this evening hadn't ended the way I thought it had.

"Oh," I said. "Okay, then."

Brandon quickly reached out to grip my hand. "No, no, it's not like that, Red. I—do you mind if I come over?"

I brightened. "Sure."

He delivered an ear-splitting grin that practically lifted my heart out of my chest.

"Great," he said. Then he shifted uneasily. "But we'll have to travel separately. I already had the concierge here call you a separate town car just after mine. Miranda...well, Kieran thinks there's a good chance she put a P.I. on me. It wouldn't be good for you or me if she saw pictures of us together."

There was an awkward pause at the mention of Brandon's still-pending divorce, a long process that his ex-wife had been stringing out for years, but which was undoubtedly taking even longer now that she had discovered my presence in his life. Part of me didn't completely blame her; Brandon Sterling was a hard man to get rid of once you'd let him in.

I looked back at the restaurant with sudden clarity. The Martin, aside from being expensive and impressive, also had excellent security. No wonder Brandon had wanted to meet here.

"I'd like to say that if it's too much for you, you can leave," Brandon said quietly as he reached out to stroke my hand shyly. "But I'm just too selfish for that, I guess. Or else not strong enough."

I said nothing. I couldn't promise that I would forget everything that had happened between us, or even that I would be okay with the fact that he wasn't yet divorced. But I wasn't going anywhere again.

Brandon pulled me to him and tipped my head up.

"Are you really here?" he asked as he brushed a thumb across the outer edge of my jaw and then toyed with the strand of my hair that kept falling out.

Behind us, the maître 'd studiously turned around.

My mouth quirked. "I am," I said. "But these things...we do have stuff to work out." My stomach clenched. I hated to admit it, but there were things I would have to tell him too.

"We *can* work it out, Skylar," Brandon said vehemently. The arm around my waist squeezed, like he was afraid I'd bolt.

"I want to," I said softly.

I placed my own hand on his cheek, tracing my fingers across the stubble covering the strong bones of his cheeks and jaw. My thumb brushed over his full mouth, and he bit it lightly before letting go. Something else tightened deep in my belly.

"We *will*," he stated firmly.

Brandon kissed me again, more softly than before, but no less potent. It was the kind of kiss that tasted of love, not lust, the kind that could last for hours. The kind I could completely lose myself in.

Much to my regret, however, Brandon broke away. "Wait five minutes, then go out to take the next town car that pulls up. I'll see you at your place. Wait in the lobby for me, will you?"

I nodded, and he strode through the doors out to his car. I looked out the window for any signs of a flash or even the reflection of a lens.

If there was someone watching Brandon, they did a good job staying invisible.

My heart sunk a little as I watched the Mercedes drive off. We weren't doing anything wrong, and yet...some part of me felt like a dirty secret. Which in a way, I realized with a cringe, I had been all the time.

~

Chapter 10

Twenty minutes later, I exited a town car after trying and failing to tip the driver, who had already been generously paid and then some. Brandon arrived a few more minutes after that, and rushed into the building as soon as I opened the door for him.

"Hey," he said with an awkward half-smile. "Thanks for waiting. I'm sorry about the run-around."

I shrugged. "It's fine."

We glanced around the homely lobby of my apartment building, one of the older ones around the North End. It might have been decent once, but the black-and-white tiled floors were covered with a thin layer of grime, and the once-white walls were equally dingy and cracked in places. A row of stained brass mailboxes lined the wall across from a staircase made of abused white granite. It was a far sight from the big, fancy house on Beacon Street.

Brandon, however, didn't seem to notice. He followed me up the two flights of stairs to my floor, humming with recognition while his sharp eyes took in everything.

"I hope your neighbors don't threaten to call the cops on me again," he said as I unlocked my door.

I giggled. "I doubt it. Just don't go yelling my name at two a.m."

"Only if you promise not to run away," Brandon said, reaching around my waist and pulling me backward against him.

His touch seemed to melt away a few layers of awkwardness, and I softened into his warm body against my back. I didn't know what we were doing, exactly. In the space of an hour things between us had gone from being defined, if miserable, to completely nebulous, although hopeful.

"Deal," I said, and opened the door.

I flipped on the lights inside, and Brandon looked around curiously.

"Roommate?" he asked, nodding at Eric's bedroom door, which stood open and revealed a plain, queen-sized bed made up with gray linens. His bed was even neater than mine. Eric was nothing if not fastidious.

"Yes," I said as I removed my coat and hung it on the small row hooks by the door. "He's a new associate of yours, actually."

"*He?*"

I turned around to find Brandon now frowning in the direction of Eric's bedroom, as if he expected Don Juan de Marco to walk out of there.

I smirked. "You're not going to turn into the gorilla-jealous type, are you? Because I'm not the one who had a secret wife for four months."

Brandon exhaled heavily through his nose. "All right, all right," he relented. "I guess I deserve that. But if he tries anything, he's fired."

"Oh, he'll definitely try something. Just not on me. He's practically my brother."

Brandon didn't appear comforted by the thought. After pulling off his suit jacket and hanging it next to mine, he examined the tiny living area, taking in the sofa, the TV, the kitchenette, and two-person table. It didn't take long. He turned back to me.

"It's nice," he said. "Smaller than your last place."

I glanced around and shrugged. "It's temporary." I had promised Eric we would only be in this situation until my dad was done with his treatment and I could afford a place of my own.

"When did you move in?"

"Last weekend."

It took Brandon exactly five seconds to walk around the small space, the leather soles of his shoes whispering across the worn wood floors while he checked out the windows, the peekaboo view down the brick-corridored street, the interior of the bathroom. When he was done, he smiled.

"It's nice," he said again. "Where's your room?"

I pointed toward the closed door behind him, and after I nodded that he could go in, he opened the door to peek in there too.

"Did you paint it yourself?" he asked after I turned on the light.

"Yes."

Behind him, I stood unaccountably nervous in the doorway. My furniture had all arrived; now, instead of an empty room with a futon on the floor, everything looked nicely put together, even if the space was a bit cramped.

"What's that?" Brandon pointed at the piano in the corner. It was still closed and covered with a blanket; I hadn't touched it since its arrival.

"My mother sent it," I replied. I sat down on the corner of my bed. "A graduation gift, I guess."

"Your mother? You mean the one who..."

"I don't talk to very much because she abandoned my dad and me? Yeah, that's the one."

Brandon frowned at the instrument, then walked to the piano, as if touching it through the faded blanket would make it more real.

"Why do you think she gave it to you now?" he asked.

I kicked my shoes off and pulled my knees up under my chin, tucking my skirt up behind them. "I don't know, to be honest. She says she's coming to town next month and wants to see me."

Brandon nodded. "Yeah, there are a lot of events going on in July." He looked up, suddenly alert. "They aren't involved with the DNC, are they?"

I raised my shoulders. "I have no clue. Why?"

"No reason."

We fell into an awkward silence again as I was reminded just how little I still knew about the world Brandon inhabited most days. I had thought I knew him so well, but the reality was that the few months we had together occurred inside a cocoon, a world encased in his luxurious house on the Commons, consisting mostly of his couch or his bed, where we alternately worked, studied, made love, and only occasionally emerged for a meal or two. I hadn't met any of his regular friends and acquaintances, and he had only ever met Jane, my best friend, once or twice.

I sighed. I didn't know what we were doing right now, but if it was actually going to work, there was some serious truth-telling to be had. At least, the truths we could share, I noted with a pang.

Would it have had blue eyes or green? Red hair or blond?

The questions rose in my mind before I could stop, and I shuddered. My heart contracted as I willed the thought away. I hated keeping something so big from Brandon, but I didn't even know where we were going right now. I wasn't ready to take the chance that something I did could push him away again. *Maybe I'm too selfish*, he said. Maybe I was too selfish too.

"You're awfully quiet over there, Red," Brandon said. "Could I convince you to play for me? It's been a while."

I blinked, surprised by the request. Slowly, I shook my head. "Not now."

I hadn't actually played since the last night I'd spent at his house, when he'd surprised me with a lavish piano before asking me to move in with him. And I'd said yes too, but less than twelve hours later had met his wife, when she had walked in on us in a fairly compromising position. And by compromising, I mean completely naked and all over each other in the middle of his kitchen.

"What happened to the piano at your house?" I wondered.

Brandon sat down at the far end of the bed and leaned back into a stack of throw pillows. He chewed his lip for a moment before replying.

"I sent it back. You said it was too big anyway, remember?"

I nodded. It had been insanely big, a concert grand fit for Carnegie Hall, not someone's living room. Easily the most insane of all the crazy gifts he'd tried to give me. My fingers strayed to the silver cuff, the only one of those gifts I'd accepted, the one he'd given to say goodbye.

"I guess your mom beat me to the replacement," Brandon said regretfully, watching my fingers.

I looked back at the piano. "Well, don't worry about it. I'm not sure I'm going to keep it anyway. It feels funny to accept such a massive gift from her."

Brandon smirked. "I'm glad I'm not the only one you have a problem accepting gifts from."

I rolled my eyes. "Nope, just the one I refuse them from the most."

"Come here."

Brandon sat up and tried to tug me next to him, but I pulled my arm out of his grasp, opting to stay at the end of the bed and face him instead. He watched carefully.

"You want to talk," he observed. "Why don't you just say what's on your mind, Red?"

I narrowed my eyes.

"She's on the chase now," Brandon mock-narrated my thoughts.

I rolled my eyes. "You don't think we need to talk?"

"I'm guessing you'd like some better explanations about Miranda. And maybe about Messina too. Am I right?"

I crossed my arms irritably, but nodded, short and quick.

Brandon laid back into the pillows. How could he could make himself at home so easily? Even in my own room, I felt completely out of place in this moment.

"All right, then," he said. "I'm an open book. What do you want to know?"

"I want to know why you never told me about Miranda."

The question popped out before I had time to think, surprising even me. I would have predicted my first question would have been about Messina. But no, I realized, I was still pretty damn upset about the fact that Brandon was married and had chosen not to tell me.

He sighed. "Going for the jugular, aren't you?"

"Don't do that," I snapped. "Don't do that thing where you deflect my questions and try to be charming."

He rubbed a hand back through his hair and sighed. "Yeah. All right. Well, it's kind of obvious, isn't it? I knew you wouldn't stick around if you knew the truth, and I was already too in love with you to want to take that risk." He blinked with wide, guileless eyes, as if to say, "it's the truth."

I watched him for a moment more, and once I determined that he wasn't lying, my shoulders relaxed at least a half-inch.

"You should have told me," I said, to which Brandon nodded.

"Yeah," he agreed. "I should have. Would have saved us both the last two months."

"So what's the status on it?"

"There's an arbitration meeting in three weeks," Brandon replied. He looked at me hopefully. "I swear it, Red, just three weeks."

"Three weeks of what?"

He twisted his mouth into an odd, uncertain expression. "Well...it probably would be best if you and I weren't seen together until she signs the papers, for one. You probably picked up on it already, but Miranda has a jealous streak, and it makes her...unpredictable."

I pressed my lips together, remembering her contorted, angry face when she had walked in on me and Brandon in the most intimate of positions. But then she had been unnervingly calm. Miranda Sterling was the kind of person who obviously didn't get angry; she just got even.

"Maybe we should just hold off until then," I said, even though it physically pained me to say it.

I wasn't sure what we were deciding here, although clearly, we both wanted to be together. But I didn't want to be with someone who was still legally tied to someone else. And I didn't want to screw things up for Brandon either.

"*No,*" Brandon said vehemently, sitting up fully and scooting so he was close to me and his knees were touching my toes.

I tucked my knees tighter against my chest. He tipped my chin around, forcing me to look at him. I pulled away, out of his grasp again, but remained close.

"Please, Skylar," Brandon said, blue eyes searching, but a bit icy. "Don't run again."

We stared at each other for a few moments, with tension between us so thick you could practically see it. Brandon's gaze broke first, drifting down to my lips, which parted almost instinctively in response. He leaned toward them. But just before our lips met, I turned my cheek. As much as I wanted to lose myself in his touch, it was just another form of distraction.

"I'm just hungry. Can we eat?"

"Um, yeah. Of course." Slightly confused, Brandon stood and helped me up too.

He followed me back into the kitchen, where I went about taking Eric's plain white dishes out of the cabinets and setting them on the counter. Brandon put our food onto the plates, and watched with obvious approval while I shuffled around, setting the table, pulling out wine glasses, and putting on some music.

"Hey!" he crowed happily when the familiar opening of "Thunder Road" came on. "Springsteen! My man!"

I grinned from where I stood, adjusting the volume on the mini speakers on the counter. "It's just an unplugged version. I figured the original would probably be a bit much for dinner."

In response, all I got was another massive grin, the kind that made my heart speed up. When Brandon looked at me like that, all the problems we had faded that much more.

"Come here," he said. He placed a broad hand at my waist and held my other hand so we were swaying slowly with Springsteen's soft melody. "'Show a little faith, there's magic in the night'," he crooned gently into my ear.

"'You ain't a beauty, but hey, you're all right'," I sang back. We were so cheesy, but I didn't care a bit.

Brandon leaned back, clearly surprised I knew the words. "I didn't know you were a Springsteen fan, Red."

I chuckled. "I wouldn't say that, necessarily. But everyone who grew up in the Tri-State area knows the words to 'Thunder Road'. And I went to school with a *lot* of kids from New Jersey who really liked The Boss, Bon Jovi, and Journey."

"Sounds like my kind of crowd," Brandon said, with a waggle of his dark blond brows.

"God, you're old," I joked.

He laughed and pulled me close so we could continue moving with the gentle guitar and Springsteen's earnest, raspy voice. I closed my eyes, content to lay my head on Brandon's firm chest. More weight fell from my shoulders as I breathed in his scent. Brandon didn't just feel good; he felt like home. My skirt swished about my knees, and Brandon's hand tightened at my waist while the other dropped my hand and clasped behind my neck, cradling me close. I buried my face into his shirt and hummed, as content as I'd ever been in my life.

As the harmonica sang at the back end of the song, Brandon framed my face with his hands and forced me to look up at him.

"I really want to kiss you, Red," he said with a rueful smile as his thumbs fluttered over my lips. "Will you let me?"

Something in my heart melted when he asked that way. Brandon was usually the kind of man to just take what he wanted, and it usually pissed me off. He had approached our relationship from the beginning with all the finesse of a bull in a china shop. And here he was, requesting something as a benign as a kiss.

Still, I could see the determination in his eyes, a hardness that wasn't there before. I wanted desperately for it to disappear.

"Okay," I said softly.

He bent down to touch his lips to mine, one arm wrapping tightly about my ribcage, the other hand weaving into my hair. This wasn't a kiss that was just about sex, although it promised that and more, eventually. It was a kiss that was sad and happy all at once, tentative, passionate, tense, and yearning. Our tongues slowly mingled as our hands began to explore each other again.

When we finally let each other go, I was surprised to see Brandon's eyes glistening as much as mine.

I grinned. "You're such a softy," I teased, but didn't move my hands from his shoulders.

Brandon gave a light-hearted shrug. "The man's a poet. And I've been listening to *way* too much 'Red-headed Woman'," he said. He kissed me gently on the forehead. "Now come on, let's eat."

~

We finished our dinner quickly, and then Brandon insisted on helping me with the dishes. He was a bit clumsy washing them, and ended up getting quite a bit of soap and water on his expensive clothes. At one point, when I came back from taking out the garbage, I reentered the apartment to find him dabbing his tie with a paper towel, but while a large dollop of soap bubble bobbed in his hair.

I giggled.

He looked up. "What?"

I walked in and reached up to wipe away the bubbles. "You made a bit of a mess of yourself here, Mr. Clean."

I was expecting a sharp retort, but instead, Brandon quickly captured my wrist and pinned it behind my back as he walked me quickly against the wall.

"Did I?" he asked as he leaned in to kiss me again.

This kiss was far less gentle than the one before, and I couldn't help but moan slightly in his warm embrace.

"How about we make a different mess?"

I snorted. "Good one."

"Do I sound like I'm joking?" he murmured into my ear before biting softly on the lobe.

Lust immediately shot right to my core. Suddenly I was acutely aware of just how long it had been since we were together, last weekend notwithstanding.

"Oh—" I breathed aloud as his teeth found the soft skin of my neck.

Brandon dropped my arm behind my back and used both hands to pick me up, leveraging me against the wall so my legs were wrapped around his waist.

"You wore the skirt on purpose, didn't you?" he asked before his lips captured mine again in a much more forceful kiss. "You know what your legs do to me."

Before I could answer, he was kissing me again. He shoved me against the wall, pressing all of himself into me, only the fabric of his trouser between us.

I gasped. "Brandon!"

"Shh, baby, I got you," he murmured into my ear before plundering my mouth once more.

"No," I gasped again in between breathy moans. "Brandon, stop."

Breathing heavily, he pulled away with a strangled expression. "What? Red, what is it?"

I bit my lip and took a deep breath, ignoring the pang of guilt in my belly. Regretfully, I slid my legs back to the floor and shuffled around the couch to put some space between us. Brandon turned to follow like a cat on the hunt, but stopped when he saw my expression. He stood on the other side of a small arm chair, his hands grasping its top so hard his knuckles turned white.

"Skylar..." he said slowly, as if working to measure his patience. "Do we need to talk more? You need to tell me something, baby?"

The guilt blossomed even more.

Blue eyes or green?

Did he know why I couldn't do this tonight? No, he couldn't know. He was just confused because he wasn't getting his normal reaction from me. I took a deep breath. I could do this. I didn't know how, but I could put him off. Somehow.

"You want me," I said awkwardly and bit my lip.

Brandon blinked and cocked his head. "You have no idea," he said, then gave me a look that clearly indicated if there hadn't been a leather loveseat in between us, I'd be back up against the wall.

I cleared my throat, doing my best to ignored the throbbing between my legs. I flopped on the couch, pulled a cushion into my lap, and squeezed as I tried again.

"If you thought...I wasn't planning to...I-didn't-invite-you-up-here-to-have-sex," I said all at once.

I stared down at the pillow as I flushed bright red. When I finally looked up again, Brandon's eyebrows were raised in clear surprise, and his grip on the chair relaxed. He rubbed his chin thoughtfully.

"Um...okay..." he said. "I don't want to say I wasn't expecting it, but..."

"You were expecting it," I finished.

"No," he said softly. Then, more strongly: "*No.*"

Brandon came to sit next to me, took my hands in his, and turned me so that I was facing him directly.

"Tell me what's going through your head," he commanded.

I gulped. This wasn't a conversation I ever anticipated having with him. In an odd way, the fact that I couldn't physically have sex for at least one more week was probably a blessing in disguise. Brandon and I would be forced to talk through our problems before we got lost in each other's bodies again. But the bad part was, I couldn't tell him just why we had to wait. I mean, I could...but a voice inside my head kept whispering: What if he doesn't forgive you? I was just barely getting him back. I didn't think I could take losing him all over again.

Suddenly sick to my stomach, I took a deep breath.

"It's like this," I started. "We have a lot to work through. And I want to make sure we actually do work through it before I–"

"Risk getting your heart broken again?" Brandon broke in. His brow quirked. "Yeah, I know the feeling."

I bit my lip. "So, you're okay with waiting a bit? Until we...you know."

"Fuck like rabbits?"

I rolled my eyes and shoved him lightly on the shoulder. "That wasn't exactly what I was going to say, but, yeah, basically. I just...tend to get lost in you. That way."

Brandon caught my hand and nuzzled it, then lightly kissed each finger, each knuckle, each pad of my palm.

"It's been eight weeks and four days since I was last inside you, Skylar," he said solemnly before he held my hand to his nose and inhaled.

I gulped. "Y-you counted the days?" I was suddenly finding it hard to find my voice as his tongue tickled my skin.

Brandon lightly bit my knuckle before letting my hand drop back to my lap. He leaned in slowly, so that his lips just grazed the edge of my ear. "Baby, I've been counting the *minutes*."

A pang of lust shot through me almost immediately at his words, ending right in that spot I knew I couldn't let him reach. I closed my eyes and hissed a breath out between my teeth.

"But I'll wait," Brandon continued as he started massaging my hand as if nothing had happened. "If you need some time—" he stopped and gave me a sharkish grin. "And you can actually be that patient, of course--I'll wait. I'm not losing you again, Red."

Before I could reply that he would never lose me—not if I could help it—the door to the apartment opened, and Eric stomped in. He was clearly a little worse for wear: fitted gray T-shirt wrinkled in places (likely from being left on the floor for too long), light blond hair tousled past the point of looking good. He stopped short when he realized I was on the couch with company.

"Oh, hey, Cros, I didn't realize you had a date—oh, shit!"

Eric almost tripped over his large feet when he got an eyeful of who was sitting next to me, one long arm stretched carefully around the back of the sofa, the other familiar hand on my knee. I looked down and tried to brush it off; Brandon's fingers took a stronger grip.

"Hey, um, this is Brandon Sterling," I said weakly as I stood up, forcing Brandon to release my knee.

Brandon immediately stood too and took the few steps across the room. "Hi there," he said with an outstretched hand to Eric.

Eric stared at the hand for a moment, then seemed to come to his senses about who exactly was standing in the middle of his apartment.

"Mr. Sterling, of course," he said in a hurry as he returned the firm handshake. "I'm Eric der Vries, your, um—"

"Newest junior associate," Brandon finished kindly. "Pending your bar exam results, of course. We're happy to have you on board, Eric. Nice to meet you in person."

"Thanks. I'm very excited about starting up after I take the bar," Eric said before catching my "get out of here" look over Brandon's shoulder. He turned back to Brandon and flashed his best interview smile despite looking like he had picked all of his clothes out of a laundry hamper.

"Anyway, sorry. I can see you and Skylar are in the middle of something. I'll just...be in my room."

He gave me and Brandon one last awkward glance before scuttling to his bedroom. Brandon turned back to me with an amused look, then slung an arm over my shoulder as I came to stand next to him.

"I should probably go," he said regretfully. "I can't stay here. Not with a new employee." Then, leaning down so his mouth was right next to my ear: "Not with the noises you make."

I shivered, and not because I was cold. It was for the best. I couldn't go home with him yet since his ex-wife might be watching, and we had to wait regardless until I could *really* spend the night anyway. The pang of guilt blossomed again in my gut. Tell him, I thought.

"It's okay," I murmured as I tipped my head up.

"I'll see you tomorrow?" Brandon asked in between kisses that were steadily turning into something more.

I laughed. "Tomorrow," I said, then gently pushed him away.

As he grabbed his jacket off the rungs, he gave me that thousand-watt grin that blinded me to just about everything else.

"See ya, Red," Brandon said as he snuck one last mischievous kiss, making me laugh out loud.

I watched him circle down the stairwell until I heard his footsteps echo out of the building. Then I stepped back into my apartment and closed the door. I wrapped my arms around my waist, both recalling his touch and giving myself a bit of comfort. It was painful to see him go, but at least this time I didn't have to focus solely on the fantasies. This time I knew that eventually I'd have the real thing back, even if it scared me, still not knowing exactly what we were or how we were going to do it. But it also felt really fucking amazing to know that he'd be back again tomorrow.

~

Chapter 11

"Okay, so new house rule," Eric said the next morning as he finished making his coffee.

He walked over to where I was on the couch, enjoying my own cup of tea and leafing through our assignment study materials for the weekend. I pushed my glasses up my nose. I was dressed in my typical Saturday morning attire: yoga pants and an oversized T-shirt. Outside it was a fine late-spring day, and I was already a bit grumpy that I had to stay in and study.

"Fine. What's the new rule?"

Eric flopped onto the couch next to me and kicked his socked feet onto the small wooden coffee table. "No bosses in the apartment."

I huffed and dropped my pencil into my open book. "Yeah. I'm sorry about the surprise. But honestly, we don't have anywhere else to go."

"What are you talking about, Cros? I've been to that museum he calls a house. You telling me all ten thousand square feet are taken?"

"No, no," I said. "It's because his divorce is in the final stages of mediation, and apparently his ex is having him tracked by a P.I. We can't be seen together, and his house is probably being watched round the clock."

"So what, now you're fifteen years old, running around behind your parents' backs?" Eric said with a smirk. "Do we need to take shifts with a sock on the door? Your boyfriend owns the Earth, Cros. Tell him to book a damn hotel."

I cringed. "Ew. Because that wouldn't make me feel more like a creepy mistress. It's bad enough he's still technically married." I turned to Eric with my best pleading face. "Come on. We can't go to his place for another three weeks. Then the papers are signed, and that's the end."

Eric slurped on his coffee. "It's a good line, I'll give him that. I should use it the next time a girl wants to come home with me. 'Sorry, babe, but my ex has my place watched by a private eye.'"

I slugged him halfheartedly on the shoulder. "Stop. It's true."

Eric raised a light blond brow and scratched his chin. "You sure about that? Some guys will say a lot of things to keep women away from their places. I should know."

I knew his heart was in the right place. A New Yorker like me, Eric was a cynic, convinced that everyone was a con artist. And it was true that Brandon wasn't always the most forthcoming of people. Some of his secrets had nearly destroyed us, and we weren't exactly out of the woods yet. But then I thought about how warmly he had invited me into his home before, even asked me to move in with him. No, it wasn't in him to make up tales just to keep me at arm's length; if anything, he had a tendency to go overboard bringing me close.

"It's the truth," I said confidently. "I'm sure of it."

Eric sighed, but nodded sympathetically. "Okay. But can you at least send me a text first when he's here? And maybe keep it to your bedroom? I don't really want to walk in on the two of you macking on the couch again, and I'd prefer if he didn't see me when I still smell like lubricant and my date's perfume."

"Ewwwww!" I cried as I whacked him with a throw pillow. "Too much information!"

Eric laughed, but tucked the pillow safely behind him. "I just need him to like me. Got it?"

I squeezed his shoulder. "I'll talk you up, don't worry. I'll be your biggest fan."

"I knew you were going to say that," Eric said, but his face quickly screwed up in horror. "Not too much, Crosby. The last thing I need is my boss thinking his girlfriend has a thing for his new associate."

Eric's eyes grew wide as he obviously imagined a jealous Brandon. I couldn't help but giggle, which earned me a brown-eyed glare.

"Sorry," I said. "I'll keep it tame."

Eric shook his head. "So what's up with the reunion anyway? I thought the two of you had broken up."

Before I could answer, there was a curt knock at the door. I looked to Eric, who just frowned, confused.

I stood. "I guess I'll get that."

I opened the door to the last person I expected to be standing on my door stoop. Jane, my best friend and former roommate, tapped a combat-booted toe impatiently on our mat, multi-ringed fingers clenched and raised to knock again. She was dressed in a typical Jane outfit: ripped, black skinny jeans, an old CBGB T-shirt, masses of leather bracelets around both wrists, and her signature cat-eyed glasses. The only discernible difference was that her short black bob was no longer spiky and asymmetrical, but had been cut to one uniform length—more office appropriate, I guessed.

"Aaah!" I screamed.

Jane immediately grinned and screamed back, causing Eric to plug his ears while my best friend and I attacked each other with hugs.

"You're here!" I cried.

"I'm here!" Jane echoed, and we hopped around in a circle while hugging tightly.

"What are you doing here?" I demanded as I let her go.

Jane reached behind her and wheeled a small suitcase into the apartment, kicking our door shut.

"Clearly I am here to help you sort out the mess of your life. By the way, the lock on your building entrance is broken." She glanced at Eric, who still sat on the couch, staring at her with hilarious bewilderment. "What's up, man-whore?"

Eric immediately recovered his blasé expression. "Hey. Good to see you too, Jane."

He picked up one of the study packets on the coffee table and continued to sip his drink as if Jane's sudden appearance was completely run-of-the-mill. Jane just rolled her eyes and mimed a hand-job.

"Whatever," she said. "You have me until tomorrow night. I figure we can spend the morning studying, and then take a break this afternoon, do a bit more, and then go out tonight." She looked behind her at the packets Eric was using. "Good, you guys are going through BarPrep too. We can work together, since the first unit is all federal statutes. That is, if Captain Underpants over there can tear himself away from his weekly un-dresser."

"You hard up, Jane?" Eric asked without even looking up from his work. "Because I could probably help you out if you're interested."

"Like an iceberg. I'll pass on the VD, thanks."

I bounced between them like I was watching a tennis match, but before I could say anything to break it up, Jane linked arms with me.

"Come on, show me your room, chick," she said. "We'll leave the human hormone to his masturbation studies until we're done gossiping."

~

"So your dad really doesn't believe you about that Katie bitch?"

After three hours of studying, Jane and I had decided to walk down to Haymarket to enjoy the sunny spring day and peruse the stalls of produce. It was the kind of day that made me love living in Boston. Just enough warmth bounced off the cobblestoned streets, and I could smell the briny water sloshing around the piers on the other side of Government Center and Faneuil Hall. I could walk around in nothing but my favorite jeans, a gray T-shirt, and a pair of sandals, my hair thrown into a casual braid down my back.

I shrugged as I looked over a display of peppers, drifting my fingers over their red and yellow skins. I had finished recounting to my friend the events of the past twenty-four hours, including Brandon's and my reconciliation, as well as the awkward conversation I'd had with my dad earlier that morning. My epiphany about Katie Corleone hadn't been taken well. It probably hadn't helped that I could hear her squealing in his ear while I talked.

"Yeah, it's...kind of nuts. I mean, I know it's just a suspicion on my part, but I don't like it. Not to mention that he really shouldn't be getting into a relationship when he's in the middle of recovery. You should have heard him, Jane. He got so mad when I suggested even the possibility that she was in cahoots with Messina."

Jane gave a low whistle and shook her head. "It's probably hard for him. Single guy, gimpy hand, lives with his mother. He probably got a bit of tail when he was playing piano, but now... She's probably got his dick so locked down right now you'd need a nitroglycerin to break that safe." She nudged my shoulder when she caught my obvious disgust. "Oh, stop with the sourpuss, Skylar! He's a musician in New York. What did you think was happening?"

I continued to scowl, but as much as I hated to admit it, Jane was probably right. I examined an eggplant, turning it back and forth.

"Come on. What are you going to do with that? Microwave it?" Jane pulled the eggplant out of my hand and set it back with the others.

I turned to her, annoyed. "I might cook it," I said, picking it back up. "You don't know."

"I know that Richie Rich's favorite food is eggplant parmesan." Jane batted her eyelashes knowingly. "And I also know that in three years, you never once used our stove for purposes other than boiling water."

I rolled my eyes, but put the eggplant back in the bin. I had forgotten just how annoying it could be living with someone who knew all of my secrets.

"Eric doesn't make fun of me for my lack of kitchen expertise."

"Yet, my love. *Yet* being the key word there."

We continued to stroll through the marketplace, looking at the bright rows of vegetables and the other stalls hawking various crafts and wares. My gaze landed on a couple: a tall blond man with a woman about my height. The man had a baby strapped to his chest. He leaned down to kiss the woman, and my heart squeezed, a feeling that was becoming all too familiar.

"So, last night. You didn't tell Brandon? About...you know?"

"I know I should," I said quietly as we continued to walk.

"It's your choice, Sky," Jane said. "I'm not judging. Really."

I sighed and continued to weave through the crowd listlessly, no longer interested in taking in the sights. Jane followed, and eventually we were making our way through the downtown area and into the Commons, with the Public Garden just up ahead. She said nothing while we waited with other pedestrians to cross into the park, just walked next to me, sipping the iced coffee she'd picked up at the market, until we wandered around the duck pond and took a bench not far from the bronze "Make Way for Ducklings" statues.

I stared at the baby ducks and glanced around the park. There seemed to be kids everywhere today.

"Look," Jane said, breaking the silence. "I'm not saying it was the wrong choice. No one is saying that. I'm just saying, if what you said is true...if you guys are trying to start again with a fresh slate, then honesty is going to be key. You're so mad at him for holding all that stuff back, Sky. How do you think he'll feel if he finds out you hid this from him?"

"Yeah, but it's not really his business, is it?" I said, although the pit in my stomach was telling me otherwise. "It's my body, not his."

"Yeah, but it would have been his kid."

Jane shrugged and spread her thin arms out on the bench back behind us. She wore a massive pair of purple sunglasses, and leaned back

113

to face the sunshine. "Real talk. If this were just some dude you were messing around with, or even worse, a piece of shit like Patrick, I'd say 'fuck, no' and 'good riddance.' It wouldn't matter because *he* wouldn't matter. But this is Brandon we're talking about." She turned to me. "He matters, right?"

I nodded, looking at the ducks on the water, some of them trailed by clusters of ducklings. "Of course he matters. He matters more than anyone."

"Well, then, you have to tell him," Jane said simply as she leaned back again.

I slouched in my seat and covered my face with my hands, then pushed them back into my hair. My braid was falling out, and I wound the loose hair around my fist and tugged meditatively.

"He might not forgive me for it," I said. It was the first time I had said it out loud, and even just the words made me feel like my body was iced over. It was petrifying.

"I've seen the way that man looks at you, Sky. He would forgive you for state treason."

"He'll think I did it to hurt him," I said, sitting up again.

"That's ridiculous. You weren't even talking to him at the time. How would something he wasn't going to know hurt him?"

I toed a loose rock on the ground. "You don't get it. Brandon...he wants kids. Like, a lot. Enough to stay married to someone like Miranda for *years* hoping they would conceive. It broke his heart that they couldn't have children. And if he knew what I did—"

"Stop." Jane put a gentle hand on my shoulder.

I looked at her with glassy eyes. I wasn't quite as cry-happy as a few weeks ago, but the tears were still always just below the surface, especially when I thought about hurting Brandon.

"You did what was best for you in that moment," she said, pushing up her glasses so I could see her face. I was touched; Jane couldn't see anything without her prescriptions. "Especially if he's the kind of man who expects you to sacrifice your entire life—and let's be real, it *would* have been *your* life that was sacrificed, not his. It would have been your body on the line if you'd stayed as sick as you were, your career you would have had to put on hold indefinitely, not to mention the whole process of actually having the baby and healing from that." She shuddered. "Two words, my friend: vaginal tearing. If that doesn't put the fear of God in you, I don't know what will."

Apparently living with her OBGYN cousin had enlightened Jane to some of the more visceral parts of giving birth.

"I would have managed," I said.

"Plus, he wasn't going to stop working at his big job to stay home with a baby, and meanwhile, you would have had to jump out of the race before you even got started?" Jane wrapped her thin arm around my shoulder and squeezed. "You'll get your chance together now. A real one, where you can build the foundation you both need so badly. If—" she paused, looking meaningfully at me—"*if* you can stop being a chicken shit and just be up front with him."

I stared down at my hands, now clasped in my lap. We were so close to his house, just across the park and a block north. I could do it now; walk up, ring his bell, and continue the catharsis we'd started last night. We could begin anew, with total honesty.

A flash caught my eye: someone was taking a photo of their kids splashing in the water. I shook my head. No, I definitely couldn't just walk up to the house. Not with someone potentially watching. I couldn't lay this kind of burden on Brandon when he had so many other stresses with Miranda, and I wasn't going to force it on him just to alleviate my own guilt. It was my burden to bear until I knew he could handle it. Until I knew we both could, together.

"I'll tell him," I said finally. "When it's the right time, I will."

Jane pursed her lips. She opened her mouth as if she wanted to say something, but then thought better of it. Before she could formulate her reply, my phone buzzed in my purse. I pulled it out; there was a text from Brandon.

"Mr. Monopoly?" Jane asked, not even looking to see who it was. She flipped her shades back down to look out at the pond again.

I flipped through the text. "He wants to know if I'm free tonight."

Jane jerked her head at me. "Sky, you *better* not say yes."

I chuckled. "Of course not! My best friend is paying me a visit. I'm not about to bail on that."

I was rewarded by a very cat-who-ate-the-cream smile from Jane.

"As it should be," she said haughtily.

I tapped a quick reply to Brandon, letting him know I was busy. A second later, I received another text.

"He says to tell you he's going to crash the party," I said, somewhat annoyed. Talk about a rock and a hard place.

"Give me that," Jane said, snatching my phone out of my hand. "Someone needs a lesson in the laws of female friendship."

Before I could stop her, she dialed Brandon's number. He, of course, picked up right away. I watched, half-horrified, half-delighted as my best friend eviscerated my boyfriend.

"Hey, Moneybags," she said. "How's it hanging? Hey, a bit of a PSA for you: boyfriends don't get to cut in on girl time, especially not when said girls now live a thousand miles apart. Haven't you heard of 'chicks before dicks?'....Yes, it was last minute....Yes, we are going out tonight. It's Saturday night, and I'm not a shut-in....Yes, I plan to get some act— wait, that is none of your business, Sterling!"

Jane looked to where I was watching, utterly transfixed.

"Uh-huh," she continued. "Uh-huh. All right, fine. But if he's a dud, I'm kicking you out. Only one of us gets to sleep in Skylar's bed tonight, and if she has to choose, she's choosing me...Great Scott...Starts at ten...And before you try to butt in there too, no, you can't come for dinner."

With that, she held the phone out to me with a somewhat dazed look on her face.

"I think your boyfriend just cross-examined me into inviting him out with us and Eric tonight," she said. Then an evil smile spread across her face. "Oh please, let *me* tell Captain Chlamydia that he gets to party with his boss tonight."

I took the phone and put it to my ear with a grin. "Hey. Sorry about that. What are you up to?"

"No apologies needed." Brandon's voice was low and warm over the phone. "You just provided a welcome interruption of a golf game."

"You play golf?" I made a face at Jane, who immediately started fake snoring.

Brandon chuckled. "Only sometimes, I promise. Usually when I have deals with old men to close."

"Is something important happening today?"

"I can neither confirm nor deny that statement," he said good-humoredly. Which meant yes, and also that it was likely related to the upcoming IPO of Sterling Ventures.

"What did you say to Jane?" I asked. "I think you broke her."

On the other end of the line, Brandon laughed, a deep, throaty sound that made me thrill from top to bottom.

"I can be very persuasive when I want to," was all he said.

"So you're going to come to the show with us tonight? Do you have time for that sort of thing?" Brandon was one of the busiest people I knew. His calendar would rival the President's.

"I've barely seen you for two months," Brandon said. "I'll make time. I'll meet you there around ten."

"Sounds good," I said, even though the reminder that we couldn't be seen around together dampened my enthusiasm a bit.

"Bye, beautiful."

I put my phone back in my purse. Jane stood up and stretched her tall frame to the sky, muttering "motherfucker" under her breath. Then she turned to me.

"He must be an absolute terror in court," she said. "Shall we head back? I'd like to get a bit more studying in before we go out tonight. Secured Transactions is kicking my ass."

Now a bit more energized, I was ready to get my work out of the way so I could enjoy myself. But I still glanced behind me as we left, thinking of the big, gray-stone house that stood beyond the trees, and the man inside who was waiting for me to come back to him completely.

~

Chapter 12

Red? Or black?

I stood in front of my closet, mentally debating which shoes to wear. The show we were going to see after dinner was Jane's choice: an all-girl band that covered late seventies punk. I didn't mind The Clash, so I was game, although Eric had been bitching all afternoon.

"If I wanted to listen to a high-pitched version of 'London Calling', I'd teach it to my four-year-old niece," he said as he strode into my bedroom.

He looked his usual dapper self, if slightly more casual than normal in light-washed jeans, a dark-gray T-shirt, and a pair of multi-colored Asics. He sat at my desk, crossed one leg elegantly over the other, and started playing with my Eiffel Tower paperweight.

Jane looked up from where she sat at the head of my bed, flipping through some flashcards. She had barely changed her outfit, only switching to slightly more torn skinny jeans and a shirt that was sleeveless.

"Don't be such a Sad Sally. You had your chance to vote, and you abstained. It's simple democracy."

"I was in the bathroom," Eric retorted.

"No one said you had to go." Jane flipped over another card and scowled. "But I'd be happy to inform Mr. Sterling that you decided to stand him up this evening. I'm sure your boss would love that."

"Can you guys give it a rest?" I asked as I finished sliding on two different shoes. "Since you're both here, help me pick."

One was a chunky red sandal with a block heel I'd gotten at a flea market last summer; the other was one of my favorite black ankle boots with the silver toe. I wore high-waisted, dark-wash skinny jeans, rolled up slightly at the ankle, and a cropped top with wide, black-and-white horizontal stripes. My hair, tossed into a messy ponytail, revealed the two sets of studs in my ears, and I had Brandon's thick silver cuff on my wrist. It was a more retro look than I would normally go for, but more importantly, it was comfortable and cool. It was going to be hot inside the club, so I wasn't interested in wearing anything too binding or suffocating.

Jane pursed her lips and looked at both, nodding. "I see what you're doing there. Sort of a Debbie Reynolds versus Debbie Harry kind of choice, isn't it?"

"Don't you have anything less clunky?" Eric asked with a nonplussed shrug. "Stilettos would be hot."

With a withering glance at Eric, Jane said, "Pay no attention to Justin Bieber. He liked his women teetering so they are easily immobilized."

Eric scowled. "I resent that."

Jane tipped her head toward my right foot. "Obviously the red. They go with the whole Bettie Page vibe you've got going on. Nicely done, by the way."

Then she opened my nightstand drawer and threw a handful of condoms at Eric. Two hit him in the face.

"Jane!" I yelped. "What the hell?"

Jane smirked at Eric, who just glowered while he gathered up the multi-colored packages.

"I thought he needed some help with his accessories too," she said sweetly.

"That's so thoughtful, Jane," Eric said as he dropped the condoms on my desk. "So kind of you to help a guy stay safe."

"Oh, they're not for your safety," Jane retorted. "They're for whatever godforsaken girl you convince to let you up her skirt. Just remember, Eric, no means no."

I rolled my eyes. "You guys are impossible."

I pulled the boot off and grabbed the other sandal, opting for height since my date stood nearly a foot taller than me.

"Come here, Ms. Pin-up," Jane said.

She pulled her lanky limbs up from the bed and went to my desk, where I kept the small box containing my spare selection of cosmetics. She pushed Eric out of the seat and shoved me down in his place. Eric just scoffed and stalked out to wait in the living room, but I did catch his quick brown eyes flicker back to Jane for a second before leaving.

"Mascara and lips," Jane dictated as she squatted down to fix my makeup.

I obediently looked up while she touched on mascara. Jane was a whiz with cosmetics; she'd been fixing my face since we met.

"Thanks," I said. "I can't go out anymore, you know, now that I don't have you to do this for me."

She grabbed lip liner and lipstick and motioned for me to open my mouth slightly so she could apply them.

"I have to make you miss me for something," Jane teased as she drew the bright red around my mouth. "Brandon's not going to be able to see anything else when he looks at you. The only thing that'll go through his head is 'fuck that P.I.'."

I didn't respond. I didn't want to think about the fact that I wouldn't be able to go home with Brandon for multiple reasons. Jane had already heard all about our public relations problem. Just the fact that he had agreed to meet me in a crowded bar, no matter how dark it would be, was a risk.

She pulled back with satisfaction, and I smacked my lips in the mirror.

"You missed your calling, Janey," I said appreciatively. "You should have been a makeup artist."

"Nah, I'm more of a glamor-by-night-only kind of gal these days," she said, looking at her work with approval. "I had to get rid of my streaks and cut my hair all the same length. Something about a preferred court attire." She scowled. "Fascists."

I put the lipstick into my cross-body purse and stood up. "All right. Let's get Eric and head out. And you—be nice!"

~

After a short, but effective pub crawl that meandered through most of Allston, we ended up at Great Scott just after the warm-up act's set, around ten. Jane and Eric had gotten along surprising well all evening, and Jane had amazingly stayed with us the entire time instead of picking up men at the bars. It was ironic, really, that she spent so much time giving Eric shit about habits that matched her own.

Considering that the band was only in the beginning stages of setting up their equipment, the venue wasn't terribly crowded, and we were able to find stools at one of the small tables in the middle, right next to one of the tall wood pillars that held up the roof.

"Pitcher?" Eric asked, pointing two fingers at Jane and me.

"I'll share one with you," Jane said.

"I'll stick with whiskey soda," I said.

Eric ducked into the crowd toward the bar, and I caught Jane watching him for a moment before she swiveled back to me.

I raised a brow. "You're looking pretty hard in that direction, Janey," I said. "And the two of you have been awfully friendly tonight. I haven't heard you call him 'Petri Dish' once."

Jane rolled her eyes and scoffed. "Please," she said. "Been there, got tested for it." She scrunched her face up, however, in a look that was slightly regretful. "It *would* help if he weren't so damn cute, though."

I glanced back at Eric. He wasn't exactly my type: lanky and way too much of a player. But I could see the appeal, just like most of the other women in the bar. The guy had charisma.

"He's got a cute butt," I conceded.

"Whose butt are you looking at?"

I twirled around to find Brandon standing behind me, wearing a pair of black jeans, black Converse, and a plain white T-shirt. He looked like he had walked out of a James Dean movie. I wanted to devour him.

"Hi," I said with a grin, while I completely ignored his question. "You're here."

"I'm here." He said leaned down to give me a brief, urgent kiss that still managed to warm me to my toes. "Hey there, Jane. Welcome back."

"Hi, Brandon," Jane replied as she accepted his polite kiss on the cheek. She looked him over critically, tapping her chin with a black-painted fingernail. "You going to a rumble later on? You look like a West Side Story extra."

Brandon rolled his eyes, but stuck his fingers into his pockets. The movement made his triceps test the constraints of his rather thin T-shirt. "Glad to see you still have your unique sense of humor, Jane."

"You just have too many people kissing your ass all the time, Sterling," Jane said sweetly as she slid off her stool. "I work for the government now, so you better be careful. You might have to kiss my ass one of these days."

"Where are you going?" I asked. "You don't have to leave. This is our night out. He's just a bystander."

"Thanks!" Brandon said, pretending to be hurt.

Jane just smiled as she looked between the two of us. "No, it's okay. I'm toasted right now, so you know there's only one cure for that. Locate wherever Eric parked the pitcher and find some fun of my own."

She turned and surveyed the club, which was quickly filling up with people, and zeroed in on a decent-looking guy about ten feet from us. He noticed her too, and held up his drink.

"And there's my fun now," Jane said. "See you later, kids." And with that, she walked around Brandon, snapping her fingers as she sang: "When you're a Jet, you're a jet all the way, from your first cigarette to your last dyin' day!"

Brandon watched with skeptical amusement until Jane had disappeared into the crowd. Then his blue eyes seared over me as he took in my uncharacteristically revealing shirt and Jane's makeup job. I blushed, an effect that was likely only exacerbated by already having a few drinks.

He let out a low whistle, his wide brow furrowed as if in pain. "God *damn*. I don't know if it's because I've barely seen you in the last two months, but...Jesus. You're not going to make this going-slow thing easy on me, are you, Red?"

I gave him a shy smile and didn't answer, just reached over and pulled him to me by the edge of his shirt. Like Jane, I was a bit toasted.

"I said go slow," I whispered as he came close enough to be nose to nose, "not be monks."

Brandon gave me a wicked grin. "Sounds good to me," he said, and lowered his lips to mine.

"Ahem."

We broke apart, somewhat irritably, to find Eric standing next to us with a full pitcher, two pint glasses, and my whiskey soda, looking obviously uncomfortable with catching his boss and his roommate making out for the second time in twenty-four hours. Brandon stepped away, and I gratefully accepted the drink.

"Thanks," I said. "Next round's on me."

"Uh huh," Eric said. "Where did Jane go?" He scanned the growing crowd.

"She went...exploring," I said.

For some reason, it felt odd to tell Eric that Jane was chasing tail. I knew he was under no pretense about Jane's nocturnal habits, but there was something about the way he'd been looking at her all night that made me hold back.

Eric looked awkwardly back at Brandon and me, then gave Brandon a fake interview smile.

"Mr. Sterling," he said. "It's nice to see you again."

"Nice to see you too, Eric."

Brandon shook his outstretched hand, then sat down on the stool behind me and scooted my seat backward so I was cradled between his legs. I settled against him, practically purring at the feel of his warm skin through his thin T-shirt. I leaned onto his shoulder, and Brandon wrapped an arm around my waist, tugging me even closer so he could gently kiss my neck.

"Right," said Eric with thinly veiled discomfort. "I'm going to go bring Jane her beer."

I couldn't blame him. It had to be hard watching your employer and your roommate cozy up together, but in my half-drunk state, I didn't have much of a desire to hold back. Not after craving this man's touch for over two months.

Without waiting for a reply, Eric started to weave through the crowd, clearly eager to be rid of us.

Brandon chuckled. "I think we offended your roommate's delicate constitution," he said before biting lightly on my earlobe.

His thumb started to toy over the bared skin of my stomach. I shivered, and not because I was cold.

"He's not offended," I said, even as I leaned into Brandon's deft touch. "Just wait until he's found his girl-of-the-night. He's just weirded out because you're his boss." I closed my eyes briefly as Brandon's tongue touched the skin right behind my ear. Then they opened again as something else occurred to me. "Why don't you tell him to call you Brandon? It might be less weird if he didn't have to say 'Mr. Sterling' every time he saw you."

"I will, eventually. It's just kind of fun to fuck with him."

I twisted my head around, and Brandon flashed a wolfish grin.

"You are so bad," I chided, even though I couldn't hide my own smile.

Brandon immediately captured my chin with his free hand and pulled me in for another brief kiss. "Want me to prove it?" he growled.

He kissed me again, this time much deeper and much longer. The arm around my stomach locked around my mid-section, a trap I didn't ever want to escape. Brandon's hand rested over my stomach, and his fingers teased the top of my jeans, dipping under the coarse material and then briefly back out.

Brandon groaned and broke away. I turned in his arms to face him and leaned back against the table. He looked me over again and rubbed a hand over his face.

"Slow, huh?"

I just bit my lip and nodded, even though it was just as hard for me to keep my hands off him. Still, I didn't really have a choice, I reminded myself with a pang of guilt that I pushed away. This was just how it had to be for another week or two.

He groaned again. "You're killing me here, Red. You couldn't have just worn a burlap sack or something?"

I giggled and took a sip of whiskey. "I'll wrap a bedsheet around me like a toga next time."

Brandon squinted, like he was trying to imagine me in the get-up, then shook his head. "Nope, it's no use. You'd be smokin' hot in anything." With another brief kiss and a frustrated grunt, he pushed off the table. "I'm going to get a drink."

The lights in the club dimmed, and a cheer rose from the gathered crowd as the band took the small stage. I slid off my stool and stood as tall as I could, buoyed by the extra height of my sandals. The club was getting hotter by the minute, stoked by the crush of bodies and the hot stage lights.

With the harsh thrum of the infectious baseline, the band launched immediately into a cover of "I Wanna Be Sedated," familiar enough that even punk virgins like myself would know it. I found myself bobbing my head in time with the music and finishing my drink much faster than I probably should have.

A hand slipped around my waist; Brandon had returned, sipping on a pint of beer. He set another whiskey soda and a water on the table beside us.

"Thought you might need a refill," he called into my ear.

"Thanks."

I took the water gratefully and drank half of it in one gulp. I was starting to feel pretty buzzed, but not so much that I was too out of it to have a good time. Brandon watched with clear approval as I downed the rest of my water before picking up my drink.

"They're pretty good," he shouted.

I nodded; it was really too loud to have any kind of conversation. Every so often I got a flash of Jane moshing at the front of the crowd while Eric lurked a few people back. Brandon's hand returned to my waist, and I was all too aware of the fact that there was nothing between my bare skin and the slightly callused pads of his fingertips. Despite the sheen of sweat on my forehead, I broke out in goosebumps.

I didn't know most of the songs played, but the band was solid and full of energy. More and more, however, I became increasingly conscious of the play of Brandon's fingers at my waist. After he finished his beer, he had rested both hands at my hips, sometimes pulling me close to fold his arms under my breasts, but mostly just keeping me close while his fingers played with my shirt, my navel, the lines of my stomach.

At one point, when the band broke into a slow cover of The Clash's "Lover's Rock," Brandon pushed my hair so it hung down one shoulder and gave him access to the other. His nose trailed up and down my neck. Suddenly I couldn't move, locked in his embrace and in the feel of his lips. His thumbs slid under the tops of my jeans, thumbnail grazing just at the edge of my lace underwear.

He hummed low, vibrating his stubbled cheek across the soft skin just under my jaw. I couldn't help but arch against him, pressing against the hardness I could now feel very clearly against my back.

"You're playing with fire there, Red," he murmured.

The light scratch of his stubble made me arch again, and this time a low moan escaped my throat. His hands clenched at my jeans, then moved around my waist and down to squeeze my ass.

"Brandon," I breathed suddenly unable to speak clearly.

All of me seemed to be standing erect for him; I was glad we were in the middle of a dark room, since my skin was likely the color of my hair. Brandon moved his hand back around my waist, up to the edge of my cropped tank, where his fingers slid just under, teasing at the edge of my bra, and then back down again to tug on my waistband.

"What is it, Red?" he asked as he continued to torment.

The band didn't exist anymore. No one existed anymore. And I couldn't take this torture for one more second.

I turned around in his arms, and wrapped my arms around his neck and pulled him down for a kiss. Although he was surprised at first, it didn't take him long to get equally wrapped up in me, reaching down to grab my ass hard as his mouth opened hungrily. We were so eager to get closer, uncaring of the fact that we were basically devouring each other in a room full of people.

The song came to an end, and Brandon stopped with it. Even in the dim light of the club, his eyes flashed and it almost looked like he was vibrating. "Come with me."

Without waiting for a response, he practically dragged me through the horde of bodies. We continued past the entrance of the club where a doorman was still checking IDs, and down a dark hallway. Brandon shuffled past the bathrooms, turning knobs on other doors, checking for someplace, any place where we could escape.

The fourth door in the hall opened, and we tumbled into a closet that seemed to be filled with shelves of music equipment and cleaning materials. Brandon grinned with a lopsided smile that was equal parts lust and mirth. I opened my mouth to protest, but he wasn't in the mood to listen. He shut the door, enclosing us in darkness. Then he attacked.

While his fingers had only flirted earlier, now they were everywhere: in my hair, down the back of my jeans, under my shirt. My shirt was yanked up and over the lace cups of my bra, giving Brandon access to the soft, sensitive nubs that hardened under the thin fabric. His lips fastened to one, sucking while I pawed at the hem of his T-shirt. My fingers met thick ridges of muscle, and when I moaned at the contact, he returned to plunder my mouth again. He palmed my breasts roughly, grunting against my tongue while our bodies banging into the shelves and knocked over invisible objects.

"Fuck," Brandon gasped against my lips. "Fuck, I want you *so* fucking bad right now, Skylar. You have no fucking clue."

Then he broke away, his hands drifting down my ribs and waist like he was tracing the shape of Coke bottle.

"I want to make you come," he said as his hands found the zipper of my jeans.

The deep timbre of his voice seemed to fill the small space and vibrated through my chest. The first time we'd ever completely had sex had been in the deserted stairwell of an MIT building, where he'd turned

126

me against the wall and taken me, suddenly and forcefully. I hadn't argued. But the frank admission of his intentions now turned me on even more.

"Do it," I murmured as I pulled him down for another deep kiss.

Brandon didn't need any more encouragement. His hands were frenzied storm, undoing my jeans in a few quick, torrid movements and wrenching the coarse material to my knees. He soon found me, playing briefly over my clit before dipping down with the clear intent to slip inside. I stiffened slightly and urged his hand back up so that he only touched what was safe.

"Just there," I said in between kisses.

Brandon's mouth stilled for a moment. "You sure?" he asked even as his fingers started to find a consistent rhythm that definitely worked.

I arched against his hand, my eyes fluttering in the dark at the familiar pulse growing inside me. At some point, Brandon had learned to do this better than I ever could, and it was getting hard to think straight.

"When you're inside me, I want, um, *you* inside me," I fibbed through shallow breaths.

I wanted that to happen right now more than anything, but I had to wait. I couldn't see what he looked like, and maybe it was for the best he couldn't see me. He would probably see the guilt written all over me, fighting with the desire his quick fingers were creating.

"Your wish is my command," Brandon said as he quickened the pace.

His teeth trailed over the top edge of my ear, nibbling slightly before his mouth moved lower to suck at my neck, hard enough to leave a mark.

"Ah!" I cried at the sudden mix of pain and pleasure. His fingers found a more consistent rhythm, and my hips began to rock with them, as if of their own accord.

"The last two months," Brandon growled. "Every day. Every day I've dreamed of this body. This body is mine, Skylar. Do you hear me? Every orgasm. Every ache. Every pull. *Mine.*"

I shuddered, climbing closer and closer to my climax. But even if his words pushed me closer to the edge, they drove other desires too. As his mouth found me again with a kiss that was almost painful, my hands tore at his belt buckle. He grunted in surprise as I unfastened his jeans and my hand took hold of him.

"*Mine* too," I murmured as I started to move my hand up and down his considerable length, matching the rhythm he had already set.

I could feel, rather than see, Brandon's mouth fall open, lips powerless as we worked each other's bodies. I could hear people moving in the hallway, could feel the vibrations of the band's insistent rhythms through the flimsy door. But here in this closet, his touch, my touch, we consumed each other. With each small caress, we brought each other closer to finishing, mouth to mouth, tongue to tongue, groan to groan.

"Fuck!" Brandon finally left out a hoarse yelp. His head fell over my shoulder and pressed into the door at my back. "Are you close?"

His thumb pressed slightly harder, then he seized my clit between two fingers and squeezed.

"Brandon!" I cried out.

I bit his shoulder through his shirt, which seemed to push him over the edge, and both of our bodies tensed together, finding our finish as waves of mutual pleasure overtook us. Brandon muffled both of our cries with a kiss as I fell apart under his hand. A few seconds later, my upper thigh was covered with his release.

After we had managed to catch our breaths, the jiggling of the doorknob snapped us both out of our post-orgasmic dazes. It appeared to be a drunk concert-goer looking for a bathroom. Whoever it was soon tromped away, but suddenly I was very aware of the fact that I was standing in a custodial closet, shirt above my tits, pants at my knees, and thighs smeared with the sticky residue of Brandon's pleasure.

Brandon swallowed as he refastened his jeans, then pulled out his phone to shine a light around the dark, humid space.

"Aha!" he exclaimed when he found a stack of spare paper towels.

I cleaned myself off, then awkwardly reassembled my clothes while Brandon rubbed nervously at the back of his neck. It wasn't until I looked up again to find him watching me adjust my bra with lust written all over his features again that I realized I had no need to feel uncomfortable. When he caught me looking, his mouth twitched.

"Slow, huh?" he whispered with a half-smile.

I bit my lip. "Slow for us?"

We could never seem to keep our hands off each other, even in those moments when I hated his guts. That had never been the problem.

"Can we get out of here?" Brandon asked as he leaned in for another kiss. "I don't want to be arrested for public lewdness."

"We're not having sex tonight," I said as he nibbled on my neck. I'd have said the man was insatiable, but I was feeling the same way.

With a reluctant groan, Brandon stood up straight. "Can I at least stay over?" he asked. At my expression, he held his hands up in mock-submission. "No funny business, I promise." He blinked, his eyes wide. "I just want to be with you, Red. I miss you."

I leaned into him. We needed to take things slow physically, but that didn't mean I didn't want to be around him just as much.

"Okay," I relented. "You can come over."

"Great. You leave first and get a cab back to your apartment. I'll follow in my car."

Checking first to see if I was completely redressed, Brandon opened the door and guided me out. There were a few other people in the hall looking for bathrooms, but no one seemed to care that we had just emerged from a closet together.

"Got everything?" Brandon asked.

I checked for my purse, made sure nothing had fallen out. "Yep."

"Good. Here's for the cab."

Before I could stop him, Brandon pressed a crisp fifty into my hand. With the effects of two whiskeys running through me, I was too slow to summon a rebuke before Brandon guided me to the club entrance and asked the doorman to hail me a cab.

"I'll see you there, Red," he said, with a brief stamp before nudging me out the door.

A car was waiting for me when I reached the curb. I glanced back to where Brandon was peering from the interior shadows, likely checking for signs of a tail. I waved at him, and he waved back with a rueful smile. Then I was shut into the cab, alone and on my way home.

~

Chapter 13

Hot. I was hot. Every part of me felt like a ripe, sweating peach. I opened my eyes; thin streams of sunshine escaped through the blinds of my one small window. In my cloudy, hungover state, they felt like needles piercing my eyeballs. I looked down my body, to find myself thoroughly and completely wrapped up in man. Well, that explained the suffocating heat.

Brandon stirred. The arm across my chest and the leg over my hip just wound tighter, and he buried his face further into my hair. Part of me relished his touch, enjoyed the warmth of his skin, the familiar scent of him. The other part of me just wanted his giant, sticky limbs *off*.

That part won out. As slowly as I could, I slid from under his embrace, doing what I could to replace my body with a few of the pillows.

It had been an interesting night. When we had come back from the show, Brandon was fully primed to do more of what had happened in the broom closet. He had watched me move around the apartment with the focus of a jungle predator. After being tossed onto my bed not once, but twice, I had elected to change into my pajama shorts and an old New York Giants T-shirt in the bathroom, much to Brandon's obvious disappointment. Unfortunately, he didn't play fair. When I returned, he had stripped completely down to his boxer briefs, looking more like an underwear model than a CEO as he splayed his long, tanned body across my bed.

"You keep looking at me like that, I'm not going to be able to keep my hands to myself, Red," Brandon had said with a leer.

I bit my lip. "You're not exactly making it easy for me either. No one asked you to hop in my bed looking like David Beckham in an underwear ad."

For that I got another thousand-watt grin. "I never said I'd make it easy. Get over here. I'll let you keep those cute little shorts on, I swear."

He stayed true to his word, taking things as slow as I wanted. It was like spending the night together as if we were sixteen and our parents were in the next room. Frustrating, but also completely a turn-on.

And now it was a little awkward.

Brandon stirred again as an old wood floorboard creaked under my feet. I froze. He raised an arm over his head and blinked lazily awake.

"Morning," he said slowly as he caught sight of me.

He propped his head up on one ridiculously defined arm and smiled. My insides tightened. Anyone who looked like that first thing in the morning should be locked up.

"Hey," I said, raising a shy hand to my face, which probably had pillow-crease marks across one cheek. "Good morning."

I slumped into my desk chair, feeling unaccountably shy. Unlike the days when we used to spend weekends together, our conversation was stunted. Brandon was guarded, and I was too. The fact was, we had hurt each other badly, and there was going to be a certain amount of time needed to heal those wounds, which seemed a lot fresher at the moment.

Brandon sat up completely, and I flushed as the sheet fell down, revealing the cut lines of his torso. He smiled wider at my reaction; seriously, it was really unfair that I couldn't hide a damn thing I was thinking.

"What are you doing over there?" A long arm beckoned me. "Come back to bed."

I obeyed. Brandon draped a familiar hand about my legs and massaged my bare thigh.

"You don't make it easy for a guy," he murmured at the touch. "You shouldn't be allowed to walk around in shorts like these."

His hand moved to my inner thigh, fingers finding the hem of my admittedly microscopic shorts. My breath picked up a notch, and I bit my lip. Brandon smiled, then pulled his hand away, much to my obvious frustration.

"You set the rules, babe," he said as he leaned back into the pillows. He pulled me down to lay on his chest. "Anytime you want to break them, you let me know."

I sighed contentedly, happy to have resumed contact with his warm body even though I'd felt suffocated by it before. His hand drifted up my back and started playing with my hair, and we laid there a moment, content in each other's company. But the comfort was short lived.

Green eyes or blue?

It was the question that wouldn't go away, and that guilt that never seemed to dissipate completely blossomed in my gut all over again.

"You all right?" Brandon asked, as if sensing my sudden change of temperament.

I opened my mouth.

A loud buzzing of my phone on the nightstand tore through the room. Brandon handed it to me; it was a text from Bubbe, asking how my week had gone. Her message was a reminder of what I had left in New York, and also of other things Brandon and I still had not discussed.

I sighed, closed the screen, and pushed myself back off Brandon's chest, ignoring his disappointed grunt. As if on cue, his phone also buzzed on the windowsill, revealing several messages that had gone unanswered last night and this morning. No rest for weary CEOs.

I pulled on my vintage Levi's and a black tank top. Brandon watched appreciatively, but once he realized I really wasn't coming back to the bed, he sighed and got up himself. I stumbled at the sight of his almost-naked body in its full glory: v-shaped abdominal muscles, square pectorals, long, lean thighs and calves that all flexed as he stretched his hands to the ceiling.

He caught me ogling and flashed another grin. "We could still break some rules, Red." He clearly wanted to, if the tent in his briefs was any indication.

I licked my suddenly dry lips, then shook my head and finished hooking on an earring. "Not yet," was all I could manage as I turned away to hide my intense blush. Instead I focused on taming my bedhead into a bun. The man really did things to me I couldn't control.

Brandon chuckled, but I could hear him putting on the clothes he'd draped over the end of the bed post the night before. Then he was behind me, wrapping my shoulders with his strong arms as he kissed my cheek.

"I miss you," he murmured, echoing the sweet admission he'd repeated throughout the night. "What are you thinking?"

He watched me through the mirror, his eyes looking impossibly blue in the early morning light. We stared at each other, green eyes meeting blue, daring the other to speak first. The issues between us bloomed. Guilt dropped in my stomach like a log.

Green eyes or blue?

I broke first and pressed a kiss to the forearms folded around me.

"The call was from my grandmother," I said. "She checks in every few days. We're worried about my dad."

Brandon's brow furrowed with concern, and he released my shoulders so he could back up and sit on the edge of my bed to listen. I sat down on my desk chair and turned to face him.

"What's going on?" he asked quietly.

I bit my lip. "I'm not sure we should get into it." Things between us were so fresh and tenuous. I didn't want to ruin it.

Brandon pressed his lips together and sighed. "Skylar, this is why we split up in the first place. Because you wouldn't let me help you."

I frowned. "No, we split up because you wouldn't respect my limits. I asked you not to get involved, and you did, behind my back. My entire family is paying for it now. Every time I see a call from Bubbe or my dad, I'm afraid that it's going to be another notice that Dad's in the hospital again, or something even worse. You put those extra-big targets on our backs, Brandon."

"Skylar, I'm pretty sure your dad got into gambling without my help," Brandon replied quietly, although he had the decency to look contrite right after the words left his mouth.

I crossed my arms and glared. "I'm aware that my dad has a problem, thanks. You forget that I've been here before. And see, when my dad was just a poor sanitation worker with a kid in college, these assholes let us alone once he paid his debts. They had bigger fish to fry. But now they found the biggest fish, which means they're not going to let up. And my family is just a bunch of sitting ducks, waiting there to be picked off."

My hands shook at the thought, and I couldn't help my voice cracking at the end.

Brandon opened his mouth as if to argue back, then closed it firmly. "You're right," he said finally, surprising me completely. "I'm sorry."

"You are?"

This wasn't usually how these discussions went for us. Usually, they ended with us acting like stubborn mules, unable to compromise and spouting off at each other. I'd actually smacked Brandon more than once. I know, not my finest moments.

"Yeah," Brandon conceded. He pushed a hand through his hair, gripping a moment at the crown of his head. "But Skylar, believe me when I say this: I would never let anything happen to your family. The

133

Messinas aren't the ones with the real power here. They might want my money for what, some fancy cars? To pay off some dirty cops? I guarantee they have no idea what that money can really do."

My skin prickled at his words. "What is that supposed to mean?"

Brandon suddenly found a nonexistent piece of lint on his jeans extremely interesting.

"Brandon!" I protested. "This is exactly what I'm talking about! I want this to work, but you can't hide things from me. We have to be honest with each other no matter what. And I have to have the final say about what happens with my family."

He sighed. "Fine. To start, you should know that I removed the trust in Messina's name from the divorce agreement. Miranda started asking questions anyway, so it was better that I paid your family's debt in bulk instead. So yes, I gave Messina a larger payment to stay away from your family, but that's it. And I did take pains to route it in a way that he might just think it came from your dad instead of me."

I rubbed my forehead. Suddenly I had a massive headache.

"Brandon. I know you don't really think that worked. Victor Messina probably started sniffing you out the second you produced a paper bag full of cash like a damn magician."

"Probably," Brandon admitted. "But it was a start." He looked up with big eyes. "You should probably know that after you told me about your dad's, um, new friend, I arranged for a security detail to watch the house in Brooklyn. And, ah, you too."

I gaped around my room as if Inspector Gadget was about to pop out of my closet. "What?!"

He had the decency to look ashamed, but I recognized the set of his jaw when Brandon wasn't going to change his mind.

"I did it during dinner on Friday," he said. "Listen, you just finished telling me how scared you are that someone is going to hurt your family again. I'm just doing what needs to be done to make sure it doesn't happen."

"I don't need a security detail. Talk about a breach of privacy, Brandon!"

I turned back to my desk in a huff. I pulled the hair band out of my hair and started brushing violently. It only made it bush up, but I didn't care. I needed something to do.

Brandon continued to watch me in the mirror.

"Skylar, come on," he said, "This is me, a guy who is currently being followed everywhere by a private investigator hired by my crazy ex-wife. Do you think I *want* to invade your privacy?"

"She's not your ex yet," I countered petulantly as I attacked the left side of my head.

"You say you know how these kinds of people work. I do too, Red, and probably better than you. I used to run with thugs like him when I was younger. And when they want something, they don't go after the guy with the money. They go after the people he cares about. Messina would go after the people I care about, and that's *you*, more than anything else." Behind me, Brandon sighed. "Will you turn around and look at me, please?"

I stilled, but set my brush down on the desktop and did as he asked. I started braiding my hair into a thick rope. Brandon leaned over and braced his hands on his knees so he could look directly at me.

"They don't report to me unless something bad happens," he said plainly. "No one is spying on you or tracking anything other than your safety. I wouldn't do that to you. Do you believe me, Red?"

His voice was imploring, but also hard with tension. We were trying to heal, but he was still a slightly colder version of the man I had fallen in love with. I hadn't thought about the obvious stresses in his life, particularly with negotiating a divorce from someone who obviously didn't want to be divorced. And on top of that, he had been trying to help my family even when we weren't technically together. I certainly wasn't always a peach either.

"I believe you," I said.

"Good. Look, I figured you wouldn't want a bodyguard, so surveillance was the next best thing. But if you really don't want it, I'll call it off," he said, although he obviously wanted to do anything but that.

I looked down at my hands. I really didn't like the idea of being followed around everywhere I went, even if I could understand his concern. Regardless of his promise that he wasn't spying, it still felt like an overstep.

"How about this," I said. "Keep whoever is in Brooklyn there for now, but remove the Boston guys. I actually do feel better knowing someone is looking out for Bubbe and my dad. If I feel any hint of anything weird here, you can assign someone to me. Will that work?"

Brandon chewed on his lower lip for a moment, clearly wanting to insist on his original agenda. But finally, he clapped his hands together and looked straight at me.

"Deal," he said.

"And no going around my back with other plans."

He gave me a shy, guilty smile that just about broke my resolve to force him to keep his hands to himself for a while.

"Deal," he said again. "Now get over here."

He pulled me from the chair to stand in between his legs, then wrapped his big hands around my hips and pressed his lips into my stomach. The sweet gesture made my heart ache. *Green eyes or blue?* My fingers threaded into his hair automatically, and I sighed.

"Thank you for letting me help," Brandon murmured into the cotton of my shirt.

His hands floated down to squeeze my ass briefly, then let go when my stomach grumbled. He looked up, blue eyes ablaze with happiness and humor. I pushed his few locks of hair off his forehead. It was getting just slightly too long again, curling around his ears the same way it did when I'd first met him. We gazed at each other, entranced by the obvious love flowing between us, until my stomach grumbled again.

Brandon laughed and stood up. "Come on, Red," he said. "Let's get you some food. And then, unfortunately, I have to get going."

"Another golf meeting?" I teased as I followed him out of the bedroom. A quick glance at the empty couch told me Jane must have found someone to go home with last night.

"Not quite," Brandon said as he went to the refrigerator. "Tennis court this time." He darted a quick glance at me over his shoulder. "You don't play, do you?"

I shook my head as I pulled a box of tea and my jar of honey out of the cupboard. "There aren't a lot of tennis courts in Flatbush."

He gave me a knowing half-smile then turned back to his search. "I feel you. Not a lot in Dorchester either. I didn't learn until I was married."

The word dropped between us like a mini-grenade—the fact that he had been and still was married to another woman. And not to just anyone. The kind of woman who belonged to a tennis club and who probably played golf too. Who wore real pearls as casual jewelry and only drank white wine and colorless liquor. I had seen Miranda Sterling née Keith. She was the kind of woman who never had a hair out of place, even in a wind storm. She was imperious and impossibly beautiful.

But Brandon didn't love her, and most likely never really had. And I had a choice to make—stand with him while he finished cleaning up the mess of his youth, or leave him, just like everyone else had. I had already tried the wrong version of that decision; I wasn't going to do it again.

He put the milk he had grabbed on the kitchen counter and welcomed me when I came to stand in front of him. I smiled and reached up to clasp his cheeks between my palms.

"I love you," I told him, knowing that it was true.

The words hadn't been said much since we had gotten back together—maybe once or twice in a fury. Brandon stilled for a moment, taking in the words before his face split with a massive grin. It was the thousand-watt smile I loved, the one that seemed to make an entire room light up without a single light bulb.

"I'm glad to hear it," he said finally. "And in case you were wondering, I love you too. Like fucking crazy."

I grinned back, then went up on my tiptoes to give him a brief kiss, which he turned into something much more thorough when he picked me up and set me on the counter. His kiss was no longer sweet—it yearned for something I couldn't quite put words to. His hands were just finding their way underneath my shirt when a door opened up behind us with a loud squeak.

Brandon's hand innocently moved back to my waist. I looked over Brandon's shoulder to find Jane creeping out of Eric's room wearing nothing but an oversized T-shirt. Her black bob stuck out in all number of directions, smudges of makeup outlined her puffy eyes, and a red pillow mark slashed across her cheek. It wasn't until she had pushed her glasses on her face that she realized she had an audience. Her mouth dropped open as her eyes darted between us, then closed with a scowl.

"Not one word," she pronounced slowly, then shuffled to the bathroom and shut the door firmly behind her.

Brandon looked to me, eyes now full of mirth.

"I guess she had a good night too." He leaned down to kiss me again, this time more tamely. "Looks like you've got some things to handle this morning, and I've got to get going. You guys have nothing to eat."

"Sorry about that. I'll pick up some groceries for next time."

"You going to keep house for me, Red?" Brandon joked as he walked to the door to pick up his shoes, then sat down at our small table to put them on.

I hopped off the counter and shrugged. "It wouldn't be so hard to have some food on hand if you're going to be here more often."

"What I should do is just rent you your own apartment so we can have some privacy," he said. "If, "he added with a churlish grin right when I was about to protest, "I thought you'd ever take it." He stood up and walked back to where I stood and smacked me with another brief, but thorough kiss. "I'll just have to wait until I can get you to move in with me again."

I was about to argue that I'd never actually moved in with him to begin with, but was interrupted by Jane skittering out of the bathroom and into my bedroom, presumably to find a pair of pants in the overnight bag she'd left in there.

Brandon looked back to me with an arched brow. "I'll call you later?" he asked. "I have to go out of town this week for a few days to meet with some investors, but I'll be back on Thursday. Can I claim Friday night again next week?"

I smiled. "Sounds good."

"Perfect." He grabbed his keys, wallet, and phone from the table. With a quick, panty-dropping grin from the door, he was gone.

~

Chapter 14

On Wednesday afternoon, I left my doctor's office in Cambridge with an extra spring in my step. After getting a check-up, I had been cleared for pretty much any physical activity again (including the kind that Brandon was clearly dying for, if his texts were any indication). On top of that, the IUD that the doctor in New York had inserted was good to go. There would be no more scares or decisions like this again in my immediate future, and for the first time, I felt like I could begin to move on from the black hole of the last month. At least, I could try.

But there it was again: that strange feeling like I was being watched. In the middle of the sidewalk, I froze, trying to figure out where it was coming from, but I saw nothing out of the ordinary among the red brick buildings. I was starting to feel like I was going crazy. Frowning, I took out my phone to send Brandon a text.

Me: is there still security following me around?

There are benefits to dating someone who is basically married to his phone. One of them is near-instantaneous communication.

Brandon: no one was ever following u, Red. they were just watching the apartment.

Me: ...

Brandon: relax. u r completely alone and unsafe. why do u ask?

I glanced around, but still there was nothing but the busy din of sun-drenched tourists and summer students filling the intersection. I really was going crazy.

Me: just checking. love you.

Brandon: u have no idea.

With a smile, I put the phone back in my purse.

"Hey, Skylar!"

I whirled around, my sage-green jersey skirt floating up with the motion. I shoved it down and looked for the owner of the voice, casting my hand over my eyes like a visor.

Jared smiled as he jogged across the street in a momentary lull of traffic, looking golf-course ready in a pair of chino shorts and a red polo shirt with a turned-up collar.

"Hey!" he greeted me as he leaned in to kiss my cheek. "What are you doing up here?"

"Doctor's appointment." I gestured at the nondescript brick building behind me.

"Everything okay?" Jared looked me up and down, as if trying to determine for himself what I might be hiding. His eyes flickered to the brass sign that clearly stated "Cambridge Obstetrics and Gynecology."

I chewed on my lower lip as I followed his glance. "Um, yeah. Everything is fine. Just getting checked out, you know? What about you? What are you doing up here?" I was eager to shift the conversation away from my reproductive health.

"Oh, I still live in the neighborhood," Jared replied with an easy smile as he shoved one hand through his floppy brown hair and adjusted his aviator sunglasses. "Porter Square, remember?"

I nodded. Jared had the means to live alone in a one-bedroom apartment in one of the most expensive neighborhoods in Boston, and had been doing so throughout his days as a poor law student.

"I was actually just picking up a late lunch before heading to your place for our study group. Do you want a ride?"

I blinked. "Oh, that's right! I'm sorry, I had completely forgotten you were coming over today."

Jared frowned. "Is it a bad day? I mean, we can reschedule if you want, although we do have a lot to get through this week. I could use the help."

I shook my head and clutched my purse to my chest, stepping closer to Jared as a large group of students crowded the sidewalk. "No, no need to do that. Does Eric at least remember that you're coming?"

Jared nodded. "Yeah, we were talking about it in the car on the way back from class today, remember?" He peered at me curiously. "You sure you're okay?"

I didn't say that I had been nervous about my doctor's appointment. I knew there was little chance that any complications had arisen, but too much time on Google had put all sorts of terrors in my head.

"Just a lot going on these days," I said obliquely. "But I'll take you up on that ride if you're offering. Save me getting stuck on the Red Line again."

I followed him to where the now-familiar BMW was parked in a small lot a few blocks away. Jared held my door open for me as I slid into my seat. He winked after I sat down and closed the door.

"So, small world," he said once we were on our way. "I didn't know your stepdad was Maurice Jadot."

I snapped my head up. "How did you know that?"

Jared smiled easily as he steered onto Mass. Ave. "My grandfather mentioned it the other night. Apparently, Maurice requested a meeting with him. Grandfather said he's fishing for clients in Boston."

I frowned. That was a little bit odd. Maurice worked for BNP Paribas, a massive bank headquartered in Paris. They had a big branch in New York, but as far as I knew, only had a small presence in Boston, and I couldn't for the life of me think why they would be interested in a tax law firm. Maurice was deputy CEO of the bank. Getting involved with what was essentially a satellite office was below him.

But it wasn't the only thing that was bothering me.

"Why does your family know who I am?"

Jared quirked his mouth. "Are you always this suspicious?"

I opened my mouth, then shut it again. With everything that had recently happened with my family, my instincts were verging on conspiracy-theorist levels. Poor Jared was about as harmful as a golden retriever.

"Sorry," I mumbled. "New Yorker. It's in the blood."

Jared laughed, a full-bellied shout that was almost too much for the remark. I smiled back anyway. At least he thought I was funny.

"But really," I said, "I am curious why your family knows my name."

Jared gave me a particularly boyish glance. "I, um, might have mentioned you a few times," he admitted. "I did have kind of a crush on you, if you remember."

The innocence in his eyes shifted for a minute to something slightly more aggressive.

I flushed and looked down to where I was clutched the thin leather straps of my purse. "Oh."

"Anyway," Jared pivoted easily, turning the conversation as easily as he turned onto Memorial Drive. "So, your mom is coming to visit? You must be excited. Isn't she some kind of hotshot artist?"

When we'd gone out on our one date, Jared had been particularly interested in my mother's "profession," although I hadn't been very forthcoming about the fact that she'd abandoned me and my father in supposed pursuit of that art. It was a bitter subject, especially since I also knew she hadn't really done a lot in the last several years.

"I think she's mostly just involved with her family," I said as I stared out the window.

Across the Charles River I could see the tall brick buildings of Back Bay, slowly giving way to the rows of ivy-covered brownstones clustered in Beacon Hill. It was one of my favorite neighborhoods in Boston, had been even before I became intimately acquainted with one of its most affluent residents. Brandon's house was so close.

"Are you planning to see her while she's here?" Jared pulled me out of my reverie as he steered past the MIT campus.

"Um, I don't know," I said, turning back. "We're not very close. Although she did contact me a few weeks ago. Sent me a graduation gift, actually."

"Oh yeah? What did you get? Not a car, I know that. Let me guess: a down payment on an apartment, maybe?"

I furrowed my eyebrows when I realized he wasn't joking. Jared's family clearly had some money, and, like a lot of my affluent Harvard classmates, frequently assumed that most of us had the same kind of wealth. He had a better reason for that assumption now that he knew who my stepfather was, and the truth was that Janette's gift *was* pretty damn extravagant, but still...it seemed a bit tone-deaf.

"Um, no," I said. "It was a piano."

"Oh, cool. Do you play?"

I nodded.

"That's so cool," Jared said again. "Maybe you can play for me sometime."

When I didn't respond, he drummed his fingers on the edge of the steering wheel while I continued to watch the river.

"So do you mind if I ask what happened with you and Sterling? I still can't believe he let you go, the loon."

I shifted uncomfortably in my seat. There wasn't anything specific about Jared's comments that were that awful, but something about the way he said them made me feel like prey. I bit my lip. Brandon and I were supposed to be keeping things on the down-low. But at the same time, Jared was a friend, and I'd already blown him off once before about Brandon. There was just something about the way he looked at me...it made me afraid of how he'd react if I did it again.

"It's complicated," was all I said. "I don't know that he did, really."

Jared pushed his sunglasses on top of his head. The movement made his hair stick out like floppy, light-brown ears so that he resembled a golden retriever even more.

"What does that mean?" he asked.

I shrugged. "It's...we're...I don't know. You probably know that he's married, right?"

Jared nodded. "My grandfather was actually really good friends with Stan Keith, Miranda's father. Our families have known each other for years. I was actually really surprised when I saw you and Sterling together, to tell you the truth, because she's always talking about him."

I cringed. Jared was on a first-name basis with Brandon's wife. And yeah, that night at the symphony had probably looked suspect to a lot of people who had known about Brandon's marital status. Everyone, it turned out, but me.

"Right. Well, then you probably know that they're in the process of getting a divorce. We're...taking a pause until it's finished."

It seemed safe enough to say. Let him know I wasn't really available without blowing Brandon's cover.

"I know what most people know," Jared replied as he turned off the highway. "That he filed a few years ago and hasn't done much since to move it along."

"That's because his wife wants to contest it," I countered. "She's nuts and won't let him go."

Jared just gave a skeptical shrug. "Is that what he said?"

"That's not fair."

Jared shrugged again. "I don't know him, but I do know Miranda. She's not a psycho. Maybe that's just what he's telling you."

We sat in awkward silence again while Jared drove down the congested streets by the Garden and into the North End. I crossed my arms over my stomach and tried not to let the seeds of doubt plant in my mind. Brandon and I were just starting to rebuild what we had. I

143

wasn't going to let some rich kid who was clearly on the wrong side of the situation poison that process.

We drove down my crooked, cobbled street, and Jared easily found a parking space. The guy had the best parking karma I'd ever seen. After he turned off the engine, he gave me a sympathetic look.

"I'll say one more thing, and then I'll leave it alone. I think you can do better, Skylar. I think you deserve better."

Someone like you? I wanted to ask. But instead I continued to sit with my mouth pressed into a thin line as I stared at the soft green fabric of my skirt. Jared reached out to squeeze my fist for a second, but when I didn't respond, he pulled his hand back.

"All right," he said with a little more acerbity. "Message received. Should we go up and get to work?"

I gave a brief nod, then turned to let myself out of the car. There wasn't anything more I could say, and we needed to focus on the bar exam instead of my complex love life.

Jared followed me up to the apartment, where Eric was already sitting in the living area with his study materials spread over the coffee table.

"Hey, sports fans!" Eric greeted us. "I got the homework divided into threes. I figure we can teach it to each other and then do a review. Thoughts?"

"Sounds good to me," Jared said as he joined Eric on the couch.

"I'm just going to change clothes," I said, and headed to my room, ignoring the way Jared's eyes followed me.

While I changed into a pair of cozy black harem pants and a gray tank top, my phone buzzed on my bureau: another text from Brandon.

Brandon: so i never asked: how's the day, beautiful?

I smiled half-heartedly, even though I knew he couldn't see it. No matter how hard I tried to ignore them, Jared's words still rankled.

Me: Good. study session in a few. what's on your agenda this afternoon?

Brandon: a barrel of laughs. I'd rather be studying for the bar again.

Before I could ask what he meant, my phone buzzed again, this time with a photograph. I opened it up to see a screenshot of Brandon's schedule, where most of the afternoon had been blocked off with "mediation with Miranda."

This time my smile was genuine. Jared had no idea what he was talking about.

Me: good luck.

I tossed my other clothes into my laundry basket. My phone buzzed again, and we traded a few more texts.

Brandon: we're on for Friday?

Me: yes.

Brandon: I made a reservation. 7 o'clock here.

A few seconds later I received a map pinning a Brazilian restaurant in Brighton called João's. I flipped through the menu. I'd never been there, although Boston did have a pretty big Brazilian community. It didn't look like a fancy place, which I was happy to see. Before I could reply as much, my phone buzzed once more.

Brandon: what r u wearing? can i get a hot pic to get me through the day?

I bit my lip, then typed out a quick reply.

Me: r u srsly asking me to sext u before your divorce meeting?

The reply was instantaneous.

Brandon: That might be the only thing that WILL get me through it.

I giggled, then sent one more text.

Me: I'll show u mine if u show me yours.

I put my phone down on my desk and started winding my hair into a loose bun at the crown of my head. Our third-floor apartment was heating up in the summer sun, and we didn't have an air conditioner. That was going to have to change soon.

My phone buzzed again, and when I swiped to reveal the message, I was glad to be sitting down, since the picture Brandon sent made my knees feel like Jell-O. It was selfie shot he'd taken down his be-suited body. He had untucked his white dress shirt and unbuttoned from the bottom, spread aside with his black tie to reveal the washboard abs he knew made me drool. Below, one big hand rested on the front of his pants, grabbing an obvious erection.

145

I bit my lip and squirmed, suddenly very aware of the fact that I had just been cleared for sex.

My phone vibrated again in my hand.

Brandon: Your turn, Red.

I pushed up from my seat and stood in front of the mirror mounted over the vanity desk. I decided to go for a similar look. I'd show him mine, as I said. I pulled up the bottom of my tank, revealing my own flat stomach and the cut of my hip bones set off by my low-slung pants. For good measure, I pulled the shirt high enough to reveal the underside of one breast, since I'd forgone a bra for comfort. Then, just because I knew it would torture Brandon, I put my glasses on, bit my bottom lip, and took the picture.

"Crosby!" Eric yelled from the living room. "You coming?"

After checking that I didn't look like a complete alien in my photo, I fixed my shirt and pressed send.

"Keep your pants on," I said as I walked back to the living room. "I'm coming, I'm coming." I set my phone on the table and picked up the study packet Eric had prepared for me. "Ready?

My phone buzzed, and Jared's gaze flickered down to the message clearly displayed on the front.

Brandon: daaaaaaammmmmnnn. u know how to tease a guy.

I flushed and snatched the phone off the table.

"Come on, boys," I said, unable to meet Jared's sharp glance. "Let's get to work. This exam isn't going to pass itself."

~

The rest of the afternoon passed easily, and when dinnertime rolled around, Jared happily volunteered to order pizza while we plowed through the rest of the assignments for the week and got a few days ahead on the course readings. I didn't miss the way Jared occasionally peeked curiously every time my phone buzzed, but he didn't say anything more about Brandon, and I had to admit that studying together as a group worked well. At this rate, we'd all pass easily.

Sometime past nine, Jared left with a smile and a "See you tomorrow."

"You're going to have to be careful with that one, Crosby," Eric remarked from the couch as I shut the door.

I turned around with a frown. "What? Why?"

Eric stretched his long arms out across the back of the sofa and gave me a look that basically said, "Seriously?"

I rolled my eyes. "We're just friends."

Eric snorted. "Um, *you're* his friend. I just carpool. But that guy is definitely looking for something more, and as nice as he seems, he's not the kind of guy who likes to hear no. He looked like he wanted to kill me when I pointed out his mistake on the statute of limitations question."

"He knows about Brandon," I said as I picked up the empty pizza boxes and started breaking them down. "He knows I'm not interested that way."

"Does he?"

I set the flattened boxes on our small kitchen table, then came back to take a seat on the couch next to Eric.

"He does," I said as I shuffled together the notes I'd taken.

Eric did the same, but sent me a considerable side-eye while doing it.

"He *does*," I insisted when I stood up with my books and notes.

"Whatever you say, Cros," Eric said with his usual practiced nonchalance.

"That's rich, considering the studied denial in *your* love life at the moment."

It hadn't escaped me that since last week, Eric had been in his room every night by ten o'clock, and there had been distinct radio silence from my friend in Chicago.

"I don't know what you are talking about," he said with a sly grin.

I just shook my head and brought my notes into my room. When I came out, Eric was flipping channels on the TV.

"I think we deserve some mind-numbing television," he said. "Westworld? Or the Sox game?"

My phone buzzed in my hand as I sat down. A text from Brandon: another semi-dirty picture of him lying in bed in nothing but his boxer briefs, giving me a look that should have melted my phone.

"A bit of advice," Eric said without even looking at me. "Maybe next week, you can hold off on the sexting with my boss until after study session is over. Might make Jared a little less...um...aware of you."

I frowned. "What do you mean?"

Eric turned to me, lolling his blond head against the back of the couch. "Everything shows on your face, Cros. And I do mean everything."

Almost immediately I turned bright red. Eric chuckled and gave me a friendly pat on the knee as he turned back to the TV.

"Don't worry," he said. "It was actually kind of funny watching Jared look like he wanted to vomit every time you got a dirty text."

"You could tell?!" I screeched. "Am I really that bad?"

Eric flipped the channel back to the Sox game, and the blare of Fenway filled the room.

"That last message must have been a doozy," he confirmed with another cheeky grin.

I groaned into my hands. I normally wasn't quite so awful about masking my emotions, but when it came to Brandon, it was looking more and more like a lost cause.

~

Chapter 15

João's wasn't a restaurant I knew, and I ended up getting lost on my way there. I took the B Line to Allston, passing the club where I'd been just last week, but then had to continue walking down Allston Street for several blocks. As the streets became less and less crowded, that feeling came back again—the one like I was being followed. It was hard to shake—you don't grow up as a woman in a large city without knowing that feeling of a stranger on your tail. I wouldn't be able to count the number of times I'd been catcalled or even tracked for multiple blocks by men in New York. Losing a creepy stalker was a survival skill in an urban jungle.

But these days that sense was clearly off. Twice I stopped suddenly and whirled around in the evening twilight, but each time there was no one there, just empty sidewalks disappearing into the dusk.

"You're going crazy, Crosby," I muttered to myself as I turned down another quiet street and finally found the restaurant.

I stood outside for a moment, looking at the place with some skepticism. It was barely discernible as a restaurant, marked only by a small sign in the window and the glass door that had a menu taped to it. I doubled-checked the address Brandon had texted me. This was definitely the place.

The bell that sounded at my entrance rang through the empty room like a siren. A head popped out of a door in the back which I presumed was the kitchen. The man who spotted me looked momentarily surprised at my presence, then his body followed his head as he walked out to welcome me.

"*Aló, senhorina*," he said in a language I guessed was Portuguese. "You are here for dinner?"

I looked around the restaurant, which was really just a plain white room with clusters of metal tables and chairs scattered around it. It was also empty.

"Um, I think so," I said. "There was supposed to be a reservation. Under Sterling."

"Yes!" the man said, clapping his hands together. "He is in the back table."

I looked around the man to the single occupied table in the far corner, where Brandon was hunched over a few papers, so lost in his work he hadn't even registered my arrival. But as he sensed my presence innately, he looked up and grinned, his smile lighting up the dank room.

"Hey, beautiful!" he glowed as he shuffled his papers to the side and stood up as I walked over.

The papers were a few messy drawings of some kind of contraption. The sight made me smile—for all of his glamorous façade, Brandon was really just a big nerd who liked messing with wires in his spare time.

"You look...wow. As always."

I glanced down at my simple black T-shirt dress and the red slip-on sneakers. Knowing we weren't going anywhere fancy, I'd opted for casual comfort.

"Thanks," I said as I accepted his kiss. "You look good too."

Brandon was dressed as simply as I was in a pair of jeans, a red T-shirt, and his favorite worn Sox hat. I had to smile. For once we looked like an average young couple, not a mismatched pairing of a high-powered CEO and a not-quite-minted lawyer. But the fact that we were in a restaurant that was completely empty on a Friday night wouldn't let me relax completely.

"Um, Brandon?" I asked as we sat down. "You...you did call off the security, didn't you?"

Brandon frowned, clearly confused. "Yeah, of course. Why do you keep asking me that?"

I shrugged and held my arms around my middle. "No reason. You know me, suspicious New Yorker."

If he got a whiff that I was worried, I'd definitely have a security detail following my every move. I *really* didn't want that. Instead I looked around the restaurant.

"This place is weird. It feels like a front for something."

Brandon blinked at me for a second, then suddenly burst out laughing.

"A front?" he asked with a huge grin. "Christ." He looked around, as if noticing for the first time that we were literally the only customers there. "Yeah, I guess I can see that. But, ah, no, Red. The Brazilian barbecue here is wicked good. I..." He looked a bit sheepish, pulled off his hat and started to worry it between his hands. "It's not a front. I just bought out the place for the night so we wouldn't be watched."

Suddenly the restaurant seemed about three times larger. It was a compliment, in a way, that Brandon would buy a restaurant's entire night's worth of business just to take me out. But it was also a demonstration of the extravagant lengths he was taking to keep me a secret. I clasped my arms over my chest, studied the wrinkles in the dingy white tablecloth, and tried to swallow back the tears rising unbidden.

"Red. What is it?"

I looked up, but still didn't answer. I didn't want to make things harder for him than they had to be.

"It's weird, isn't it?" Brandon asked. He sighed and pushed his hat backwards over his flattened blond curls. "Damn."

I shrugged, knowing I had no talent for hiding my feelings. Brandon's features scrunched with sympathy; the movement made the small lines around his eyes and between his brows show up.

"I'm sorry," he said quietly. "Miranda just knows too many people. It's either someplace like this or The Martin, where I know for sure I can pay for confidentiality." He looked up, eyes pools of worry. "Would you rather just go back to your place? We don't have to go out."

I sighed and placed my hands on the table. "I'll just be happy when this is all over."

Brandon reached out and covered my hand with his large one. He brushed his fingertip over my oval-shaped nailbeds. "Not long now, Red. We're supposed to be signing the final papers in less than two weeks."

"Let's just eat," I said. I pulled my hands back to my lap.

Brandon studied me for a minute, then suddenly stood up from the table.

"Fuck this," he pronounced as he pulled me up, his accent large and pronounced. "I can do better. And you're not some dirty little secret, you're the love of my fuckin' life."

I glanced around the restaurant, but there was no one there to notice the outburst. Brandon leaned down and stamped a hard kiss on my lips.

"I'm not going to run around like a scared mouse just because Miranda's looking for dirt," he said.

While he tugged me toward the back of the restaurant, Brandon took out his phone, swiped through a few apps, and then pushed the door open into the kitchen. The waiter and the cook (there were apparently only two employees in the entire restaurant) looked up from where they were sharing a cigarette by the window. Our dinners were simmering on the massive stovetop. Admittedly, they did smell delicious.

Brandon slapped several hundred-dollar bills on the counter.

"That's for the food and your trouble," he told them. "St. Mary's up the street runs a soup kitchen on Fridays. I'm sure they'd appreciate the extras."

The waiter reached out cautiously and took the bills while the cook nodded at Brandon's suggestion.

"*Sim*, of course," he said as he waved us away.

I gave them a grim smile while Brandon opened the back door into an alley. Like a spy, he glanced down both ends of the street before pulling me out to follow toward Allston Street. An unfamiliar Prius pulled up at the curb, and immediately we hopped in.

"Whose car is this?" I asked once we were on our way. I had no idea what was happening, but Brandon seemed to be in charge.

In return I received a massive Cheshire grin. "What?" he said. "You've never heard of Uber?"

I couldn't help but laugh despite the stoic expression of the driver.

"So, what subpar restaurant are we going to instead?" I joked.

Brandon gave me a grim smile back. "Well, the food will be good, I promise you that."

~

Twenty minutes later, after a stop at the grocery store to pick up some flowers and a premade pie, we pulled up in front of a small blue colonial on a quiet street in Somerville. It was the kind of street that reminded me of Flatbush, the neighborhood in Brooklyn where I'd grown up. Close to the city, yet still a street dominated by single-family houses, most of them barred from the sidewalk by chain-linked fences and even a few trees. A couple of lights shone brightly through the windows of the house, which, though small, had obviously been carefully kept up over the years.

The Prius drove off, leaving us standing in front of the small wood fence that bordered the house and a tiny yard that had been planted with rose bushes and azaleas. Brandon took my hand so that I could face him.

"You up for a family dinner?" he asked shyly. "Friday is usually chicken."

I glanced back at the house, full of epiphany. Of course. This was the house where Brandon had lived with his foster parents between the ages of twelve and twenty or so. I had once met Ray Petersen, the crotchety old MIT professor who seemed to view Brandon more as a lost intellectual commodity than a son. I had heard better things about Susan, Brandon's foster mother, but had never had the pleasure of meeting her.

"*The* chicken?" I asked.

Brandon had once told me a story about Susan's special roasted chicken and how the way Ray, normally a taciturn, emotionless man, looked at her when she made it helped Brandon realize just what he was missing in his own marriage. It was a funny thing to say, but Susan's chicken meant love to Brandon Sterling. So of course, I couldn't wait to taste it.

Brandon just grinned. "If we're lucky. But I'm warning you, Susan isn't going to let up with the questions."

I faced the house with determination, eager to be among people—especially the people who knew Brandon better than anyone else. "Bring on the cross-examination."

Brandon let me up the short walk through a dimly lit yard that was lined with flower beds and hanging baskets on the front porch. One of Petersens definitely had a green thumb, I noted as velvety purple petunias brushed my shoulder.

Brandon knocked on the white front door, and we waited. It was a marked difference from the way I would enter my family's house. If I ever knocked on the front door, Bubbe would probably start wondering if I had been hit in the head.

"I'm getting it!"

A muffled, gruff voice sounded from within, and we heard the obvious stomps of Brandon's foster father, Ray. Beside me, Brandon's tall form stiffened.

The door swung open.

"What is it? Oh, Bran!"

We were met by the clearly confused face of Ray, who was dressed nearly the same as the night I met him, nearly four months before, in a pair of practical khaki pants and a plaid, slightly threadbare button-down shirt with the sleeves rolled up. He pushed his frameless glasses up his straight nose and surveyed both Brandon and me as if we were potentially here to burn his house down.

"Hi, Ray," Brandon said in a tone I recognized from the last time we saw his foster father: resigned and hopeful all at the same time.

Ray glanced at me. "Who's this?"

I reached out a hand. "Skylar Crosby, sir. We met a few months ago in your office."

Ray screwed up his ungroomed white eyebrows, but clearly had no recollection of the event. Brandon took my extended hand and squeezed. I squeezed back, hoping he'd understand that I didn't take offense. Ray Petersen's opinion of me wasn't really the one that counted anyway.

"We were hoping to crash dinner," Brandon said. "We brought dessert. And some beer if you can hide it from Susan."

Ray screwed his face up again in disapproving glare, but stepped aside and took the paper bag containing the six-pack of PBR Brandon had selected. Brandon set the dessert, a chocolate cream pie, on the small entry table next to the door and turned to help me remove my denim jacket after we entered the house. The room opened into a homely living room lined with bookshelves. A small television set was in one corner, and a burgundy couch faced an unlit fireplace.

"Ray! Who is it?"

A woman's voice floated down a hallway, out of which shone a few lights that, if the smell was any indication, clearly led to a kitchen. A few other darkened doors on the right likely led to bathrooms, closets, maybe an office. The woman appeared in the hallway: short and compact with a navy-blue apron tied around her waist. She caught sight of who had just entered her house, and threw her hands up.

"Brandon!" she cried and raced down the hallway.

Close up, Susan Petersen looked a lot younger than her husband, although some of it might have just been their personalities. With his bright white hair, stodgy glasses, and stooped posture, Ray looked to be well over seventy, maybe even seventy-five. Susan, on the other hand, had an appearance of youth that couldn't just be erased by time alone. Her skin, a tawny color that belied years in the garden, and shoulder-length wavy hair that was still more light-brown than gray, made her look no more than her mid-to-late fifties. She would have strongly resembled a sparrow, chirping down the hall and around her family, had it not been for the clear blue eyes that matched her foster son's. Ray Petersen might have held his foster son at arm's length, but Brandon was clearly the apple of Susan's eye. I was thrilled to see it.

"*You*," she said fondly as she grabbed Brandon around the middle with a warm embrace.

Brandon smiled and pressed a kiss into Susan's mussed hair, but I could see the mirth in his eyes as he hugged his foster mother. That is, until he looked to Ray, who was staring grimly at the two of them.

"Are you finished?" Ray asked.

I frowned. What a grump.

Susan stepped back, but continued to pat Brandon over the arms and shoulders, even reaching up on her tiptoes to fix his hair where it stuck out from under his backwards bill.

"What are you doing here?" she asked. "This is such a surprise!" Then her warm yet sharp glance turned to me, as if she had just realized I was there. "And who do we have here, Bran?"

Brandon turned to me with a grin and pulled me in front of him.

"Susan," he said as he set his hands on my shoulders. "I want you to meet someone really special. This is Skylar Crosby, my girlfriend."

Susan quirked her eyebrows at Brandon, then looked at me with open curiosity.

"Girlfriend?" she repeated with obvious awe. Her infectious grin transformed her face. "Well, well, well. It's very nice to meet you, Skylar. My, you are a lovely little thing, aren't you? Look at all that beautiful hair! Ray, could you imagine if these two had kids? Beautiful, just beautiful."

Blue eyes or green?

I pushed the guilt away and focused on the situation at hand. "It's lovely to meet you as well, Mrs. Petersen," I said.

I reached out to shake her hand, but she pulled me in for a tight hug instead.

"Does your wife know you've got a 'girlfriend'?" Ray asked behind us.

Brandon jerked his head to his foster father. "Really?"

Ray crossed his arms. "Does this one know about the mess you're in right now, Bran? Trying to divorce a woman who won't have it?"

155

I blinked between them and noticed immediately the way that Susan's spritely demeanor shuttered when her husband spoke.

"Ray," she hissed. "No need to throw that wet blanket on the evening!"

"She knows everything," Brandon said evenly. "And she also knows that it's almost over."

"I've heard that before," Ray grumbled before turning down the hall. "Well, come on then," he called to the three of us. "Chicken's on the table and getting cold. Hopefully we'll have enough."

"Oh, hush," Susan said as she shepherded Brandon and me to follow Ray. "There's plenty," she assured me as we turned into the kitchen.

She wasn't lying. Along with a massive roasted chicken, there was a large bowl of buttery mashed potatoes and a salad that would have obviously fed a lot more than just her and Ray. If I hadn't known better, I would have thought that Susan was expecting us. But when I saw her beaming at Brandon, I realized that his tendency to prepare for visitors who might stop by wasn't unique; it was a learned trait from the woman who helped raise him.

"This looks amazing, Mrs. Petersen," I said truthfully as she set out two extra plates and silverware around the small kitchen table. It was the kind of spread that would rival Bubbe's Sunday brunches.

"Oh, honey, you call me Susan," she said with a wink. "We're casual around here. And help yourself before Brandon eats it all up."

"I'm not that bad anymore," Brandon protested even as he spooned a mountain of potatoes onto his plate.

"No, you're not," Susan agreed. "Used to be you'd eat everything at the table plus whatever I had left in the fridge." She looked pointedly at me. "If the two of you have kids, you'll have to have a separate savings account for this one's son."

My stomach immediately clenched again at the second mention of kids, so I focused on unfolding my napkin across my lap.

"Susan!" Brandon chided as he caught my strained expression. "I'd appreciate it if you didn't scare Skylar off."

"Brandon, you've met my grandmother," I said. "This is nothing."

Brandon conceded the fact, and started serving everyone chicken.

"So, you've met Skylar's family too?" Susan asked innocently, although she didn't bother to mask her clear interest. "Are you from Boston too, dear?"

I shook my head as I accepted a chicken wing onto my plate. "No, New York. Brooklyn, actually."

"And what brought you up here?"

"Skylar just finished law school at Harvard," Brandon said proudly.

"And is that how the two of you met?" Susan asked, blinking between the two of us. "At a Harvard event?"

Brandon glanced at me and grinned. "No. We met by chance one snowy night. Skylar got trapped in my house in a storm. It was kismet."

The heat in his eyes caused my heart to thump just a bit louder. Susan blinked cheerily between the two of us, the dimples in her cheeks growing deeper. Ray just took a bite of his chicken and looked bored until Susan elbowed him in the ribs.

"Ow!" he cried, rubbing his side irritably.

"Do you remember what it was like to be in love like this?" Susan asked still beaming at us. "Just look at them."

Ray did, but his look was more of a glower. Brandon caught it and set his fork down on his plate.

"Why don't you just spit it out, Ray?" he said.

Ray mirrored his foster son by setting his fork down on the table too. "All right, then, I will. This is ridiculous. You're getting involved with this young woman when you've got a whole host of things to clean up in your own life, most of which I have to read about in the gossip columns. It's embarrassing."

"You read the gossip columns, Ray?" Brandon teased with a raised brow. "That *is* embarrassing."

"That's not what I meant!" Ray barked. "The point is that I'd like to know when you're going to get your act together and make something real of yourself."

I balked. What the hell was going on? Brandon, for his part, just rubbed a tired hand over his face and groaned.

"And, there it is," he said. "That's right. I've accomplished exactly nothing my life. You know, besides building two of the most successful businesses in New England."

Brandon slouched in his chair and laid a heavy arm on the back of my seat. I had a clear vision of what he must have been like as a teenager, going head to head with Ray on a nightly basis. Susan just took a bite of chicken and chewed it for a very long time.

"See, this has always been your problem, Bran—" Ray started.

"Here we go," Brandon said under his breath as he sat up again to eat.

"That's right, and I won't stop saying it. You think that money means the same thing as real accomplishments. You took that brain of yours and capitalized on it, getting embroiled with that ridiculous family along the way, instead of making real contributions to the world like I know you're capable of."

Ray finished his diatribe and bent to keep eating while Susan just looked on sadly.

"It's a waste," Ray mumbled through a mouthful of potatoes. "Always has been."

Brandon exhaled forcefully out of his nose, while Susan bit her lip sympathetically, clearly having watched this exchange countless times before. I, however, hadn't, and it was infuriating.

"But he does make real contributions!" I burst out.

All three other heads at the table swiveled toward me. A flush immediately bloomed across my face, and I took a deep breath. This wasn't how I'd wanted to play the first meeting with Brandon's parents, but I couldn't sit by silently.

"I'm sorry," I continued, trying my hardest to ignore Ray's hard stare.

He was formidable in his own way, but I'd also been raised by Bubbe, not to mention having grown up in New York City and attending the most rigorous law school in the world. I could handle a few hard looks, and I could dish them out too.

"I just can't sit by and let you call Brandon a waste," I said.

"Skylar," Brandon said, reaching for my hand under the table. "You don't have to do this."

"Yes, I do," I told him, and caught an approving glance from Susan. I turned back to Ray. "Do you know what Brandon does for this city? He uses his money, his time, for so much good. His firm basically funds an entire pro-bono center at Harvard for low-income families. He gives away millions of dollars every year to charities, including an outreach program that scouts gifted kids like him from disadvantaged neighborhoods and gives them access to the kind of educational experiences he got from you two. And then, of course, there's his lab."

Ray frowned, but perked up visibly. "Lab? What lab."

I turned to Brandon, who seemed to be trying his hardest to melt his large form into the floor. His features, tinged pink, were set in stone. I couldn't tell if he was pleased, embarrassed, or angry. Maybe a bit of all three.

"He should know," I said to him.

Brandon waved a hand around the table. "You're on a roll," he said, refusing to meet my eyes like an embarrassed teenager. "By all means, keep going."

"Brandon, you hush. You've found someone who's proud of you," Susan said as she beamed at me. "And I, for one, enjoy hearing all of this, since you don't tell me a thing about it. Continue, dear."

So I did, with a grim glance at Brandon, whose expression I still couldn't read. "Okay, well, he has this workshop on the top floor of his house." I turned back to Ray, who looked utterly confounded by this revelation. "You'd probably love it, Dr. Petersen. He makes these...I don't even know what to call them. Contraptions. Inventions. Amazing things he could sell, but he doesn't, because he's just interested in building them for the sake of building. Brandon, you should show him those drawings in your bag."

I took a deep breath. Brandon sad nothing, but his hand squeezed mine tightly and didn't let go. Okay, that was a good sign.

"Whatever you want to say about him, you can't call him a waste, Dr. Petersen. Your son—"

I tripped over the word, not sure if I should say that or not to a man who had never fully adopted Brandon. But the word fit. Ray Petersen was the closest thing to a father that Brandon had ever had.

"Brandon," I clarified, "is one of the most brilliant, accomplished, *contributing* people I have ever met, by any standard. And that's all there is to it."

I finally looked up to the stone-still man next to me. Brandon's expression had barely moved, but now his eyes glowed, glittering, cerulean jewels of gratitude.

"Thank you," he mouthed silently.

I just smiled back. Then we both turned to Ray and Susan, who were staring at us with mutually dumbfounded expressions, although Susan's had more than a tinge of pride in it as well.

"Well," she said finally. "I guess that *is* that. Brandon, you hold on to this one. And I hope you can show her the same kind of support she's giving you."

Brandon kissed me lightly on the forehead. "Oh, I plan to," he said, although his eyes never left mine.

He bent again to his food. With a quick glance to Ray and Susan, I did the same, willing the insistent flush to fade from my cheeks. Sometimes I *really* hated my Irish blood.

"And what does Miranda say...about...this?" Ray finally broke in again, pointing a long finger at me.

Brandon set his fork back on his plate. Mid-bite, Susan followed suit.

"*This* is a person, not an object on a goddamn shelf, Ray," he said, nostrils flaring. "So you can start by speaking to her with the respect she is afforded therein."

"Cut the lawyer speak, Bran. You know what I'm talking about."

"Well, to start, it's none of Miranda's damn business. We've been legally separated for over three years. She doesn't get to dictate my personal life anymore."

"Hasn't stopped her before," Ray put in.

"Well, I'm stopping her now," Brandon snapped. "Besides...sometimes you can't control when you fall in love. Isn't that right, Ray?"

I couldn't quite suppress the smile and the warm feeling his words caused in my chest. Ray opened his mouth, then shut it tightly while Susan gave him a sly smile.

"I see," was all he said before taking a mouthful of potatoes.

"Anyway, Skylar is only one of the reasons I wanted to come by tonight," Brandon said before another awkward lull hit the table. "I have some news. And I wanted to share it with the three people who are most important to me."

All of us looked up curiously. This was new to me too.

Brandon took a deep breath. "I've been approached by some DNC representatives. They've asked me to run for office next year. For Mayor of Boston."

Susan raised both hands to her mouth in surprise, dropping her fork on her plate with a clink. Ray, of course, only had a hard stare as he processed the news. I, however, felt like I couldn't move. Mayor? Right now Brandon looked more like an off-duty construction worker than one of the most influential people in Boston.

"Oh," Susan said, eyes clearly gleaming with pride. "Oh, *my*. My Brandon? Mayor?" She looked to Ray, grabbing excitedly at his shirt sleeve. "You know what will happen, don't you? He'll win—just look at those dimples. And soon it's going to be the White House."

"What's driving this?" Ray asked pointedly. "Where is this coming from?"

I turned to Brandon. These were questions I also had.

Brandon swallowed his food and took a breath. "Well, it's like you said, Ray," he said. "I want to do more than just stockpile money. They asked, and the timing seems right."

"How can the timing be right when you're in the middle of a divorce?" Ray demanded. "And what about your companies? Are you going to run them and the city at the same time? Or will you be one of those politicians who doesn't care about obvious conflicts of interest?"

I raised an eyebrow. Also valid questions.

Brandon exhaled again through his nose. "Well, to start, I haven't actually decided to do it, and if I do, I won't be announcing anything immediately. And as for the businesses, well, I'd step away from the firm if I decided to run, and I'm in the process of divesting from Ventures anyway just to settle things with Miranda."

"What?" I finally found my voice, clogged as it was in shock.

Apparently that's what he'd been doing on the golf courses and tennis courts. But for someone worth as much as Brandon, divestiture was insane. It would require the liquidation of his shares in Ventures—essentially selling his business to the highest bidder. Depending on how long he took to do it (and he likely would not have long if he was trying to settle the divorce soon), he would take an enormous personal loss. Hundreds of millions, potentially.

He squeezed my hand, then looked back to Ray and Susan. "Look, I've been asked, but I haven't answered. Because the truth is, this would affect all of you. The press will be interested in where I came from and who I spend my time with. So, I won't do this without your support. All of you."

The three of us blinked at him, unsure of what to say. Brandon, to his credit, sat like a statue, waiting patiently for our responses.

Finally, Ray cleared his throat. "If it's what you want...I suppose we support you. Is that right, Sue?"

Beside him, Susan broke into a wide smile. "Of course, Bran. Oh! I'm *so* proud!"

Brandon grinned at her, then looked down at me carefully. "What do you think?" he asked quietly.

For once, I wasn't blushing when the table's attention was on me. Instead, I felt numb, like my skin had lost all color. This was massive news, and I had no idea how to process it. We were just starting to find our footing again. What was I supposed to say?

"I don't know," I said softly. "I need to think about it."

Brandon nodded sympathetically. "Okay, that's fair." Then he turned to Susan. "All right then. I believe we brought some dessert if anyone's ready."

"Of course!" Susan said, bouncing up from her chair. "It's time to celebrate!"

I offered a weak smile, but my insides felt like sawdust. Celebrate...was this news worth the celebration? I didn't know. I hoped so.

~

Chapter 16

After we finished dinner, Ray and Brandon adjourned to Ray's office to go over the ins and outs of his potential campaign. Ray was clearly not a man who liked changes or surprises, so when he demanded some extra time with Brandon, I wasn't surprised when Brandon gave me an apologetic smile and agreed. Although I still had questions myself and would have loved to take part in the conversation, it was clear that Brandon needed some time alone with his foster father.

So instead, I allowed myself to be steered upstairs to tour the rest of the small house with Susan, who showed me the master bedroom, the bathroom, and the bedroom that had once been Brandon's.

"I'm surprised you kept so much of it intact," I said as I walked around the room curiously.

Half of the room had clearly been converted to a crafting space for Susan. A sewing table was set up next to several large shelving units filled with materials for assorted projects. I had glanced at them briefly, but that sort of thing was like a foreign language to me. Other than my musical abilities, I didn't really have a creative bone in my body.

The other half of the room, however, still looked like the bedroom of a broody teenage boy. The extra-long single bed still had the faded blue-and-white plaid bedding and Star Wars-themed sheets. There was a desk, which Brandon had told me before used to be Ray's in his grad school days, which was piled with the clutter of Brandon's youth: stacks of comic books, sci-fi novels, an old boom-box, and a shelf full of CDs and cassette tapes. Old Red Sox posters hung over the bed, as well as a few pictures of a teenage Brandon in various baseball uniforms.

I smiled as I drifted my fingers over the tapes, lingering on several different Springsteen albums. Brandon had told me the story about how Susan bought it for him when he'd come to live with them. If there was a soundtrack to Brandon's life, it was these tapes.

I turned to Susan. "I feel like I just dropped back in time. Like if I closed my eyes, little Brandon would be right here."

Susan chuckled and touched one of the pictures lovingly. "Well, he wasn't ever little. Already six feet tall when he came to live with us. This was taken that day."

She ran a finger over the edge of a brass-framed photo of the three of them in front of their house: a tall, gangly preteen standing between a much younger Ray and Susan. I leaned in to examine the picture. Brandon's hair was even longer then, reaching nearly to his collar. He looked overly thin, even for that age, all elbows and knees, newly grown shoulders hunched over. He didn't smile in the picture, instead looked at the photographer with a blank, almost desperate stare that was still, even with the lack of focus, penetratingly blue.

"He came after his mother was incarcerated for the last time," Susan said as she traced his face. "Poor dear. He was so hot and cold. One moment he'd be the angriest thing you ever saw, and the next the absolute sweetest." She sighed. "You should have seen him when I took him to the comic shop for the first time. You would have thought I'd given him a winning lottery ticket, when it was only a few tapes and posters."

"He told me about that trip to Newbury Comics," I said with a smile. "Obviously it meant a lot to him."

Susan nodded, still entranced with the picture. "Oh. Well. He deserved it, the poor boy." She shuddered and looked at me. "Has he told you much about before he came here?"

"A little. About his mom and dad some, and how she died."

Brandon had told me about his mother during one of our first dates. She was a drug addict while his father was an abusive criminal. On more than one stint during his childhood, he'd been removed from her custody when she was deemed unfit to watch him. Three years after he had come to live with the Petersens, she had tried to get back custody one last time. Since Brandon was fifteen and his foster parents were willing to let him stay, the judge had given Brandon his say. He had chosen the Petersens. Two days later, his mother had died of an overdose.

Susan whistled and looked at me with a new appreciation. "Goodness. I didn't think anyone else knew about that except for us and Kieran. I'm not even sure Miranda really knows. Do you know Kieran?"

"She was my mentor in law school. I'm actually starting at her firm after the bar."

"Well, if she vouched for you, that means more to Brandon than just about anything. She's been a really good friend to him over the years. One of his only real ones."

Susan pointed to another photo tacked onto the corkboard over the desk. I followed her finger to a picture of a teenage Brandon and Kieran that must have been taken close to twenty years ago.

In this photo, their skinny arms were around each other's shoulders. It was far sight from the polished, professional appearances both of them maintained in their jobs as two of Boston's best attorneys; Kieran was rocking a nearly shaved, Sinead O'Connor-looking haircut, and wearing a pair of stonewashed jeans and a loose men's shirt. Brandon had filled out quite a bit from the first photo, but still with the long, lithe muscles of a teenager evident even through his baseball uniform and backwards hat. Kieran was making a face at the camera while Brandon was flashing his trademark smile. Both of them, however, had eyes that were much older than your average seventeen-year-old's.

"Were they ever...involved?" I wondered. I had never noticed anything resembling romantic affection when they talked about each other, but Brandon and Kieran clearly cared about each other a great deal.

Susan shook her head. "Oh, no. Only ever friends. Brandon always said Kieran was basically his sister. She didn't have it easy either, poor thing. Hers was a single working mom, so she basically raised herself, from what I understand."

Susan reached across the desk and picked up a picture of Brandon in a baseball uniform and smiled. "When he came to us, the social worker told us he had been abused. Not just by the people who ran the homes he stayed in, but sometimes by the other boys who lived there. He was just getting big enough that he could defend himself against...the worst of them."

I shuddered at the thought of what she was alluding to. "Did he...ever talk about it with anyone?"

Susan smiled sweetly, but there was sadness in her eyes. "Not to us, just a therapist. That was part of the requirements of allowing him to stay. He was very...difficult in the beginning. And it was clear to both Ray and me that he could never meet any of his potential with all that anger in the way."

"Potential like becoming the youngest graduate ever of MIT?"

I was exaggerating a bit, but not by much. It was no secret that despite being angry, Brandon was also a bit of a wunderkind, which was part of why he had attracted Ray's attention in the first place. He's graduated from high school at sixteen and gone straight to MIT, where Ray taught. Yet for all of the academic support his foster father had provided for him, Brandon had never gotten what he truly needed from a parent: love.

"Yes, well," Susan said, not without some bitterness. "I had my reasons for wanting to keep Brandon here, and my husband had his." It seemed that she was somewhat critical of Ray's motives as well.

"Susan?"

She looked up at me with a kind expression that would have put anyone at ease. It was sad that she'd never been able to have children of her own. Susan was the definition of maternal.

"Yes, dear?"

"Why...why didn't you and Ray formally adopt Brandon? After his mom passed, that is?"

She opened and closed her mouth and reached back to adjust the barrette holding her hair back. "I, well, I..." She sighed and gave me a look that screamed guilt. "I wanted to. But by that point, Ray said it would have been a waste of time and money to petition the court. And Brandon, well, he still had a father out there, Skylar."

"You mean the father who used to beat him with household tools?" I asked.

Susan had the decency to look ashamed, and I immediately felt bad. I took a seat on the twin mattress, and she sat down beside me.

"It was different in those days," she said. "If I could go back and change things, I would. But Skylar, dear, Brandon was a very different person at sixteen than he is now. Very angry. Very aloof. Most of the time we barely saw him. There was a time when I was legitimately afraid that he was going to follow both of his family's footsteps."

I looked at the photo of Brandon and Kieran. It was hard to imagine the smiling young man in the picture being angry.

Susan followed my gaze and smiled. "It was Kieran, you know, who put the bug in him to play baseball and keep going to school. He was so very smart, but he used to hang around with the worst kids, always getting into trouble. Luckily, he'd see Kieran there too. And you know Kieran. She won't put up with anyone's nonsense, much less Brandon's." Susan smiled fondly. "A lot like you, actually."

Then she turned serious. "Skylar, Brandon isn't someone who's had a lot of love in his life, even from that godforsaken wife of his." Her petite feature wrinkled momentarily with distaste, but then her eyes twinkled back at me. "I'm so glad to see that he's found someone else who can see just how special he is, and not just for his money or his brains."

She reached out to clasp my hand with her small one, and I squeezed it back.

"You could still do it," I said. "Adopt him, I mean."

Susan chuckled. "Adopt a thirty-seven-year-old man? Can you imagine Ray's response for that?"

I tipped my head from side to side, as if weighing the possibilities. "It's not like you'd have to pay for it. You know enough lawyers now, after all. If you want, I'd take care of all the paperwork for you. I actually specialized in family law, and I work on a bunch of CPS and child custody stuff last quarter with Kieran. This would actually be really easy because Brandon can give his own consent." I paused. "I think it would mean a lot to him."

Susan sat there for a moment, her small hands on mine with a tightened grip. She was quiet, but the spark in her eyes told me she liked the idea. She liked it very much. But instead of agreeing to do it, she just sighed and stood up.

"We'll see," was all she said.

I stood up and followed her out of the room, pausing again to take in some of the more recent photos in the upstairs halls. One in particular caught my eyes: a candid photo of Brandon and Ray at his college graduation. He was maybe twenty, still so young, dressed in a cap and gown, towering over Ray. The photo was taken next to the Charles River, and Ray was looking up at Brandon with something that actually resembled love. Brandon's face, however, was pensive as he looked out over the river toward the Boston skyline beyond him. He was on the precipice, you could tell, of great things, but still kept his arm securely around the aging man at his side. He never stopped caring about the people around him, no matter how they treated him.

"My favorite thing about Brandon isn't his successes. It's his heart," I murmured to Susan. "Once you see that about him, he's just so easy to love."

Beside me, Susan smiled. "That he is, my dear. That he is."

~

"Susan seems a lot younger than Ray," I remarked later, once we had been picked up by another Uber driver to take us back to my apartment in the North End.

It was an easy way to play a shell game with potential spies, we'd decided, so Brandon had sent David driving his fancy Mercedes all over the city so that we wouldn't have to take separate cars home. I had sent a quick text to Eric letting him know we were coming over. In response, I'd received a gif of Roadrunner hightailing away.

Brandon smiled at me, eager to converse. He was obviously conscious of the fact that I was still processing the evening. This was the first thing I'd said since we'd left the Petersens.

"Yeah, she's almost twenty years younger," he replied.

"So that stuff about falling in love and control?"

Brandon snorted. "Oh, it's just a petty jab. Ray has always thought I was too impulsive, that I wear my heart on my sleeve. But Susan was his student. It nearly cost him his career, and he ended up transferring schools just to get away from the department gossip." Brandon chuckled. "And it's not like he was a young, impulsive man. He was two years older than I am now when they met. And married."

I gawked with wide eyes. "And she was..."

"Nineteen," Brandon said. "Sort of makes our age difference seem like nothing, huh?"

"Not to mention makes him a bit of a hypocrite about the whole divorce thing."

I thought bitterly of the multiple times now when Ray had characterized my presence in Brandon's life as little more than a dalliance, someone who would only complicate things even more for him.

Brandon shrugged. "Honestly, I think that's *why* he's so hard on me. Because he knows what it's like to be stuck between two relationships."

The thought made me tense. I saw the look on Miranda's face when she'd walked in on Brandon and me. It hadn't been the face of someone who had been separated for three years. It had been the face of someone, as Ray put it, who "wasn't having it."

"Are you stuck between us?" I wondered.

Brandon reached into my lap and picked up my hand, then kissed it lightly across the knuckles. He sighed, and the tiny lines around his eyes crinkled.

"I don't want to be." He turned to me then with a solemn expression. "We'll get through it."

I didn't say anything. I still felt somewhat shell-shocked. To be truthful, I often felt that way around Brandon, someone who had the gravity of the sun. But I didn't know how to take all of this. Increasingly it was looking like our relationship was going to be more of an inconvenience than anything else. What kind of political candidate would run for office fresh off a divorce and with a twenty-something girlfriend?

"Skylar," Brandon interrupting my ruminating. "I meant what I said in there. I won't do this without you."

I sat still. I had so many questions, but none of which I was ready to say. What did this mean for us? Would he have to keep me a secret even longer? How would it work if we ended up together for an even longer time...even (and I wasn't ready to consider it yet) marriage? And then there was the matter of my visit to the clinic only a month before...would anyone find out?

"Will I have to give up my career?" I asked finally.

It seemed like the most important point. I had absolutely no desire to be a housewife-turned-politician's wife, dedicated to making babies in order to fulfill the average voter's fantasy of the American nuclear family. That wasn't why I went to law school.

Brandon snorted. "Absolutely not. It's not like Michelle Obama stopped working when her husband ran for office. Hell, by most accounts she was a better lawyer than he was."

"She had to eventually," I pointed out. "She had to be 'mom in chief' when he became president."

The blood drained from my face as I imagined myself chasing kids around the White House, having to watch my speech all the time and constantly have my picture taken.

Brandon tipped his head, then turned to face me. "Listen to me," he said. "I will not do this if you don't want me to, Red. Absolutely not."

"But you want to do it." It wasn't a question.

Brandon shrugged. "I'm intrigued. As much as I hate to admit it, I think Ray sometimes has a point. I could be using my life for something more important. Maybe this is it."

I understood the feeling. I had left a burgeoning career on Wall Street to attend law school in the first place. I still wasn't a hundred percent sure what I wanted to do with my new degree, but passing the bar and keeping my dad out of trouble was a first step. After that...well, I had some other decisions to make.

"I just need time to think about it some more," I said finally.

I turned away and pressed my face against the cold glass of the window. Cambridge flew by as the car wound through the back streets to Boston proper. Beside me, Brandon kept hold of my hand, pressing his fingers into the pads of my palm meditatively.

"All I want is you, Red."

I turned back to find Brandon watching me, blue eyes full of concern. And full of love. The numbness in my heart that had been there since he'd made his massive announcement started to dissolve.

"Do you believe me when I say that?" he asked, reaching his other hand out to cup my cheek.

Instinctually, I leaned into it, closing my eyes as I basked in the feel of his warm palm on my skin. This part was the easy part. When it was just us, skin to skin, face to face. He was so easy to love, and I was learning to accept the fact that he loved me too.

"Yes," I said, without a doubt. "I do." It was just all the other stuff that was so difficult to figure out.

Brandon relaxed, and pulled me into his side so he could cradle me into his chest and stroke my hair.

"Good," he said. Then after a few more seconds, for the second time that night: "Fuck it."

He pulled out his phone and opened the Uber app. He typed in a difference address, then looked to the driver.

"Change of plans, my friend. I've got a new address for you."

~

Chapter 17

It wasn't until the driver steered right past the big house on Beacon Street that I realized Brandon hadn't given the driver his home address. My heart sank. For a minute, I'd thought he was going to take me home with him instead of sneaking into my building like a thief. But, of course, that would be too risky. If his ex-wife was watching him, someone was likely camped out by the house, waiting for Brandon to return.

"I had to give it up," Brandon interrupted my thoughts.

I looked back at him. "What?"

"It's part of the divorce agreement that she's supposed to sign."

I pressed my lips together, surprised by the ambivalence I felt. On the one hand, I was sort of happy the place would be gone. It was a palace that had always made me a bit uncomfortable with its opulence, which I now realized more reflected Miranda's expensive taste than Brandon's. Plus, it was the house where he had lived with her, even if just intermittently, and where she had discovered us together.

But it was also a house where I had fallen in love with Brandon. We had first met in its enormous living room, when I had been stranded in his basement during a snowstorm and wandered upstairs to find cell phone service. We had spent countless hours making love in almost every room, and just lounging together in various other spots as well. Just before Miranda had walked in on us, I had agreed to move in there with him.

There was that feeling again—that feeling of being railroaded, blindsided by the pure force of Brandon Sterling in my life. I knew it wasn't really any of my business what he did with his property, but all of the changes were so intense. Would we ever have those moments again where we could just relax? Where we could exist on equal terms?

"Red?" Brandon interrupted my thoughts, tipped my face to look back at him. "The next time I find a home, I want it to be with you. Because *you're* home to me, Skylar. That's all there is to it."

I relished in the warmth that seeped through my entire body with his words. Everything still felt very overwhelming, but when Brandon looked at me like that, anything felt possible. Maybe I just needed to focus on that.

The car pulled to a stop in front of a large apartment building just a few blocks from Copley Square, close to where Sterling Grove and Kiefer Knightly were both located. Brandon's door opened, and we were greeted by the jovial face of a middle-aged doorman.

"Welcome, Mr. Sterling," he said.

"Hi, Gordon." Brandon looked at me. "Will you come up?" he asked hopefully.

I smoothed my hair, looked warily out the car door and then back at him. "Won't we be spotted? Isn't there someone watching?"

"I doubt it. I sent David to Rhode Island and back." He pressed his lips together, then leaned down to touch his nose to mine. "I don't give a shit anyway."

It was bravado, but I appreciated it anyway. "I'll have the driver take me around to the service entrance if there is one," I said, and gave him a brief kiss. "Go. You'll make Big Brother suspicious if you linger here too long."

Brandon's mouth twisted reluctantly, but he gave a short nod. "Other side of the block. There's a garage entrance. Code 24821."

He kissed me back, more thoroughly this time, then closed the door. I ignored the pit that swelled in my stomach as the driver took me around to the garage.

I entered the building easily and then found my way through the service hall into the nicest lobby I had ever seen. The interior was all white and glass, decorated with white marble flooring and massive, modern chandeliers that hung from twenty-foot ceilings. Brandon was waiting for me while he chatted up Gordon the doorman.

"Hey," he said with a bright smile as I approached. He took my hand and pulled me into the crook of his shoulder. "Gordon, this is my girl, Skylar Crosby. She's allowed up anytime."

Gordon gave me a friendly nod. "I'll put her on the list, Mr. Sterling."

I followed Brandon to the elevators, still taking in the mirrors and glass. Everything shined, like we were in the middle of a prism.

"Funny, I never would have put you in a place like this," I said. A million reflections of myself echoing between the twin banks of mirrored elevator doors.

"Yeah, well. Don't hold it against me." Brandon took my hand and kissed my knuckles. "It's a rental."

Once inside the elevator, Brandon punched in a code before the doors closed again. We went up. And up. And up. Until finally the doors opened directly into an enormous penthouse apartment. Brandon placed his keys, wallet, phone, and hat on a small table near the elevator doors. I stepped inside curiously.

The apartment was basically one open room, a wide space that took up one corner of the building's top floor. Two out of the four long walls consisted of floor-to-ceiling windows that showcased a panoramic view of Back Bay and the Charles River. Boston twinkled from twenty-seven stories below.

After Brandon flipped on the lights, I took in the rest of the apartment. A kitchen was built against one of the interior walls, complete with a spacious granite-covered island and breakfast bar. The other interior wall was hung with several pieces of modern art, split by a hallway entrance that likely led to bedrooms, bathrooms, guestrooms, or an office.

The open living space was clearly designed around the view. Gleaming slate floors covered all of it, with a spare, modern dining set taking over one corner and an angular, steel-gray sectional couch oriented with two black leather armchairs in the other. A few other cloistered seating arrangements dotted the perimeter of the place, but mostly it was just spacious.

And kind of a box. A beautiful glass box, but a box nonetheless. It was the opposite of where I ever would have expected Brandon Sterling to live.

"What do you think?" Brandon asked behind me.

I turned to him. "I...kind of hate it."

Brandon sighed, almost as if he were relieved to hear me admit it. "Me too." He shrugged, looking around. "Margie found it last minute. It's a place to live."

"It just doesn't feel like you. It's so cold." I glanced around at the hard metal fixtures and the gray and white color scheme. "What happened to fireplaces in every room? And big comfy couches?"

Brandon just gave me a rueful half smile and walked into to the kitchen. I took a seat at the bar as he found us something to drink.

"Tea?" he asked. "Or something stronger?" He held up a bottle of Lagavulin and two glasses.

I nodded gleefully. "Ooh, you've got the good stuff."

I was rewarded with a grin that immediately warmed up the entire chilly room.

"I keep it around in case someone special stops by," Brandon said.

So he still hadn't given up that habit. At the big house on Beacon Street, he had kept an entire room full of bachelor-style furniture and accessories for old friends who never came. He wasn't normally a scotch drinker, generally preferring IPAs or maybe a bourbon or brandy. That scotch was for me, a girl who, up until just a few weeks ago, wasn't supposed to be coming back. My heart twisted a little at the thought.

Brandon poured us each a few fingers of the golden-brown liquid, then added a splash of water.

"Do you mind sitting here? The dining table makes me feel like I'm at a board meeting, and those couches are really uncomfortable," he said as he sat next to me at the bar.

Suddenly I couldn't bear the distance between us anymore. I craved our intimacy, the feeling of just *fitting* together. I slid off my stool. "Come here."

I grabbed ahold of his shirt sleeves and pulled him to me for a kiss. My fingers threaded through his soft, curls. Instinctively, he wrapped his big arms around my small frame to engulf me in his scent, in his body.

At last, I let go, and took my seat. Brandon watched with a sly half-grin, as if already a little drunk.

"What was that for?" he asked as he sat back down, although he scooted much closer and set a hand on my knee as he took a sip of his drink.

"That was for the scotch," I said with a wink.

He laughed.

"Did you keep it here knowing we were going to get back together?"

Brandon was silent for a second, conveniently taking another drink. He swallowed, opened his mouth, closed it, then opened it again.

"I hoped," he said finally with a concessive shrug. "A man can dream, Red."

That was Brandon in a nutshell. A man who dreamed. He'd dreamed his whole life, of a family, of a better life, of a job, of money, of his firm,

174

even of a family at one point...and of me. And now there was nothing to hold me back from showing him that I had dreams of him too.

We sat there, sipping our drinks, watching each other as a silence fell between us. He's been to my apartment a few times in the last few weeks, but we hadn't been fully intimate yet, always because I had put on the brakes. But now there was nothing to hold me back. *Blue eyes or green?* Now was also the perfect time to tell him.

I took a deep breath and opened my mouth.

"I'm sorry," Brandon interrupted. "You're too far away."

He dragged my stool even closer so that I was basically wedged between his knees. He picked up my hands and kissed them solemnly, one by one, then set them down in my lap, so he could cup my face.

"It's been a hell of a night, Red," he said. "I just need to keep kissing you right now."

His blue eyes were bright and curious. I hadn't said much since leaving the Petersens' house, and Brandon was clearly a bit nervous, considering the bomb he'd dropped. I didn't say anything, instead just fisted his shirt and pulled him to me.

He took my mouth slowly, continued the soft thoroughness that had characterized our kiss moments before. But now I was the one who couldn't get close enough. Suddenly the fact that it had been months since we had last *really* slept together seemed absolutely unbearable. I needed Brandon inside me, and I needed it right now.

He seemed to feel my sudden urgency. His mouth opened hungrily as his hands clenched at my waist. With a grunt, he reached down under my ass and lifted me up onto the countertop so that I was eye to eye with him.

"You," he murmured in between kisses as his hands ran insistently up and down my bare thighs, pushing the flimsy material of my dress farther up.

"You," I groaned back as I sucked on his full lower lip.

My hands naturally rose to grasp at the ends of his hair. Brandon's deft hands drifted up my sides, slipping over the cotton to cup my breasts, my ribs, the muscles in my back, my waist. He played with the hem again, but retreated. He was waiting for me to give him the okay to move forward.

I broke the kiss then, and Brandon stared, licking his swollen lips.

"Too fast?" he asked, out of breath.

His gripped the edge of the counter so hard that his knuckles turned white. I glanced down at them and back at him. It looked like he was physically struggling not to touch me. I felt the same.

Without blinking I reached down and pulled my dress over my head. He stared at my suddenly bared, lightly freckled skin, his mouth dropped open slightly.

"Christ, Skylar," he croaked as his gaze dragged up and down my body. "You are so beautiful it hurts." He blinked, blue eyes wide and glistening. "Say something."

I didn't. His look, his words made me feel too full. I was so overwhelmed by him—it was a feeling that never seemed to stop with Brandon—and the number of emotions swirling in me were too complicated to say. I craved clarity, and in this moment, the only thing that promised to do that was his body.

"Come here," I murmured finally.

I pawed his shirt over his head, eager to feel his skin on mine. I groaned as I found my payload: the smooth muscles of his chest, that broad expanse that I drew my fingers across before shoving them over his shoulders to pull him closer, skin to skin. With a grunt, he grasped my thighs again, eliciting a moan through his kiss with every deep knead of my flesh.

"God," he finally breathed as his mouth trailed down my neck, kissing, biting, licking until he could bury his face between my breasts. "I never stop wanting you," he groaned into the soft skin there. He kissed me again.

I reached behind to unsnap my bra. His muscles flexed all the way down his ridged stomach with tension as the bra fell to the floor. He stared hungrily where the tips of my hardened nipples grazed his chest, shuddered, then voraciously took them into his mouth, one at a time. As if acting of their own accord, my hips gyrated against his, eager to find some union there.

"Fuck!" he breathed as his stiff length pressed through his jeans and my underwear. The hands at my ass squeezed even harder. "I need you. Right fucking now."

"I don't want to wait," I said into a salty sheen of sweat on his shoulder. I licked it. He tasted delicious.

A split second later, he had shredded the thin lace of my underwear and was busily shoving his pants down his legs.

"Shit," he muttered. "I...hold on. Condoms are in the other room."

I wilted slightly at his words as he pulled out of my grasp. Brandon noticed the small movement and stood tall.

"What's wrong?" he asked.

I bit my lip. If he needed a condom, did that mean he had slept with other people? Did he think *I* had slept with someone else?

You tried, I reminded myself.

As if he could read my doubts, Brandon returned to stand between my legs, eyes dark and searching. "I haven't been with anyone else," he said quietly. "I couldn't."

I gulped. Relief washed over me, although his muscles tensed even more. He was clearly wondering the same thing about me.

"Neither have I," I whispered.

My hands trailed over the contours of his muscles: the elegant lines of his neck, over his deltoids, the curves of his defined biceps and triceps. He was so beautiful, with the grace of an athlete.

He searched me for a moment, as if looking for something I might have to hide. The tension in his body released, though his hands on my thighs still gripped with urgency.

"Are you...are you still on the pill?"

I shook my head. He started to step away, but I grasped his wrist.

"IUD," I said softly. "A few weeks ago."

His face turned feral. "Thank Christ."

Before I could respond, I was picked up from the counter and heaved over his large shoulder.

"Aaah!" I cried, but Brandon just laughed as he hoofed me down the hallway to a door he kicked open. I was dumped on a huge blue bed, sumptuous and soft.

Brandon kneeled between my legs with a look that said all jokes were done. His fist wrapped around his erection, which he meditatively rubbed as he perused my body. When his eyes met mine again, they were dark and demanding.

He leaned over and slid his palm between my breasts, over my belly, and down my clit with just enough pressure to make my hips jump off the bed. Then he rubbed his length against the slick space between my legs, never entering, just teasing, causing my hips to arch even further, begging him to enter.

"Not yet."

He stood up, still massaging himself. I watched the movements of his hand. He was teasing me, on purpose, but for what reason, I didn't know. Brandon read my expression knowingly.

"Turn over," he ordered.

Obediently, I flipped onto my belly, then looked back over my shoulder just in time to see his eyes dilate at the change of view. He moved back between my legs, his free hand drifting up the interior of my limbs until he reached my ass, to which he then gave a quick slap.

I jumped, and my breathing picked up. My hair flipped over one shoulder as I looked back at him.

"Really?" I asked. "It's going to be like that?"

Brandon just bent over my body, pressing himself against my skin as he gave me a quick, biting kiss.

"Really," he replied. "Now, get up on your knees and touch yourself."

I obeyed, my hand snaking under my hips to find my clit while my face pressed into the soft dark blue of the duvet. The fabric muffled my moans as the feel of him pushing just slightly into me from behind.

"Christ," Brandon muttered again as he pushed in further. Both of his hands took solid handfuls of my ass, pulling me toward him so he could sink in all the way. "Fuck. You feel so fucking good, Skylar."

I gasped at the feel of him, and my fingers, as if of their own accord, picked up the pace.

"Fuck," I whimpered into the cotton. "Brandon...I....need to..."

"Not yet," he growled as he pulled out.

"No!" I cried out at the sudden loss. We were just getting started!

In response, all I got was another quick slap on the ass, hard enough to make me jump. I cried out, but just as much out of pleasure as anything else.

"You're going to come when I let you come," Brandon growled as he flipped me back over and knocked my hand away. "Hands up. Now."

Obediently, I raised my hands over the bed, feeling his gaze like fire.

"Clasp your hands together. *Don't* move."

My skin prickled all over with anticipation as I followed his orders. I hadn't seen this side of Brandon before, and while normally I wouldn't have said I had a dominant fetish, I was so starved for him that I would have done just about anything he said.

With firm hands, Brandon pushed my knees apart so he could stand between my legs and survey my body like some kind of conqueror. He pulled my legs up around his hips so that just the tip of him brushed against my entrance. I squirmed as my hips pressed forward to take him. His hand found my ass with another loud crack.

"I said don't move."

With every bit of self-control I could muster, my palms squeezed together over my head as I stilled the rest of my body. Everything pulsed.

Brandon trailed a hand down my torso, over my breasts, belly, down to the sensitive spot that ached for him. Every muscle in my body tensed as I worked overtime not to rise into him. He looked on with satisfaction.

"You want me to touch you, don't you, baby?" he asked with a wicked smile.

His thumb flicked over my clit, and my hips jerked slightly.

"Please," I whimpered, tortured by the way he lingered, teasing at my entrance, teasing at my clit.

"Please what?"

I hardly knew. They were gentle, but his ministrations were agony.

"Please—you—I—" My words came out stunted, half-formed.

Without warning, Brandon shoved himself fully inside.

"Fuck!" he barked.

"*Oh!*" I shouted.

He pummeled into me with a few sharp, intense thrusts before pulling out just as suddenly.

"No!" I yelped at the sudden absence, but then the thumb on my clit started to work, and I melted back into the sheet. "Please," I begged again as he brought my body closer to its edge. Seriously, the way the man used his fingers should have been illegal.

My body tensed again, this time preparing to let go completely. He pulled his hand away.

"Hey!" I shouted, slamming my hands on the mattress in frustration.

I glared up at him, and he chuckled, although from the way the bricked muscles of his torso were flexed, he was having a difficult time maintaining his control too. He covered me with his body, silenced my cries with kisses.

"Do you have any idea how gorgeous you are right when you're about to come?" he murmured into my ear.

His long length slid into me again. I moaned and tried to tilt my hips to bring him in even deeper. I craved those deep, punishing thrusts from before. My hands were no longer clasped, instead grabbing angrily at the sheets. But he kept his slow, steady pace, finding a rhythm with his body as he caged me with his warmth.

"Your whole body seizes up," he continued, his deep voice vibrating against my ear. "Your eyes get so wide, I could get lost in them. Your mouth opens, a perfect, fuckable 'O'. Sometimes I can't decide whether I want to fuck your mouth or your pussy." He paused over me, closing his eyes as if in pain. "*Fuck*, Skylar. You feel...*fuck*."

"Brandon," I whimpered as I raised my mouth up, looking for a kiss. "*Please*." I didn't know how much more of this I could take.

His eyes popped open, their bright blue searing into me. He pushed up to his knees and continued to move, somehow finding a way to sink deeper, to touch the darkest parts of me with every merciless drive of his hips.

"Yesssss," I hissed as he found a harsher rhythm that would undo me completely. "Keep going. Don't stop."

My hand drifted down my body to find my clit, but Brandon slapped it away.

My eyes blinked open, confused. "What—"

"Not this time, Red," he said, his breath ragged and harsh with his effort as his hips started to move even faster.

Beneath his assault, my limbs began to shake, hips jerking involuntarily to meet his. I writhed, desperate for contact, every nerve in my body alight and yearning for the simple touch that would send me soaring.

Brandon just pressed his hand, palm down firmly over my center to still me against his onslaught.

"*No!*" he said sharply. "Tonight's pleasure is *mine*."

He rammed so hard I yelped in response. Once, twice, three more times. But just when I thought the feel of him would push me past that point of no return, he pulled out with a shout and released himself all over my stomach, fisting his length while his groan filled the room.

Our eyes met, flashing something almost dangerous in the dark-lit room. After a few minutes, once we had both caught our breaths, Brandon pushed off the bed and walked into the en suite bathroom. I lay there, my entire body still tensed for a release I wasn't going to get. Casting an eye toward the closed bathroom door, I contemplated just finishing myself off. But something made me stop. This felt like a penance, one that maybe I deserved. Brandon could read me like a book; how often had I been lost in thought only for him to anticipate my worries before I'd even had a chance to speak them aloud.

Maybe he knows.

Could he?

Blue eyes or green?

When he returned, I cleaned myself up with the damp cloth he brought, then curled into a ball under the covers. Brandon slid into bed, but didn't gather me close like he used to. Instead, he faced me, with at least a foot of space in between us. It might as well have been a mile.

We didn't say anything, just let the sound of our breaths fill the room. A few streams of moonlight soared through the blinds, casting long shadows over the sharp lines of Brandon's face. He just watched me, with a curious expression I couldn't quite read. There was love there—there was always love there—but it was guarded. Mixed with something that looked like curiosity, fear, maybe even a bit of quiet, lingering anger.

Several times Brandon opened his mouth as if to speak, but he always closed it again. I just hugged the covers tightly to my chest and pulled my knees closer. Eventually the silence overcame us both and we fell asleep.

~

Chapter 18

Brandon left early the next morning for one of his six a.m. runs. Although I knew he wouldn't like it, I couldn't sleep after he left, so I ended up getting dressed and heading back to the North End, where I spent the rest of the weekend holed up studying. We traded a few texts through the morning, but it was clear that both of us needed some space. Things had gotten very real.

As much as I wanted it to, the comfort and lightness that had always seemed such an integral part of our relationship still hadn't returned completely. Darker elements loomed. We craved each other, but there were pains we were both trying to purge with our bodies instead of words. The truth was, we had both hurt the other badly. It would simply take time to work through all of the complications.

Late Sunday afternoon, while I was finishing my weekend homework, my cell phone buzzed loudly on my desk. It seemed that Brandon was finally ready for a real conversation. That was good, because so was I.

"What's up?" I answered.

"Nothing much. Just finishing up some things for a few meetings tomorrow. I needed to catch up on a lot of stuff this weekend."

It was an unspoken acknowledgment of the fact that I'd left early Saturday morning and he had been fine with it. I missed the days when I would camp out at his house for days at a time, but we clearly weren't there yet.

"Anyway, I had a thought," Brandon said.

I pulled my knees up onto my chair and rested my chin on them. "What's that?" I asked, happy to hear the fondness in his voice. His texts through the weekend had been friendly and flirtatious, but nothing matched his deep voice.

"Sterling Grove is sponsoring a few tables at the New England Children's Advocacy Gala next Saturday. Want to go?"

I sat up straight. This was a far cry from sneaking into hole-in-the-wall restaurants. This was the same group I'd mentioned to Ray and Susan the other night. It was the center of his philanthropy efforts, one of the only things that I had found on his Wikipedia page before we had even dated.

"You want to go to a benefit together?"

My heart rose at the thought. Maybe it wasn't as important to keep me hidden as he'd originally thought. I was already so heartily sick of being incognito, I would have accompanied him to a party even if I was only allowed to wear pajamas.

Brandon sighed audibly on the other end of the line. In the background was the noise of what sounded like a baseball game on television. I could see him sitting on his uncomfortable couch watching the game on the flat screen mounted over the fireplace. Alone in his palace in the sky.

"Ah, well. Sort of," he said lamely. "I was thinking Eric could bring you as his date. I'll have Margie throw him a ticket at one of the firm's tables."

I deflated.

"What does that mean?" I asked as I hugged my knees closer. "How would we go together if you can't be seen with me?"

"Skylar," Brandon said gently. "It's two weeks until the papers get signed."

"I've heard that before," I mumbled, staring up at the ceiling. Like the rest of my apartment, it was old, the one part of the room I hadn't tackled with paint. Cracks ran through the plaster.

"Skylar. I'm trying here."

I sighed. "I know, I know. I just...why should I even go, then? Having to be around you and pretend like we're not involved sounds like a terrible way to spend the evening. I see how women look at you, even when you're practically all over me. This will drive me nuts."

"It's not going to be like that," Brandon insisted. "I know it's not ideal, but the NECA is a really important cause to me. I'm on the board of directors, and it's one of the top charities I support."

I glanced at myself in the mirror curiously. "Just how many charities *do* you support?"

"Um...twenty-eight? I think? I'd have to ask Margie to be sure. I'm only on the board of five, though."

I blew a long raspberry between my lips. "How did I end up with a married saint?"

"Not a saint, Red. Just a sinner trying to redeem himself."

"How very Catholic of you," I replied dryly.

"Half of Boston is Catholic, babe. Even if you're not in the church, you're still practically confirmed just by association."

I snorted, but the joke fell flat.

"I'm not a perfect man, Skylar," Brandon said, his voice slightly sad.

"No one says you have to be." I doodled a heart on the margin of my textbook. "I'm not perfect either."

"Maybe not," he said softly. "But you might be perfect for me."

My heart squeezed in my chest at his words, and I smiled a little bit. But one question still remained.

"Is...Miranda...going to be there?"

I hated even saying her name. Over the last thirty-six hours I'd managed to push her out of my mind most of the time. When I did see her smirking, refined features, I'd usually just think of Brandon, whose face could always distract. This time, though, that wouldn't work.

"I'd be shocked," Brandon said. "The NECA isn't really her thing, and everyone from Sterling Grove hates her guts. Mark will be there. He loves giving her shit and isn't afraid to do it to her face."

I couldn't help but chuckle at that. I had only seen Mark Grove, the other name partner of Sterling Grove, in passing when I worked as an intern at Brandon's firm, but I already liked him. He was short, spry, and sharp-faced, a bulldog with an acute bite. I could easily imagine him cutting Miranda Sterling's stately entitlement down to size.

"Kiefer Knightly has a table, so Kieran will probably be there too," Brandon continued as a cheering crowd sounded behind him. "But more importantly, there are some people I'd like you to meet."

"Who people?" I blinked with realization. "DNC people?"

We hadn't talked any more about the bomb he'd dropped at the Petersens' house. I knew that Brandon had been waiting for me to broach the topic; he'd been dropping obvious lures, like random discussions of local political issues, all weekend via text.

"It's a way for you to see what it's all about." I could hear the longing in Brandon's voice. "Please, Red. For me?"

How was I supposed to say no to that?

"All right," I mumbled. "I'll go."

He laughed, his relief palpable even through the phone. I couldn't help but grin into the mirror.

"I'll have Margie send a car for you and Eric," Brandon said in a much lighter tone. "And babe? Thank you."

I couldn't help it. I grinned. It felt too good making him happy.

~

Later that evening I was video chatting with Jane while folding laundry. Like me, she had been deep in study mode through the weekend and was desperate for some best-friend time. We had to make do with screen versions of each other while I decompressed from the weekend.

From what I could see on the screen, Jane had turned her cousin's spare room into study central, with a mountain of notes splayed around her bed. Her mostly black, punk-inspired wardrobe was hanging on a rack behind her, and the menagerie of hair products she used was piled on a small dresser. It was actually pretty funny seeing her semi-Goth paraphernalia scattered around a room that was otherwise decorated with pink roses and ruffles.

My insides squeezed. Eric was a good roommate, but sometimes I really missed having my best friend around all the time.

"Any more news about Princess Godfather?" Jane asked, popping her spiky-haired head into view again before ducking out of the frame to put away some clothes. It was laundry night for her too.

I blew a massive sigh while I folded another shirt.

"Dad still thinks I'm nuts about Katie," I said. "She's got him stuck in her damn spider web. I'm going to have to go down there and confront them myself, I know it."

"That sounds...potentially dangerous," Jane replied from across her room. "Especially if she really is involved with Messina and his henchmen. I know you're not going to like this, but what about asking Brandon? Didn't you say he already has security watching your family? Why not just have them check her out?"

I paused, holding a black shirt up against my body and checking myself in the mirror. "Goddamn it. I think that stupid dryer shrunk this shirt."

I turned back to the computer, where Jane had framed her face with a filter that made her look like a unicorn. I laughed, and she gave me a cross-eyed grin, then took it off.

"I've thought about that, too," I admitted. "He would probably do it, but I don't want to get him more involved than he already is. What if this mess gets back to him? What if it costs him his bid for mayor?"

The idea still twisted my stomach into knots. Between my father's drama, Miranda's potential vendetta, and my recent personal choices, I felt like one big skeleton in Brandon's closet, which already had enough skeletons by itself. He hadn't even brought up that he was also trying to negotiate the fact that Miranda had served as a false alibi for him when he was just a twenty-year-old kid. That was the beginning of their relationship, and no doubt part of the divorce had to involve a non-disclosure agreement. Considering his goals for public office, her silence was paramount to his success. I couldn't get in the way of that.

"I still think you should ask him," Jane interrupted my thoughts. "Just like I think you need to tell him about —"

"I know, I know," I cut her off. "But now I'm wondering if it's a good time."

"Sky..."

"Look at everything else we are having to deal with right now!" I cried, tossing several pairs of unmatched socks up into the air in frustration. "We're trying to rebuild our relationship in the middle of all of this shit. If we were smart, we'd just wait until everything settles down. Until Miranda signs the papers and I pass the bar and he's done running for whatever office he wants to run for and my dad is finally stable. And as if that weren't enough, I got a message today confirming that Janette is actually going to show up this week. Kids in tow and everything."

Jane whistled. Even Jane had never met my mother, whose presence in my life was so sporadic she seemed more a product of my imagination than an actual family member. I flopped backward onto the bed, suddenly exhausted. I felt like I was trying to sprint through a marathon.

"Sky?" Jane said finally.

"What?"

"Sit up, will you? This is a nice view, but I have something to say to your face, not your hoo-ha."

I scrambled back up, and tipped the screen so it showed my face clearly. "Sorry. That better?"

Jane smiled. "You have a nice mug. I like to see it when I drop pieces of life-altering wisdom."

"And what wisdom would that be?"

Jane took a dramatic pause, but then suddenly looked much more serious.

"It's not ever going to get easier," she stated clearly. "You and Brandon are complicated people. That's just who you are."

I frowned. "What is that supposed to mean?"

Jane shrugged, her frank yet friendly expression emanating good will through the screen.

"It means you need to grow up, chick. Stop hiding from the truth and face the music. Together."

"Is that what you're going to do?"

Jane's eyes grew wide behind her large black frames, and then she shut them completely. "I haven't the foggiest idea what you are talking about."

I glanced into the living room to make sure that Eric couldn't hear our conversation. But his bedroom door was safely shut, and I could hear the thump of electronic music.

I looked back to the screen. "I think you know exactly what I'm talking about. I've just been nice enough to give you time to bring it up, but since you're not, I'm going to have to do the dirty work."

Jane grimaced. "It was just one night. We've done it before."

"That was three years ago, and it was a month, not a night. Plus, the two of you were strangers then. That is clearly not the case now."

"The boy is a walking PSA against STIs," Jane replied as she ducked out of the frame.

"And yet you slept with him." I held a sly finger to my lips and cocked an eyebrow. "'Methinks the lady doth protest too much.'"

"Stop doing that; you look like a James Bond villain." Jane popped up again and pulled her glasses off so she could squeeze the bridge of her nose. "Look, it doesn't really matter, does it? I live in Chicago; he lives in Boston. We're all about to start the busiest years of our lives. And your roommate, bless his skanky ass, is good in the sack, but shit at intimacy."

"So exactly like you, you're saying?" I said as I folded a pair of jeans.

"Oh, don't be so proud of yourself," Jane said. "These emotional barriers are constructed by choice. When I'm ready, I'll take 'em down and dive right in. Eric isn't even aware he has walls up. He isn't aware of anything but his penis."

I glanced back in the direction of Eric's room again, where the door still remained safely shut. The music, however, had gone down. He might have gone to bed. Alone. Same as the last seven days.

"I think you're wrong about that, my friend," I said. "But that's all I'm going to say. It's your business, the two of you. I'm just enjoying my front row seat."

"Don't get too excited," Jane said with a significant eye roll. "It's not going to happen again." She shook her head, refusing to look directly into the camera. "A tiger doesn't change its stripes, Sky. Once a slut, always a slut."

I couldn't help but wonder if she wasn't just talking about Eric.

~

Chapter 19

The week passed uneventfully, with class in the morning and afternoons spent studying. Brandon was traveling for most of it, and other than a few study sessions with Jared, Eric and I mostly kept to our rooms to focus on a particularly difficult section of our class. By the time the weekend rolled around, I was more than ready for a reprieve.

Just as Eric and I walked through the door on Friday evening after spending the afternoon studying at Jared's apartment, my cell phone buzzed in my messenger bag. I pulled it out and frowned at an unfamiliar number.

"Hello?" I answered.

Eric walked into the kitchen to get a drink.

"Skylar? My goodness, darling, is that really you?"

The voice was friendly, female, and also made my skin crackle.

"Skylar?" she asked again. "It's Janette. Are you there, darling?"

The buzzer to the front door cut through the room. I turned to Eric, who was nursing a beer. I nodded my head at the door, and covered the receiver end of the phone.

"It's Brandon. Can you let him in, please? I have to take this."

Eric grumbled unintelligibly to himself, but nonetheless trudged over to answer the buzzer. I didn't blame him; I hadn't even met the partners at Kiefer Knightly yet, but I certainly wouldn't be thrilled if they were sleeping over every weekend.

"Thank you," I mouthed, trying to look appropriately apologetic.

Eric nodded, and I took a seat at our small kitchen table.

"Janette?" I said. "Sorry about that. You still there?"

"Yes, darling, I'm here. How *are* you? You sound absolutely marvelous."

"Um, I'm fine." I stared at the lacquered wood tabletop. My mother was the kind of person who acted like she was your best friend in the world when she actually took the time to speak to you. The rest of the time, you didn't exist. It didn't matter if you'd known her for years. It didn't matter if you were her blood.

"Did you receive your graduation gift? I picked it out myself. Well, a man from a piano shop in Boston did, but I spoke to him myself about it."

This was also typical Janette: assuming accolades for normal actions that most people would just do without a single thought. I didn't know what she wanted me to say. Making a phone call didn't make her a saint, and especially not after being largely absent for most of my life.

"Yes, I got it," I said. "It was definitely a surprise."

"I'm glad you liked it!" Janette exclaimed, despite the fact that I'd said no such thing.

I mean, it was certainly a nice piano and all, but aside from the fact that I'd barely be able to play it between studying and respecting the noise restrictions of an apartment building, there was also the awkwardness of receiving an extravagant gift from someone who barely knew me.

The apartment door opened, and another person with a penchant for extravagant and at times inappropriate gifts strode in, stern until he found me, at which point I was rewarded with an ear-splitting grin that raised the wattage of the room by at least ten points.

Janette continued to gab about the piano, but I barely listened, happy instead to ogle Brandon. He had clearly come from work, still dressed in the remnants of a summer suit: light gray pants and a starched white dress shirt, a dark red tie loosened around an unbuttoned collar. He tossed his jacket and briefcase on the couch and made a beeline toward me.

"Hey, beautiful," he whispered as he engulfed me from behind.

His nose and mouth unerringly found that sensitive spot just below my ear, and I arched against him while Janette continued her chatter.

"So what do you think, darling?" Janette was asking.

"Hmm? What's that?" I murmured, closing my eyes as Brandon's tongue touched my earlobe.

"In two weeks. The Cape. I'd love for you to meet Annabelle and Christoph."

"Um, yeah. I'll think about it," I said, half-dreaming as Brandon pushed my hair off my other shoulder and resumed his work on the other side. Honestly, I should have known better than to have any conversation while under the spell of Brandon's deft touch.

"And tomorrow sounds good for dinner?"

"I can't," I said, with minimal coherence. "I have an event. I'm going to a benefit with my—"

The sudden absence of Brandon's mouth interrupted my train of thought. I turned to him, and the tight shake of his head informed me I shouldn't tell anyone about him.

I frowned. "My roommate. I'm going with my roommate."

Brandon gave me a contrite smile. I slipped off my stool, wandering in the direction of my bedroom, ignoring the frown behind me.

"A benefit? It wouldn't be the NECA gala, would it?" Janette was asking.

I paused with my arm braced on the doorframe. No one could say Janette didn't have intuition—just in the wrong way. She could track fancy events like a bloodhound, but had no ability to gauge the moods of her daughter.

"Yeah, that's the one," I said. "Why?"

"Well, we were invited to that by one of Maurice's business associates. So, I suppose we will see you there. What fun!"

Before I could answer, I was swept off my feet, suddenly hostage in Brandon's strong arms.

"Don't run away from me," he murmured into my ear, and then bit my earlobe before taking my mouth with a kiss that was at once tender and insistent.

"Oh! I've just had the best idea!" Janette was saying in my other ear, loud enough that Brandon could hear her. "Let's go shopping tomorrow. We'll make a girl's day of it. Get something fabulous to wear and have our hair done before the benefit. What time do you say? I'll have a car pick you up."

"Get rid of her," Brandon growled as we collapsed on my bed together, he on his back, me now sprawled over him. He kissed me again, hard and fast. "Now."

"What?"

My breath was shallow, and I could barely hear Janette's jabbering as I was once again smothered in a kiss.

With a devilish grin, Brandon snatched the phone out of my grasp. "She'll be ready at ten," he barked without breaking his gaze, and before I could say anything, had ended the call and tossed my phone onto my bedside table.

"Come here," he ordered.

And, of course, I did.

~

About twenty after ten in the morning on Saturday, a town car dropped me off in front of Swish, one of the many stores on Newbury Street that catered to Boston's elite. It was one of those stores I'd never had any reason to enter, since most things inside cost more than my rent.

Brandon had left early that morning to meet with his trainer after we had spent the night making out instead of having sex. It wasn't for lack of wanting, but I didn't press the issue, and neither did he. It was like we were content just be together, yearning somehow for a closeness that still wouldn't come.

So in the morning, Brandon left, but not before we had a minor argument about the wad of cash he'd tried to shove into my purse.

"*I'm* the one who wants you to come," he'd insisted over and over again. "Let me pay for your damn dress!"

"No one is going to pay for anything but me!" I'd yelled back, at one point literally throwing the bills at him in a confetti of green and white.

Eric, of course, had walked out of his bedroom right at that moment. He had gone right back in. Brandon finally left, cash and all, muttering something about a "gorgeous, stubborn ass" that I'd chosen not to hear.

So here I was, already having decided that no matter what happened this morning, I'd go to Macy's for a reasonably priced knockoff. It was hard not to be irritated. I needed to be studying instead of playing Pretty Woman with my estranged mother.

"Courage," I muttered to myself, and walked up the steps of the brownstone building.

Swish was the kind of shop that demonstrated its affluence by having as few items of clothing as possible on display. Its merchandise was treated like art, presented one piece at a time against a minimalist decor. I stood in the entrance of the store, a bland white space that was bigger than it looked from the outside, and immediately found my mother at the far end, gabbing with the saleswoman like they were best friends.

Janette looked the same as she always had: tall and willowy, with light brown hair tied up into a tasteful chignon at the base of her neck, dressed in deceptively simple clothing made of the best possible fabrics. Today she wore a pair of white summer slacks, a navy silk tunic that had just enough design quirks to make her look more like an artist than a socialite, and enough tasteful gold jewelry at her wrists and ears to demonstrate her wealth without being gauche about it.

Despite being raised in New York (albeit on the Upper East Side), Janette looked very French. And very rich. She looked up and spotted me, raising her hand and causing the gold bangles at her wrist to fall downward with an audible clink.

"Skylar! Darling! Come here and let me see you! How long has it been, my love? Three years? Four years?"

It had been five, actually. But who was counting?

As I crossed the nearly empty shop, Janette turned to the saleswoman, placing a hand on her shoulder familiarly. I recognized it as a common tactic of Janette's. Within five minutes, she'd be on a first-name basis with a Saudi prince.

"Just look at her, Denise," she said. "Isn't she absolutely stunning?"

I rolled my eyes, but smiled politely once I reached them. It was hard to take that kind of compliment from my mother. Considering how alike we looked, she was really complimenting herself more than anything. Although we had the striking difference of height and coloring (I had inherited my father's diminutive stature and his father's freckles and flaming red hair), looking at Janette's face was like looking at my own: the same slanted green eyes, the same heart-shaped mouth, the same button nose that was slightly rounded at the end.

"Hi, Mom," I greeted her with air kisses she usually offered.

"Janette, darling, Janette. You know the rules. This is my daughter, Denise, but you can't tell a soul. I'm not old enough to have a daughter this age, am I?"

Denise smiled conspiratorially as she looked me over. "Definitely not, Janette. I would have guessed sisters. Maybe even twins."

It was physically impossible not to roll my eyes again.

"Have you found a dress already?" I asked hopefully, looking past her at the rack of clothes. Maybe this wouldn't take very long.

"Oh, no, darling, we're just getting started. Now, I had Denise pull these ones for you, although it's been so long that I don't really know what your taste is. I guessed on your size, of course."

Janette scanned me up and down as if to gather my taste in formalwear from the cropped black pants and black T-shirt I was wearing. When she got to my slightly scuffed ballerina flats, she raised a plucked brow.

"How charmingly...down-to-earth you look. But perhaps we should pick out some other clothes too. We can't have you entering society looking like the Audrey Hepburn before she got her makeover."

"You don't need to worry about that," I said as I followed her across the shop. "I'm a twenty-six-year-old lawyer, not a teenager getting ready for cotillion."

Janette sighed as she examined the fabric of a beige summer sweater. "I do regret that," she admitted. "That we never had you formally announced in society. You would have made a lovely debutante."

I remained quiet. It didn't seem worth the effort to point out that the reason I had never "come out" in society (if I'd even wanted to) was because she had skipped town again and the Chambers family had never actually recognized me. I couldn't even remember which husband she'd been on at that point. Third or fourth, it didn't matter. All of them had long been more important to Janette than her own child. Until, it seemed, she had new ones with her current and most long-lasting husband.

"Anyway," she said. "It's not about coming out, my love. It's about fitting in. You've got the pedigree—you're *my* daughter, after all. But you can't show up places looking like a ragamuffin. I know that's the style these days with young people, but I don't care what people say. Appearances *do* matter."

I looked down at my simple outfit. It wasn't Gucci or anything, but I didn't think my clothes were anything to be sneered at. One plus of the study-abroad year I'd spent in Paris (ironically seeking a relationship with my mother, who'd never shown interest in reciprocating at that point either) was that I'd paid attention to the basic tenets of French style: simple, classic silhouettes and good material.

"And really, you'll need to get used to it, won't you?" Janette remarked as she paged through a few other shirts.

I frowned as I trailed behind her. "What do you mean?"

Janette smiled at me, brilliant and white, the kind of smile that only comes from cosmetically enhanced dental work. "Well, I just assumed, you know. Brandon Sterling is one of the biggest donors on the East Coast. Excellent choice, by the way. He's still married, of course, but that's not a real obstacle. Miranda—horrible woman—can't hold on forever."

I opened my mouth and closed it again. "How did you know about us?"

There was no use in denying it; she was a stranger, but she was, after all, my mother. I was more concerned that Brandon and I hadn't been as discreet as we'd thought.

Janette waved my concern away as she pulled a diaphanous white silk blouse off a rack and held it up to my body. "Oh, a mother has her ways. You don't need to worry, dearest, your secret is safe with me." She returned the blouse and winked. "That was him on the phone last night, wasn't it?" Janette asked, her big green eyes suddenly sharp with interest.

I frowned. "Um..."

"Let's dish. How long has it been serious? Men don't get territorial like that if it's not, you know. I'm impressed, darling. He really is such a catch!"

"Um..."

"You know, if we play our cards right, I could help you get a proposal by the end of the summer. Miranda used to be pretty, but she can't compete with you." Janette sighed and tapped my chin wistfully. "Effervescence of youth. Can't be replaced, much as we might try."

"What are you *talking* about?" I asked, shaking off her finger as I finally found my voice. How did she know about this? Where was she getting her information? "Proposal? Marriage? I'm nowhere near thinking about—"

"Pish, don't fret," Janette cut me off. "You'll get frown lines. Do you always take everything so seriously? Now, it's your grandmother you should be talking to about marriage. She's more excited about it than I am."

I huffed. Of course Bubbe was the culprit. She was so over the moon about Brandon, and she loved sticking it to Janette. When Janette had called for my number, Bubbe likely couldn't resist telling her that Danny's daughter, the garbage collector's daughter, was dating a billionaire. I considered what would happen if Brandon decided to get into politics as well. I was going to have to have a serious talk with my grandmother.

Denise approached.

"Janette," she said as if she was my mother's friend from school. "Everything in the dressing rooms is ready now. We've got mimosas this morning too."

Janette clapped her hands like a school girl. "Fun!" she said and grasped my hands. "Let's try some things on, shall we?"

And hour later, I was half drunk on champagne at eleven in the morning, wearing a dress that would easily cost more than two months' rent, and standing on a small platform in front of a three-sided mirror at the back of the shop. There was a small mountain of dresses still hanging on our rack, not to mention the various separates Janette had already made me try on. I'd vetoed everything on account of cost.

I felt ridiculous. Janette sat on the couch in front of me, champagne glass in hand as she gabbed with Denise. She'd made a quick choice of a blush-colored dress that was now hanging from a rack by the cash register, waiting to be sent to the in-house tailor for rushed alterations. I, on the other hand, suffered from no such luck under my mother's scrutiny.

"This is insane," I insisted for what felt like the thousandth time. "I am not paying three-thousand dollars for a dress I will wear exactly once."

Janette waved her hand at me, although her nostrils flared slightly. "It doesn't matter, I keep telling you." She cocked her head at me. "What do you think, Denise? I feel like that color washes her out."

Standing beside Janette, Denise nodded in agreement. "She needs a softer green with that skin and hair. The chartreuse isn't doing her any favors."

Janette nodded. "Get the Grecian one, then. The sage color?"

Denise nodded and disappeared into the back of the store. Janette stood up and walked to me, then turned me to face the mirrors, where she looked at me through their reflection.

"Darling," she said evenly. "Please stop."

"Stop what?" I asked petulantly. I crossed my arms over my chest.

"Stop protesting every time you try something on. You sound dreadfully poor, and you're embarrassing yourself."

"I *am* poor, Janette."

"Well, that's not what the trust fund I gave you would indicate. Wasn't it enough to pay for school, and then some? Besides, you're not paying for this; *I* am."

I stared at the ground, then finally looked back at her through the mirror.

"I'm uncomfortable with this," I said as plainly as I could. "To be frank, Janette, it feels really inappropriate to accept such extravagant gifts from you. We barely know each other."

Janette stood still for a moment, the turned to look at me directly. She set a delicate hand on my shoulder.

"Please let me," she said quietly. "I think we both know it's the very least I can do, considering..." she trailed off, unwilling to finish. We could both easily fill in the blanks.

I'd seen that look before—the one where remorse for all the wrongs she'd done over the years seeped through her normally buoyant face. She had deployed it more than once over the years, usually in order to assuage a sudden burden of guilt. My mother acted like she was full of air, but in reality, she knew just how to manipulate people to ease her own weak moral compass. I was really no better than Dad, who couldn't ever quite say no to her. Not until the very end.

"Okay," I finally relented. "You can buy me a dress. But no matching separates. I'm twenty-six, not seventy-six. Bubbe wears sweater sets, for crying out loud."

Janette blinked, then burst out laughing. "Of course, of course!" she agreed with glee. "But you'll let me pay for the salon too, all right? Oh, darling, we are going to have *such* fun!"

~

Chapter 20

Eric and I arrived at the gala with Janette and Maurice, whose driver had picked us up so we could all travel together. Eric was decked out in a tuxedo that he actually owned. I shouldn't have been surprised. I often forgot about it, but his family was part of the same Upper East Side set that Janette came from.

"I just love Beth, your mother," Janette said once we were on our way. "She's a bit older than me, of course, but what a darling."

"I'll tell her you said hello," Eric replied with the subtle, practiced politeness of someone who had been having these kinds of conversations his entire life.

I listened curiously; it was possible I could learn something from Eric. Maurice, who hadn't stopped speaking on his cell phone once, ignored the rest of us as he prattled on in French. He had a typical Parisian accent and spoke very quickly; even with my mostly fluent French, I found him difficult to understand.

"Now, let's get a look at my gorgeous girl," Janette said, turning to me. "Well, I can't see a thing with that shawl on. Wherever did you get it?"

She tugged off the light, gold-threaded scarf I used to cover my shoulders. I sniffed. It was a hand-me-down from Bubbe, who had bought plenty of my clothes growing up from secondhand stores. The scarf fell around my hips, and Janette nodded in approval as she looked me over.

The Grecian-style, moss-green gown did fit perfectly. The satin fabric draped over one shoulder and left the other bare, while the gold-corded bodice cinched my waist smaller than it already was. A hidden slit in the skirt would tease my leg every now and then, but the dress's sex appeal came mostly from the way it made me look like I'd been wrapped in luxurious green sheets, leaving most of my body to the imagination.

Janette had insisted on a beaded gold clutch and strappy gold sandals to go with the dress, and we had spent several more hours that afternoon having our hair and makeup done. Janette had instructed the hairdresser to create barrel rolls out of my masses of red, which had then been pinned at the crown of my head and set with two thin, gold headbands, much like a Greek statue. The makeup artist had drawn subtle gold tints around my eyes, complemented by otherwise natural makeup. I felt a bit like a dress-up doll, but I couldn't deny the effects.

"Yes, I'm glad we went with that one," Janette said. "But something *is* missing, isn't it?" She reached down and fingered the pounded silver cuff on my wrist. "This is nice, but it doesn't really go with the dress, does it? The accents aren't silver."

Self-consciously, I looked at the sturdy bracelet Brandon had given me. It felt like an anchor against a impending storm.

"Luckily, I came prepared," Janette said as she reached into her small purse and pulled out a pair of thin gold cuffs and a set of diamond-drop earrings. "Put these on. They'll show off your darling little wrists. I'll keep your bracelet in my purse."

"That's all right," I murmured, reluctantly sliding it off my wrist and putting it in my own clutch.

Eric snorted. Janette had worn me down throughout the day. She watched with pride as I put on her jewelry.

"There," she said once I was finished. "Now you're perfect."

Beside me, Eric gave my hand a compatriotic squeeze. Obviously, he understood this weirdly superficial praise that seemed nested in tacit critique; if his mother was anything like Janette, he had dealt with it his entire life.

"Thanks," I said. Maybe I looked perfect, but as we pulled up to an event full of people whom I essentially had to hide from, I felt anything but.

The limo drove past a gatehouse onto an expansive, tree-lined estate, and I gawked openly.

"You'd better shut your mouth before we get there, dear," Janette said knowingly.

Eric chuckled. Maurice shot me a sideways glance and continued chattering in French.

We joined a line of cars dropping off pairs of glamorous attendees at the entrance. My palms started to sweat. The house—if you could even call it that—was bigger than my entire apartment building, and built in a style that would look more at home on an English manor than the middle of Brookline.

"Who lives here?" I asked incredulously.

"Oh, Rick Avery owns it now. He founded Nike, I think. Or was it Reebok? I really don't know, some enormous shoe company. Isn't that right, Maury?" Janette asked.

Maurice nodded, but didn't stop his chatter to answer. Our limo stopped in front of the mansion's grand entrance, and one of the several servants standing outside in tuxedos stepped forward to open the door.

"Onward and upward, darling," Janette said as she scooted out.

Eric and I followed, and Maurice shuffled after us, finally putting his phone away.

"You got this, Cros," Eric whispered, tucking my wrist into the crook of his elbow.

"Did you do this a lot growing up?" I asked quietly as we walked toward the entrance.

"Every freaking weekend," he muttered. "Stick by me. I'll keep you safe from the wolves."

We followed other well-dressed attendees into the house. It was the kind of place that looked more like a castle than a home. Massive double doors opened into a domed hall that could have fit Bubbe's entire house inside. A huge winding staircase curved around the space, and past that was a reception room for large events like these.

We followed the crowds there, where tables, a stage, and a live band were set up for the event. Black-tied servers scurried around with trays of food and champagne. Everything was elegant, tasteful, and bright, and also screamed of wealth.

Maurice almost immediately found someone he knew and quickly abandoned the three of us against the wall. I could see now why an event like this was more likely to be held at a private residence than a grand hotel room. These were some of the richest people in New England, even the world. Their homes were nicer than any hotel, and no doubt potential backroom dealing would require privacy that wouldn't be found at the Ritz.

"Are you all right?" Janette asked beside me.

My fingers clutched Eric's sleeve, and I stood, frozen. Fitting, really, since I'd basically been styled exactly like several of the mock-Greek statues around the room's perimeter.

"I don't know what I'm doing here," I admitted.

It was like being in the showroom of Tiffany's, full of diamonds. That's what wealth actually did to people, I realized: it created a blinding veneer. It wasn't just the jewelry, although there was plenty of that. The diamond earrings I had borrowed from Janette were actually ridiculously understated.

Everything about these people seemed to glitter. Their clothes, sumptuous and tailored, weren't sewn from cheap poly-blends, but lavish silks and charmeuse. Their skin gleamed with high-quality skin products and dermatological treatments. Their nails were freshly manicured, their hair blown out, their teeth whitened and capped. Faces pulled taught, wrinkles erased, cheeks plumped. They walked about the room with the grace and confidence of people who know the world was under their control.

Suddenly I was very, very grateful that Janette had insisted on the shopping trip.

"Is that one of the Red Sox?" I wondered aloud.

Beside me, Eric nodded. "Johnny Caron. Solid stats this year."

"Brandon's a fan," I murmured, thinking first that I should get his autograph for him, then realizing how ridiculous that was when in this room, Brandon was just as famous as the man, or more.

Janette watched with a gaze that looked almost hungry. "Maurice is trying to get him to invest. I should go introduce myself." And with that, she disappeared through the crowd, slippery as a fish.

"You should drink something," Eric said. "Immediately."

He snagged me a glass of the cheap champagne that had been circulating on trays. I tipped it back in one go.

"There you go," Eric said after putting down his own and grabbing two more from another passing server. He handed me one. "Takes the edge off, doesn't it?"

"How did you do this all the time?" I gasped after downing the second one. The bubbles fizzed in my stomach, calming and amplifying my nerves at the same time. I needed to burp, but at least I didn't want to throw up anymore.

"Oh, my liver has built up a good tolerance over the years."

"No, I mean *this*." I waved my hand at the opulent buzz. "These people. Talking to them. Everyone judging."

Eric shrugged. "They're like cats. Act like you love them, they'll treat you like shit. Treat them like shit, and they'll worship the ground you walk on."

"Is that where you learned your game?" I wondered, noticing already how some of the younger women were looking at Eric. "I can go find our table. I don't want to cramp your style."

To my surprise, Eric scowled. "These are the last kinds of women I will *ever* get involved with again," he said vehemently. "They are the worst. Manipulative bitches, all of them."

"Wow, that's a first. I've never known you to pass on available tail." Coincidentally, I'd also noticed that he had spent every night of the last two weeks alone in his bedroom, home every night by ten. "I don't suppose that has anything to do with a certain best friend of mine, does it?"

The champagne was starting to get to me.

"Please," Eric scoffed. "I know where I stand there. Jane thinks of me as a walking vibrator. No more, no less."

I watched him thoughtfully, but his poker face gave away nothing. Hmm. Curious.

"So..." Eric looked down at me again with concern. "Your mother. What's she after?"

I blinked in surprise at his uncharacteristic directness.

"Cros," he said impatiently, "I grew up around people like these my entire life. I know when they want something, and your mother is looking at you like you're a piece of prime rib. What's she after?"

I shook my head, my face growing hot. "I really...I mean, you're probably right. But if I had to guess, I'd say redemption, maybe. She usually grows a temporary conscience about once every five years, pokes around my dad or me until she feels better about herself, and then splits."

Eric nodded, but his face was pensive as we watched Janette cozy up to a circle of attendees, most of them men.

"If you say so," he said. "I don't know. I just...I smell a rat."

"And what about you?" I asked, nudging his shoulder. "Do I need to be guarding you against all of these vicious predators?"

Eric just snorted and polished off his champagne. We gave our glasses to a server and went to find our seats. The Sterling tables had all been set with name tags. Brandon hadn't arrived yet, but he was placed next to several other names I recognized: Mark Grove, a few of the other equity partners at Sterling Grove, and some political heavy hitters around Boston. I, however, had been relegated to the table full of younger associates with Eric. I wasn't surprised by the arrangement, but it still hurt. A lot.

Across the room, I spotted Kieran, who stood with a small circle of men dressed in suits. Unlike most of the other women in the room, she had eschewed a formal dress in favor of a fitted white tuxedo with a blazing ruby brooch, the same color as her lips, pinned to her lapel. Her dark hair was pulled back as severely as ever. She stood out as much for her confidence as for her unusual formalwear.

She waved briefly, clearly surprised to see me, then returned to her conversation. I wilted a little in my seat. I don't know what I had been expecting. I wasn't Kieran's friend; I was her subordinate, and someone who should probably be at home studying for the bar, not socializing at fancy events.

Nearly three hours later, I was drunk. Dinner had come and gone, speeches and donations had been made, and Eric had finally left so he could get up early to study. I hadn't seen Janette and Maurice the entire evening; they were too busy hobnobbing with Boston's elite to bother. So much for seeking redemption. The most elite of them all, my "date" who wasn't really my date, was still nowhere to be seen.

Eric offered to share a cab, but I had demurred, saying I'd wait for another thirty minutes before going home. That, unfortunately, had left me little else to do but sip on continuous glasses of champagne. It had been an hour since then.

I'd left my phone at home, not having been able to fit it into the tiny purse, which could barely hold my lip gloss, some cards and cash, and my bracelet. Watching Janette dance with one of the lesser Red Sox after Maurice disappeared, I sat at my table, feeling very sorry for myself. I pulled the silver bracelet out of my clutch and toyed with it, running my fingers over the engraving. It only made me feel more alone. What was I even doing here?

"Skylar?"

I turned around to see another surprising, yet familiar face.

Dressed in black-tie attire, Jared looked a far sight from the preppy student from class. It actually made perfect sense that he would be here, considering his family's roots in Boston society and politics.

"What are you doing here?" I asked anyway, my words slightly slurring as I accepted his kiss on my cheek.

Jared, clearly having had a few drinks himself, didn't seem to care that I was so shocked. He looked me over with obvious appreciation.

"That's, um, a dress, Skylar."

I glanced down. Everything was mostly in place, but in my inebriated state, the slit of the gauzy fabric had opened clearly to reveal most of my left leg as it was crossed over my right. Maybe it was because at that point, I was fairly furious with being stood up, but the show of skin didn't bother me. I made no move to close the fabric.

"You look bored," Jared said as he sat down next to me. His glance flickered to my leg again, but came right back up to look me in the eye and didn't move. "I saw that you came with Eric, but then he left. Are you waiting for someone?"

He quirked an eyebrow, and it was obvious that he wanted me to admit that I was here for Brandon. But no one was supposed to know that. Plus, Brandon wasn't even here.

"No," I said finally and tipped back the remainder of my sixth glass of champagne. "I came with my mother and her husband too, but they seem to be preoccupied. I was actually going to leave soon."

I stood up abruptly, but had to grab the table as blood rushed from my head. I brushed out the creases of my dress, which fell more modestly around my legs again, then glanced around for my clutch to put the bracelet back in it. The movement caused my head to spin a little.

When I finally straightened up again, I found Jared standing too, looking somewhat amused.

"You all right there?" he asked.

"I'm *fine*," I said with enough effort that I swayed a little.

"Well, then you can't leave without giving me a dance first," Jared said, putting a hand at my elbow to steady me. "Do me the honor? I'll go slow, I promise."

I looked at the hand and then back up at him. Jared actually looked amazing. He wore a standard black tux and had brushed his light brown hair back, and the effect made him look a little like James Bond. He smirked at my obvious appraisal.

"Only if it's *really* slow," I agreed.

I set my clutch on the table and allowed him to lead me to the dance floor, which was starting to clear out. The more powerful people had adjourned for back room dealing, and everyone else was wilting from the champagne. Jared pulled me securely, but not indecently, against him, settled a hand at my waist, and began to lead me around the floor in a tepid box step. He wasn't a terrible dancer—certainly better than me.

"So, don't take this the wrong way," he said as he turned me under his arm. "But whoever decided to let you sit at that table by yourself was an idiot. You and Eric haven't..."

"No," I said quickly. "Still just roommates."

"And your mom doesn't seem too interested in keeping you company because..."

I rolled my eyes as he pulled me close again. Jared was taller than I realized: over six feet. Not as muscular as Brandon, but he still filled out his tuxedo.

"We're not close," I said. "It was sort of an accident that she was coming to this thing anyway."

"So...Sterling stood you up, huh?"

Now the elephant had been addressed. Great.

I leaned back so I could smile at him, hoping to pivot away from the question. "Do I stick out that much?"

"Well, yeah, but in a way that probably wouldn't be polite to talk about in public." Jared swung me around for another turn.

I shrugged. In my drunken state, the compliment felt good. Better than being stood up, that was for sure.

"So, why didn't you call me after our date last winter, Skylar?" Jared asked, changing the subject once again.

I raised an eyebrow. "I don't remember you being this direct."

He gave a good-natured wink. "I have nothing to lose. So what happened?"

I sighed. I considered the awkward night when Jared had run into Brandon and me at the symphony, on Valentine's Day, no less. I had blown him off to see Brandon, and Jared had discovered us there. Not my finest moment.

"I'm sorry about that," I said. "I...got wrapped up in...you know."

Jared nodded. "Yeah. I guess I can see that," he said, not without some bitterness. "The way my sisters talk about him, you'd think he was the second coming or the devil himself, depending on whether or not Miranda's around."

His hand tightened at my waist as he pulled me just a bit closer, so that my breasts grazed the front of his chest. Still not enough to be indecent, but the subtle maneuver didn't escape me.

"I'll say it again," he said into my ear. "He's an idiot for standing you up. If I got to be your escort tonight..." He leaned back again with a look that was more sharp than gentle. "I'd never leave your side."

We stared at each other for a moment, no longer moving with the music. Jared's brown eyes suddenly seemed more intense than I'd imagined him capable of. Safe, sweet Jared was gone. For the first time all evening, I didn't feel like abandoned trash, but I wasn't sure I liked this attention either.

Jared smirked. Then he closed his eyes and leaned in.

Wait, what?

I leaned back a solid six inches away from his face. I was drunk, but I wasn't that drunk. Jared opened his eyes, now darkened with something I didn't like at all.

"Whaaaat are you doing?" I asked, trying and failing not to slur my speech.

"That's an excellent question."

At the sound of the familiar deep voice, I dropped Jared's hand and stepped away like he was made of fire. I whirled around, which made the room spin like a top. When it stopped, there was Brandon, standing in front of us, looking like every penny of his net worth.

"Hi," I said weakly, and fell into his strong arms.

~

Chapter 21

He looked incredible, as always. Brandon was dressed in an all-black tuxedo with a finely embroidered vest. The dark color only set off the natural glow of his skin and hair, which emanated health in a way that most of the glittering people in the room were trying to fake. The monochromatic ensemble gave him a rakish look when compared to someone like Jared, who immediately looked more like a prom attendee than an Ian Fleming character.

"Hey," Jared stepped back with his hands up. "I didn't know, man. I'm sorry."

He didn't know? Yeah, right.

Brandon darted a quick glare at him. "Aren't you George's kid? I'm surprised you would come here. This isn't really your side of the aisle."

I glanced between them curiously. This wasn't technically a DNC event, but a lot of the attendees were there to unofficially discuss politics. Jared's family, however, was staunchly conservative.

Jared puffed up visibly. "My family doesn't play party politics," he said with a curious set to his jaw. "My father's not a party hack like *some* people interested in office. If he wants to support a cause like this, he will, and I'll stand with him."

"That's good," Brandon said calmly, letting the jab slide off his shoulder. "Always nice to hear about representatives growing spines for once. Hopefully George will teach his son what he's so recently learned."

Jared's face bloomed a bright red, and he shook visibly. With a nasty look at Brandon, he reached out to squeeze my hand, but I pulled away. I was drunk, but I wasn't interested in poking the bear who had finally arrived.

"I'll see you on Monday, Skylar," Jared said with another pointed look at Brandon. "I'm really enjoying the fact that we get to spend so much time together these days. And don't worry. *I'll* be right on time."

Before I could reply, Jared slipped away between the tables. I turned to Brandon, preparing for an onslaught.

"Nothing happened," I started.

"Relax," he said quietly. "I saw you pull away." He looked at me with sad blue eyes. "But I can't help but wonder why you were dancing with him in the first place."

I frowned. "It was just dancing with a friend. I was bored. And alone."

"You didn't look bored. And he didn't look like a friend."

I glared. "You have no standing here to be pissed off. You weren't the one whose date stood you up for three fucking hours."

"I did not stand you up, Skylar!" Brandon tried and failed to keep his voice down.

He glanced around the hall. We hadn't gotten any attention yet, but we would soon. I couldn't care less.

"I had a meeting in New York today, and there was a massive accident on the 93. If you had had your phone with you, you would know that and could have just gone home."

"You didn't think to contact one of your many admirers?" I retorted. "Every person here is donating gobs of money to your favorite charity so they can have the next mayor in their pocket. It was a giant circle jerk in here, every single one of them getting off to you."

"Whatever." Brandon ground his teeth meditatively. "Doesn't mean my girlfriend needs to get physical with every guy in the room. Especially not a little prepubescent shit like him."

"Girlfriend? That's rich." I crossed my arms over my chest. "We both know I'm closer to something else at the moment."

The vein in Brandon's neck popped as he clenched his teeth. "Don't start, Skylar. You're drunk. You know I hate it when you talk about yourself like that."

"If the shoe fits."

The thing was, even though the words were intended to make him feel bad, they just made me feel even worse. I was realizing just how much I hated this arrangement—I hated being his dirty little secret.

Brandon exhaled long and heavily through his teeth. Then, with sudden determination, he snatched my hand and dragged me out of the main hall, much to the interest of the attendees still around. Luckily, they seemed even more intoxicated than I was.

"Where are we going!" I yelped, trying and failing to free my hand as I scooted unwillingly behind him down one of the long corridors leading off the hall, past several closed doors. I smacked him on the shoulder with my clutch. "Brandon! I'm not going to have sex with you here!"

He came to an abrupt stop in front of a large wood door.

"Will you keep your voice down?" he hissed. "That's not what I'm doing!"

I snatched my hand back and cradled it against my chest, lest he make another grab for it. "Then what *are* we doing? I'm still really fucking mad at you!"

"You're so fuckin' difficult, you know that?" Brandon looked at me with a hard gaze that gradually softened. "But I love you anyway." He leaned down and smacked a brief, intense kiss on my lips. "I'm sorry, okay? And not for nothing, but you look insanely hot in that dress."

Oh. I dropped my hand and swallowed. "Thanks. I think."

Brandon picked my hand up and kissed my palm gently. "Come on, Red. There are some people I need to talk to, and I want you to see what this is all about. Then we can leave, and I'll show you just how sorry I really am for being late."

Before I could say anything else, he set a broad palm against the door and pushed.

As soon as we stepped into the room, the chatter comprised of predominantly male voices came to an immediate halt. Several pairs of eyes shot to Brandon's and my still-clasped hands. Brandon just squeezed tighter.

"Sterling!" A deep voice called out from across the room. "You made it. Traffic didn't kill you getting back from New York, did it?"

At that, the din resumed, and Brandon steered us toward the owner of the voice, a trim, younger man with graying black hair. He stood next to a set of bookshelves with a few other men, including my stepfather, Maurice.

"Hi, Maurice," I murmured as I joined them.

Maurice just gave a curt nod and glanced at the hand that Brandon still held.

"Skylar," Brandon said, pulling my attention away, "I'd like you to meet Cory Stewart. He's the guy who will be my campaign manager if I decide to run. For now, he's in charge of PR at Ventures."

I reached out to shake Cory's hand, ignoring his sharp concern. Everything about him was sharp, actually. His posture under the black and white tuxedo was ramrod-straight; his face, with pointed angles, a razor-edged nose, and beady eyes that darted up and down my person with lightning-quick judgment, had the warmth of a steel knife.

"Pleased to meet you," I said with a forced smile.

"And you," he replied. He looked anything but pleased, and darted a quick look at Brandon. "Listen, buddy, I hate to break it to you, but we're going to have to save introductions for later. You've got a room full of people here who only want to know the answer to one question: are you running?"

Again, the room silenced as everyone turned to hear the answer. After a few bemused moments, Brandon just cracked a smile.

"You're a crafty one," he said, shaking a finger at his maybe-campaign manager. "Can you believe this guy?" he asked the room. "Could charm someone out of their last kidney, I swear."

The room erupted in low laughter, and its occupants once again turned back to their conversations, satisfied that Brandon's decision wouldn't be made tonight. I looked on curiously. I hadn't realized just how many people were invested in his plans.

"Well, since you're determined to keep us all in suspense, can I convince you to meet a couple of prospective donors?" Cory asked. "If your...friend here doesn't mind letting you go for a few?"

Brandon looked down at me.

"Do you mind?" he asked. "You can stay with me if you want. But this is just networking around the room."

"It's actually pretty boring," Cory added. He was trying to sound friendly, but I could feel, rather than hear the tension in his words. He wasn't happy I was there.

Brandon just waited patiently and squeezed my hand again. I squeezed back, then let it go.

"It's okay," I said.

I meant it. For the first time that evening, I actually wanted to sit back and observe. This was the real reason that Brandon had asked me to come.

He leaned down like he was going to kiss me on the cheek, but then clearly thought better of it and straightened. I tried to convince myself it didn't matter.

"I won't be long," he said. "There's someone with drinks around here. Get comfortable."

I located a server taking orders for the kitchen. I wouldn't be having any more alcohol tonight, but I could definitely use some water.

"Go ahead," I said. "I'll be fine."

I took a seat on one of the large Chesterfield chairs that sat around the perimeter of the room. It was a library or study of some sort, a rich man's version of intellectualism, with the dark wood, built-in shelving, and large, masculine furniture.

"I didn't know it was public news."

I turned from my observations to Maurice, who took a seat in the chair next to me and sipped what looked like brandy. I was surprised he was actually speaking to me; he'd barely acknowledged my presence all evening.

In a roomful of uptight New Englanders, Maurice looked irrevocably French. With his lithe, diminutive stature and a head full of salt-and-pepper hair, he wore a classic black tuxedo with a black tie instead of a standard bowtie. With a nose that was a little too long and dark eyes that sunk into his face with Gallic circles, Maurice was handsome in a patrician sort of way. However, I had yet to see him smile.

"What news?" I asked.

"That my stepdaughter is involved with Brandon Sterling," Maurice replied evenly in his thick Parisian accent. He watched me with cold calculation. "Janette," he said, "she told me that you knew him, but the way she talked, it seemed...how do you say...a dalliance?"

I frowned, unsure of what I was supposed to say here. I didn't consider Maurice family, even though technically we were, and I'd as much as admitted my relationship to Janette. But despite the fact that with a simple hand hold, Brandon had basically told everyone in the room that we were involved in some way, I didn't know what I was at liberty to say. I didn't know what they thought.

"No," I finally said. "Not a dalliance. I've never been one to...dally." The word sounded as awkward as it felt.

Maurice crossed one leg elegantly over the other. "I see. And what do you think of all of this?" His accent was incredibly pronounced, perhaps an effect of the brandy. "Are you interested in being a part of politics?"

I looked at the crowd of people who now surrounded Brandon. Tall and strong, with his head of gold hair, he was the sun to their orbit, a center of gravity that drew them all in. It wasn't hard to see why. He exuded both charisma and a kind of genuine goodness that would attract anyone. If he chose to run for mayor, I had no problem seeing it happen. Nor, it appeared, did anyone else.

"I don't know," I answered, and that was the truth. But I was willing to figure it out in the end. Brandon was my sun too.

"I see," Maurice said again as he swished his brandy in its sifter. "I see."

Before I could reply, a pair of white pants appeared in front of us. I looked up and gulped. Kieran, looking anything but happy.

"Hi-hi," I managed to stutter.

She didn't move, just peered grimly down at me.

"Hello," she said. "I was surprised to see you out there. I'm shocked to see you in here."

I had to force myself to maintain eye contact. Kieran's piercing stare was one of the most formidable I knew. She glanced at Maurice, who just held up his drink in a sleepy salutation.

"This is my stepfather, Maurice Jadot," I said, gesturing in his direction.

Kieran acknowledged Maurice with a curt nod before leaning down a little more closely to me.

"You shouldn't be in here," she said bluntly. "It's not good for him to be seen with you."

"You make me sound like some call girl," I said bitterly.

"If his *wife* ever gets wind that you were here, and she *will*, that's basically what everyone here will think of you," Kieran retorted. "Skylar, I'm doing my best to get him out of this marriage so that you can be together the way I know you both want, but you are not making it easy by showing up here."

"He asked me to come," I protested weakly. "He said it was important. What was I supposed to say? No?"

A thin, raised brow told me that was exactly what I was supposed to say.

"You should know better than anyone else that Brandon has a habit of doing stupid things for people he loves," Kieran said. "So you need to think about his best interests better than he does. And right now, that means you should go before people get the wrong idea, and definitely before Miranda shows up."

I crossed my arms defiantly. "He said she wasn't going to come. I wouldn't be here if that were a possibility."

"Miranda has a habit of showing up in a lot of places Brandon thinks she won't," Kieran said dryly. With a flash in her dark eyes, she looked around the room. "You'd be better off to remember that."

As if her words were a clear omen, the door to the study burst open, and another magnetic field of charisma entered. The chatter quieted.

"Hello! Oh, hello, nice to see you, Henry! Love that ascot!"

I froze at the sound of a voice I had only heard twice before. Both times were burned into my memory. All the blood drained from my head.

Next to me, Kieran stood up to her full height and closed her eyes in anticipation.

"Fuck," she said so low no one else but I could have heard her. She looked at me. "You need to *go*." Then she darted through the crowd, presumably to distract the newest guest at the party.

This wasn't happening. Just when I thought the night couldn't get any worse, it absolutely did.

I stood up to see Miranda Sterling née Keith giving people air kisses as she moved about the room. She looked, as ever, like a movie star, dressed in a red column dress that fit her long, lithe form like a glove. Her thick brown hair was pulled back at her neck to reveal a massive wreath of diamonds that paired with the ones at her ears. Her full lips were painted a bright red to match the dress. She looked like she had walked off a *Vogue* cover, like money, charm, and confidence. Everything I wasn't.

"Bran, darling, I made it after all!"

By now the room had gone completely silent, as everyone looked to where Brandon stood, still surrounded by Cory and several others. I was never so glad that I was watching Brandon the moment she spoke, as I was able to see the look of complete and utter shock on his face. He

213

hadn't known she would be here. He never would have invited me; perhaps he wouldn't have come himself.

I started to edge my way around the perimeter, wary of Maurice's curious gaze as I did. Miranda and I were two of only a few women in a room full of men. We stood out just by virtue of our dresses in a sea of black tuxedos. I needed to get out of here before I was noticed.

As Miranda continued to chatter, I wove through the room, doing my best to take advantage of my short stature. The study, unfortunately, wasn't crowded quite enough to hide me. Miranda Sterling's sharp gray eyes zeroed on me just as I was about to reach the door.

"Oh, hello!" she crowed with a wicked smile. "If it isn't our little red-haired Calypso!"

To an outsider, her tone might have sounded friendly, as if she were complimenting the Grecian style of my dress, but at least three people in the room knew exactly what she was referring to: Calypso was the Greek nymph who had tried to steal Odysseus from his wife, Penelope.

My face flooded the same color as her dress. Brandon tried unsuccessfully to elbow his way through the group that had cornered him.

"Miranda, that's enough," he called, but his voice only brought more attention to the situation.

"I...I'm going to go," I said to them both, eager to escape the prying eyes surrounding me.

Thank God that most of them didn't know my name. The confrontation between Miranda Sterling and her husband's anonymous, red-haired mistress was bad enough.

"That's probably for the best," Miranda agreed with a critical nod. Her eyes flashed, hateful and bright. "No one here likes cheap goods."

"Miranda!"

I didn't stay to see Brandon's reaction. With my face turning hotter at Miranda's ugly words and the hum of the gathering picking up behind me, I stepped out of the room. As soon as the door closed, I picked up my skirts and ran.

~

214

Chapter 22

By the time I reached my tiny apartment, the buzz of alcohol had completely worn off, but the heady feeling of the evening hadn't. I sent Brandon a quick text to let him know I was home and that I'd talk to him tomorrow.

But after I pulled off the ridiculous dress, I took one glance at my small space and knew I couldn't stay there. I had two choices: I could roam the city at night by myself and have even more to drink (which probably wasn't the best idea). Or I could take this adrenaline and use it productively.

I grabbed my gym bag and chose the latter.

It was well after midnight when I swam my last lap at my gym, which was thankfully open all night. Only diehard gym rats were in the building; I was the only one in the three-lane pool.

All vestiges of alcohol had evaporated. I could see the evening for what it was: a medium-sized disaster, but not necessarily one I had to flip out about. There would definitely be fallout, but I intended to make sure that Brandon listened to Kieran from now on. I was done being humiliated by his ex-wife.

I finished my last flip-turn and soared through the water, making it halfway down the twenty-five-meters before I surfaced for air. There was someone standing at the end of my lane—likely one of the gym staff sent to kick me out of the pool for the night. I swam quickly to the end, pushing myself until my muscles started to shake. I reached for the concrete edge with my final stroke and pulled myself up to catch my breath.

I pushed my goggles over my swim cap, and it was then I got a look at the shiny black oxfords in front of me. Definitely not the sneakers of your average gym attendant. I yanked my cap and goggles completely off and looked up.

Brandon towered above me, broad shoulders still looking indecently handsome in the all-black shirt and embroidered vest. The top two buttons of his shirt were undone, and the black bow tie lay loose on either side of his collar. His jacket was gone, and his hands were shoved deep into his pockets. His hair was mussed, like he'd been running his hands through it too much, gold waves in haphazard pieces around his forehead. The wavering reflection of the pool water cast deep shadows under the strong lines of his cheekbones and jaw.

He pulled his hands out of his pockets and crossed his arms. "Having a nice swim?"

He squatted down so our faces were only a foot or so apart, close enough that I could see the slight perspiration on his forehead from standing in the humid pool room. His eyes glowed bright like tiger's, despite their brilliant blue, but the faint lines over his brow told me he was tired.

I bit my lip, treading water. "It was all right. How did you know I was here?"

Brandon sighed, his features unreadable. "You didn't answer your phone after you texted me, so I went to your place. Eric told me where you went."

I blanched. "You woke up Eric?" He couldn't have liked that.

Brandon sighed and rocked back and forth on his heels. "I'm his boss. He was happy to accommodate."

I pulled my damp hair out of its bun, happy to relieve the weight. It fell in thick ropes around my shoulders, causing water to trail over my skin. It was a far cry from my earlier, more glamorous look. My face was bare, wet, and likely had goggle marks around my eyes. My sport bikini wasn't the skimpiest of suits, but the rough intake of Brandon's breath told me it was alluring enough. He looked like he wanted to eat me.

Good, I thought. Fair's fair.

Finally, Brandon blew out a long sigh. "Why did you leave?"

I cocked my head in disbelief. "Come on. Staying wasn't an option."

"I got that. But why didn't you wait for me?"

I pressed off the ledge with my feet, but kept my grip on the concrete, arms straight while the water swished around me. Without moving, I should have been cold, but Brandon's presence lit a fire inside me.

"I had some things to think about, and you were busy." I looked up. "I'm not at your beck and call, you know."

Brandon exhaled heavily through his nostrils and rocked backward onto his heels again. "No one thinks that, Skylar."

"It sure felt that way tonight," I said. "Sitting around waiting for you for two hours, put in a corner like inconvenient arm candy, then forced to flee when your wife busts in."

"You didn't need to run off like that. You knew I'd come back for you. Come on, Skylar."

"I didn't run off," I corrected him, even though I literally did run. "I told you I was going, and then I told you I was home and I'd talk to you later."

"Well, it's not like you have the best track record of following through on those kinds of promises."

His words were almost as bitter as mine, and I flinched, thinking of when I'd left him, still in my bed, to run away to Brooklyn after I'd discovered his divorce papers. He had a point, but he also wasn't the one who had to accept all of this somewhat passively. I wasn't planning to leave him again, but it was still a lot to take. Especially tonight.

We stared at each other, bristling and irritated. Finally, eager to break the stare-off, I pushed off the wall with my feet to float on my back. I stretched toward the opposite end of the pool, arching in a way that made my breasts peak toward the ceiling, then flipped backward until I popped up again through the water. When I surfaced, Brandon was watching intently, a different kind of fire in his ice-blue eyes. Did he wanted to strangle me or eat me alive? It was hard to tell the difference.

"I know what you're doing," he said finally, low and almost menacing.

I continued to tread water, then flipped over again, slowing my movements even more. "Do you?"

"Get out of there, will you?" Brandon reached a hand out, beckoning me to swim back.

I just stared at it. "No," I said. "I'm not done with my workout."

I rolled backward through the water once more, then resurfaced to find Brandon standing up. His face looked like murder, but the tenting in his pants spoke of something else.

"Get out of the pool, Red," Brandon said, barely concealing his frustration.

"Stop telling me what to do."

"I'm not joking. Get out."

"No."

"Get out of the fuckin' pool, Skylar!" Brandon shouted, his South Boston accent out in full force. He thrust both hands into his hair and yanked. "Fuck!"

I just kept treading while sounds of the water lapping on the sides of the pool filled the space between us. Brandon stared at me, then dropped his hands.

"Fine," he said as he started to remove his vest. "Have it your way." He unbuttoned his shirt and tossed them both on the lounge chair next to him.

"What are you doing?" I asked as he started pulling off his shoes and socks, which then joined the clothes.

"What do you think?" Brandon snapped as he unbuckled his belt. "You won't come out, so I'm coming in."

"In your underwear?"

He pulled off his pants and threw them on top of his other things. He now stood in front of me in nothing but his boxer briefs, his perfectly sculpted body, including his sizable erection, on display for anyone to see. The reflected light glimmered over the broad lines of his shoulders and pectorals, the v-shaped muscles of his abdomen, the lean, long shapes of his thighs. Now he was the one who looked like a Greek statue.

I bit my lip, willing the heat building in my core to calm down.

"Well, it's either that or nothing at all," Brandon said just before he jumped in with a splash.

Tall as he was, he didn't need to tread water, but he still dipped underwater and surfaced like some kind of mythical sea god. The water glistened on his muscles as he tracked me like a shark.

My legs somehow kept circling, but the rest of me stilled. I wasn't in the mood to be pounced on, as Brandon sometimes did. He often used sex as a Band-Aid, and right now, I wasn't okay with that, even if the water droplets sliding over his pecs were getting me pretty hot and bothered.

My instincts took over: fight or flight. I dove underneath the blue lane barrier and swam to the corner of the pool. Before I could climb up the ladder, though, I found myself caged by two tanned, rock-hard arms.

"I don't think so."

Brandon's voice vibrated in my ear, and I froze. I turned slowly, and he released his grip on the ladder, backing off just enough so that I could turn around. His gaze bored into me like a drill. But it wasn't just the intensity in his eyes that pinned me to the ledge; it was the hurt there as well.

"You can't keep doing this," Brandon said in a low, taut voice.

Around me, his body was pulled tight as a drum. The evening had taken a toll on him too.

"You can't keep running away every time I do something you don't like."

"I don't—"

"You *do*," he cut me off gently.

We were close enough that he didn't need to raise his voice. Around me, his muscles flexed even more.

"Every time. My office. The airport. After you found out about Miranda, about Messina's payoff. That night at the club. And now tonight. If I railroad, Red, you run."

I heard my grandmother's words to me in Brooklyn after I had escaped there in April. She had compared me to my mother, who couldn't even stand beside me for the length of a party. And now I was becoming just like her.

"My life is complicated," Brandon continued. "I know that. I know it's not easy for you. But I am *yours*, Skylar, body and soul. But I can't be yours if you're not mine too."

I gulped. Bubbe was right. Brandon was right. I didn't have to act like everything was okay tonight, but I shouldn't have run. I should have stayed and dealt with things like an adult. Like the partner I wanted to be.

I leaned my forehead on his shoulder.

"I'm sorry," I whispered into his damp skin. "You're right."

"I'm right?"

I lifted my head and smirked. "Don't get too excited, Casanova. You screwed up too, leaving me there for three whole hours. But yeah...you have a point. We can't rebuild our relationship if I'm running away."

Almost immediately, the tension in Brandon's muscles relaxed, although he kept his arms propped on the ledge beside my shoulders, refusing to let me go.

"I'm...glad you agree," he said as he leaned down to kiss me gently on the lips.

The quick connection, which started out innocently, ignited the smoldering fire between us. My mouth opened hungrily, and when his tongue touched mine, my entire body shivered.

Brandon pulled back, a different kind of spark in his impossibly blue eyes. His gaze slid over the visible parts of my body: over the wet surfaces of my shoulders, my neck, the hint of cleavage at the top of my bikini. Slowly, he reached a finger and traced the edge of the spandex, following the border of the top along the strap, down across the sensitive skin of my upper breasts, and up the other strap until his hand came up to cup me behind the neck.

I couldn't move. I was like a startled deer, caught in his headlights.

"In the mood to be teased, Red?" he asked as his finger played with the straps behind my back. "You in the mood for games?"

He pressed his warm, hard body into me against the ladder. Only the thin fabric of his underwear and my bikini separated us. I could feel him straining through it, even as the corded muscles at his neck also strained with the tension of holding back. His blue eyes glowed into my green as we breathed into each other's space, allowing our bodies to touch, but neither of us willing to make the first move.

"I-I don't know," I stuttered.

Slowly, one side of his mouth and then the other rose in a wicked smile that made my insides flip over. And again. Brandon leaned in further. I wanted desperately to kiss him, but I couldn't move. Kiss me, I willed him. Show me you want me.

To my disappointment, his hand fell from my neck into the water, fingertips drifting up and down the dip of my waist, the sensitive skin of my thighs, toying with the elastic band of my bikini bottoms.

"Spread your legs," he ordered.

Breathlessly, I obeyed. His thumbs hooked the interior edge of my suit and slid up and down the elastic, finding slight contact with the center of me under the fabric.

"You hate it when I tell you what to do." Brandon's voice became distractingly low as he dipped his mouth near my ear. "But you like it when I boss you around like this, don't you, baby?"

I couldn't deny it. It went against every urge I had for control, but maybe it was the desire to let go of that control that attracted me so much to Brandon. His ability to manipulate my pleasure seemed as important to him as his own. I didn't like it anywhere else in my life, but with him, it was...freeing.

His fingers tugged aside my suit so that I was fully exposed under the water, while his other hand spread my legs wider.

"Hold this to the side," he said, guiding my hand down to keep the fabric out of his way.

Together we watched through the ripples of water as his fingers found me. One slipped in and out of my heated center, followed by another as his thumb found my clit and started to move in slow, teasing circles. If I hadn't been propped on his hand, I would have fallen under water.

"Brandon."

My voice started to fade as my body instinctively melted toward him. I didn't just want his touch. I wanted his mouth. I wanted everything.

The hand on my thigh gripped hard while the other continued its work. Still only inches from his hard chest, my nipples pebbled through the thin material of my suit. Brandon leaned down to nip one briefly through the fabric, causing me to moan as his fingers picked up their pace.

"That's it, baby. Does it feel good?" He leaned in again to growl in my ear. "Do you like it when I fuck you with my hand? Right here, where anyone could see you?"

I whimpered into his neck, then bit hard enough that Brandon gasped. He shoved his steel length against my inner thigh. He wanted me just as badly as I wanted him. He thrusted more forcefully with his fingers, and his thumb found a more insistent rhythm on my clit, driving me further and further to the edge of my undoing.

But just as my body was starting to approach its point of no return, he pulled his hand away and tugged my suit back into place.

"What are you doing?" I gasped. Not again! "No! I was just about to—"

I didn't finish my sentence as large hands found my thighs, and with a splash, I was tossed up onto the ledge. Brandon pulled himself out of the pool, then practically dragged me off the floor toward the men's locker rooms.

"Brandon, we can't—"

"No, *I* can't," he barked as he whirled around. "Wait, that is."

He yanked my entire body against his with a kiss that utterly and completely gutted me, an urgent attack with a relentless tongue and bruising lips. His hands grabbed my ass hard enough that I'd likely see finger-shaped bruises there in the morning, but the brutality only made me groan louder.

Before I could stop him, Brandon bent down, grabbed me like I weighed nothing, and hoofed me in the direction of the locker rooms. My arms wrapped around his head in a death grip. I couldn't get close enough.

Our mouths firmly attached, Brandon kicked open the door to the men's locker room and carried me into one of the shower stalls. Hot water sprayed over us in a warm embrace as we made short work of each other's clothes: my bikini landed on the floor with a wet splat right next to his soaking briefs.

"Fuck," Brandon breathed as he stared at my naked body. "Fuck, you are so goddamn beautiful."

His gaze fell down my stomach, my legs, resting a moment between them before coming back up to my eyes.

"Come here," he growled as he hoisted me up again, pulling my legs back around his waist. He was warm—the man was always warm—and his desire was thick and hard against my stomach.

"Oh, *God*!" I cried out as he slammed into me against the shower tiles, entering me hard and fast.

My arms flailed, looking for something to stabilize me against his onslaught, seeking purchase in the muscles of his neck and the wet curls pasted onto his head.

"No, baby, that's *me*," Brandon snarled with a sharp nip at my neck. "And don't you forget it."

He took my lips again, his tongue demanding as much as the rest of his body. We feasted on each other as every thrust brought us each higher, closer to our mutual edge.

"Use your hand, baby," Brandon breathed between ragged breaths. "I got you."

His fingers dug into my ass, biceps bulging as he continued to pummel me under the shower spray. I somehow detached one hand from its death grip in his hair and slid it down between our bodies.

Brandon moaned as he felt it reach its goal, the apex of my pleasure right next to our joining.

"That's it, baby. Touch yourself. I want to feel you come...God, Skylar!"

He started to move faster, and my body responded in kind, all the nerves alight with each unforgiving thrust, each quick twitch of my fingertips.

"Brandon!" I moaned, losing my voice completely.

I bit his shoulder, and his cries echoed off the tiles.

"Fuck, baby." Brandon voice was hoarse, ragged, almost as if in pain. "I'm...*fuck*, you feel good."

"I'm close," I whimpered, steadily losing my ability to hold on to him. "So close. Please."

"It's okay, baby, I got you. Let it go."

Brandon rammed me up against the wall one, two, three more times before I fell apart completely, hands falling to the side, limbs shaking in his strong grip. He closed his mouth over mine, cutting off my cries as he pulsed and found his own intense release.

"Jesus," Brandon whispered as our bodies melted together.

We were both gasping, completely out of breath. But before I could reply, the door into the showers opened, and the high squeak of sneakers echoed across the rubber-tiled floors.

Brandon and I stood like statues as the water ran over our still-joined bodies. The sneakers walked around the showers while the attendant whistled a tune under his breath. I bit into Brandon's shoulder, trying not to laugh until the footsteps retreated and the clear creak of the locker room door signaled the attendant's exit.

We let go of our breaths in a barrage of laughter. Then Brandon released my thighs, slipping out of me with a grunt as my feet fell to the floor. The roar of the shower filled the space between us as he pressed his forehead to mine, hands slipping lovingly down the length of my body, dipping about my waist and back up my ribcage and breasts until they cupped my face.

"It's only you," he promised with a sweet, slow kiss. "It's only ever been you."

I pulled him closer, wanting the warm feeling to last forever.

In my heart, I knew it wasn't true. We both had past lives that sometimes interfered with the present, real struggles and pains that still hadn't been dealt with properly. But I was determined to do it together, not alone. If we loved each other this much, everything just had to work out. The universe wouldn't be that cruel.

~

Chapter 23

Brandon and I spent Sunday locked in his apartment, alternately working and distracting each other. There was no talk about Miranda, the gala, or his candidacy; we both seemed content to pretend none of them existed. I even managed to keep the guilt over my own secrets at bay, eager as I was to feel normal with Brandon again.

On Monday morning, I surprised Eric by showing up in front of our apartment for the carpool to Andover.

"Thought you might have gotten, um, different transportation," Eric said when he found me waiting in the building lobby with my messenger bag and a to-go cup of tea.

I took a sip of my drink. "Well, Brandon tried. But he knows better than to pick that fight with me."

"I heard the party ended eventfully."

I tapped my sandaled foot on the ground. "Who's talking?"

Eric shrugged. "Oh, you know. The good old Sterling Grove rumor mill." He looked knowingly at me. "Is it true that you were making out with Jared on the dance floor and that Sterling punched him in the face?"

"Great," I groaned, "just great."

This was exactly what I wanted to avoid. A lot of the staff at Sterling Grove knew me and would now assume that I had been sleeping with their married boss while I was interning for the firm last year. The truth was that I hadn't gotten involved with Brandon until I had finished. I hadn't even met him until I was almost out the door.

"For the record," I clarified, "Jared and I were just dancing. Then Brandon arrived, so I stopped. Nothing happened."

"So you weren't thrown out of one of the back rooms by his wife either? Someone saw you booking it out of there."

A flush rose over my shoulders and up my neck as I studied the cracked tiles of the lobby floor.

Eric nodded sympathetically. "I see. Sorry."

I looked up. "Well. It is what it is."

"So does that mean the cat's out of the bag and he won't be sneaking into the apartment anymore?" Eric asked hopefully. "I'm assuming you stayed at his place through the weekend."

I frowned. "I don't know. Maybe. We haven't really talked about it."

"You should probably get on that, Cros."

Before I could reply, Jared's BMW pulled up, and we filed outside. Through the rearview mirror, Jared watched me get into the backseat with surprise.

"Well, hi there," he said. "I'm shocked you were allowed out of your cage."

"You're my ride," I replied evenly. "Unless you'd like me to take the train..."

Jared shrugged, although he looked like he was tempted to tell me to leave. "I'm fine if you are."

After he shut his door, Eric looked between us dubiously. "Nothing happened, huh?"

Jared just watched me through the mirror, waiting for me to take the lead. His brown eyes were darker than usual.

"Nothing," I repeated. "Let's go."

~

The class passed uneventfully, with me and Eric sitting relatively far from Jared, who pointedly took a seat at the opposite side of classroom. The car ride back to Boston was equally uneventful. I sat in the back seat, staring out the window while Eric and Jared argued about the upcoming Red Sox-Yankees game.

It was when the car pulled up in front of our building and Eric stepped out that Jared turned around to look at me directly for the first time.

"Can we grab some lunch?" he asked abruptly.

I stopped, one leg already out of the car. Eric had entered the building.

"I feel bad about what happened on Saturday," Jared said. "Let me make it up to you? You have to eat anyway."

His brown eyes looked so earnest, like a puppy dog. Jared had always been a nice guy. He didn't deserve to be treated like a pariah, and I didn't want him to feel used either.

My stomach rumbled loudly.

"Sure," I said. "Let me put my stuff away while you park. Want to get sandwiches at Angelo's and eat by the water? The breeze would feel really nice today."

Jared nodded. "Sounds good. I'll meet you there."

Twenty minutes later, we were sitting on a park bench looking out at the harbor, watching seagulls swoop around the tourists throwing breadcrumbs. The gorgeous June day invited me to wear sandals and a sundress. Summer was well on its way, but not quite at the point where Boston was hideously humid.

Jared had been doing his best to make pleasant small talk, and he was a lot better at it than I was. We'd covered all the basic topics: the weather, our class, the instructor's funny haircut. But as we tucked into our Italian subs, the conversation hit an awkward lull that was only partially filled by the squawking gulls.

"So about the gala," Jared said finally.

I swallowed my bite and gave a grim smile. "Yeah?"

"Everything okay there? I saw you run out."

I flushed red. "Um, yeah. It's fine now."

"It really doesn't bother you he's married?" Jared asked before taking a large bite of his sandwich.

I sighed. "They're separated and going through a divorce, like I said."

Jared raised a light brown brow. "That's not what Miranda says."

"They *are*," I insisted. "I've seen the papers, and I work for his divorce attorney. Miranda's supposed to sign them in a few weeks."

My stomach fell as I realized that almost certainly wasn't true anymore. And this was a conversation I was going to have to keep having every time someone brought up Brandon's marital status. I sounded like a pathetic cliché, like the other woman who was constantly trying to convince everyone that her married lover really *did* love her.

Except Brandon did. I was sure of it, just as I was sure he was doing everything to extricate himself from a very difficult situation. But that knowledge didn't always make dealing with it much easier.

Jared didn't say anything for a few more moments, just looked at me with something dangerously close to pity. I focused on the worn planks of the pier, hoping that I could pass off my watery eyes as the effect of the wind coming off the water.

"Look, it's really none of my business, Skylar," Jared said, "but I care about you. And well, I think you deserve more than just to be on the sidelines. You're the kind of girl who should be shown off."

He reached over carefully and took my hand in his. I stared down at our clasped hands with indifference. His compassion was nice, but something about the way he talked about me, like I was some sort of trophy, irked.

I turned to say that to his face, but ended up turning into a kiss likely meant for my cheek. His lips collided awkwardly with mine, and I froze. Three things immediately went through my brain: One, I felt absolutely nothing. Two, Jared was putting his arms around my waist to pull me closer. Three, this time he couldn't blame it on alcohol.

I set my hands on his chest and pushed him away firmly. His arms fell, and he scooted several inches down the bench.

"Jared," I said. "What are you doing? At the party, I just wrote it off as you being drunk, but this..."

"I was trying to kiss you on the cheek," he said lamely.

"You shouldn't be trying to kiss me at all! I'm involved with someone. You know this."

"Someone who treats you like crap. I know loads of guys like him, Skylar. They use girls like you and throw them away. He doesn't care about you!"

I stood up, scooping my sandwich off the bench and putting it back into its plastic bag. "I need to go."

"Skylar, wait!"

Jared followed me across the pier, leaving his food to be attacked by seagulls. He caught up with me as I turned down one of the cobbled streets leading back to the North End, where the crooked brick buildings blocked out the noise of the city.

"Look," I said, although I didn't stop walking. "You've been a good friend. You are nice, and you deserve to find someone special. But that someone isn't me. I'm *taken*. So really, don't waste your time."

"Waste my time? Seems like you should look in the mirror, don't you think?" Jared sneered, his bland features turning suddenly nasty. "Look, I know Miranda and her family. We aren't the kind of people who take no for an answer. We don't have to."

I whirled around. "What is *that* supposed to mean?"

Jared avoided my glare. "Nothing. It means nothing."

"It didn't sound like nothing."

He pressed his thin lips together, causing a crinkle between his brows. "Look. I'm just saying...I'm sorry. Really, I am. It won't happen again, I promise."

I crossed my arms and balanced my weight to one side. "You mean that?"

Jared held his hands out from his body in a gesture of mock surrender. "Completely," he said. "Can we just be friends?"

I raised an eyebrow. "Can you do that? No more funny business?"

Jared crossed his heart and held up his hand in a salute. "Scout's honor. I just care about you. That's not a bad thing, is it?"

I placed my hand on my hip and pursed my lips. Then I rolled my eyes.

"I can't believe I'm friends with a boy scout," I said, "Come on. You can eat another sandwich in my apartment. Then we should probably study for the rest of the afternoon."

~

Which is what we did. There were no more mentions of Brandon, although I didn't miss Jared's veiled glances whenever I checked my text messages.

Around six, Jared and Eric ducked out to pick up some pizza for dinner while I picked up the refuse from our study session. My phone rang in the bedroom, and I shuffled in to pick it up.

"Hi, Bubbe. Everything okay?" I said as I tucked the phone under my ear and went back out to continue cleaning up our scratch paper and leftover snacks.

I tensed myself for her response. Ever since receiving her frantic phone call in March telling me Dad was in the hospital after being severely beaten, there was a part of me that prepared for the worst.

"Everything is fine, *bubbela*," she said. "Can't I call my granddaughter to check in?"

I smiled as I tossed the scrap paper in our recycling bin. "Of course, you can. What's new?"

I listened at the kitchen table as she started rattling about the everyday minutia of her and my dad's life in Brooklyn. She talked for about twenty minutes, and was just finishing up when Eric and Jared returned with dinner.

"And you, Skylar?" Bubbe asked. "Are you...feeling better?"

I glanced behind me at Jared and Eric, who were taking seats back on the couch and setting out the pizza. Bubbe and I hadn't had a direct conversation about the fact that I had been pregnant and had also chosen to end the pregnancy. I hadn't admitted it outright, and she hadn't come out and said she knew, but there had been some signs that she was in on the secret.

"Yes," I said. "I'm fine now. Everything is...back to normal. I'm feeling much better, thanks."

"Good, good. Just wanted to make sure." Bubbe paused. "There is one thing, though..."

"Bubbe, I can't really talk very long," I said as I stood up and stretched. I was hungry, and the pizza smelled really good. "Is it urgent?"

"I was just thinking about Katie."

My dander flew up, and I sat right back down. The screech of the chair leg caused both Eric and Jared to jump in their seats.

"Everything okay?" Jared mouthed at me.

I nodded and flapped at hand at him to be quiet.

"What's going on?" I asked Bubbe.

"Nothing, nothing. I mean, not nothing, but nothing."

"Bubbe," I said. "Today..."

"Don't take that tone with me, young lady. I'll get to it when I'm good and ready."

I sighed, and propped my chin in my hand. There was nothing I could do but wait her out when she got like this.

"I...it's probably nothing. But I saw her the other day. At the store. She was shopping, and let me tell you, Skylar, that woman knows nothing about nutrition. Nothing but junk food in her cart! What if she and my Danny get married? Is he supposed to survive off of potato chips and sugary soda?"

"Bubbe," I said again, rubbing a frustrated hand over my forehead. "Did you call me because you were concerned about Katie Corleone's grocery habits?"

"Skylar, you have never been patient, and that is going to be your end."

I just closed my eyes and waited.

"As I was saying, I saw her at the store, buying all of this junk. And then a man's voice called her name. He said, 'Katie, honey!' So of course

I followed her to see who this man was. I was very careful not to be seen."

I had no problem imagining my tiny grandmother creeping around the aisles of the Associated Supermarket, peeking through the towers of kosher pickles like a private eye. No doubt she fancied herself a regular Nancy Drew.

"So she went up to this man, and he kissed her on the cheek, *bubbela*, and put a *very* friendly hand around her waist while they walked down the aisle. He even touched her on the *tuchus!*"

Her thick Brooklyn accent was becoming more pronounced, and she was peppering her speech with Yiddish, both sure signs of excitement. I frowned as Eric and Jared chatted amiably on the couch.

"What did the guy look like, Bubbe?"

My heart sank in my chest as she described a short, portly man with a round belly and receding hairline. She hadn't gotten a good look at his face, but when she said that Katie had called him "Vic", I knew exactly who it was. Proof positive that my dad's girlfriend was a close associate of Victor Messina, the thug who had almost cost my father his life just a few months before.

"Shit," I muttered under my breath.

My dad had stubbornly refused to listen to all suspicions I had about the woman, and I'd been putting off going down there and confronting her myself.

"What?" Bubbe asked. "What's the matter? I knew she was bad news. I just...your father, Skylar...he's been playing piano again still...and she always seems to make him so happy."

"I know," I said regretfully. "I know. But Bubbe, she's no good. I'll come down this weekend and talk to dad and Katie. But you can't say anything to spook her, understand? I mean it."

There was a silence on the other end of the line. Restraint wasn't Bubbe's strong suit, especially when it came to her son. But at last she sighed.

"All right," she said. "But only if you come this weekend and take care of it. You promise?"

"I promise, Bubbe," I said. And I hated that at this point, that was really all I could do.

~

Chapter 24

On Friday, right after class, I found myself riding to New York in the back of Brandon's Mercedes while his driver, David, chatted amiably in the front with an extra bodyguard that Brandon had hired for the night.

Brandon had insisted on accompanying me to New York himself. After trying and failing throughout the week to convince me that going was a bad idea, he'd been just as stubborn about the fact that he was going too. I couldn't lie; I was sort of happy to see that he was willing to travel with me outside of his apartment. He hadn't heard from Miranda since last weekend, but that didn't mean he wouldn't. Kieran assured him she was expecting a call from Miranda's lawyers daily. Brooklyn, in other words, was a good distraction.

The security Brandon had assigned to my family had helpfully supplied the fact that Katie had her hair done every Friday afternoon at a salon in East New York, which made my job easy. The only people who would be in a salon would be other women—a potentially safer environment than trying to confront her somewhere else. Brandon wanted to go in with me, but I convinced him that he would only attract attention just by being a tall, handsome, obviously wealthy man standing in a roomful of money-hungry women.

We spent most of drive down working peacefully together. Brandon participated in several conference calls while I sat in the opposite corner studying, trying (and failing) to ignore the way his fingers massaged my feet propped in his lap. I was dreading the task I was on my way to do, but the car ride down was the most normal I had felt with Brandon in months.

We pulled up in front of Connie's Cutz just after five, when Katie's appointment supposedly began.

"Are you sure I can't go in?" Brandon asked again as I opened the door.

I turned to him. "Yes. Like I said, you'll only call more attention to yourself. If she's a pawn for Messina, it's better that she doesn't know you're in the picture. Besides, maybe I can handle this woman to woman."

Brandon watched me regretfully, then finally nodded. He leaned in and threaded a big hand around the nape of my neck.

"Come here," he said, and he pulled me close for a quick, but very thorough kiss. "I'm right here if you need me, and Andy is going to stand just outside the shop. Be careful."

"I'll be fine," I murmured. Then I kissed him again, and stepped out of the car.

The shop door jangled with a bell when I entered, causing the five women inside to swivel quickly at my presence. Four of them boasted identically massive heads of long, barrel-curled hair, all teased and styled to at least four inches above their scalps.

I had known girls like this my whole life. They were the remnants of a certain part of Brooklyn that yearned for the New York of the seventies and eighties: big-haired Italian girls who wore their acrylic nails and pancaked makeup like armor. They attached themselves to the small-time crooks of the neighborhood, bragging to each other about the newest rock or Gucci bag their boyfriends had bought them with dirty money. Some of them ended up married to these guys; others were content just to be sidepieces. They were walking clichés, caricatures inspired from *The Sopranos* and *Goodfellas*, but with none of the glamor.

Two of the women sat together in the back of the shop, chattering happily while one did the other's nails. Another lounged in an empty seat while a fourth stood at the shampoo station. Katie Corleone lay there with her head in a sink.

"Can I help you?"

The woman who was currently wrist-deep in Katie's hair looked me up and down with a critical, faux-lashed eye. Her ashy, bottle-blonde hair was partially piled on the crown of her head, the rest flowing down her back in a cascade of dry ringlets. Like the rest of the women there, she wore a revealing, ostentatious outfit: leopard-print skinny jeans, a black tank top that revealed more of her red bra than it concealed, and sky-high gold heels that couldn't possibly be comfortable to wear all day in a salon.

I had to force myself not to follow her gaze. In my simple black pants, loose gray tank, and flat sandals, my hair tossed into a messy bun, I was clearly not a part of this tribe. But I wasn't here to fit in. I was here for my dad.

"I'm looking for Katie," I said.

"Who's asking?" said the woman with a quick glance down at her client.

Steeling myself, I stepped farther inside. "Skylar Crosby. I'm Danny's daughter."

Katie pulled herself up to look at me, her wet hair falling onto her plastic-covered shoulders with a splat.

"Hi Skylar!" she greeted me with enthusiasm that obviously masked both surprise and irritation. "Girls, this is Danny's daughter. Ain't she gorgeous?" She sighed with a terrifically fake smile. "She's so lucky she can pull off that natural look."

"That's one way to put it," one of the women at the nail station said, and the other snickered.

"Listen, sweetie, can this wait?" Katie asked, pointing to her soaking hair good-naturedly. Without her bouffant, she looked like a wet rat with a face painted like a doll's. "A girl's got to take care of herself to impress her man. You know how it is."

"Does she?" the woman at the empty hair station wondered a little too loudly to be under her breath, causing another round of low laughter to flutter around the shop.

"Um, sorry, but it can't wait," I said more loudly than I intended.

I forced myself to walk all the way to the back of the shop, ignoring the stare stabbing my back as I came to stand next to Katie.

"This won't take long," I said. "I just came to tell you to leave my dad alone."

The hum of the shop stopped completely, and Katie's pleasantness evaporated.

"Excuse me?" she asked in a way that clearly wasn't a question. "Just who do you think you are?"

"His daughter," I said, puffing up my chest even though I stood close to six inches shorter than the hairdresser next to me.

"And why is it you don't want your dad to be happy?" Katie asked with a nasty grin. "I don't think he'll want me to leave him alone, honey. Danny likes me too much."

The other women in the shop cackled and whistled. My stomach turned at the memory of my dad all over this ridiculous woman.

"Look, my grandmother saw you with Victor," I said, putting my cards on the table. "You're not really interested in my dad. He's a garbage collector who can't even play in his band anymore because Victor messed him up so much. He's twenty years older than you, has no money, and lives with his ma. You've obviously been sent by Victor to get him into trouble again, and I'm asking you, if you have any decency, to stop. Please stop."

I took a deep breath. All of the women stared at me, their plump lips dropped to the floor.

"He has nothing more to give," I said quietly, now pleading rather than dictating. A catfight wouldn't work here. They had me in numbers, and they'd dig in their claws. It was better to play dead. "If Victor's looking for another payout...he needs to know there's nothing left."

"Who do you think you're foolin', honey?" Katie asked, apparently having decided to abandon all pretense. "Nothin' left? Ain't you got a rich boyfriend? Victor *knows* there's a lot more there. And if he don't get it, well...let's just say your dad and grandmother might not have a place to live pretty soon." She turned to her friends. "It's a shame really. It's a nice house, just a few blocks from here."

I fought the sick feeling that was growing in my stomach.

"You can tell him that's not an option anymore," I said. "That connection is gone. And if he feels okay with tossing an old lady and her maimed son out onto the street, then he's going straight to hell."

Katie shrugged.

"Ain't you a fancy lawyer now?" she asked, her smile laced with daggers. "That's what Danny's always sayin'. He can't stop braggin' about his daughter and her fancy Harvard degree." She glanced at her friends, who were looking at me with arched, heavily plucked brows. "I think you'll be able to find plenty of funds when they become necessary."

"When will that be?" I asked with a dry mouth. I couldn't help myself.

"Oh, your dad's holding out better than most, I'll give him that. He's actually tryin' to make this whole rehab thing work. But..." She flipped a long-nailed finger around the room whimsically. "Once an addict, always an addict. He'll come back to the track. They always do."

My heart sank. This was the wrong tactic; I should have known better. Appealing to Katie's better nature was never going to work. The best thing I could do would be to get my family the hell out of New York. A lot easier said than done.

Before I could leave, the shop door jangled open again.

"Skylar?"

My heart fell even further when I heard his voice. Along with the rest of the women, I turned around to find Brandon standing awkwardly in the shop entrance, looking way better in his simple white T-shirt and jeans than anyone had any right to. He wore his favorite Red Sox cap, the curled brim pulled low over his face. From afar, he might have looked like any other regular neighborhood guy coming off a construction shift or a delivery route. But it didn't really matter how he dressed; Brandon couldn't mask the confidence in his shoulders, the determined set of his chiseled jaw. No hat could hide his natural magnetism.

"Hot *damn*," someone breathed behind me. I knew without looking that all these women were practically panting.

"Skylar?" Brandon said again as his blue eyes zeroed in on me. "Everything okay?"

I closed my eyes. Shit.

"It's fine," I said in a voice that sounded anything but. "We should go."

"Who's your friend, sweetie?" Katie asked behind me, saccharine-sweet. She raised a hand. "I'm Katie. How you doin' handsome? What do we call you?"

Her voice was friendly, but I knew exactly what she was doing. Every single thing she saw was going to be reported right back to Messina, and he would know exactly whom she'd seen. My entire story was completely blown.

Brandon darted a quick blue glance at her and the other women, then landed back me.

"You ready to leave?" he asked, ignoring Katie.

His question jarred me out of my frozen position.

"Yes." I wove my way back through the shop and grabbed his hand. "We need to go."

"Oh, Skylar?"

Katie's voice stopped me as I tugged Brandon toward the door. I turned around. She might still have looked like a drowned rat, but she looked like a smug drowned rat. She looked down at Brandon's wrist,

237

which bore the single giveaway of who he was: his shiny, expensive Rolex watch.

"I'll tell Victor he has nothing to worry about," she said with a particularly evil smile.

I bit my lip. Brandon tensed.

"Please," I said. For what, I didn't know.

"You know," Katie said, looking at Brandon with a desire she didn't bother to mask. Then her eyes flashed, all kindness evaporated. "For an educated broad, you're pretty fuckin' stupid."

I gulped and said nothing. Right then, I couldn't deny it.

~

Brandon sat quietly with me on short drive to my family's house. David navigated the backstreets of Brooklyn silently, while Andy, the bodyguard, was basically a piece of furniture. We pulled to a stop outside of my family's brown house. The sagging eaves seemed to bear a little more weight in the coming twilight.

Brandon looked up to the front seat. "Guys, can you give us a minute?"

With a brief nod at us through the rearview mirror, David left the car, followed by Andy. Their solid forms leaned against the side of the doors outside, blocking some of the excess sunlight. Brandon turned to where I sat, still numbed by the exchange in the shop.

"You have to let me help," he said quietly.

"You already did," I replied more bitterly than I intended. "That's why I'm in this mess."

Brandon sighed with a sharp look. "No, we're in this mess because your dad is an addict and got entangled with the wrong people."

"Yeah, but now they know about you." I clasped my hands in my lap, suddenly very interested in the tiny wrinkles on my knuckles.

"Skylar, did you really think they wouldn't figure that out?"

I looked up. I felt completely sick. "You can't get involved. You're trying to run for office. What if Miranda catches wind of this? Your career, your life...it could all get screwed up if you start buying people off like—"

"Do you really think that's the only option?" Brandon cut in gently. He picked up one of my hands and sandwiched it with his. "Sometimes I think you forget just who—what—I am. You see me as a normal guy,

238

and while I love that about you, the truth is, babe, I'm just not." He took a deep breath and continued. "This guy has absolutely no idea what kind of power I have. And I can make his life a living fucking hell if I want to."

He tugged a little on my arm, begging me to turn toward him.

"You can't do this on your own, Red," he said as he tucked a strand of hair behind my ear. "Let me in."

The gesture broke me. I was so incredibly powerless in this situation, in everything lately, and more than that, it seemed like whatever I did only made things worse. I started to shake against the soft leather seat. Brandon grasped my wrists and gathered me quickly against his strong, solid form, warm through the thin cotton of his shirt.

Green eyes or blue? The question came unbidden, and I pushed it away with a sniff. It wasn't important now, not with everything going on.

"Shh," Brandon hummed, pressing my head into his shoulder and stroking my hair. "It's going to be okay. Nothing is going to happen to you. Nothing is going to happen to your family. I promise."

He held me tight, forcing me to inhale his sweet, almond-laced scent. Soon, the shakes subsided, and I started to feel halfway normal again. He was right. At some point, I realized, I needed to stop holding so tightly onto everything and let Brandon in.

"Okay," I mumbled into his chest. "We'll do it together?"

Brandon pressed his lips into my hair, and I could feel him nod against the top of my head.

"Always," he murmured.

After we sat for a few more moments, I felt strong enough to get moving.

"Well, we'd better go in," I said. I nodded behind me at my family's house. "If we don't have dinner before heading back to Boston, my grandmother will make stew of us both."

Looking over my shoulder, Brandon smiled. "I'm actually pretty excited to see Bubbe again," he admitted. "I've been dreaming about that blintz of hers."

"I think tonight she's making brisket."

Brandon grinned. "Sounds great!"

I laughed. "Remember that while she's giving you the third degree."

I joked, but as we walked toward the house I grew up in, I closed my eyes to relish in the feeling. I forgot sometimes how good it felt to have the people I loved all safe around me in one place. Now that Brandon was here with me again, it felt like home.

~

After finding out that Brandon and I were going to be stopping by that evening, Bubbe had pretended to be nonchalant on the phone. But I knew better. She had been rooting for me and "that handsome *goy*" to work out from the beginning, so it was not too much of a surprise to find that she had spent the rest of her afternoon making a traditional Shabbat dinner, the likes of which I hadn't seen since I was a small child.

Brandon and I walked into the house and were immediately bowled over by the rich smells. A quick glance in the kitchen revealed not one but two freshly baked loaves of challah bread sitting on the counter, a massive salad and a zucchini kugel on the table, and, from the smell of it, her brisket slow-cooking in the oven.

I was a little amused. Bubbe was the only practicing Jew in our house, and Shabbat dinner was a rare occurrence. Dad only attended temple when Bubbe guilted him into it every few years, and considering the fact that my mother wasn't even Jewish at all, I only really considered myself part of that tribe by association. This was definitely a meal designed to impress our guest.

"Are you going to sing *Kabbalat Shabbat* for us?" I joked as we entered the kitchen.

Bubbe, who was lost in concentration as she checked whatever sauce she was making over the stove, jumped. She turned around with a hand held to her heart, then pointed her wooden spoon at me.

"I ought to, you little minx, you. If I could do it without your father falling asleep, I would. Now come here and give me a kiss."

Brandon and I both did as she said, and she grasped us each around the neck for a brief hug.

"Hello, handsome," she greeted Brandon. "*Oy gevalt*, did you get taller since May, or am I shrinking?" She pressed a hand against his chest and looked him over with obvious approval. "Such a big, strong man. So wonderful to see you again, Brandon."

240

I thought he might be embarrassed by her comments, but Brandon's massive grin over Bubbe's small form lit up the room. He seemed to enjoy my grandmother as much as I did.

"Sit down, sit down," she urged us after several pinches of Brandon's cheeks. "I'm almost done here. Danny's just getting dressed."

Brandon and I obediently sat at the table, and Brandon nodded when I offered him a glass of wine from the open bottle.

"You really didn't have to make all of this, Bubbe," I said, taking in the massive spread once again. "It's too much."

"Well, it's not so often I get to have my granddaughter and her handsome friend here for Shabbat dinner," Bubbe said from the stove. "Speaking of...did you...accomplish what you came here for?"

She glanced toward the doorway of the kitchen, as if expecting my dad to bound through at any moment. Under the table, Brandon grasped my knee.

He cleared his throat. "We did, Mrs. Crosby," he said. "But we both think it's time to tell Danny what you saw at the grocery store."

Bubbe's face fell at the thought, but she nodded her head.

"What happened at the grocery store?"

We all swung around to find my dad standing in the doorway. I brightened at the sight of him; he looked better than I'd seen him in months. When I'd left for Boston, he was still in his bathrobe. Now he was dressed like his normal self in a pair of ironed, if faded, navy blue chinos and a plaid button-down shirt that he had actually tucked in. He even wore shoes and a belt, and mustache was neatly trimmed.

He still cradled his broken hand against his chest, but other than the still-fresh surgical scars over the top, it looked almost normal again. But I knew he had another month before he could really go back to work, and his disability was running out; it would take another year before he could even think about getting full range of motion back. It was just another reason why he would be better off with me in Boston, where I could take care of him.

"Hey kid," Dad greeted me with a kiss on the cheek before reaching over to shake Brandon's hand—with his left, I noticed. "How you doin', Brandon? Nice to see you again."

Dad winked at me, then took a seat at the table and poured himself a glass of wine. We all leaned back as Bubbe set a mountain of brisket in

241

the center of the table. She took her own seat and poured a glass of wine for herself.

Dad looked warily around the table, which had become oddly quiet.

"Anyone want to tell me what's going on?" he asked, wrinkling his nose so his mustache scrunched over his lips.

I sighed and looked at Bubbe. "Go ahead, Bubbe. Tell him."

Bubbe looked like she would rather do anything else, but she set her wine glass on the table and proceeded to describe what she had seen between Katie and Victor. I continued the tale with the exchange in the shop. By the time we were finished, Dad looked like he was going to be ill.

"God," he said under his breath. "God, I have been so damn stupid."

He pulled his napkin in between his hands, twisting and turning the faded fabric while he processed. When he looked up, his expression was pained.

"You've been trying to tell me this for weeks, and I didn't believe you, Pips."

I took a big gulp of wine. Underneath the table, Brandon's hand squeezed my knee again.

I sighed. "It doesn't matter. She was so nice to you, Dad. I don't blame *you* for anything."

It wasn't completely true, but blaming him for an addiction and for ignoring the reservations of his family wasn't going to help.

Dad shook his head. "I'm sorry," he kept saying. "So damn sorry." He placed the napkin on the table with a slight bang of his wrist. "Well, one thing's for sure: she's toast. I ain't getting mixed up with Victor Messina again. I learned my lesson." He held up his crippled hand.

I nodded. "That's good, Dad. But Brandon wants to help too, and this time we're going to let him do it the right way. He wants to hire an investigator to help with the D.A.'s case against Messina. In the meantime, he's already assigned some extra security to watch the house. They should go with you and Bubbe when you're out and about. Especially when you go to Nick's."

I didn't like the fact that my dad still insisted on spending most of his free evenings at a small jazz club that Victor Messina sometimes frequented, but it was also where his band played. We wouldn't know for a long time whether or not he'd ever be able to play the piano with them again, but asking him not to be there when they performed would have been asking him to tear out his own heart. Music was what made my dad tick.

"Oh, Brandon, that's very nice of you," Dad said, already shaking his head, "but it's too much. I'll just make sure I steer clear of Victor."

"It's really no problem, Danny," Brandon started to say, but I cut him off.

"Dad." I reached out and put a hand gently on top of his scarred one. He flinched slightly, but I didn't put any weight on it as I traced the raw lines with my thumb. "Let him help. Brandon's...basically one of the family now."

I didn't have to look to see Bubbe's thrilled look at those words, because Brandon's wide smile caught me first. Trying not to grin myself, I just continued.

"I don't want to have to worry about you and Bubbe while I work to support this family," I said. "Okay?"

Dad ran his free index finger along the edge of the table, smoothing nonexistent wrinkles in the worn tablecloth. Finally, he looked up.

"Okay," he relented. "Whatever you say, Pips."

The tension around the table melted away. I put my hand back into my lap and looked at Bubbe, whose face was shining with relief.

"All right, then," she said as she reached to grab the serving spoon in the center of the table. "Let's eat."

~

Chapter 25

It seemed I couldn't quite get away from family. Brandon and I went back to New York after enjoying the delicious spread that Bubbe laid out Friday night, despite her many attempts to convince us to stay the night. When she promised blintzes, I could tell that Brandon was tempted.

Unfortunately, I had none of my study materials with me, and on top of that, Janette had already cornered me and Brandon into brunch the next day. She and I had traded a few phone-calls over the week, and she had been insistent on getting more quality time with me so I could meet my half-siblings. It was hard to say no to that.

"Your mom's in town?" Dad had asked, trying and failing to mask his obvious curiosity when we had mentioned it on the way back out to the car after dinner.

"With her husband and kids," I had said in a tone that I hoped told him to leave it.

Dad definitely didn't need to fall down the Janette Chambers black hole again. He was already vulnerable enough. Behind us, Bubbe had rubbed her forehead and muttered something about a "*shiksa* hussy." She couldn't stand my mother, having been forced to fill her role in Dad's and my lives for the last twenty-six years. It probably didn't help that she was being shirked for a brunch date with Janette.

~

"You really don't have to come," I said again as David pulled the car up in front of the Stillwater Hotel just before eleven. "It's not exactly private."

We were having brunch in the hotel restaurant, a swanky spot that catered to wealthy businessmen and local politicians. We would be on full display to many of the same people who, if they hadn't been present at last weekend's benefit, would have almost certainly heard about the drama.

Brandon picked up my hand and kissed my knuckles, nipping at the last one in a way that made my skin prickle with something much more than nerves. Although he'd woken me up that morning with attention that had should have sated any desire I felt, I was still humming for more.

"Our cover's blown now, Red," he said with a lopsided smile. "Silver lining is, we don't have to hide anymore." He cupped my face, running a thumb over the contours of my lips. "Come on. Let me meet the rest of your family. I promise they'll like me."

I smiled into his kiss, trying and failing to curb the mounting desire his lips and tongue caused. Just as I was starting to curl my fingers into the hair at the nape of his neck, he pulled away with a satisfied, cat-who-ate-the-canary grin. He watched with obvious satisfaction as I struggled to fix my hair and smooth my dress.

"Easy for you," I muttered as we stepped out of the car. "It would take a tornado to make you look like less than a million dollars. One kiss and I look like a windswept tomato."

Brandon laughed and glanced down at his outfit. He wore a perfectly pressed, blue and white gingham shirt and navy pants, paired with a cognac-colored belt and matching shoes. His wavy blond hair was combed back, and his bright blue eyes matched the color of the sky. He looked picture perfect for a Saturday brunch. I looked reasonably nice in my gray sundress and brown sandals, but I couldn't light a candle to him.

He wrapped a long arm around my waist and pulled me close for another kiss. "I'm nothing compared to you, Red."

We were led to a table in the middle of the crowded restaurant where Janette, Maurice, and two children sat. Of course Janette had requested the most visible spot in the restaurant. She was always one who basked in the attention of others.

"Brandon!" she cried as she hopped out of her seat.

Tasteful as ever, she wore a light floral skirt and green silk shirt that brought out the color of her—our—eyes, her light brown hair tied at the nape of her neck. Pearl-and-diamond earrings swung from her ears, matching the necklace she wore and the sparkling tennis bracelet at her wrist. Maurice wore tailored slacks and a button-down white shirt, and the children, from what I could see, both wore equally prim outfits. They were the perfect picture of an upper-class French family.

Janette leaned in to accept a kiss on the cheek from Brandon, who then reached across the table to shake Maurice's hand before sitting down. I accepted French-style, double-cheek kisses from both Janette and Maurice with some surprise; this was the friendliest Maurice had ever been to me. The two children at the table, a boy and girl who weren't older than ten, watched all of us.

"So good of you both to join us," Janette said as we all took our seats. "*Mes petites puces, ça c'est votre sœur*," she introduced me to the children. "Skylar, this is Annabelle and Christoph."

Despite the endearments their mother used to address them, neither child responded to her, choosing instead to watch me with open curiosity.

"You may have to brush up on your French a bit, darling," Janette said to me. "They're still learning English."

"My English is very good, *Maman*," a small voice with a very thick Parisian accent piped up from across the table. The older child, the girl, looked pointedly at her mother with clear green eyes she'd inherited from Janette, just like me. "And Christoph can understand everything, even if he still cannot say very much."

Beside her, the little boy, whose fringe of brown hair topped a pair of wide brown eyes, nodded broadly as he sipped from a plastic cup with a straw.

Janette cleared her throat and took a sip of her drink, which looked like a mimosa. "They go to a very good school."

A waiter came by to take our orders and deliver drinks. I hoped that another round of mimosas and food would calm everyone's nerves.

"So, what are you doing in town?" Brandon asked Maurice after the waiter had left. "Boston seems a little outside of your scope at BNP."

He had taken my hand again under the table and held it securely on his lap.

"Maurice is here to help the new BNP Boston office negotiate an expansion. They are trying to land Rick Avery's portfolio," Janette said before Maurice could respond. She looked coquettishly at Brandon. "Of course, I'm sure he wouldn't mind a meeting with the CEO of Sterling Ventures as well."

"*Tais-toi*, Janette," Maurice cut her off sharply. "Pay no mind to my wife," he said more jocularly to Brandon with an extremely Gallic roll of his eyes. "She often speaks without thinking."

His French pretensions aside, I was starting to get a good handle on Maurice. Despite his glamor and cool, nonplussed appearance, he was just like so many other chauvinist men I'd encountered in the finance

246

sector who treated women like accessories. He had barely spoken to me, his actual stepdaughter, at all since arriving in Boston, and only then to inquire about Brandon.

Beside him, Janette just took another long sip from her drink. For the first time in a long time, I felt sorry for her.

"Are you here long?" I asked Maurice, mostly to deflect the criticism from my mother.

Maurice looked at me as if he had just noticed I was sitting at the table, and gave another supremely French shrug. "It depends. These things take time, I cannot say for sure." He looked back at Brandon with a smile. "Enough to enjoy everything this wonderful city has to offer."

"At least a few more weeks," Janette added eagerly. "We will probably go down to New York for a spell so the children can meet my family, of course, but mostly we want to enjoy Boston."

I ground my teeth. Aside from their obvious pandering to Brandon, this was a sore subject. I was permanently iced out from the Chambers clan; my conception out of wedlock, when Janette and my father were only seventeen, nearly cost her membership in that family to begin with. The only part of that life I had ever seen was the small trust fund that Janette had set up—mostly, I think, to avoid any problems with child support payments and to keep my family quiet about me: the dirty little secret.

"We were just in New York yesterday," Brandon volunteered with a worried glance my way. My discomfort must have been written all over my face. "Down visiting Skylar's dad. Her grandmother made this amazing dinner for us."

Janette looked up, her cup poised in midair. "Oh?" she asked with a pretense of casualness that failed miserably. "And how is Danny?"

I clenched the stem of my champagne glass tighter than necessary. "He's fine."

Janette blinked, her big green eyes that mirrored mine blank and innocent. "And is Sarah still cooking those enormous meals? She always did make enough to feed an army. I swear, whenever I stayed in that house, I always gained at least ten pounds."

She chortled at Maurice, who only watched with his typically bored expression. I just sipped my mimosa. I wasn't really interested in hearing her jokes about the family she'd toyed with over and over again. Brandon cleared his throat, pulling the table's attention.

"Do you have any plans other than staying in the city?" he asked. "Poor Annabelle and Christoph can't find the inside of a hotel room that interesting."

The kids' faces perked noticeably when he mentioned their names; Annabelle already looked half in love with Brandon, and Christoph was staring at him like he was a superhero.

Brandon flashed them a toothy grin, and they both collapsed in giggles. Maurice shot a stern look at his children, who immediately straightened up and quieted down. They were clearly well trained; I couldn't help but wonder by what means.

"The children have a nanny to keep them occupied during the day," Janette clarified with a short smile. "But we were considering taking some excursions up the coast. Maine, perhaps. Kennebunkport—isn't that where the Bushes have a place? Brandon, have you ever been there?"

Brandon nodded. "I have, although only once or twice. When I go to the coast, I usually spend my time at the Cape. I have a house there, actually."

Janette's eyes gleamed. "Oh, Cape Cod! Yes, we were considering that as well. It would also be terrific fun to show the children where their ancestors came from." She winked at me as she continued: "My father's family emigrated on the Mayflower, you see. My mother's were mostly Dutch, of course—cousins of the Stuyvesants, actually, but my father's people actually came originally from Massachusetts."

She spread her slender hands over the table and peered around the room proudly, as if the crowded space of the hotel represented the cold rock where the pilgrims originally landed. Beside her, Maurice continued to looked bored, and both Annabelle and Christoph were frowning in confusion.

"Well, you're welcome to come for a visit," Brandon offered cordially as he leaned back to make room for the server, who had just arrived with another round of drinks.

I jerked my head at him. What? He caught my look and winked.

"I may not have it much longer, so we might as well put it to good use," he continued before taking a sip of his coffee. "It would be a good time for Skylar and the kids to get to know each other."

"Oh, that would be *wonderful!*" Janette exclaimed. "Children, wouldn't that just be wonderful!"

She leaned over to touch Annabelle's shoulder; the girl just looked at the hand, but then looked back at Brandon, eyes shining.

"Oh please, *Papa*," she addressed Maurice almost formally. "May we go?"

Christoph, who had yet to say anything, also turned to his father with pleading eyes.

Maurice, for his part, no longer looked bored, but extremely interested as he surveyed Brandon. His sharp eyes flickered back and forth between us, as if gauging our connection. Then he gave another Gallic shrug, and sat back in his chair.

"If it is not too much of an imposition," he said as he picked up his espresso cup.

The kids practically jumped out of their seats in excitement. Janette continued to jabber about the possibilities for the trip, while Maurice and I stared at each other with mirrored looks of shock. Somehow, before our eggs had even arrived, my estranged mother, her family, my married boyfriend and I were all scheduled to go to Cape Cod for the upcoming Fourth-of-July weekend.

~

"Are you okay?" Brandon asked later when we were on our way back to the North End.

I had insisted on going back to my apartment. I had too much to do, and I wasn't interested in spending the day in the icy penthouse. Surprisingly, Brandon didn't fight me on it, and actually asked if he could come with me. It seemed he really did hate that apartment as much as he said. Or, I also suspected, he could feel the fissures the last few days had caused and was trying to compensate.

Beside him, I shrugged while I watched Boston passing through the tinted window. "Does it matter now?"

Brandon reached for my hand. "I should have asked first. I'm sorry."

I sighed, but let him toy with my fingers. "It's fine, I guess. It will be nice to get to know Annabelle and Christoph. Maybe I can convince Janette and Maurice to let me take them somewhere, just them and me. They seem to be on a pretty tight leash."

Brandon nodded. "I bet they'd like that."

"I still can't believe you invited them over to your house," I teased. "My weirdo mother and her robot husband."

"I just want to help," Brandon said. He still held my hand as he massaged his thumbs around the bones. "They're your family, and they want to know you." His blue eyes were wide. "Not everyone is as lucky as you, Red."

I watched him for a moment, letting his words sink in. Brandon gleamed so brightly among most people, it was easy to forget the dark circumstances he came from. His mother, who had died of a drug overdose when he was just a teenager, had neglected him so much that he had been in and out of group homes for most of his childhood. His father, an abusive man, had been in jail multiple times and was currently serving a twenty-year sentence. The only real family that Brandon had were the Petersens, and despite Susan's attempts to be close, Ray wasn't exactly a big ball of warmth.

"You're right," I said. "It's a nice idea. It will be fun."

"We'll make a long weekend of it," Brandon said. "You can bring your stuff and study, and I wouldn't mind you seeing the place again before I have to sell it."

The reminder of the divorce proceedings settled a pit again in my stomach.

"So Miranda...she's still going ahead with everything as planned?" I asked.

A part of me hoped that maybe this sudden invitation, and Brandon's recent willingness to accompany me openly everywhere, was a sign that things had improved. Maybe Miranda had simply accepted that he was moving on. Maybe she was ready to move on too.

But Brandon heaved a big sigh and pulled me into his side. "I don't really want to talk about it right now," he admitted before pressing a kiss into the top of my head. "She's...making things difficult again. I'm not sure exactly to what extent."

My heart sank. I knew it was too good to be true. I curled my fingers around the crisp cotton of his shirt and inhaled his fresh, warm scent.

"I'm sorry," I said. "I'm making things more difficult for you."

He pulled back so he could look directly at me. His blue eyes were fathomless, even in the dimmed lighting in the car. My clenched stomach eased a little.

"Don't be," he said. "I'm not."

As he pressed a soft kiss to my lips, I conceded. I could be stressed. I could be fearful. But I couldn't be sorry now. Not for us. Not ever.

~

Chapter 26

Despite my best plans to convince Eric to join me on my impromptu family vacation, he pled the need to study through the long weekend, and I couldn't argue with that. I'd have to compartmentalize my time carefully through the weekend just to make sure I didn't fall behind. With the bar exam only three weeks away, I couldn't afford to waste time, and I was pushing it with this weekend in the first place.

But although I could have canceled, I found I didn't want to. Despite all of the complications in our lives, Brandon and I were learning to deal with them together, and I didn't want to dismiss that progress.

In the interest of my time constraints, Brandon insisted on flying me out to Cape Cod via helicopter on Friday. I'd initially fought it, but it wasn't hard that for him to convince me to take advantage of his generosity for once. I couldn't study on the bus, and I needed all the time I could get.

I landed on a massive grass compound just after three in the afternoon on Friday. I had spent most of the short trip in awe, with headphones protecting my ears from the roar of the rotors while I watched the coastline through the glass windows.

When I stepped out of the helicopter, the combination of the wind coming off the waterfront and the whir of the rotor blades plastered my hair against my face. When I finally managed to tame it into a ponytail, I found Brandon jogging across the lawn. The wind pressed the fabric of his T-shirt and jeans against his torso in a way that left little to the imagination, his tanned skin healthy against the white of his shirt. Even with the vivid green of the grass, the bright blue of the sky, and the glow of the sunlight, his smile still outshone everything.

"Hey!"

I was picked up off the ground and swung around several times. I wrapped my arms around Brandon's neck and laughed.

"Welcome to the Cape!" he yelled over the rotors with another grin and a hearty kiss. He set me down and accepted the bags from the pilot in exchange for what was likely a sizable tip. "Thanks, Tony!"

The pilot nodded. "Anytime, Mr. Sterling! You enjoy your vacation, Miss Crosby!"

I followed Brandon across the lawn, forced to hold the edges of my skirt as the helicopter started taking off. It wasn't until it was well on its way that I was able to let go of the fabric and look around the property as we walked.

Brandon's house stood on several acres of land that created a luxurious solitude in the crowded Northeast. The property included a bluff overlooking a small bay, and was mostly scattered with trees around the big green lawn. It eventually dipped down to a beach of white sand and a rocky edge, Brandon informed me, though I couldn't see it from where we walked.

The house itself was large but not enormous, and of typical Cape Cod style: a simple, square shape covered with weathered gray shingles and white shutters and trim. It boasted a wrap-around porch and a deck that extended a good thirty feet onto the lawn. There was a kidney-shaped pool behind the deck, along with basketball and tennis courts beyond that.

Brandon led me up the deck stairs and through French doors that opened into a spacious living room. Everything was bright and airy, with high, white-beamed ceilings and a rustic, open floor plan. A living room situated around a large stone fireplace opened directly into a chef's kitchen, next to which was a farmhouse table that could seat at least twelve.

Like all of the spaces Brandon inhabited, it was big, but unlike his penthouse rental and the opulent mansion on the Commons, this house actually felt lived in. Although the kitchen was luxurious, the appliances were likely fifteen or twenty years old. The furniture, mostly leather sofas and weathered wood pieces, looked well used.

Brandon dropped my bags inside the French doors and pulled me to his body. He had been in Washington D.C. all week on business and had flown directly here. We hadn't been able to see each other since Sunday. There had been chats and texts, of course, but things felt...tenuous again. I wondered if we would ever get rid of that feeling completely.

Blue eyes or green? Shut up, I thought to myself.

"I missed you this week," Brandon murmured as he wrapped me up in his kiss.

I smiled against his lips and bit down on the bottom one lightly.

"Me too," I said. "Thanks for the helicopter ride, by the way. That was ridiculously fun."

Brandon winked. "Anytime. I don't want to wait for you any longer than I have to."

I closed my eyes, luxuriating in his familiar, almond-laced scent. Maybe I'd regret not spending the holiday weekend holed up with my study guide, but I was thrilled to be here right now.

"Come on, Red," Brandon said. "Let me give you a tour."

My hand clasped firmly in his, Brandon took me around the rest of house. Aside from the great room, the bottom floor also included a TV lounge and an office that was clearly Brandon's domain, plastered with Red Sox paraphernalia and a bunch of Star Wars collectibles. The desk was covered with a mess of papers and two open laptop computers. I glanced around with a smile—this was a side of Brandon I loved so much: the hometown boy, the Red Sox fan, the closeted dork who couldn't quite manage to pick up his workspace.

The tour continued upstairs, through a hallway lined with three guest bedrooms, all with en suite bathrooms, and stopped at the master suite at the end. A pair of double-doors opened into a room that included a white king-sized bed against a wall that faced an atrium-style window looking over the bay. A glass door opened to a smaller private deck and a set of sun-bleached Adirondack chairs.

I turned back to Brandon, who stood in the doorway of the room, watching me as I checked everything out. I grinned.

"This place is amazing," I said.

His face exploded with a grin.

"I'm glad you like it," he admitted. "It's kind of my favorite place on the planet."

I found myself looking for signs of Miranda; after all, they owned this house together. I walked up to the atrium window and pressed my fingertips against the glass panes while I looked at the water. Had they had good memories here together? They must have. I couldn't imagine being unhappy in a place like this.

As if he could read my thoughts, Brandon came up behind me and wrapped his long arms around my waist, leaning down to set his jaw on my shoulder.

"Don't think about her," he said.

"How do you always know?" I wondered.

"I can see it all over your face, Red."

I sighed and tried to turn in his arms, but he held me still, forcing me to continue looking at the view. I sighed.

"It's her place too, isn't it?"

Brandon finally loosened his grip so I could turn around, but he kept me pressed against his hard chest.

"It's mostly mine," he said. "She never liked it here."

I frowned, remembering some comment she had made so long ago about seeing her family at the Cape. "She didn't?"

Brandon shook his head. "Her family owns a place near Provincetown. She doesn't like how isolated this place is, so most of the time she wanted to stay over there."

"So why are you giving it to her in the divorce agreement?" I asked. "You were going to give her all of your property."

Brandon shrugged and rubbed my back meditatively. "A lot has changed since then. Six months ago, the most important thing to me was keeping my companies intact. But now I'll probably have to divest anyway, not to mention..."

I watched curiously as he trailed off. "Not to mention what?"

He cocked his head shyly. It made me want to tackle him onto the bed, except I wanted to know the end of his sentence.

"Not to mention that now I have more important things to fight for," he said with a hopeful gaze. "Maybe there are things worth keeping if they are important to you too. To us."

"Oh."

We gazed at each other, letting the gravity of his words, those others "things" sink in.

I looked around at the room. "So, the decor, then..."

Brandon gave me a lopsided smile. "Would you believe me if I said I pored over design magazines trying to find the perfect lamp?"

In response, I just raised my eyebrow. He laughed and dropped a kiss.

"I bought the property as is," he said. "I'll tell the previous owners you like it."

With yet another brief kiss, he released me from his embrace and took my hand again.

"You hungry?" he asked.

As he spoke, my stomach let out a loud growl. He laughed again, and it filled the room with even more light.

"Come on," Brandon said. "Let's feed you, and then I can show you the grounds."

~

We spent the next few hours exploring the property while Brandon pointed out all of his favorite spots: the cluster of driftwood that was perfect for reading on nice days and the tennis court where we could play doubles with Janette and Maurice. My eyes grew wide at that one; I'd played tennis maybe three times in my life.

"Don't worry, babe, I'll teach you," Brandon said with a laugh.

I couldn't help but laugh with him. He was different here, somehow. Lighter. Happier. It was infectious.

He led me into a small grove of oak trees on one edge of the property's bluff. At the end, there was another set of several deck chairs and a dining area underneath the of the trees. A tire swing had been hung from one of the trees.

"Indulging your inner child?" I asked as I hopped on it and swayed back and forth.

It was the kind of swing any kid would have dreamed of. As a city kid myself, I had often imagined living in rural place like this, with a swing of my own from this kind of tree. I closed my eyes in the sunlight shining through the leaves.

"Or one I might have one day."

My stomach dropped with his words. The slight squeak of the swing's chain fill the sudden silence.

"I think about it with you." Brandon came to stand in front of me, letting the swing come to a stop against his thighs. He held the chains that anchored the tire in each of his hands. "Do you ever think about it with me?"

I gulped. He was watching me very carefully, and I prayed the sudden guilt that had bloomed in my belly wasn't written all over my face—or at least that Brandon wouldn't be able to read it as clearly as he could normally. I forced myself to inhale and exhale. Brandon cocked his head.

"Too much?" he asked. He shook his head with a bitter laugh and rubbed his chin. "Of course it's too much. We just got back together a few weeks ago." He gave a sardonic smile. "'Too much' is my middle name, isn't it?"

The disappointment and obvious sadness on his face broke my heart.

"*No*," I said forcefully. I slid off the swing, and pulled him close to me by his shirt, standing on my tiptoes so I could wrap my arms around his head. "I think about it too," I said, hoping our faces were close enough that he wouldn't be able to see all of my conflicting emotions. "I think about it all the time."

"Yeah?" Brandon looked out meditatively over the blue water. A few seagulls cried out in the distance. "Sometimes I think it's crazy. What would I know about being a dad? I have absolutely nothing in the way of model. My father's still in jail for one of his many crimes, and Ray, well, you've met him."

He bit his lip, and my heart practically cracked in half.

"Hey." I picked up his hand and brought it to my lips. "You don't need models. Look at you. You are one of the kindest, most generous people I've ever met. Brandon, you'd be a wonderful father, I know it."

Even as I said the words, my heart physically throbbed. He *would* be a wonderful father one day. And in another life, he might have been on his way by now.

Blue eyes or green? Now was the time to tell him. We were alone, there was nowhere to run, no one to interrupt us.

"Brandon, I need to tell you something," I said, feeling sick even as I said the words.

Brandon looked down at me, eyes gray-blue and broody, but...maybe not surprised. "What's that?"

Do it, you coward! My conscience screamed at me, sounding irritatingly like Jane. I opened my mouth, but when I caught his wide blue gaze, nothing came out. I choked.

"Last May..." I tried again.

Brandon's brows quirked in confusion. "Yeah?"

I shut my mouth, then opened it again. "I was so...I was...miserable. Without you. I just realized...Brandon, I just love you. So, *so* much."

Chicken. No, I was going to do this. I had to.

But before I could speak again, Brandon swept me off the ground and sat us down in a surprisingly smooth motion, pulled me on top of his lap so that my knees straddled his hips. His hands settled on my waist, thumbs stroking lightly over the thin fabric of my cotton dress.

"Are you trying to fix me again, Skylar?" he asked in a low voice, echoing the same question he had said just after the first time he'd brought me to meet Ray.

I'd given him praise then too. The question had let to our frantic first coupling in the stairwell of the MIT electrical engineering building, a forceful condemnation of any suggestion of charity. In his own way, Brandon was even worse than I was at taking compliments or gifts. This time, however, I wasn't afraid to say how much I felt for him. I could at least be honest about that.

I cupped his face gently, gazing into the blue eyes that were subtly riddled with a life of pain that Brandon worked so hard to overcome.

"Aren't you trying to fix me too?" I asked softly, running my thumbs over his cheekbones. "Aren't we trying to fix each other?"

Brandon gazed, blue eyes unblinking, his jaw set tight. He took a deep breath, then exhaled slightly. His hands rose up my back, and he pulled me in for a kiss that started slowly, then quickly grew into something much more passionate.

"Yes," he said hoarsely as he tried to get closer. "Yes, we are."

He kissed me again, with lips that quickly turned primal. It was so easy to lose myself in the tongue that wrapped around mine and made me forget where I was.

His hand slipped around the back of my head, tangled in my hair while the other drifted over the rise and fall of my breasts through the cotton. Brandon's fingers whispered over the fabric, plucked at the buttons until one by one, they fell open, baring my breasts in the late afternoon sun. He looked down to where he palmed both my breasts lightly.

"You are so incredibly beautiful," he pronounced while his thumbs drifted over my nipples.

Although his touch had me aching for more, I still looked around, aware of the fact that the only protection we had from prying eyes was our relative isolation and the scattering of trees.

"Relax, baby," Brandon said, reading my mind again, as was his uncanny talent. "This property is ten acres. There's no one around."

He pulled his shirt over his head and tossed it onto the ground, then drew me back so we were skin to skin in the cool grass. I burrowed in the cocoon of his chest, the warm muscles against my skin, the familiar smattering of hair soft against my face. I kissed the divot between his pectorals, and he shuddered.

He rolled me onto my back, and his mouth trailed down the side of my neck, nipping and biting while he twisted his tongue with some mystery of sweet torment. Eventually he returned to my breasts, and pulled one taut curve between his teeth, causing a ripple of tension to vibrate through me.

"Brandon," I moaned.

My hands threaded into his hair to keep him close. One of his hands drifted lower, pushing up the hem of my skirt to find the flesh beneath. He was so big, blocking out the rest of the world. Keeping me safe.

"Skylar," he murmured against my breast before switching to the other side.

His fingers found the edge of my panties and pulled them off.

"Please," I whimpered against his ear before I seized the edge of it between my teeth and bit lightly.

Brandon hissed, then unbuckled his own pants. When the heavy weight of him was freed in the damp warmth between my thighs, we both gasped at the sudden contact. Brandon took my mouth, sucking voraciously on my lower lip as he adjusted his hips until—*aaaah!*—he found entry.

"Fuuuuck," he swore as he sank into me, slowly, surely.

I gripped his shoulders as my body adjusted to his girth, but sighed into his warm skin. Nothing felt better than him. Nothing felt better than this.

"Tell me what you need," he croaked as he pressed me further into the grass. "Tell me what you want."

From my vantage point, I had the full, sun-drenched view of his impressive physique. I ran my hand over him and rotated my hips, taking him deeper and causing him to hiss again.

"I just need you," I said as I slipped one hand between my legs. Brandon's eyes zeroed in on the moment, dilated sapphires as he watched my fingers find my clit and move in tandem with his hips.

Our bodies had reunited before, but this was different. It was slower, less frenzied. No forceful joining in his bed, no frenzied coupling in a public bathroom. No withholding, no games. Our eyes met, and neither of us could look away as we found our rhythm together, bodies rocking, joining, warm and light and free under the open sky.

As if of its own accord, my other hand ran up Brandon's chest to cup his face, torn as it was between pain and ecstasy.

"Brandon," I whispered.

He thrust deeper, and the lines on his brow deepened. "Skylar."

The fingers on my clit twitched. I gripped the edge of his jaw, forcing him to look at me.

"I love you," I breathed, the words floating on the air between us.

Brandon's eyes flew open, and his entire body clenched in response.

"God!" he cried, matching the calls of the seagulls looping through the sky behind us.

He throbbed within me, and I arched in response. I pressed hard on my clit, and Brandon took one, two, three more deep thrusts before we both exploded together, our bodies joining in a tangled mass of light and love.

"Skylar!" he called as he collapsed against my shoulder.

"Brandon!" My body shook under him.

And we trembled, slowing to shudders, until there was no more Brandon, no more Skylar. There was only us.

~

The sun was a warm blanket over my shoulders, and the distant sound of waves and seagulls combined with the hushed breeze through the grass-covered dunes lulled me partially to sleep on Brandon's chest. That feeling was finally back—that one we had worked so hard for before everything had come crashing down last spring. In this moment, I was perfectly content.

Before I had found out about Miranda, and before she had found out about us, Brandon has asked me to move in with him. And despite how overwhelmed I was by his wealth and his life—feelings that I would probably struggle with for a long time—the answer had been easy. I had wanted to share a life with Brandon, share a home with him, because somehow, I had known that Brandon *was* my home. He was where I belonged.

I didn't know if he would ever ask me that again, although he had mentioned it in passing. Likely not until he had his life straightened out, until he was fully divorced and determined his future in politics. But if he did, I knew the answer would be the same. No matter where he was, where he needed to be, I'd want to be there with him. He was home.

Which made what I needed to do all the more difficult. And all the more necessary.

Oh God, I thought as a ball of fear took root in my stomach. I pressed myself up, causing him to groan against the movement.

"Don't," he mumbled, already half asleep in his equally content, post-coital haze.

I kissed him lightly on the chest, but still sat up.

"Why?" he asked as he opened one lazy blue eye.

I smiled nervously and twirled a few strands of my hair. "I have to tell you something," I tried again.

A dark blond brow quirked. "Now?"

I took a deep breath. I might lose everything, or I might gain everything. But either way, Jane was right. I couldn't keep it to myself if I wanted us to be real. I opened my mouth to speak.

The sound of a loud car horn broke through the air.

Brandon tipped his head toward the house, then smirked back at me. "Looks like the cavalry has arrived."

I wilted. Shit. My mother really did have the best timing. The car honked again insistently, and I tugged my dress back over my shoulders.

"I'm coming, I'm coming," I mumbled to myself.

Brandon chuckled while he pulled on his jeans and T-shirt. The car honked a third time, and now I could hear Janette's "helloooos" echoing over the lawn along with Annabelle and Christoph's curious voices.

"On our way!" Brandon shouted with a laugh as he slipped on his flip-flops. Then he looked back at me with sudden concern. "Wait. What was it you wanted to tell me?"

Tying my hair on top of my head, I froze, mouth open.

"I...just that I love you. Again."

The words came out before I could stop them, and immediately the ball of fear shrank to a tiny clenched fist. That wouldn't go away, I knew. It had been there for the last month and a half. But this wasn't the right time to talk about it, and I couldn't bring myself to kill Brandon's happy mood.

Brandon's megawatt smile lit up the entire wood despite the fact that we were out in the direct sunlight. He leaned in to give me a hearty, all-encompassing kiss and didn't release me until the car horn blasted for a fourth time and we were both completely out of breath.

"I love you too, Red," he said with another brief smack. "Now let's go welcome your family before they burn the place down."

~

Chapter 27

The weekend passed smoothly, almost to the point where I forgot I was spending it with my estranged mother. Annabelle and Christoph happily spent most of the time in the pool, watched over by Marie, the middle-aged French nanny. Janette seemed happy to sketch while she sunbathed on the deck, and Maurice was delighted to find another tennis player in Brandon. I was able to spend the mornings studying in Brandon's office, interrupted only occasionally when he would check on me with a cup of tea. Only one kiss turned into something else that we needed to lock the door for.

When I came out to the yard around lunchtime on Monday, our last day, Brandon and Maurice were finishing their usual morning match. Janette was lounging at the pool while the children dove for rings at the bottom. She peered up at me through a pair of oversized Chanel sunglasses, poised in a sleek black maillot like Bridget Bardot.

"Back from studying. Amazing, a daughter of mine could be such a bookworm."

I pulled off my light gray cover-up and tossed it onto the other lounge next to her. "I didn't know that was a bad thing."

"Well, at least you've kept yourself nice and trim." Janette looked up and down my body with blatant inspection. "Of course, you've got those genes on both sides, haven't you? Danny always was a handsome little thing."

I fought the urge to put back on the cover-up. I had noticed her making remarks about Annabelle's slightly round, eight-year-old physique and meant to say something it about it anyway, but Brandon had suggested that it wasn't the best way to continue rebuilding my relationship with my estranged mother.

"Is that what I'm doing here?" I had asked in bed last night.

He'd shrugged. "What else?"

What else indeed?

"Do you know, I think you would look perfectly marvelous as a blonde," Janette continued. "With our green eyes...it's just a shame you inherited your grandfather's hair. And skin, as it were. Let's hope if you and Brandon ever have children, those genes skip another generation."

I looked down warily at the light speckles that decorated the skin my modest blue-gray bikini didn't cover. Despite the umbrella-sized straw hat I wore in the sun, the last two days of playing on the beach and in the pool had caused an avalanche of freckles to erupt all over my body. Normally I wasn't too conscious of them, but Janette's frank appraisal made me more aware than usual of my Irish complexion.

"You know, there are procedures that can remove freckles, darling," Janette said, pushing her sunglasses onto her forehead to examine more closely some of the spots on my thighs. "I'm sure we could find a top-notch dermatologist in Boston to take care of them for you. I'd pay, of course."

"Don't you remove a single spot, Janette," Brandon interrupted. "She's perfect as is."

He loped up the deck and scooped me to his side for a sweaty kiss. Janette watched us with keen interest, then slid her glasses back over her porcelain nose.

"Who won?" I asked as I stepped away from Brandon, more just to benefit from the view than because I didn't want to touch him. His white tennis shirt and hairline were both damp from the game, and the shirt stuck to his lean muscles.

"I tried to let Maurice have it in the end, but he forced me to take it. Straight sets." He looked back at Maurice. "You all right back there, Maury?"

I had to stifle a laugh at the familiar nickname, which seemed more appropriate for a used-car salesman than a suave French businessman. Maurice approached, looking considerably worse for wear. His normally immovable gray hair stood up in a few places, and his tanned face was bright red under the sweat that also soaked through his blue shirt.

He grimaced. "It was a good match."

Clearly, Maurice didn't like losing. I didn't blame him, but I could have told him two days ago that Brandon, one of the most competitive people I knew, not to mention a natural athlete, never lost. I had learned that the hard way more than once.

Brandon hopped from foot to foot, swinging his racket toward a phantom ball. "It *was* a good match," he repeated. "What do you say, Red? You up next?"

I shook my head, holding my hands out as if to block him. "Ohh, no. I learned my lesson yesterday."

"I could teach you to be better. I'm a *very* effective instructor." Brandon waggled his brows at me prominently in a way that made me giggle.

"Brandon!" Annabelle called from the pool. "Will you come swimming with us now? *S'il vous plaît?*"

Every afternoon after his tennis match with their dad, Brandon had demonstrated to Annabelle and Christoph his excellent impressions of various sea creatures. This generally led to countless games of *Jaws* that basically consisted of us chasing the kids around the pool while they giggled uncontrollably. Maurice and Janette often disappeared around this time, Maurice to work in their guestroom, Janette to the expensive Pilates studio in a nearby town. I didn't mind when they left, although I did wonder sometimes what kept them so long to get ready for their daily "errands." Sometimes they hovered upstairs for hours before they left. Brandon guessed they were probably getting it on and teased me for thinking too much about it.

Today would be even better. It was Marie's afternoon off, and I had volunteered to take the kids beachcombing in Chatham before the firework display that night. Unfortunately, Brandon also had to spend the afternoon working. I didn't mind too much, though; I was eager to get some time with the kids by myself.

But first things first.

Brandon pulled off his shirt, his perspiring, cut torso gleaming in the sun. Behind him, Janette snuck a peek over the rims of her glasses. I hid a smile; she was only six or seven years older than him, and I couldn't really blame her for looking. He *was* quite a sight.

"*Papa, vous aussi?*" Christoph's small voice piped up behind his sister.

They were both hanging onto a life-sized, alligator-shaped floaty that Brandon had bought for them yesterday in the village. The creature had already been used as a whale, a boat, a spaceship, and a subway train.

Maurice looked at his children as if he had just realized they were there, then curtly shook his head. Christoph's face fell, but his quick recovery indicated he hadn't expected his father to join them in the first place.

"Well, I'm coming in!" Brandon yelled, and to the children's giggling surprise, he launched cannonball-style into the center of the pool.

The massive splash sprayed me, Maurice, and Janette. Janette shrieked, and Maurice rolled his eyes.

I laughed. "Me too!" I jumped in to chase the kids with Brandon.

"*Comme pisser dans un violon*," Maurice muttered to himself as he brushed the stray drops of water off his tennis kit. He zipped his racket forcefully into its case, then strode into the house, mumbling more grumpy French idioms under his breath.

Janette stood up.

"I think I'll get ready for the afternoon too," she said as she put on her caftan. "I've got a spinning class in the village at two." She pushed her sunglasses on top of her head to look at me, where I was carrying Christoph on my back. "Are you really going to be okay with them for the entire afternoon? I can tell Marie to come back, you know, if you need a break."

I rolled my eyes. I wished I could be surprised that Janette found it strange to want to spend time with her children, but my life had taught me otherwise.

"We'll be GREAT!" I yelled before I tossed Christoph off my back to send him flying in the pool with a squeal. "Enjoy your class. We'll meet you in the village for dinner."

Janette glanced at all of us with a dubious expression, then shrugged. "As you wish. *Ciao*, darlings. Listen to your sister and be good."

The kids ignored her, too focused on Brandon's stalking underwater form to answer. Janette left, equally unperturbed.

After chasing the kids for a while Brandon hopped up to where I sat at the edge of the pool and wrapped a wet arm around my waist.

"You going to be all right with them all afternoon?" he asked as he nuzzled my cheek. "I feel bad I have to work."

I leaned into his lips and smiled. "Why does everyone keep asking me that? We'll be great. I'm actually really excited to spend the day just us. It's their last day, and I want it to be special."

While my time with Janette and Maurice had been mostly lukewarm and cordial, the last two days had allowed me to truly bond with my siblings. They were adorable kids, and I was already trying to figure out how to see them more often. Brandon had hatched a plan to convince

Maurice to send them to one of the boarding schools in the area instead of the school they currently attended in Switzerland.

In response, I got another kiss on the neck. "I don't know how well I'm going to concentrate," he said, "knowing that you're running around town in this."

His hands dropped low to play with the side-ties of my bikini bottoms. It wasn't a terribly skimpy suit, but it was flattering and showed off my curves well. My breath caught in my throat; it had been incredibly hard keeping our hands to ourselves until we were behind closed doors each night. More than once Brandon had dragged me upstairs in the middle of the afternoon to discuss some "business" only to tackle me onto the bed.

"*Touché!*" Christoph yelped, slapping Brandon on the butt with a loud, wet thwack!

Brandon jumped, the momentary spell between us broken.

"That's it! One last round of King of the Mountain!" he cried, turning around and diving back into the water after the shrieking, laughing children.

I grinned and dove after them. This weekend wasn't anything I'd expected, but I was happier than I'd been in months.

~

A few hours later, I was shepherding the kids into town after beachcombing and sand castle-building on Brandon's property. Chatham was packed for the holiday, but luckily most of the tourists were at some of the other neighboring towns to view the larger fireworks displays. This was apparently the first year that Lighthouse Beach would have a display, so while the beach was already starting to fill with onlookers, it wouldn't have nearly the crowds that would be at Orleans or Hyannis.

My phone buzzed in my purse, and I pulled it out to find Brandon calling.

"Hey," I said. Christoph and Annabelle stopped at the window of a closed toy store, giving me a moment to chat.

"Hey, beautiful." Brandon's voice was tense and frustrated.

I frowned at my reflection in the shop window. "What's wrong?"

He sighed loudly enough that I could hear him, even on the busy street. "We're kind of wrapped up in some things here. Maurice asked me to help him with this...deal...he's trying to put together, and it's taking

267

more time than I thought. We're nowhere near done. Do you mind taking the kids to dinner without us?"

I glanced down at Annabelle and Christoph, who were currently debating whether American dollhouses were better than French ones.

"No, it's fine," I said. "They've been great. Are you sure you can't just take a break, though? You have to eat."

"Unfortunately, not," Brandon paused for a moment. "I'll tell you more later. We'll meet you on the beach for the fireworks, okay? Try to get a spot near one of the lifeguard stations so I can find you."

"Okay," I said. "I hope everything is all right."

He heaved another great sigh. "It will be. I think."

We hung up, and I found the kids looking at me expectantly. I pasted on the biggest smile I could. To hell with the fancy farm-to-table place Janette had chosen. If there were ever kids in need of fast food, it was these guys.

"*Vous aimez des hamburgers?*" I asked.

The instant grins on their faces told me everything I needed to know.

Fifteen minutes later, we were comfortably ensconced at a picnic table outside a local diner, watching tourists ambling around Chatham while we enjoyed our very American meals of burgers, fries, and chocolate milkshakes.

"I'm so glad you guys were able to visit," I said for what must have been the fifth or sixth time that weekend. I meant it, too. "I'll really miss you when you go back to France. You'll have to come back and visit."

"Oh, we are not going home," Christoph said casually before taking a monster bite of his burger. For such a small kid, he ate a lot. "Not until *Papa* can get us back our house."

I frowned, French fry in midair. "What's wrong with your house?"

"Well, it's not ours right now. The big men come to take our furniture," Christoph continued before taking a long pull on his milkshake.

"*Idiot!*" Annabelle hissed next to him. "*On ne doit rien dire!*"

"You keep forgetting that I can understand you," I remarked calmly, causing Annabelle's face to turn bright red. "What is it you're not supposed to tell me?"

Christoph stared at his sister, then shrugged. "*C'est notre sœur.*" She *is* our sister, he reminded Annabelle.

Annabelle sighed. "*Donc,* we had to move. *Papa* thinks I don't know that he is in trouble, but I do. The...how do you say...*le conduit?* For the air?"

She looked to me for help.

"The vent?" I guessed.

She nodded, satisfied. "*Oui,* the vent in his office, it connected to my room at home. I could hear a lot that he didn't know." She looked at me with sudden terror. "You will not tell?"

I placed a hand over her small one and tried to look reassuring. "Sisters don't tell on their sisters."

Annabelle's small shoulders relaxed, and she smiled. "*Bon,*" she said.

"So, what did you hear?" I asked before I took another bite of my burger.

An uneasy look crossed her face. "I don't like to listen to him fight with *Maman.* But I know she was very angry with him about something he did. She said that if he did not get our money back, she would find a way to do it without him. The men came to take our things the next week, and Papa says we are here to try to fix it." She looked up, her large brown eyes full of questions. "Do you know what he needs to fix, Skylar?"

Both of the children's faces zeroed in on me, unblinking. Clearly, they were both extremely concerned with their father's situation, what little they knew of it. I gulped.

"Um, no," I said, although now I was certainly curious. Maybe this was what was keeping Brandon.

When Christoph looked like he might cry, I gave him my best "don't worry" smile. I set my burger down and reach across the table for both of their hands.

"I'm sure we'll figure it out," I said.

It was all I could say. Both the kids nodded and went back to their meals. Their normal chatter returned as we started speculating about what kinds of designs the fireworks would have.

After dinner, we went to the beach and laid out a blanket. We had bought some cupcakes from a shop in town, and the kids were happy to lay with me, telling stories about France while we waited for the fireworks to begin.

"I wish you came to our house in France," Christoph said. "When you lived there too, I mean."

I squeezed his shoulder. He was a small boy for his age, but solid.

"It's probably better this way," I said. "When I lived in Paris, you were only a baby. You wouldn't have remembered me."

"I would remember," Christoph said.

"Me too," Annabelle echoed, and they both burrowed closer to my sides as we watched the sky above us change colors in the twilight.

Just as the sky turned dark and the crowd was starting to hum with anticipation of the main event, Brandon, Maurice, and Janette appeared, bearing flashlights.

"Finally!" Janette cried as we scrambled up. "I thought we'd never find you! Skylar, darling, you really should check your cell phone more often."

Maurice and Janette sat in the front of the blanket, with Annabelle and Christoph on either side of them. Maurice made no move to touch either of his children, but I noticed Christoph sidling closer and closer to his father until their knees touched. Only then did the boy sit still.

Brandon landed on the blanket beside me with a huff just as the fireworks began over the water. Even in the din, I didn't miss the way he kept glaring at Maurice and Janette.

"Everything okay?" I asked, nudging his shoulder. "I thought you would be here earlier."

I pressed my nose into the crook of his neck and inhaled. His scent was so calming. Brandon reached a hand to briefly clasp my face to him, then pressed an absent kiss on my cheek before releasing me.

"It's...I'll tell you about it later," he murmured into my ear after another sharp look at Maurice. "But it's safe to say that Maurice and Janette aren't just here on a typical business trip."

I frowned, then dropped my face into a more neutral position when Janette peeked over her shoulder to smile at me.

"I got some vibes like that from the kids at dinner," I muttered while giving her a forced smile. "Why? What happened today?"

Brandon just shook his head and pulled me closer.

"Later," he said again. "I'll tell you later."

We continued to watch the fireworks, but the familiar knot of stress in my stomach constricted again. Would I ever be able to bring anything else to Brandon's life besides family drama? The arm around my shoulder tightened, as if Brandon could feel the tension.

"Hey," he said into my ear. "Don't worry about it. It's nothing I—we—can't handle, okay?"

I could see the fireworks reflected in his eyes, which searched mine for reassurance. He didn't want me to worry, or to bolt, most likely.

"Okay," I said, and moved further into the nook of his shoulder. I only wished my gut felt the same way.

~

Chapter 28

We left at five-thirty the next morning on a plane that Brandon had opted to charter so that we could both work (and talk) on the way back to Boston. Maurice and Janette weren't joining us, having decided to go to Martha's Vineyard for the rest of the week to visit some friends from New York.

Brandon looked visibly relieved at their decision. We had all been exhausted after the fireworks, and he'd refused to tell me anything while the Jadots were possibly within earshot. Once we were on the plane en route to Boston, he finally told me why they had missed dinner the night before.

"They kept me cornered in my office until close to ten, giving me the hard sell on why Ventures should sell out to BNP." He rubbed a tired hand over his face. "They had contracts and everything. It made no sense, especially with the two of them there. I mean, he has to know I'm in no position right now to be making those kinds of deals. It's basically an open secret now that I'm thinking of selling off."

It wasn't easy for Brandon to admit that out loud. But it was looking more and more like full divestiture from his companies would be the price of both his divorce and his entry into politics.

"Do you think he was trying to get in on the ground floor?" I wondered. "Capture some of Ventures' best investments before anyone else does?"

Brandon shrugged. "Maybe. But I would have expected a lot more subtlety about it. You know, I think he's really in some deep shit at BNP. I've never had someone and his wife sell me together on a deal before. And definitely not for three hours. Christ, I was a prisoner in my own house."

He gave me a crooked smile and kicked his feet up on the chair facing him. One hand dropped to my thigh and squeezed lightly.

I frowned, considering. "Well, according to the kids, they had to move out of their house in Paris. I don't think they are going back anytime soon."

Brandon's brows raised, causing his forehead to wrinkle slightly. "Jesus. No wonder they seemed to desperate. Shit, think about all that time they were alone in my office!" He pulled open his laptop. "I'll get Margie on it."

"Brandon," I said, interrupting his typing.

He looked up, big eyes full of concentration, but also compassion. "What, Red?"

"You don't have to do this," I said. I knew he wouldn't stop, but I needed him to know anyway. "Whatever is going on with them, you don't need to rescue Janette and Maurice. She's...they're...it's not like Bubbe and my dad, okay? They're not our responsibility."

"Oh, I know," Brandon said grimly. "I've seen them with you. And their own kids." His eyes flashed at the mention of Annabelle and Christoph.

The truth of what was really happening hit me: that once again, Janette had duped me into believing that she had something to offer besides her true colors. Her sudden appearance and generosity after nearly ten years of sporadic-at-best communication should have been more suspect. If they were truly in financial dire straits, then the lavish gifts of the piano and clothing were even more manipulative than I'd thought. I wasn't the target: Brandon was. I could only hope they had other options and would be able to take his rebuke at face value.

"We *will* make sure those kids are taken care of, though," Brandon said.

I couldn't help but smile. Brandon had fallen in love with my little brother and sister just as much as I had. I couldn't help but wonder how much of his protectiveness was linked to the way he had *not* been able to escape his own parents when he was the same age. His experiences as a young child fed his tendency to go a little overboard trying to please the people he loved.

"So this week." Brandon flipped through his jam-packed calendar on his phone. "Dinner on Wednesday? Otherwise I probably won't be available until Sunday." He twisted his lips ruefully. "Consequences of taking four days off."

I leaned my head happily on his broad shoulder. Things really were back to normal again—back to the place where he couldn't bear to wait a week to see me. I was thrilled; I felt the same.

"Just a quick one," I said. "But FYI, I'm probably going to go back to New York next weekend to check on Dad."

273

I could feel Brandon's frown.

"I don't think that's such a good idea," he said.

"Brandon, I can't just leave him down there. He's an addict in recovery, not to mention he's dealing with the stress of healing, unemployment, and being the potential target of a mobster."

I toyed with the pages of my book; when I said everything out loud, it made me even guiltier that I hadn't stayed in New York to begin with. Everything seemed to be calm and casual in Brooklyn, but that hadn't stopped me from checking on my dad on a daily basis since my last visit. The security team Brandon had installed was getting thoroughly annoyed with my constant requests for updates. But even though there had been no word from either Katie Corleone or Victor Messina, that didn't mean they weren't still circling. It just meant they were planning their next move.

"I still think we should keep trying to convince them to relocate," Brandon said as he picked up my fidgeting hand and started to massage my fingers. The calming effect was instantaneous.

I sighed. "I keep trying. But they are both so crazy stubborn."

"How many more times does Danny have to be messed with before he realizes he needs to get out of Brooklyn?" Brandon asked irritably, his Boston accent seeping through. "Is your family so attached to New York that they are willing to risk their safety? Is your dad's life worth a band he can't play in or your grandmother's card games?"

I didn't answer. These were questions I had asked several times, and every time had them swatted away like flies. I was asking them both to give up their lives, they'd said. Hadn't they lost enough? Was it right to let Messina kick them out of their home?

"I'll keep working on it," was all I could say. "But in the meantime, I'm not going to abandon my family. If they won't come to me, I need to keep going to them." I pressed a kiss to Brandon's jaw line. He'd shaved for the first time all weekend this morning, and his skin was smooth and soft. "And don't forget: I still have the bar exam in less than three weeks. I think a weekend away from you might be a good thing. You're too much of a distraction."

"I'm a distraction, am I?"

He looked down with a devilish grin, then slyly picked the book off my lap and tossed it onto the chair across from me. I followed the book,

274

then watched as he unbuckled my seatbelt as well. I couldn't stifle my smile, but I tried to give him my best "I told you so" look.

"You're not really fighting that reputation right now," I said as his hand slipped inside my shirt and floated over my breasts, causing my nipples to stand erect through the loose fabric.

"I wasn't arguing with it, Red," Brandon said as he leaned down to nuzzle my neck. "Why don't I show you just how distracting I can be?"

~

The rest of the plane ride to Boston was basically extended foreplay, and we landed on the small runway at Logan panting like a pair of horny teenagers. Instead of going our separate ways, Brandon ended up taking me home in the back of his Mercedes and walking me up to my apartment, which took about twice as long as it should have because we kept stopping on the stairs to make out.

"I feel like I've barely been alone with you all weekend," he murmured into my neck while he ground his hips into mine beside my door.

"It's not like we didn't...you know...most of the weekend," I said, although the twist of his tongue at my neck made me lose my breath.

Brandon laughed, low and sexy, against my shoulder. He pulled back with a grin, then gave me another thorough kiss.

"You're funny," he said against my lips. "I'm the uptight New Englander, but you're the one who can't bring yourself to say that we fucked whenever we could."

I opened my mouth with a comeback, but was captured again with a kiss that took my breath away.

"I just want to be able to take my time about it again," Brandon said when he finally released me.

His hands reached down to my ass and lifted, and I moaned when his hips ground me against the wall so that my feet no longer touched the ground. His fingers tickled my most sensitive spot though the fabric of my capris. I moaned.

"What do you say?" he rumbled. "Can you come by tonight? I don't want to wait until tomorrow."

Brandon kissed me again before I could respond, and this time, I wrapped him equally up in me, grabbing greedily at the hair at the nape of his neck and biting lightly on his lower lip while my legs wound around his waist and squeezed. It didn't matter that we had just spent an entire long weekend together. I needed him just as badly.

"Tonight?" he asked again as his fingers played with my waistband, sliding under it, then back out with a regretful grunt.

"Tonight," I concurred against his soft lips.

He dropped me to the floor and adjusted the obvious bulge in his pants.

"Tonight," he repeated with a rakish grin, and left.

With a smile still on my face, I walked into the apartment. It was wiped completely away when I found Eric on the couch, completely naked and panting loudly.

"Oh! Christ!" I yelped, whirling around even as I shielded my eyes like I'd been blinded. I basically was. I'd never get the view of my roommate's jerking hips out of my head. "I *so* did not need to see your ass this early in the morning, Eric!"

"Shit!"

Behind me, I heard the telltale scrambling of limbs and shuffling of blankets and random items of clothing.

"Fuck! Where the fuck are my glasses?"

"I don't know! You're the one who threw them across the room before you pounced on me."

"Jesus, you *really* are only good for one thing, aren't you, Petri Dish?"

The familiar back-and-forth had me standing ramrod straight, although I kept my face pointed firmly at the closed door, hands plastered over my eyes.

"Jane?" I asked.

Behind me, Eric chuckled, and there was a long, loud sigh.

"Yeah, it's me," said my best friend. "You can turn around now. No more of Ken Doll's skinny ass to see."

"Ken Doll?" Eric asked. "Seriously? He's basically a eunuch."

Slowly, I turned around, still wary of what I might see. Eric had his boxers back on, while Jane just sat on the couch, wrapped in a throw blanket.

"Keep your pants on, Eric," Jane retorted. "Once, you know, you actually get them on. I wasn't talking about your junk. Just your boyish, Aryan looks."

"Whatever," Eric said with a roll of his eyes. "Hey, Crosby. Sorry. We weren't expecting you back until later."

I glanced between the two of them. Jane had the decency to avoid my gaze, but Eric just looked at me directly while wearing nothing but his boxers, oblivious to the fact that half of his hair was standing up or that he had splotches on his neck and a set of angry red scratch marks on his pale chest that looked remarkably like fingernail tracks.

"What happened to no fucking on the couch?" I demanded, trying my best not to crack a smile. My lips twitched, but that was it.

"Seriously?" Eric asked. "How many times have I come home to you sucking my boss's face?"

I shrugged. "Clothes on, my friend, clothes on. There were no bare asses anywhere near that couch. Speaking of which—" I looked back at Jane, who was sitting with her hand shoved into her bedraggled bob. "I'll expect you to take care of cleaning that blanket when you're...done with it."

She nodded and made a muffled "Of course, Sky." Eric blinked, still unabashed, then stretched his long arms up toward the ceiling.

"All right," he said. "Since we won't be finishing what we started, unless, Jane..." He nodded at his bedroom, and Jane gave him a look like he was actually insane. "Right, then," he said. "Shower for me."

It wasn't until he disappeared into the bathroom and the water started running that Jane finally looked directly at me. She found her glasses and shoved them over her face.

"That's better," she muttered. "I'd like to see your condescension with crystal clarity."

I smirked and went to sit on the couch next to her, then thought better of it and took the opposite chair instead. "Hey, I'm not judging," I said, holding my hands up innocently. "You're the one who calls him 'Petri Dish.'"

Jane leaned back into the couch and pulled the blanket up her bare form to cover her shoulders completely, so that now all I saw of her was a rumpled head with glasses.

"He's...yeah. Maybe not so much that anymore."

I raised a brow. "So, are you guys dating?"

She shot me a wide look. "Um, *no*. It's still just fucking, Sky. That's it."

"Isn't flying in for the weekend from Chicago three weeks before the bar exam a little bit more than 'just fucking?'" I asked. "And, since you're still here, presumably skipping a day of prep class? Does Eric know it's 'just fucking?'"

"Oh, like he'd want more," Jane said, not quite able to hide the bitterness in her voice. "I know the score, and he does too. You think I don't know where that thing goes when I'm not around? Trust me, I'm making him double-bag it."

I glanced back at the bathroom, where steam was starting to filter out through the bottom of the door.

"I don't know about that," I said. "I happen to know that Eric doesn't bring women home. And unless he's sneaking in quickies at the grocery store, I don't think he's meeting them anywhere else, either. All I've seen him do for the last month is eat, sleep, and study."

"Well, then it's only a matter of time. He's not going to commit to a skinny Korean girl with weird hair who lives a thousand miles away." Jane bit her lip while she stared down at the folds of the blanket.

"Janey. Since when do you talk about yourself like you're nothing?" I reached over the coffee table and gave my friend a pat on the knee. "You're the shit, and you know it."

The shower stopped. Jane tensed.

"It's just sex," she repeated, this time louder and with more surety than before. She popped an arm out of the blanket and held it wrapped around her lean form. "I'm going to shower and get dressed, and then you and I are going to a late lunch after your class, before my flight tonight. No walking dildos allowed." She looked to the still-closed bathroom door. "You got that, Mr. Clean?" she called.

The door opened, and Eric walked out in nothing but a towel wrapped around his hips, his long muscles somehow more on display despite the fact that his boxers had actually covered less of him.

"Loud and clear," he said with a grim look and disappeared into his room.

Jane followed his form, then closed her eyes tight when the door slammed shut with a loud bang. Then, with a heavy sigh, she stood up.

"It's just sex," she said like a mantra as she walked to the bathroom. "Just sex."

~

278

Chapter 29

I passed. I knew it. There was just no other way that test could have gone.

When I walked out of the Convention Center on a sunny Friday morning in late July, I felt like one of the people in Plato's "Allegory of the Cave," blinded by the bright summer sun after spending so long in the dark. Except my dark cave was prep classes and the last two days of testing.

I squinted in the late afternoon sun triumphantly. I wouldn't find out the official results of my exam for eight more weeks, but I knew I had done well. And now a weight had been lifted from my shoulders, the last step toward becoming a licensed attorney, ready to start my real life in the real world.

"Time for a motherfucking *drink*," Eric pronounced as he followed me out of the Boston Convention Center, where we had just spent the last two days in one of the enormous rooms with the other hundreds of new law grads in the Boston area.

Eric looked more than a little worse for wear. His T-shirt was rumpled, and his hair on one side was sticking out on the side, like he'd spent the last six hours pulling at it while he wrote the second-day series of essay responses on Massachusetts state law. His eyes drooped with dark circles, and despite the summer weather, he looked even paler than normal.

I probably looked just as terrible. Like most of the test-takers, I was exhausted and had forgone things like makeup or jewelry. I'd dressed comfortably, in layers of jeans and a hoodie to withstand the air-conditioned rooms. Outside, however, in the sticky, late-July heat, I quickly stripped down to my white tank top and pulled my messy hair into a loose braid, eager to get the sweaty strands off my neck.

"That guy with the cell phone during the third essay," Eric said. "I wanted to kill him. If I fail, I'm suing his ass, I swear it."

Several other classmates from our Andover and Harvard classes were also filtering out of the building. Most had the same bleary, dazed expressions that come from two straight days of testing.

"Woohoo! Time to get messed up!"

Shouts of relief started to pepper the air as more and more people emerged. If there was ever a day to let loose, this was it. Most of us were taking two weeks off for the vacation we hadn't gotten after graduating from law school in May. It was fairly typical for most firms to negotiate their associates' start dates a few weeks after the exam; no one needed a burned-out associate when they expected us to hit the ground running.

For my part, I was thrilled to have some time off. While the dramas of the spring hadn't completely disappeared, they were all basically in a holding pattern. The security team in Brooklyn confirmed that my dad was continuing with his rehabilitation and therapy regimen without any more interference from Victor Messina or Katie Corleone. Miranda had, predictably, continued to delay divorce proceedings, but had not caused any additional headaches once Brandon and I had started seeing each other more openly.

Maurice and Janette had remained in New York (presumably with her family) since the Fourth, and although Maurice continued to pester Brandon with occasional phone calls and sometimes even messengered proposals, there was no more than a few distant suggestions that we socialize with them until they returned to Boston in August. The gifts had stopped. Janette was as silent as she had ever been.

The official word from BNP was that Maurice was working at the New York office for the time being. Margie, Brandon's assistant, couldn't get any other information about why he was there. It could have been any number of things: a deal gone bad, some kind of scheme the company was trying to hide. Maurice was a large enough figure that any malfeasance could cause a scandal that would affect stock prices. My best bet was that he was being given a shot at a *mea culpa*.

He didn't talk to me much about it, but I knew that the DNC was also pressuring Brandon to make a decision about a mayoral run. The election wasn't until the following year, but they likely wanted to start fundraising. The local papers continued to speculate about his interest in politics, and a few PACs had already been started for him. I didn't miss the clench of his jaw whenever he saw a new headline. What I didn't know was what he was going to do. I wondered if he was waiting for me to make that decision first.

Like a herd of escaped livestock, close to fifty of us overtook the nearest bar, aptly named The Drunk Monk, as we'd all felt like secluded monks with our study guides for the last month.

Eric and I sat at the bar with Steve Kramer, one of our classmates, and quickly ordered several plates of bar grub along with drinks, the boys opting for a pitcher of PBR while I took my preferred drink of whiskey and soda.

"And a round of tequila shots!" Steve called out as the bartender walked away to put in our order.

"Come on, Crosby," Eric prodded when I made a face. "If there was ever a day to drink cheap liquor, this is it."

"You seem pretty sure of yourself."

Jared appeared next to us, looking only slightly less groomed than normal. The collar of his polo shirt was still starched, and the only sign that he'd also been testing for the last two days was that his khaki shorts were creased from sitting for too long. He flagged the bartender and ordered a beer, then looked down at me with a bright smile. I couldn't help but smile back as the bartender delivered everyone's drinks along with a tray full of shots.

"Onwards and upwards, counselors," Steve crowed as he reached between us and delivered shot glasses to me, Jared, and several other classmates crowding the bar.

I held up my shot along with everyone else as the adrenaline of finishing this chapter rushed through the room. We all tipped them back with howls and hoots and gleefully ordered another round.

"Keep 'em coming!" Steve shouted before throwing back a second tequila and sucking on a lime.

"And some water," I called before following suit.

I held a hand to my forehead while I sucked on my lime. Two shots in, and I was already feeling lightheaded.

"I need some food," I croaked to Eric while Jared calmly sipped his beer. "Didn't we order potato skins?"

As if on cue, the skins arrived, along with a plate of fried mozzarella and clam strips. We dug in. Fried food had never tasted so good.

"I wish Jane were here," I said to Eric after scarfing my second skin. "It isn't the same, celebrating without her."

281

"She'll be here on Friday," Eric said, as if it were completely normal that he would know that in the first place. Suddenly he found a scratch in the bar top extremely interesting.

Both Jane and Eric had been mum since the Fourth—Eric because he never said anything about his love life, and Jane because she still staunchly denied the long weekend meant anything at all. More interesting was that although I had talked to her several times in the last three weeks, she had also not mentioned a visit. Not once.

"Will she?" I asked with a raised brow. "And when was this decided?"

Eric took a gulp of his beer. "Last night. She's planning to spend her vacation in Boston."

"And is she planning to stay with us?"

Eric looked up. "What, do you want me to pay more of the rent? I didn't think you'd mind. I'm sure she was going to tell you after her exam. She's just not done until tomorrow."

He popped a piece of fried cheese into his mouth and focused on aligning his coaster and beer glass with the edge of the bar, as if knowing Jane's bar exam schedule and the fact that he would be hosting the same girl every night for two weeks wasn't completely out of the ordinary. I said nothing, just gave a hard stare while he ate.

"Okay!" he finally exploded after swallowing his food. "Jesus. If I tell you that I like her, will you stop staring a freaking hole through my forehead with those laser beams?"

He rubbed viciously at said spot, as if the pressure was literally killing him. I folded my arms with a satisfied smile at Jared, who just looked confused.

"I'm glad you can admit the truth," I said haughtily before picking up my drink.

"I'm not the one you should worry about," Eric grumbled. "You should be talking to Jane about the truth, not me."

I quirked my eyebrow, but that was all he was willing to say about the matter.

Two more shots and several rounds of drinks later, the entire bar was effectively shitfaced. I had already seen at least three soon-to-be-prominent Boston attorneys sprint to the bathrooms to throw up, and a few others had just skipped the line and dashed outside to hurl over the pier. We were messier than a frat house during Rush week.

Steve was getting sloppy with one of his BC classmates on the improvised dance floor by the juke box, and Eric was working hard not to fall off his bar stool while he checked his phone every two minutes and crooned George Michael's "Faith" every so often. Eric, as it happened, could actually sing. I was willing to bet a thousand dollars that most of his texts were drunk missives to a certain half-Korean friend of mine.

I, on the other hand, had sent my share of drunk-texts to Brandon, who was trapped in meetings at the office. Jared had kept me company at the bar and continued to ply me with alcohol and greasy food while we competed with our worst law school stories. We all sacrificed a lot to get to this point, financially and personally. The road to becoming a lawyer took a lot of time and money that most people couldn't understand. While many of our friends from college and high school were well into their careers, we were just starting now, and wouldn't be able to take a reasonable break for another several years.

"You have no *idea* what I've given up for this," I pronounced to Jared for the fifth time, sweeping my arms like great wings. I smacked the shoulder of a dancing classmate. "Sorry, girl."

"I bet I can beat you." Jared's voice was becoming increasingly slurred too. "Summer in Europe."

I snorted. "Oh, I'm so sorry, lil' rich boy, that you had to skip your special snowflake vacay." I held a thumb out, preparing to count. "Thanksgiving three years in a row. My grandmother's seventy-fifth birthday. Helping my dad through rehab. Missed every one of 'em."

Jared frowned at the last one. "Shit. I didn't know about your dad, Skylar. Everything okay?"

I tipped back the last of my fourth whiskey soda. "It will be. He's...got some issues." I turned to the bartender and signaled for another round, barely managing to keep myself on my barstool. "So, summer vacation? That's all you got for me, precious?"

Jared grinned and pushed his floppy brown hair off his forehead. "Okay, okay, no. I got a few more. My best friend's wedding. In Tahiti."

I shook my head so hard I almost fell off my stool. "Still a rich boy problem, but yeah, that had to hurt. But I got you again." I held out a second finger: "Spending time with my long-lost brother and sister this summer."

"Spending time with my aging grandmother. She's got rheumatoid arthritis, you know."

"Missing my sister's birthday party in New York," I shot back.

"Missing every party all summer long," Jared countered.

"All the money I could have been making to pay for my dad's rehab."

"All that gas money driving back and forth from Andover every day."

"A baby."

The words fell between us like a stone, tumbling out of my mouth in spectacular word-vomit before I could stop them. I stared at the ground, as if I could actually see the bomb I'd just dropped. The blood drained from my head, and I swayed on my seat. Did I really say that? No, no, I didn't. I couldn't have.

"You were pregnant?" Jared asked, all signs of friendly competition replaced with sharp curiosity.

Fuck.

"Uh, no," I said, trying and failing to stifle the flush racing up my neck and cheeks. "No, no, no. I was just trying to one-up you. I get kind of competitive like that sometimes."

I gave him a sheepish, probably useless smile. Jared was too busy calculating the months to notice.

"Was it Sterling's?" He tapped his chin, trying to process the news. "Does he know?"

I shook my head furiously, terror rising in my belly. Fuck, fuck, FUCK.

"Jared, it was a *joke*," I insisted, shifting around in my stool to try to catch his bleary, yet searching brown eyes. Do not look away, do not look away. "Look into my eyes. I. was. never. pregnant."

Did those words sound as vacant as they felt? I couldn't tell. Jared stared at me for a few more seconds, then gave a half-hearted shrug.

"All right," he said. "I hope not. That's a heck of a joke to make, Skylar."

"What's a heck of a joke?"

I turned to find Brandon elbowing his way through the crowd, standing out in his tailored suit among a crowd full of drunken, casually dressed exam-takers.

"Um, nothing," I said as I accepted his hearty kiss. "Just a dumb joke."

I pushed my glasses up my nose and shook my head infinitesimally at Jared while Brandon sat on the stool behind me. He scooted forward to straddle my seat and ordered himself an IPA. If Jared didn't think the joke was funny, Brandon definitely wouldn't like it. And, considering how well Brandon could read my face, he would probably know it wasn't a joke at all.

Jared pressed his mouth shut and took a long drink of his beer while Brandon looked him over.

"Okay, then," Brandon said. "Looks like I'm a few behind you, babe."

He pulled my frozen form against his chest. His familiar almond scent reminded me just how little I'd been able to see him in the last weeks.

"You smell good," he murmured into my ear as he brushed my braid over one shoulder to kiss me on the neck, just under my earlobe. "Like jasmine and...tequila, is it? Not usually your drink, but I'll take it."

Jared watched us with hooded eyes, then started studying the rim of his beer glass. I didn't know why he hadn't disappeared yet; considering what had happened at the gala, this wasn't going to be anything but awkward.

Brandon paid for his drink, the arm wrapped around my waist tightened. I recognized it as the territorial move it was.

"So, Jared, right?" Brandon said over my shoulder "You think you passed?"

Jared cleared his throat. "Yeah, I think so. It's a tough test, as you know, but our class was a good one. Plus, Skylar's a great study partner."

The forearm around my midsection flexed, but Brandon's smile didn't waver. He glanced down at me and pressed a kiss to my forehead.

"I bet she is," he said. "After all, my Skylar's wicked smart."

His accent was out in full, making "Skylar" sounds like "Sky-lah" and "smart" sound like "smaht". It was either an indication of his raised anxiety or a play to intimidate Jared. Considering that Jared was a rich kid from the suburbs who would be *very* familiar with the class tensions in Boston, I was guessing the latter.

"Thanks," I said, finally finding my voice again. "She's also sitting right here, so you guys can stop talking about her like she's not."

Brandon squeezed my waist again while Jared looked mildly contrite.

"So, do you have any plans for the break, Jared?" Brandon asked, affecting a kinder voice. "I'm assuming your grandfather is giving you one, right?"

I tried to elbow him, but only hit the bar. The contact sent an arrow of pain up my arm. I winced and grasped my elbow. Brandon immediately cupped the spot with his hand and started to massage like he had been planning to do that the entire time. I would have brushed him off, but it felt really, really good. *Damn it.*

Jared took a sip of his beer and cleared his throat as he took in Brandon's familiarity with my body. "Um, yeah," he said. "Two weeks off, like everyone else. I'm heading to St. Bart's with friends to blow off some steam. What about you, *Skylar*?" He looked at me as if Brandon wasn't there.

I shrugged. "Not much. I'll probably go down to visit my family in New York, take it easy for a bit."

"Actually, I had a surprise planned," Brandon said quietly enough that I wasn't sure that Jared could even hear him.

He set an envelope down in front of me. I picked it up. This wasn't grandstanding anymore; Brandon had come prepared with a gift.

I twisted around to find an adorable puppy-dog expression on Brandon's face. He looked hopeful, yet tentative. I couldn't blame him for being nervous; I didn't have the best track-record of accepting his gifts. But things were different now. We had a different level of trust, and I had finally started to let my issues about that sort of thing go.

"What is it?" I asked as I examined the envelope. "What did you do?"

"Open it," he said, blue eyes sparkling with anticipation.

Inside the envelope were several pamphlets of various locations in South France, and a slip bearing a confirmation for a flight bound to Toulouse.

"You got me a trip to France?" I stared at the papers with wide eyes, not quite believing what I saw. "Really?"

286

Slowly, like he was next to a wild animal, Brandon nodded.

"I thought maybe you'd like to make some better memories there than you did in Paris," he said. "You deserve a break, Red. You've been through a lot the last few months. If you don't want to go here, we could go somewhere else. I just thought now was a good time to get away." With a quick glance at Jared, who was still watching with an increasingly dark expression, Brandon added, "Together."

I looked at the confirmation slip again, which had both of our names on it. We were supposed to leave the day after tomorrow.

"Can you afford to take all this time?" I asked quietly. "It's not like you don't have your own stuff to deal with right now."

Brandon just pressed another chaste kiss on my cheek that promised more than it showed.

"The truth?" he asked.

I nodded.

"I might have booked our flight the second you agreed to come to dinner that night." He gave a sheepish smile. "I might have been planning this for a while."

Slowly, unbidden, an ear-splitting grin spread across my face until it felt like my cheeks were going to crack in half. Suddenly I was so excited, I was practically vibrating in my seat.

"Toulouse?" I asked again, my voice hitching up another octave. "*Really?*"

Two weeks in Toulouse. In the summer. Alone with Brandon. I literally could not think of anything better.

"For a night," Brandon said, now with a megawatt grin that mirrored my own. "Then we would go down to Marseille. Mark agreed to loan us his villa on the water."

Okay, except that. That was definitely better!

"What do you say, Red?" Brandon asked, picking up one of my hands and bringing it to his lips. "Will you go to France with me?"

The question was so formal and out-of-character for Brandon, such an obvious attempt *not* to go overboard (despite the extravagance of the gift), that my heart squeezed and my response came freely.

"Yes!" I sprang out of my seat, threw my arms around his neck, and peppered his laughing face with kisses. "Yes-yes-yes-yes-YES!"

Brandon laughed as he held me off the ground, causing a few of my classmates to turn around and smile at us.

"Well," I said with a grin to Jared as I was set back down. He looked like he was going to be sick. "I guess I'm going to France for my vacation."

Jared immediately pasted a polite smile on his face. "That sounds great," he said. Then he looked over my shoulder and waved at someone. "Excuse me. Just going to say hi to some people."

Brandon watched him go with a satisfied expression that was far too similar to a lion who had just kicked out the weaker member of the pride. I elbowed him in the gut.

"You could wipe that smug expression off your face, Sterling. It was never a contest."

"I know, Red," Brandon said. "That guy couldn't handle you anyway." His expression dropped to a frown as he considered something. "But I'm glad you're not going to be studying together anymore. I don't like the way he looks at you."

"How's that?"

Brandon looked at me with a positively predatory gleam. "Like you're something to eat."

I stared at him with my mouth open, something in his feral expression robbing me of my capacity to speak. Brandon revealed a few white teeth with a half-smile, then slipped an arm around my waist and pulled me against his tall, hard form.

"Are you ready to celebrate alone yet?" he asked with a quick nip to my earlobe.

I shuddered as his hands slid down to cup my ass and squeeze gently. I stepped out of his embrace, concerned I might combust right there in the bar, in front of all of my future colleagues, if I let Brandon keep touching me like that.

He just smiled again, baring his teeth like a lion on the hunt. I was his prey, and I couldn't be happier about it.

~

Chapter 30

I woke up the next morning with wide rays of sunlight streaming through my bedroom window. It was the one time of day where the light managed to slip between the brick buildings my window faced, and they landed directly on my eyes.

The other side of my bed was rumpled and empty. Brandon was nowhere to be seen.

I rolled to my back and stared up at the ceiling. The rest of the night had been a blur after Brandon had taken me home and we had continued "celebrating" my vacation well into the night. Perhaps it was that, or the copious amounts of water I'd drunk in between mind-bending orgasms, but I wasn't nearly as hungover as I should have been.

My door opened, and Brandon backed into the room carrying a tray of drinks and food. I was hit with a sense of déjà vu. How many times had I dreamed exactly this while we were apart?

His broad shoulders filled the small doorway, a golden expanse of muscle, clad as he was in just a pair of boxer briefs that clung to every perfect curve of his ass.

"Did Eric get a look of you like that?" I asked as I sat up, not bothering to hold my sheet against my naked body. With Brandon, I had no shame. "I'm pretty sure seeing his boss in his underwear would qualify as awkward and uncomfortable."

"He didn't. But I'm too damn hungry to care anyway."

Brandon turned around as the door shut, revealing a tray loaded with tea and bagels. His hair stood out in a wavy riot around his head; vaguely, I remembered clenching that mane a lot last night, urging him on as he feasted on my breasts and other body parts. I shivered and blushed.

He looked down at my bare breasts and the pink rising over my skin, and his friendly smile turned savage, a change also evident in the bulge in his briefs.

"On second thought, breakfast can wait."

Brandon set the tray on my side table before he crawled over the bed and completely covered me.

"Good morning," he murmured as he caged me against the bedding, positioning his long body over mine.

Considering what was currently pressed between my legs, it was a very good morning indeed. I grinned into his lips. He teased my mouth open with his soft lips and twisted his tongue around mine.

"Fuck," he murmured. "It just never stops, does it?"

"What's that?" I asked before he dove in for another kiss.

"The wanting," he said as he licked and nipped at my neck. "You. Always."

I arched into him, luxuriating in the feel of his big body.

"No," I said as my hands found their familiar clutch in his waves while his mouth moved lower to pull the tip of one breast, then the other between his lips. "It doesn't."

His reached to tug his briefs down, and kicked them and the sheets off the bed before situating himself between my thighs. I winced slightly as he entered me.

"Too much?" he asked, although by the look on his face, it wouldn't have really mattered.

"It's fine," I breathed and grabbed his ass to push him further in. "But you're not wasting time, are you?"

"I can't wait," he said with a shudder as he slid fully in. "You feel too good."

His hips moved lazily in slow, languid circles, taking time to enjoy the friction of each movement. Covered by his wide shoulders, his lips on my neck and cheeks, I luxuriated in the feel of him. Of us. There was nowhere else.

"I want to try something," he whispered in my ear. "I need...fuck, Skylar. I need all of you."

He turned me over, pushed into me again from behind once, twice, before he pulled out and tugged my hips up toward him. I tensed as I felt him nudging a bit higher, just at my other entrance, the one that pretty much no one had ever touched. Actually, scratch that—no one at all.

"What—what are you doing?" I stuttered, although to my surprise, my hips pushed back instinctively.

"All of you," Brandon murmured again as he moved away and teased me with a finger. My whole body shuddered. "Will you let me?"

"I...you..."

I couldn't speak as inch by inch, he eased himself into the unbearably tight space.

"Is this okay?" Brandon bent down to cover my back with his warm, hard body. His voice rumbled low next to my ear.

I shifted, letting my body adjust to the feel of him. "Yes," I finally breathed. "Keep—keep going."

He pushed in a bit more.

"Fuuuuuuuuck," he breathed. "Jesus *Christ*, you're tight here."

"I'm...I...Brandon...*please*..."

I could barely get out any coherent words. I was just...so...*full*. Somehow, Brandon managed to reach into the drawer of my nightstand and pull out the small bottle of lubricant I kept there. I heard the sound of the bottle being opened and a quick squirt of the cold gel, before he pulled out slightly to apply it to where our bodies met. Then he pressed back in. I gave an animal groan.

"You can take it, baby," he said as he seated himself fully. "That's it, Skylar."

Brandon started to move, slowly at first, letting me acclimate to his size and the feel of him there, but then slowly picked up the pace until eventually he was thrusting into me just as hard as he had anywhere else. His hand on my ass disturbed the quiet with a loud crack.

"Ah!" I cried, my eyes clenched against the sweet combination of pain and pleasure.

"You like that?" Brandon growled behind me. His hand slapped down again, the rest of him ramming into me mercilessly. "You like it when I give it to you hard like this? When I fuck this gorgeous ass, baby?"

"I...please..." There were no words. I literally had no words anymore, and his were going to undo me.

My hand fell limp beneath me. My whole body was starting to feel limp. Brandon leveraged my hips up slightly higher, then reached down with one hand on my clit. I moaned against the feel of his mouth on my neck, the carved muscles warm against my back.

"That's it," he murmured into my neck. His teeth latched on to my earlobe as he pressed himself deeper, harder. "*Fuck*. You can't run from me now, Skylar, can you?"

Running? Who was running?

"Brandon!" I moaned. I was so close...soooo close. "Brandon, please!"

His thumb flicked my clit. "Come," he growled. "*Now!*"

"Aaaaahhh!" I cried.

His fingers rubbed small circles, then suddenly found my clit and squeezed. The ache in my belly burst, and I unraveled in series of shudders and shakes, completely falling apart under Brandon's large, merciless form. He pistoned in and out of me at breakneck pace until both hands grabbed my ass again hard enough to leave a bruise.

'FUCK!" he yelped.

I fell forward, and he fell with me. His big form shook until slowly, finally, his body relaxed on top of me.

"Oh *God*, Skylar. I love you," he moaned as he released himself into me. "I love you so much it hurts."

I welcomed his mouth on my neck, welcomed his body on mine, welcomed his essence into every pore of me, into this place where nothing else existed but two of us. My head was a fog; the fact that Brandon had just done something to me that no one—not Patrick, my ex, not anyone—had ever done just was starting to register. He could have every part of me, and he did. Love didn't even begin to cover it.

~

I flipped open my laptop while Brandon was in the shower, pulling up a packing list I often used for long trips. Almost immediately, my Facetime started ringing: Jane, looking to video chat, likely out of guilt. No doubt Eric had informed her of our conversation yesterday.

"Hi Jane," I answered as I pushed my glasses further up my nose and my hair out of my face.

"Well, hi there, Sunshine. You look like you had a nice night. And by nice, I mean exhausted because a tycoon was banging your lights out."

Jane grinned lasciviously into the camera, and I rolled my eyes. In the small picture-in-picture, I could see the tired circles under my eyes and the way my hair basically bunched around my face in that "just-fucked" sort of way. Well, wasn't I?

"I had a *great* night," I said with a grin. "And morning. And probably afternoon too. You?"

"Well, I'm about to head into day two here of the exam."

Jane turned to her phone to show me a blurry scan of the University of Illinois Chicago campus. She flipped back to her tired-looking face and took a drink from a paper cup.

"Is that coffee or vodka?" I joked.

"Ha fucking ha. Coffee, thanks. Although a shot probably would do some good right about now. My nerves are done."

I checked the clock on my desk. "When you start?"

"Thirty minutes. I should go in, but I can't with all the nervous energy in there. Was it like that for you, all these uptight almost-lawyers basically shattering the windows with their vibes?"

I chuckled. "Pretty much. But you're going to do fantastic. You'll kick ass, like you always do."

Jane shrugged, but her teeth ground audibly through the small phone speakers. "I tell you, I'm going to need a month to recuperate after all of this. Two weeks won't do it."

"Well, I'm sure Eric can help you out with that," I said with a sly smile. "He seems *very* eager to help you unwind. Starting Friday, apparently."

Jane bit her lip and cast one eye downward. "Are you mad I didn't tell you?"

I shrugged. Maybe I was a little disappointed that Jane hadn't confided in me immediately, but she was entitled to her personal life as much as anyone else.

"Nah," I said. "I just hope you guys are being careful."

"Oh, don't you worry about that. I make the boy double-bag it."

"I meant with your heart, Janey," I said with a roll of my eyes. "And I hope for Eric's sake you're joking."

Jane didn't quite look into the camera, just covered her mouth with a smile she was obviously trying to hide. Maybe she and Eric weren't willing to admit it, but it was clear that whatever was going on between them was more than just screwing around.

"Anyway," I continued, knowing she wasn't about to spill her guts out minutes before walking into her exam. "You can make him wear as many condoms as you want without worrying about me walking in on you this time."

"What? Don't tell me we're forcing you to live in the ice palace. I'm coming as much to see you as my sex Viking."

"Aannnd now I'm imagining you and Eric while he's wearing a Viking hat. Thanks for that."

"That's not a terrible idea," Jane said, tapping her lips. She grinned. "Ooh, late graduation gift!"

I chuckled. "Just disinfect the couch before I get back, all right?"

"And where is it that you're going?" Jane demanded, all thoughts of Viking hats clearly gone.

I grinned. "Oh, you know. Brandon's taking me to France for two weeks."

Jane's eyes bugged through the screen. "Whaaat? You lucky bitch. So, you're finally going to let him use all that money to do something fun for once?"

I blinked sheepishly. "It's not like that."

"I know, I know, Sky," Jane waved away my concerns. "I just mean, I'm glad you're finally letting him spoil you a bit. It's about time. That man is so damn crazy about you, and you deserve to be loved like that. I'm happy for you, friend."

I couldn't help but grin a little at her words. "Thanks, Janey. I'm pretty happy too."

Things were still so complicated, and we hadn't even come close to sorting out all the issues in both of our family lives, but that was the truth. And today, nothing seemed like it could get in the way of that.

"So, are you going to tell him...you know...now that the pressure is off?"

Through the wall, the wall the water turned off in the bathroom. I glanced back at the computer and shook my head vehemently, all the bliss of our conversation now evaporated.

"Not the time right now, Jane."

"But, Sky, you said that—"

"Not the time, Jane!"

She frowned into the screen, worrying her lips together before she finally sighed.

"Fine," she said. "I'll say no more. Just do it. Soon. You promise?"

I just blinked, then nodded my head. She was right, I knew, but I didn't want to ruin what was finally finding its rhythm again. It had taken this long for Brandon and I to rebuild what we once had. It was too precious.

My bedroom door swung open, and Brandon came back in wearing nothing but a towel, water droplets dewing over his shoulders and chest, his mop of wet hair curling more than usual around his ears.

"Thanks for the towel, man," he called back to Eric, whom I could see clearly through the doorway, focused completely on his coffee, thin shoulders hunched over like he wanted to disappear.

Brandon kicked the door shut, then flopped next to me on the bed, which poked his lean form into the frame. "Oh. Hey, Jane," he said.

"Shit!" Jane's voice exploded as her head shook so hard her glasses came loose. "For Christ's sake, warn a girl, Casanova. You could put someone's eyes out with those abs."

Brandon tipped his head back and laughed, the movement causing his already defined muscles to bunch into tight ridges. It really wasn't fair. The man was three years from forty and looked like he had been photo-shopped.

On the screen, Jane's eyes turned wistful. She waved a hand in front of the camera. "Will you get him out of there? I don't need that in my head while I'm testing. Otherwise, all I'm going to see is A) Brandon's abs, B) Brandon's pecs, or C) Brandon's biceps. Thanks a lot, Sterling. If I fail today, it's because of you!"

"I'm moving, I'm moving. Good luck, Jane." Brandon went to where he'd stashed his stuff on top of my dresser.

"I see that dreamy look on your face, Sky," Jane teased, causing Brandon to leer back at me as he pulled on a pair of clean briefs.

The heat in his gaze caused me to blush all over again.

"Right," Jane said. "I think that's my cue to go." She quirked a smile and tipped her head. "I'm glad you're happy, chick. And Brandon?" she called out.

"Yeah, Jane?" Brandon replied as he pulled on a pair of shorts.

"Take care of my girl in France. Don't forget, Don Juan: you mess with her, it's your balls on a platter, courtesy of *moi*."

Popping back into the frame, Brandon rolled his eyes and grinned. "Loud and clear, Jane," he said before leaning down to grab a T-shirt from his overnight bag.

"Good luck, friend," I told her. "I'll see you when we get back."

"You better, chick. Love you, Sky."

"Love you too, Janey. So much."

~

Chapter 31

Our flight was at ten the next morning, so I spent the rest of the day packing and making sure I was leaving everything settled at home. I was a bit worried about leaving, but Bubbe assured me Dad was attending his therapy like clockwork and that Katie Corleone was still nowhere to be seen. He'd even continued his tinkering on the piano, and the doctors thought he would be able to go back to work in another month. Brandon had requested additional security to watch the house while we were gone; there wasn't much more we could do.

"He can barely play 'Twinkle, Twinkle, Little Star,'" Bubbe recounted Dad's progress. "But his fingers are on the keys, and that's the important thing."

I wholeheartedly agreed.

Brandon had told me to pack for a variety of activities, so when David pulled the car up in front of my building at eight a.m., I was standing next to my biggest suitcase that carried supplies for every possibility I could think of in South France, from lounging on the beach to hiking through the Pyrenees.

Brandon stepped out of the car to help me and looked at the suitcase with an amused expression.

"You know," he said as he kissed me on the cheek, "I didn't peg you for the kind of girl who would pack her entire wardrobe for a short trip."

"It's two whole weeks," I countered as David hefted the suitcase into the trunk. "And you wouldn't tell me our plans."

Brandon grinned. "That's because we have no plans, Red. It's part of the charm."

"Exactly," I said. "I need to be prepared for anything."

"You do realize that if we didn't have something, we could just buy it?"

I scowled. "No, *you* could just buy it. *I* come prepared."

Brandon just rolled his eyes, and with a hand on my back, escorted me into the car. "I forgot. I'm traveling with Ebenezer Scrooge."

I smacked him on the shoulder, and he laughed.

"I resent that," I said. "Just because I don't like to spend unnecessary money on myself doesn't mean I'm not generous with others."

"I know, I know. Take it easy." Brandon gathered me in and pressed a kiss on my lips before I could continue my protestations. "Now let's get going. Plane's waiting."

I was in for another surprise when the car pulled up at the small private airfield next to Logan International—the same airfield where I had left Brandon on our first official date, where he had tried to fly me to France once before. The memory of that night was seared into my memory. Dinner in Paris had been a lovely idea, but it was also misplaced, far too ostentatious for a first date, and had only pushed me away.

I found him watching me, looking slightly nervous.

"I thought we had tickets," I said. "Why are we here?"

Brandon grinned sheepishly. "Did you really think I want to fly commercial? This is so much easier. We'll be there in six hours instead of ten. Plus, I can try my luck with the mile-high club."

He waggled his eyebrows in a way that made him look like a horny puppy. I burst out laughing in spite of myself, and Brandon joined me. His excitement was contagious.

"Come on, Red," he said as David opened his door. "Let's see if I can get you on a plane this time without slapping me."

"Ha fucking ha," I retorted, but allowed him to help me out of the car.

A flash from outside the gates of the small airport pulled my attention to the road. A cluster of photographers was there, all of their lenses pointed directly at us.

"Mr. Sterling! Brandon!" They called. "Where are you going? Who is your friend?"

I glanced up at Brandon and found him looking at the photographers with a hard scowl.

"Who are they?" I asked as he guided me into the airport, which thankfully had tinted windows.

I wondered if they were installed partly because of the wealthy, sometimes famous people who used private airfields like this. In the plush lobby, the agents took our bags and passports.

Brandon grimaced and his broad shoulders tensed. "Paparazzi. They've been starting to follow me a bit the last few weeks, since there has been more speculation in the papers about whether or not I'm going to run. Apparently, my whereabouts are more important than things like, you know, the economy or public healthcare."

His voice dripped with sarcasm. It was clear he wasn't happy with being surveilled this way, and I couldn't blame him. I hated it when we suspected that a PI was following us around. Now we had to deal with the press too?

"*Have* you decided?" I asked, unable to help myself.

I hadn't pressured him much about the decision—in the last few weeks of studying for the bar exam, I honestly hadn't had time to think about it, and he hadn't mentioned it at all. But obviously, it was an issue that needed to be discussed, and soon.

Brandon shook his head, the small lines at his eyes crinkling as he frowned. "Not yet." He turned an awkward smile at me. "Although Cory has been riding my ass about it."

I masked a scowl at the mention of Cory, Brandon's would-be campaign manager. I hadn't spoken to him for long at the benefit last month, but I hadn't liked him very much. He was snippy and superior—basically the complete stereotype of someone who worked in politics. The idea that he would be a consistent presence in Brandon's life wasn't very appealing.

The agents announced that our plane was ready to board. Brandon took my hand with a squeeze that melted away all my reservations.

"It's time," he said. "Campaign stuff can wait. You ready for some downtime together?"

Was I ever.

I grinned. "Let's go."

~

Seven hours later, we arrived in Marseille. Five hours ahead of Boston, it was nine o'clock in the evening by the time the plane pulled to a stop on a private runway at the Marseille airport.

Brandon, as it happened, was incredibly well traveled. This shouldn't have surprised me, considering how extensive his business interests were, but it did. He always seemed like such a local boy dressed up in nice suits. So, it was somewhat of a shock when he spoke to the customs officers in surprisingly decent French.

"And here I thought I was going to have to translate," I said as we were waved easily through the gate.

He looked down at me and flashed his thousand-watt grin. "I'm not fluent or anything, but I've at least learned to say thank you when I travel," he said.

He leaned in and kissed me, a long, lingering kiss that sent sparks down to the bottom of my toes.

"Welcome to France," he murmured against my lips.

I smiled into his embrace. "*Bienvenue a France,*" I whispered. "*Merci, monsieur.*"

Brandon leaned back with a sly grin. "Yeah, I'm gonna need you to do that some more, baby. Preferably naked."

My heart thrilled, and I practically skipped out toward the street where another car was waiting for us, swishing my hips a bit more than I normally would. "*Avec ton plaisir, mon cher.*"

Brandon slammed a palm to his heart, watching me in faux pain. "You're killing me, Red. Let's get you inside before I molest you in front of customs agents."

"They won't care," I said. "They're French."

~

We pulled up in front of a house that belonged to Mark Grove, the other name partner at Brandon's law firm. I didn't know Grove well, having only seen his brusque face occasionally while I had served as an intern at the firm last year, but for some reason, the fact that he was a Francophile surprised me.

"Big time," Brandon said when I said as much. "He comes here every chance he gets. All of his wives have been French too."

"Wives?" I asked. "Just how many has he had?"

Brandon chuckled. "Oh, I don't know. Four or five, I think." He gave a sheepish shrug, like he was embarrassed on his partner's behalf. "What can I say? He's a better attorney than a husband, I guess."

"I guess," I echoed.

Brandon unlocked the door to the villa and walked inside, hefting our bags up a short flight of stairs that led us directly into the living room. Huge by European standards, the house was fairly small in contrast to Brandon's properties, with most of the first floor taken up by the living area and adjacent kitchen.

But the house made up for its lack of space with opulence; it was absolutely stunning. Done in the typical Mediterranean style of stucco exteriors and pink clay roof tiles outside, the interior was light and airy, floored with pinkish Spanish tile in an open design that made the most of the limited space by allowing the kitchen, living room, and dining area to flow together in one high-ceilinged room, punctuated by carefully chosen modern furniture. Gauzy drapes floated over picture windows at the far end of the living room, which looked out onto a wood-framed pool and a view of *Chateau d'If*, the sixteenth-century island fortress that was the setting for the *Count of Monte Cristo*.

Brandon came to stand behind me as I gazed out at the view, entranced by the moonlight flickering across the Mediterranean, glittering on the white hulls of the boats bobbing in the harbor. A gull sounded somewhere in the distance, and I sighed as Brandon slipped his hands around my waist and pulled me against his tall, strong form.

"All human wisdom is contained in these two words, 'Wait and Hope'," he quoted softly as we looked out to the harbor.

I turned in his arms, surprised. "I didn't take you for a Dumas fan."

Brandon shrugged. "I always liked the *Count of Monte Cristo*," he said. "It's a pretty kick-ass story. Guy gets mistakenly locked in a prison for twenty years, comes back, makes his fortune, and sticks it to his enemies before he takes off with the girl." He grinned at me. "Doesn't sound too bad."

The obvious parallels between his life and the count's sent ripples down my spine.

"Is that what you're doing?" I asked as I placed my palms flat over his broad chest. "Are you the Count?"

Brandon snorted. "Hardly. I'm not much for vengeance, Red. You know that."

I traced the line of his jaw. "I'm glad."

It wasn't a characteristic I liked. Vengeance had nearly cost my dad his life. I was more interested in peace.

"How about this one?" Brandon asked quietly as his hand threaded through my hair. "'Woman is sacred; the woman one loves is holy'."

"That's very parochial of you," I joked, although the words and his tone made my entire body hum.

"Lapsed Catholic," he rejoined with a shy smile.

Brandon's thumbs stroke the edges of my cheekbones as he looked down at me, dark blue eyes shining with love. I couldn't have looked away even if I wanted to.

"I've never been a religious man, Red," he said, his voice suddenly hoarse and low. "When I'm with you...I find myself praying a whole lot more than I ever did."

"Oh? Not for help, I hope."

Brandon shook his head shyly. "No. I'm too busy thanking Him for making me the luckiest bastard in the world."

His words took mine away. I wanted to tell him that his touch seared my skin and made my cells tingle, that his face was at the center of my heart. That being with him made the world make sense and turn upside down all at once.

But instead I pulled him down to me for a kiss that would say what I couldn't quite put into words. That I felt that same magical connection, one that was so much more than love. One small word couldn't begin to cover it.

Brandon's hands drifted down my waist and pulled me tight to him, the romance of the moment quickly morphing into something much more animal. I pressed back, eager for the feel of his growing arousal. He leaned in for another kiss, but we were interrupted by a loud growl of his stomach.

I broke away, laughing, and he gave a sheepish smile.

"I really want to have *you* for dinner, Red," he said with a chuckle. "But I think I might fall over first."

My own stomach grumbled back, and we both laughed again. It had been a long time since breakfast. Brandon took my hand and kissed my palm, eyes shining with the heat of a promise for more, later.

"Come on, gorgeous," he said. "Let's find some real food first. Then we can take care of that other craving."

~

"I suppose I should tell you about our plans for the trip," he said after we sat down at a busy restaurant just a few blocks away.

Mark Grove had happily provided a list of recommendations for Marseille, and this bistro, with its casual *al fresco* patio that looked out over the Old Harbor and the pink lights of the city, topped it. While in

Boston most of the restaurants would be clearing out their tables by now, ten o'clock in France was right in the middle of prime dining time.

I perused the menu and took a sip of my water. "I thought you said that the plan was that we had no plan."

Brandon tossed his head from side to side. "Well, sort of. We have options. Marseille is really central. I was thinking about going down the Italian coast or spending a few days in Spain, if you want. Or we could just stay in the bedroom too."

He leered across the table, and I took another, longer sip of water, ignoring the blush that mottled my skin. Brandon just laughed.

The waiter arrived with our bottle of wine and took our orders. I had let Brandon choose for me again, not because I couldn't read the menu, but because it was becoming a regular game between us to see if we could guess the other's preferences.

Brandon was easy: although he was usually game to try anything, he tended to prefer simpler foods. Tonight, for instance, he went with the catch of the day and a side of stewed beans and vegetables. I, on the other hand, almost invariably wanted seafood when it was available, and usually went with either the chef's special or whatever was a bit strange on the menu.

"I'm going to guess the *supions avec artichauts*," Brandon said in his slightly clunky French. He glanced at me. "Did I get it right? I figured you'd go for anything with tentacles in it."

I grinned. "On the nose."

The waiter took our orders with a curt nod, then left us with our drinks.

"Is it wrong that I want to just play it by ear?" I asked. "I've already done the backpacking thing around Europe. I was really looking forward to just relaxing. Maybe just take some day trips around the area. What about you?"

Brandon nodded. "Yeah, that sounds good. Mark told me we should definitely drive down to the Pyrenees if you're up for some hiking."

We continued to muse about various local places we could go while our food came and went, deciding in the end it would be best to rent a car for the next two weeks to do what we wanted. By the end of the meal, I had a list of possibilities sketched out on a napkin, and Brandon's face was alight with excitement. We were both giddy with wine and the thrill of being alone together—and more than ready to get back to the house.

"Two weeks," he said again as we walked up one of the steep cobbled streets together toward Mark's villa. His arm was wrapped tightly around my shoulders. "I can't believe I get two whole weeks alone with my girl. Seriously, Red, I don't think I've taken a vacation in ten years."

My arm, wrapped around his trim waist, just grasped a little tighter at his shirt, a white button-down rolled up at the sleeves. He had looked almost as delicious as my food all night, and the wine had me ready to eat him for dessert.

Brandon inhaled at the sensitive spot just behind my ear. The tip of his tongue touched the delicate skin, and I shivered.

"Come here," he said, and pulled me into a dark corner of the street. His mouth found mine easily as he pressed me into the dark space, one hand cupping my jaw as the other drifted down to my ass under my short skirt.

"Fuck," he breathed between the torrent of kisses. His hips rocked into me, and I could feel his arousal clearly through his jeans. "I need you naked. Like, yesterday."

"More," I demanded, my hands threading through his hair and pulling his mouth back to mine.

He obliged, kissing me again until we were breathless. Both his hands found their way up my skirt, gripping the flesh while he grunted. I was about two seconds from letting him take me right there in the middle of the street. It was always like this, no matter where we were.

Then I heard a click. It was low, and it might have just been the buzz of a streetlamp going out, or maybe the sound of a door shutting, or one of the myriad sounds you hear on a city street. But for some reason, it made the hair on the back of my neck stand up.

"Stop," I said, although Brandon was oblivious as he worked his mouth up and down my neck.

"Hmm?" he asked. "Jesus. How do you smell so fucking good?"

"Brandon, stop," I said, as I tapped him on the shoulder. I couldn't have said why, exactly, but I wanted to get out of the street.

With a groan, he pushed himself off the wall, then reached down with one hand to adjust himself subtly. He stared, eyes clearly dilated with lust.

"You have no idea how alluring you look right now," he said. "With your hair all curly, and your shirt half off your shoulder." He grinned, shark-like. "And knowing *I* did that makes it even more of a turn on."

The look of naked desire on his face was almost enough to make me pull him back to continue his work. But.

"Let's get inside," I said, not wanting to ruin his mood with my suspicions.

Brandon grinned again. "You don't have to tell me twice," he said, and pulled me the rest of the way up the street, where he could continue his work in private.

~

Chapter 32

I was surprised to find that Brandon was actually a good driver as he maneuvered our rented Mercedes coupe down the crooked two-lane roads that snaked around the French countryside. Over the next two weeks, we fell into a rhythm where we would wake up in the morning and enjoy tea and coffee along with some kind of breakfast (usually scrambled eggs and fruit to go with pastries from a bakery down the street). Then we'd would look at the map of France that Mark had framed on his kitchen wall and pick a destination.

"What do you think about staying here today?" Brandon asked after we'd repeated this pattern for ten days. "The Calanques trails are open; I already checked. We could hike down to one of the beaches."

We'd already been wine-tasting twice, driven all the way up to Dordogne and spend the night in a castle, and gone for a long day drive to the Pyrenees the day before. We'd been waiting for the famous national park bordering the Eastern side of Marseille to open for summer hiking for the last ten days. Because of the dry summer weather, the trails were often closed at this time of the year. Last night, however, it had rained.

I was actually more than ready to spend a day in town. Hiking down to a hidden beach where we could swim and veg together sounded fantastic.

After packing some things to bring with us, Brandon and I took a taxi to the Marseille-side trailhead of the park and started winding our way around the gorgeous cliffs of the Calanques National Park. It was the kind of place that belonged on a postcard, and I made a mental note to send one to Bubbe when we got back to town.

We walked for hours around the three-hundred-foot cliffs towering over the inlets for which the Calanques were named. The rocky white limestone speared up from the Mediterranean, and although we saw a few tourists also taking advantage of the rare summer access, we were mostly alone to enjoy the views, joke with each other, and eventually weave our way down to one of the many small, deserted beaches at the base of the cliffs.

"Holy shit," I said for the thousandth time as I dropped my pack onto the white-pebble beach with a satisfying thump.

I took a deep inhale of the salty sea air and pulled my ponytail off my neck to the feel the light breeze coming down the channel. Two walls of jagged cliffs on either side of the beach stretched for another hundred meters or so out to sea.

"You up for a little cliff dive, Red?" Brandon said as he dropped his pack and proceeded to strip off his sweat-soaked T-shirt.

I looked up from the towels I'd spread on the ground and ogled openly at his six-pack and well-defined arms. I'd seen the sight almost every day for the whole vacation, but it never failed to drop my jaw. Brandon's body was a bit tanner than usual after hiking shirtless the day before and swimming at local beaches and Mark's pool. On top of that, he'd only been shaving every few days, so his cheeks and jaw were covered with a golden growth that was delightfully scratchy whenever he kissed me.

I, on the other hand, just had more freckles than ever.

"See something you like, Red?" Brandon asked with a smirk when he caught me staring.

I shut my mouth and grinned. "Yes." I wasn't trying to hide anything.

The smirk deepened. "Didn't I satisfy you last night, green eyes? Or this morning? You're looking pretty hard over there."

I blushed and bit my lip, but didn't avert my gaze. He was just so damn beautiful. Luckily, two could play that game. Instead of responding, I stood up to remove my tank top and shorts so that I was even more exposed than him in the skimpy bikini that I'd bought in Nice. Brandon's smirk immediately (and satisfyingly) morphed into a dropped jaw and darkened pupils.

"I bet *you're* the one who won't be able to keep your hands to yourself," I countered.

Brandon's eyes, which had been blazing down my body, blinked back up. His arrogance had completely replaced the casual lust. He cocked a blond brow.

"I don't think so," he declared. He ran his hands casually up his bare stomach, knowing that the movement would make my mouth water.

"Tell you what, Red. Loser has to make dinner tonight *and* do all the dishes."

I bent down to retrieve the sunblock in my bag. Brandon and I both suffered from competitive streaks that sometimes came out with little bets or wagers. Brandon usually won. So far, I'd gotten stuck with dishes three other nights of the trip.

But not this time. I undid the halter tie of my bandeau so that my neck and shoulders were bare.

"Sounds good to me," I said.

Brandon watched suspiciously and, if the adjustments he made to the front of his shorts were any indication, a bit uncomfortably. I squeezed some of the sunblock into my hand and proceeded to apply it to my upper body, taking extra time to rub the upper expanse of my chest and over the exposed tops of my breasts. When I looked back up, Brandon's eyes had dilated considerably. He was stone-still, muscles flexed and hands clenched by his sides.

"Oh, I'm sorry," I said innocently as I continued to rub my hand slowly into the hollow between my breasts. "Did you want to help?"

Brandon just chewed on his bottom lip as I proceeded to rub the lotion down my stomach and over my thighs, fingers slipping provocatively under the edges of my bikini bottoms. I gave a few low moans just for good measure. The tenting in his swim trunks was even more pronounced. Yeah, I was going to win this bet in about two minutes.

"I know what you're doing," he said, not taking his eyes off my hands. He swallowed heavily.

"Oh?" I turned around so he could watch as I rubbed my backside, kneading at the flesh the way he liked to do behind closed doors. I looked over my shoulders at him. "Do you?"

Brandon jaw tightened visibly, and he ran a rough hand behind his neck. "Yes. And it's not going to work."

I turned back around, pressing my hands into my skin as I moved them very, very slowly up my torso and down to hook my thumbs into my swimsuit bottoms. Brandon's arousal was now bordering on indecent. I totally had this.

I smirked. "Oh really? And why is that?"

With considerable effort, Brandon tore his gaze from my body and turned toward one of the small cliffs sticking out from the beach.

"Because I've got cold water, baby," he said with a grin that seemed brighter than the sun above us.

Then he scampered up the cliff and hurled himself off the edge, landing in the sapphire waves with a giant splash. I watched in shock when he emerged, flipping water back with a flick of his head and a laugh that echoed through our little canyon.

"Come on, Red!" he called. "It feels great!"

He didn't have to ask me twice. I grinned and climbed up the cliff myself. I jumped off with a whoop, landing beside Brandon with a slightly smaller splash.

"Wooo!" I howled with glee as I burst back into the sun.

Beside me, Brandon's thousand-watt smile showed that he was as happy as I was. We were surrounded by cliffs and trees, the sky and water mirroring one another's colors in perfect harmony. No one around for what felt like miles. It was perfect.

Perfect, that is, until I realized I felt freer than I probably should. I looked down and shrieked.

"Shit!" I cried as I splashed frantically, twisting around like a dog chasing its tail.

"What? What is it?" Brandon asked, concern marring his relaxed features. "Did you see something in the water?"

"No, I *lost* something in the water!" I yelped. "My swim top. It fell off!"

I was now completely naked from the waist up. And my bandeau was nowhere in sight.

"You're kidding." Brandon stopped looking around while an impish grin spread over his face. His long arms continued to tread slowly in the waves.

"No, I'm not!" I continued to paddle around, looking for signs of my absent top while trying to keep my body below the water and out of sight.

Brandon just watched with obvious amusement, and eventually started laughing as he made his way back to the shore and sat down in the shallow surf. The more I looked, the more he laughed, his loud guffaws filling the canyon while he held his belly in check.

I glared from where I still tread water, my body submerged with the exception of my head.

"You think this is funny?" I demanded. "You're not even going to help me look?"

Brandon propped himself back on his elbows and grinned down his long body at me. "You have to admit, it's pretty hilarious, babe."

I scowled, which only made him chuckle again. "It's *not* funny. I have nothing to wear now except a sweaty tank top!"

My frustration just made him laugh harder, and when he caught me glowering at him, he collapsed back on his back, stomach shaking. That was *it*.

"All right," I called as I swam back to the beach. My feet touched the ground, and I started to walk in toward Brandon.

Brandon propped himself up on his elbows again. His eyes, which were the same color as the sky-blue waters that surrounded us, popped open as he watched my progress to shore.

"What-what are you doing?" he asked, all signs of amusement wiped from his face.

I stood up fully as I walked, topless in the afternoon sun as he stared, all signs of amusement gone. Water cascaded down my bare skin, and Brandon's gaze was riveted as I continued onto the beach.

"Maybe it's not that big of a deal," I remarked as I kneeled beside him, careful not to let any part of me touch his wet skin. "It *is* France, after all. Everyone here goes topless."

Brandon sat up fully, ignoring the tiny pebbles stuck to his elbows and back. He pushed a hand through his hair, not even bothering to shield his fascination with my naked breasts. I sat a little closer, bringing my nipples only an inch or so from his face. His mouth fell open, but he didn't move. His eyes flickered to my face, then back down. A drop of water fell off one nipple. Brandon bit his lip.

"Not...going....to work," he said with considerable effort, although he made no move away. His shorts, now soaked, did nothing to hide his arousal.

I smirked and stood up. Did he really think that's all I had? I swayed my hips as I retrieved the sun lotion, then came back to sit next to Brandon in the shallow water. He still hadn't moved, just watched silently as I squeezed another bit of lotion into my palms and rubbed them together.

"What are you doing?" he asked again after clearing his throat.

I glanced at him. "Time to reapply," I said, then started to rub the lotion over my chest again, this time making obvious circles around my breasts.

"Reapply?"

A muscle in the side of his neck ticked, and Brandon's eyes moved with the slow, deliberate movements of my hands.

"Of course," I said slowly as my palms slipped under my breasts to rub lotion there. "I have to get the newly exposed areas too."

I cupped my breasts and kneaded them softly, just as Brandon liked to do, usually when he was holding onto me from behind. His eyes widened even more as I pressed my fingers around the rounded swells, moving closer and closer to my nipples. His finger dug hard into the tiny pebbles.

"Unless," I said in a breathy voice, "you'd like to help."

I finally pressed my fingers into the hardened nubs of my nipples, coating them with just a bit of the coconut-scented lotion. I pinched them between my thumbs and forefingers. Brandon's eyes darkened into fathomless blue abysses. I moaned lightly. He lunged.

"Aaaah!" I squealed as I was tossed over a large shoulder. "I won! I won! I wo—"

My shouts were cut off when Brandon hurled me into the water.

"Ha!" I pointed triumphantly at him when I reemerged. "I won! That's dinner and dishes on you tonight, buddy!"

But my crows of victory were quickly silenced as Brandon yanked me into his arms and steered us quickly against the wall of limestone that shot up one side of the inlet. His mouth found mine with a deep, forceful kiss, and my legs immediately twisted around his waist.

"Worth it," he said before he fastened his mouth to one of my nipples and sucked. Hard.

"Ah!" I yelped. All triumph evaporated as lust exploded through me at the feel of his teeth. My hands threaded through his wet hair as he switched to the other side. "Fuck," I breathed, urging him closer.

Below the water, his fingers busied themselves with untying the sides my bikini.

"What-what are you doing?" It was my turn to speak breathlessly.

Brandon released my breast from his mouth as he tore my suit away and threw it onto a ledge above us. He attacked my mouth, sucking and nipping with the same vigor he'd just applied to my nipples.

"You didn't think you were going to get away with that, did you?" he asked in between torrid kisses, again and again. His hand slipped between us, and I felt his shorts disappear, replaced by his long length between my thighs.

"I—oh!" I cried as he found my entrance. "You're not really going to—Brandon, people could be on the trails up there. They could—oh—they could see us!"

"Like I give a shit," Brandon growled against my mouth. "Now who's winning, Red?"

And with that, he buried himself fully into my slick center, his mouth a frenzy as it moved between my mouth, my neck, my ear, and my breasts, sucking and biting as he thrust deeply into me.

"Brandon," I cried, barely managing to keep my hands in his hair. I was helpless against his onslaught—and I loved it.

He pried one of my hands from his hair and pressed it between us, urging me to find my clit while he continued to show just how much control he had over the rest of my body. I shuddered as my fingers found their familiar rhythm, and I buried my face in his powerful neck, sucking the salt water off his skin while he moved within me.

"Fuck," he hissed as his muscles tensed. "Baby, I'm close."

I quickened the pace of my fingers, and he tipped his head down for another feverish kiss.

"I want to see you come," he ordered, leveraging my body up to take him even deeper. "I want to see you scream with my dick inside you, out here, where anyone can see it."

His words, as always, were my undoing.

"Fuck," I gritted out as I strained against his merciless palms. His thick length pummeled into me. "Brandon, I'm-I'm going to come!"

"Squeeze me, baby," he ordered with one, two, three more powerful thrusts. "Now, Skylar! Let them hear you!"

I came with a cry that seemed to echo off the sides of the cliffs, followed by Brandon's strained shouts as he emptied himself into my depths. We shook together, our delirium flying off the water until we slid back into the waves as one, both of our bodies totally and completely spent.

Brandon pressed a long, languid kiss to my mouth, taking his time to savor my saltwater cries.

"God, I love you," he breathed into the space between us. "You break me, Skylar. You really do."

How could I tell him that he had invaded my entire being; that I couldn't imagine a day without him; that when I thought about my future, I saw him and nothing else? How could I say everything I felt when most of it, I couldn't put into words? Not even close.

So instead I kissed him and cupped the strong, square lines of his jaw.

"I love you," I told him back. "Only you. Always you."

Brandon's bright blue eyes shined with a brilliance that was more than just the reflection of the water. He kissed me once more with soft, tender lips, and gave me a smile of impossible sweetness.

"Always you," he repeated softly. "Always us."

~

Chapter 33

We spent the rest of the afternoon lounging around our inlet paradise. Brandon spent a fair amount of it openly staring, as I remained topless in French fashion, and several times he insisted I needed help reapplying yet another coat of sunblock. I was generally happy to let him so long as I could repay the favor.

Just as we were starting to think about the hike back to Marseille, a small boat turned into the gully that formed our small corridor of paradise. It looked like a fisherman's boat, not much more than a rowboat with a motor affixed to the end: the kind we'd seen drive past the distant end of the inlet all day but never enter. In the front stood a man with a pair of binoculars. As the boat drove close, he dropped them and started waving so wildly I genuinely thought he might fall off the small boat.

"Who's that?" I asked Brandon, who was lying on his back and reading the latest Neil Gaiman novel.

He dropped the book to his chest, then propped up on his elbows and looked to the water, his hand a visor over his face.

"What the..." he muttered. Then, with more recognition: "Oh!"

The boat came as close as it could without hitting the bottom of the lagoon, and the man hopped into the water with a splash.

"Christ, that's cold!" he yelped as he made his way to shore.

I frowned. The voice sounded familiar, but I couldn't quite place him.

"*There* you are, man. Are you trying to outrun the law or something? I have literally been looking for you all fucking day."

My jaw dropped when I finally recognized who stood in front of us, clad hilariously in slacks rolled up to his knees and a dress shirt soaked through with sweat. It was Cory Stewart, head of public relations for Sterling Ventures and Brandon's potential campaign manager. My stomach dropped. What the hell was he doing here?

Brandon looked like he was wondering the same thing. Without even looking my direction, Brandon swiped my shirt off the ground and threw it at my bare chest. After catching several of Cory's furtive glances, I obediently pulled it on.

Now that the show was over, Cory dropped next to Brandon and took a seat on the pebbled beach while he wiped sweat off his brow. The boat driver, who couldn't have been more than sixteen, tossed out an anchor and pulled a beer out of a cooler.

"I have been going in and out of this goddamn maze all day," Cory said before taking several gulps from a water bottle. "If it wasn't for the tracker on your cell phone, I never would have been able to find you."

"You have a tracker on his cell phone?" I asked sharply.

Brandon darted me a quick, blue look. "It's a precaution. With everything that's happened with your dad, I thought it might be a good idea if someone could find me in a pinch. For safety's sake, just in case something happens."

I gulped. Oh.

He turned a glare on Cory. "I'm pretty sure interrupting my vacation doesn't qualify. What are you doing here, Cory?" Brandon asked as he sat up completely and faced his subordinate.

Good question. I pushed my sunglasses on top of my head.

"There are things we need to discuss. You've been avoiding my calls," Cory replied with a pointed finger at his boss.

"It couldn't have waited another few days?" Brandon asked with a deep scowl that made me *very* glad I wasn't on its receiving end.

"Unfortunately, boss, it couldn't." Cory glanced at me as if just realizing that, apart from my breasts, I was actually there. "Maybe you should go for a swim, honey," he suggested with a smile that felt about as warm as ice water.

I quirked an eyebrow with all of the Brooklyn attitude I could muster. "Ex*cuse* me?"

Brandon placed a hand on my leg. "She's not going anywhere," he said. "Unlike you, if you don't start treating her with some respect. What the fuck, Cory?"

I swallowed, not wanting to get involved or cause trouble, even though I already *really* didn't like this guy. "Brandon, it's fine. I'll just pack up my stuff and start hiking back. You can catch up in a few minutes."

"You're not going anywhere," Brandon stated unequivocally, the hand on my thigh keeping me pinned to my towel.

I relaxed, and he released the pressure, although his hand stayed where it was. Considering how Cory was looking at me like a bug he

314

wanted to squish, I was perfectly fine with a little territorial show. I was feeling a bit territorial myself.

Cory looked back and forth between the hand and his boss's face.

"All right, fine," he said. "To be frank, things are going to shit. Gary Crown just announced he's running for mayor, which means there's yet another competitor for the DNC's endorsement. They want you, of course, but they're getting tired of waiting around. The board is yelling for a decision on the IPO or else they are threatening to vote you out, and Miranda—" he glanced back at me "—you sure you want her here?"

"Spit it out," Brandon ordered. "We don't have any secrets."

Cory blinked at me like he didn't quite believe that. I forced myself not to flinch.

"Fine. Miranda, your *wife*, just told us she is planning to take her story to the press if you don't get back to Boston. Immediately." Cory looked back to Brandon, who was now tensed and approximately the color of a tomato. "Basically, I've been dealing with a public relations shit show since you left, and I've been trying to call you for the last five days. *Five days*, man. I finally had to steal your itinerary off Margie's computer and come hunting for you."

Brandon sighed and rubbed a big hand over his forehead. The movement made the muscles in his chest and shoulder ripple.

"Do we need to go back?" I asked in a small voice, although my heart sank at the thought of it. I didn't want our vacation to end.

"No," Brandon mumbled through his fingers. He sent me a small smile. I was unconvinced.

"Boss," Cory said, but was quickly cut off.

"I said no," Brandon barked. He exhaled a long, slow breath, then looked at Cory. "Miranda's not going to say shit about what happened with Ricky O'Neill. Not about anything that matters. Otherwise she'd be in as much trouble as I would."

I gaped. I wasn't aware that anyone knew about that besides me, Miranda Sterling, and her deceased father. Sixteen years ago, Brandon had been a twenty-one-year-old financial wunderkind still spending half his time hustling pool halls with a group of friends in Dorchester, his old neighborhood. One night, they'd hustled the wrong people and found themselves in a fight that ended with the other group's ringleader, Ricky O'Neill, shot and killed. Brandon hadn't shot the gun, but he had been a target of the prosecution, only to be saved by Miranda's (false) alibi in exchange for a ten-year contract at her father's investment firm. That lie had eventually led to his romantic involvement with Miranda and their essentially loveless marriage. At least, loveless from his perspective.

Cory blew a raspberry through his thin lips and scratched his cropped hair. The actions made him look like a grumpy chimpanzee.

"Not *that* story," he said with another look my way.

Brandon cleared his throat. "You don't have to talk in euphemisms. Skylar knows everything."

Cory blinked with obvious surprise, then wiped another layer of sweat off his brow.

"Christ, it's hot," he complained. "How can you be sitting out here all day like this? It's fuckin' maniacal."

"Spit it out, Cory," Brandon said as he reached into his bag and pulled out a few bottles of water.

He opened one, took a sip, then offered it to me before tossing the other to Cory, who drank from it like a dying man in the desert.

"She wants to tell the story of you and your friend here," Cory continued after he had drained half the bottle. "Cause a fuckin' public relations nightmare, that's what she wants to do. Turn herself into the wronged woman. Listen, your little stunt at that benefit last month really fucked things up. I thought you were going to keep things quiet until the papers had been signed, man. Instead you turn around and flaunt your sidepiece all over Boston. Did you really think your *wife* was going to let her humiliate her like that and get awa—Hey!"

He wasn't able to finish his sentence before he was lifted bodily off the beach and hurled into the water. Brandon stood at the water's edge, chest heaving with the sudden effort.

"What the *fuck*, man!" Cory yowled from where he sat chest-deep in the water. He stood up with another big splash. "This is Armani! What the fuck was that for?"

Behind Brandon, I couldn't help but laugh, although I tried to cover it as a cough. I wasn't successful.

"I told you, Cory. Respect," Brandon said as he stood to his full height and crossed his arms over his chest.

"You don't pay me for respect, boss," Cory retorted as he swished back to the beach. "Ah! What the fuck is that!"

He scrambled the rest of the way out, and I had to hide my face behind my hand to stop from laughing as he circled around his body, looking for signs of sea life that might be stuck to him. Brandon didn't even bother to hide his laughter, carved abs flexing with every loud hoot. Then he pressed a brief kiss to my head before sitting easily with his arms lounged over his knees.

"Skylar's off-limits," he said to Cory, who had finally calmed down enough to accept the extra towel as he sat down next to Brandon. "You're the best at what you do, Cory, but I pay you to tell me like it is and fix shit. The insults are done if you want to keep your job."

Silently, Cory nodded, although his jaw clenched as water dripped off his chin.

"And remember that one of these days, *she* might be your boss too," Brandon said.

My stomach flipped. What did that mean?

Cory's soaked, rodent-like gaze flickered between the two of us before he cleared his throat.

"I apologize," he said through clenched teeth, although he was barely able to make eye contact with me.

"It's fine," I said. I looked back to Brandon. "It sounds like you guys have a lot to sort through. Should we start hiking back?"

"Fuck no, we're not hiking. Not if you want me out of here by tomorrow." Cory stood up, brushed the tiny pebbles off his pants, and jerked his head toward the boat.

Brandon followed his gaze, then blew out a resigned sigh. "I think Cory's right, Red. We need to get back to the house sooner rather than later." He gave me a rueful grimace. "Can you forgive me?"

Cory didn't even try to hide the disgust on his face at the question, but I just smiled and nodded.

"Of course," I said. "Whatever you need."

Brandon rewarded me with a bright smile that seemed to reflect off the impossibly clear waters in front of us, then leaned in to give me a quick, but thorough kiss. His hand snaked around my waist and gripped my shirt. The electricity mounted between us again; it was always there, just below the surface.

He released me with a grunt. "Damn," he murmured, too low for Cory to hear him. "I *was* hoping to make you scream on those rocks again before we left."

Something buzzed inside me, and I tried and failed not to blush. Brandon grinned, then turned back to Cory, who quickly resumed a bland expression.

"Well, you should probably stay for dinner," Brandon said. "Apparently, we've got some shit to take care of." He looked over his manager's shoulder to the boat driver, who was sound asleep on the bench. "That is, if our driver isn't already passed out for the evening."

"I'll fuckin' tow the boat back to Marseille myself if I have to," Cory said. "Now, let's just get your shit and go."

~

I ended up sending myself to the local market to pick up dinner, since after sitting in a boat with Cory for the twenty minutes it took to get back to town, I was heartily sick of the man. He reminded me of a cartoon rodent, one of those *Looney Tunes* characters who played slick bankers and traveling salesmen. He never stopped talking. I had absolutely no idea what Brandon saw in him, other than the fact that he seemed to be obsessed with his job, which was protecting Brandon's image, and the fact that he seemed to be good at it.

When I came back to the villa, the sun was already starting to set over the cliffs to the west of the city, and I paused for a moment on the front stoop to take it in. Pools of magenta, violet, gold, and tangerine streamed from the horizon, with craggy shapes of the cliffs blocking the rays like shadows of primeval ruins.

I sighed. Even though we still technically had a few days left, Cory's presence seemed to portend an early end of our blissful two weeks. I hugged myself close and closed my eyes, lost for a moment in the memories. Whatever stresses were coming for us, we'd always have this time. Brandon must have known we'd need it, and I was incredibly thankful for that foresight.

Voices filtered from the patio to where I stood below: Cory and Brandon, still debating how to resolve all of the drama.

"The board will keep as long as you call Karen Richards tomorrow," Cory was saying. "But you can't fuckin' forget, boss."

I moved to open the door, not wanting to eavesdrop, but stopped when I heard my name.

"Now, what about the Skylar situation?"

"What situation?" Brandon asked sharply. "You said it yourself. Miranda already knows, so it doesn't matter anymore, does it? I'm not going to skulk around like we're doing something wrong."

"So, it doesn't matter that to the Catholic half of Boston, you're absolutely doing something wrong?"

"If Miranda doesn't want to be embarrassed, she should just sign the fucking divorce papers and be done with it!"

There was a loud screech of a chair leg on tile, then footsteps pacing––Brandon's, most likely. I could easily see him pulling his hands through his hair in frustration.

"It's not just that," Cory said. "The Miranda thing...it will blow over eventually. People will figure out that she's been hanging on you for years, and I agree that at some point she's going to realize it makes her look clingy as fuck. But Brandon, you asked me to vet you, and I did."

There was a long sigh. I couldn't tell if it was Cory or Brandon.

Cory continued. "That means I had to vet her. And her family's connections to the mob don't exactly make her a great candidate for First Lady, if you know what I mean."

"Cory, I swear to fuckin' God...do you want me to toss you into the harbor this time?"

"Hey man, it has to be said! You need simple right now, man, and she is not that. She's young and hot, I'll give you that. I'd want to hit that too––"

"You can stop right the fuck there."

"Brandon, the Brooklyn D.A. has an open investigation that lists her father!" Cory protested. "Not to mention that her grandfather was basically a runner for the Gottis until he was whacked. Don't even get me started on her stepdad. Maurice Jadot is one shady fuck. All I'm saying is, there are a lot of other redheaded fish in the sea, my friend."

There was an awkward pause, filled only with the din of a car driving down the street. I froze, my insides twisted together. Say something, I thought, mentally urging Brandon to stand up for us like he'd always done. In all of my worries about the dramas in Brandon's life, I'd never considered the fact that my family's history might be his undoing as well. How naive.

I was about to walk inside when Cory spoke again.

"I see," he said to some unspoken communication.

I wished more than anything I could see the expression on Brandon's face.

"Then I have to ask," Cory continued. "Is there anything else we need to know about her? Anything else that might come up in a character attack? I'm not saying you can't run, my friend. If there's anything we know from this last election, it's that literally anyone can get into office. If I can't get *you* elected, I have absolutely no business being in marketing. But it will be a whole hell of a lot easier if we can control the narrative."

"There's nothing." Brandon's voice was pulled tight as a drum.

Cory waited a few beats, then sighed.

"All right," he said, although he clearly thought it was anything but. "Just...be careful, will you? Keep it casual. Take it slow. Maybe don't be seen making out on the street together?"

"We'll take it exactly the way it needs to go," Brandon said.

I clutched my groceries tighter to my chest. What did that mean?

But he didn't say anything else, and the conversation turned to discussing a press release planned for Ventures. I entered the house and walked up the short flight of stairs to the main floor.

Brandon and Cory both turned from their seats on the balcony, beers in hand, with completely opposite expressions: a dark cloud over Cory's pointed features, while Brandon's chiseled face brightened immediately. Even with Cory sitting there, I couldn't help but smile back. The twisting in my belly lessened.

"Hey, beautiful," Brandon said as he stood up to greet me with a kiss.

I didn't have to look at Cory's face to see the irritation at the affection.

Brandon looked eagerly into the bags I had set on the dining table. "What do we have here?"

"Oh, you know, the goods. Wine, cheese, bread, charcuterie. A bunch of local fruits and veggies." I sighed as I pulled out the food. "I'll never get enough of French markets."

Brandon walked into the kitchen to grab dishes for the three of us. Cory meandered in and looked suspiciously at the food.

"Isn't the cheese here unpasteurized?" he asked with a frown.

I rolled my eyes. "The best cheese in the world is from France. You might actually like it if you gave it a chance."

The words came out before I could stop them, and Cory flashed me another look of blatant irritation. Behind us, Brandon chuckled.

Cory narrowed his beady eyes. "I'll try it," he mumbled.

As Brandon set down our plates and glasses next to the impromptu buffet, my phone buzzed in my pocket.

"Hold on, it's Bubbe," I said, and stepped out of the room, leaving Brandon and Cory to take their loaded plates back to the balcony table.

"Hi, Bubbe," I said once I was in the bedroom. "Is everything all right?"

"Hi, sweetheart," came my grandmother's low, thickly accented voice. "Everything is fine, it's fine. We were just calling to...check when you were coming back."

I frowned as I sat down on the bed. "Really? That's all?"

There was a brief silence, then a sigh.

"Well...your father...it's nothing, but I think he'd like to see you."

There was some shuffling, like she was moving to a different room. In a slightly hushed tone, she continued.

"I just think he could use a pick-me-up from his daughter is all," Bubbe said.

"Katie hasn't been coming back around, has she?" I asked sharply, my hand twisting the edge of the bed sheets. There had been no word from the security team, but that didn't mean she wasn't texting or contacting Dad in other ways.

"No, no, no," Bubbe assured me. "Not since you were here last." She paused again, and something about the reticence in her voice made my heart beat a little faster. "But the thing is, *bubbela*," she continued, "he missed his group therapy session two days ago. He said he just went for a walk, but honey, I don't know...I couldn't reach him for several hours, and he lost the security."

My spine prickled with the thought of where my dad might have ended up, depressed, upset, and alone. I toyed with the end of my ponytail and made a decision. This had gone on long enough.

"Bubbe?"

"What, sweetheart?"

"Dad needs to get out of New York. It's time."

There was a silence, then a long sigh.

"Yes," she said sadly. "I think you're right."

"I'm going to look into a program up here for him," I said. "Brandon will help, and I'll figure out the finances. But we need to get Dad out of Brooklyn. Out of that scene, at least until his hand heals. You could come too..."

Bubbe scoffed openly, like I knew she would.

"And what would I do up in that city?" she asked. "I am a Brooklyn Jew, *bubbela*, always have been, always will be."

"You could be a Brooklyn Jew in Boston for a while," I offered, though I already knew the answer. Bubbe wouldn't leave Brooklyn as long as she had an active bone in her body.

"I'll be fine here, Skylar," she said, although she couldn't quite get rid of the sadness in her voice. "You just get everything ready for Danny. Don't worry about me."

Like that would ever happen. But instead, I just said, "All right, Bubbe. Will do. I'll call you when I get back next week, and we'll figure out the next steps, okay?"

"Okay, sweetheart. You give that handsome man of yours my love, and a kiss for you too."

I blinked. It wasn't like Bubbe to be so openly affectionate. Things must be worse than I thought.

"I will," I said softly. "My love to you and Dad."

~

The developments of the day hung over us like clouds as Brandon and I curled together beneath the gauzy canopy of the bed, the French doors left open to let in the warm night breeze. Our vacation had started out idyllically, but now the stresses of home had found us across an ocean and a sea.

We lay separately, facing each other in the moonlight. Whether it was the unexpected disruption of Cory (and the awkward dinner that had gone late into the night) or Bubbe's phone call, which I'd relayed to Brandon after Cory had left, something had shifted. The carefree mood was gone, and we were left with what remained: the joy of being together, but the knowledge that another tide of change was coming.

"I think it's good," Brandon was saying about Bubbe's and my decision. "It's progress, especially if we can convince her to move too at some point." He pressed his lips together, then nodded to himself. "I'll have Margie find an apartment for him close to a good rehabilitation center. We'll have David drive him to Boston next weekend."

"You don't need to do that," I started to say, but Brandon silenced me with an exasperated look.

"Stop," he said. "You're about to start a new job that is going to ask more of you than anything else you've ever done. I should know; I'm the one who usually does the asking."

I rolled my eyes, but I knew he was right. Come Monday, I'd soon be working close to eighty hours a week for the foreseeable future. I'd barely have time to eat, let alone go down to Brooklyn every other weekend to keep Dad out of trouble. It was why I had already admitted to Bubbe I'd let Brandon help.

"All right," I relented.

Brandon only offered a brief smile in return.

We lapsed into silence again, content just to gaze at one another. Under other circumstances, I might have found us nauseatingly sweet, but right now, I just was content to enjoy the quiet.

"God, you're beautiful," Brandon murmured for the umpteenth time on our trip. Every so often he'd interrupt our light conversation to say it, and each time, he made me blush.

I buried my face in my pillow, but couldn't keep the silly grin away. "You are ridiculous."

When I looked back at him, he was still staring at me. His tanned features were dark against the white of the pillow case, and in the moonlight, his eyes glittered like stars. He reached out a finger to trace the edge of my cheekbone.

"I'm just a man in love," he said softly.

The words warmed me all over. It was these moments that made me feel like we could last always, that nothing could break us. I wished with all of my heart that were true.

Brandon played with my fingers. Our hands were so different: mine were so long and slim compared to his big paws.

"You aren't..." he started as he stared at our interwoven hands. "Do you...you aren't hiding anything from me...are you, Skylar?"

When he looked back at me, Brandon's eyes were wide sapphires in the night, but they glowed with something other than happiness.

I hugged my pillow closer, trying and failing to ignore the pang of guilt in my stomach. *Green eyes or blue?*

"Why do you ask?"

He searched my face, then sighed and shook his head.

"No reason," he said. "Just...sometimes I get the feeling like you're maybe holding something back." He shook his head with a rueful smile. "Sorry. It's probably all in my head."

Now was the time to tell him. I had been waiting for months, waiting for a time when we weren't inundated with work drama, family drama, exam studying, and all the other excuses I'd amassed. If we were going to move forward, we had to be one hundred percent open with each other. I knew that.

But.

I opened my mouth, and nothing came out. The words clogged in my throat, and the pang in my stomach grew while my skin crawled and crackled, like it was made of glass.

Brandon had been hurt so much in his life. By his mother, his father. His foster parents, his wife. By me.

I couldn't bear to do it again.

~

Chapter 34

It was early on our last day when Brandon and I drove to Carcassonne. Cory had left early yesterday morning, giving us a final twenty-four hours together before we headed back to chaos. Instead of leaving from Marseille, we decided to lock up the villa early and fly out of the old medieval city perched on a hill above Provence, with a few hours to sightsee before our flight.

We parked the rental car at the base of the hill and meandered down one of the side streets in search of a *boulangerie* where we could get a quick breakfast that we could walk around with. We walked up the road that wound around the base of the old city. The old part of Carcassonne was an almost perfectly preserved medieval city, a cluster of turrets, towers, and medieval-themed shops all encircled by a massive stone wall.

We arrived just as the shops and inns were starting to open and meandered around the city for well over an hour, poking our heads into some of the older buildings and exploring the multiple courtyards and towers of the maze-like complex. As I watched Brandon inspect the execution block, I imagined him in a blaze of armor, gleaming silver in the sunlight. He really would have been the perfect knight.

When he caught me watching, his smile was blinding. His hair, wavy and bright, caught on the wind. Two weeks in the French sun had bleached his mop of normally dark blond a vivid gold. Comfortable and relaxed, he looked the exact opposite of the stolid attorney I had first met last January.

We picked up another few coffees and croissants before walking to the outer wall of the city to take in the view over the rest of Carcassonne.

"I have to tell you something," Brandon said as he leaned over the stone edge.

I turned to look at him. Behind him stood towers bearing bright blue flags from their conical roofs. I had no problem seeing Brandon, with his strong, tall back and sharp-lined face, as a feudal lord. He looked like a modern-day King Arthur, presiding over the streets of Camelot. It fit.

"You're going to run," I said.

He'd had that pensive look on his face all morning. Cory had left with a final admonishment to "make a fuckin' decision." Brandon couldn't put it off any longer.

The wind turned up Brandon's hair, ruffling it lightly. He rubbed a hand over his chin, which currently had about four days' worth of growth on it. I knew it would disappear before Monday, and I was sorry for it. I was enjoying the Viking-look on him, particularly when he looked at me with a clear intent to pillage.

"I am going to run," he said out loud as he looked over the stucco houses below, and beyond them to the vineyards and sunflower fields in the distance. "But only if you're on board. I can't do this without you. I don't *want* to do it without you."

I gazed out at the view with him. We didn't touch while he waited for me to process his words. But I'd had enough time to process over the last few weeks. The sunlight gleamed on the silver bracelet he'd given me, and I considered the words on the inside. We were beyond the point of pulling away. A man like Brandon Sterling wasn't made to stay behind closed doors, and I didn't want him to. It was time to get over my fears and step out with him.

"If this is what you want," I said, "then I'm with you."

Brandon gave me a cautious smile. "Really?"

I took his palm between my hands. "All in, right? Isn't that what we're doing here?"

The smile turned up to about a thousand watts.

"All in," Brandon repeated. Then he sighed and shook his head. "Mark's going to be pissed, that's for sure. So will the board of Ventures. They've all been trying to convince me not to do it." He grimaced. "I'm going to have to divest from both Ventures and Sterling Grove. I'll be able to give Miranda whatever she wants, but more importantly, I'll be free of any conflicts of interest."

I didn't miss the slight thrill in the word "free." In the last two weeks, I had started to wonder just how attached Brandon really was to his companies these days. Whenever his phone rang, as it did multiple times an hour, he almost always scowled. When I'd met him, he'd said he enjoyed his job, but the longer I knew him, the more it seemed like he wanted something different. Apparently, it was this, the mayor's mansion.

Something sunk in my heart, but I did my best to stay bright. It didn't matter whether or not I wanted him to do this. If this was his dream, then I wasn't going to stand in his way. If this was his dream, I just wanted to support him.

Brandon wrapped his fingers around mine and squeezed.

"So, if that weren't enough, I have a favor to ask you," he said.

My stomach clenched even more. That couldn't preface anything good.

"There's another event on Sunday after we get back."

I pulled my hand away, already shaking my head. "No, no, no."

"It's not going to be like last time. For starters, I'll actually show up on time." He flashed a sheepish grin, and I couldn't help but smile back.

"Brandon, I just don't think...Cory has a point. It's best if I stay out of sight until everything is settled with Miranda."

The thought of having to go back to being together incognito made me feel sick to my stomach, but it was better than the other option of inflaming Miranda to the point where she'd want to plaster our affair all over the tabloids. I could deal with a few more months of secrecy if it meant I'd get to be with Brandon in peace in the end.

But Brandon shook his head adamantly. "I'm going to announce my candidacy on Sunday," he said plainly. His eyes were wide and blue as he spoke, searching my face for a reaction. "Please, Red," he said. "I need you there."

We watched each other, letting the sound of the wind sweeping up the hillside and through the tunnels of the old city fill the space between us. A few strands of my hair escaped the braid on my shoulder, and Brandon reached out to gently push them behind my ear. We were locked in a trance, my green eyes lost in his blue pools, the earnest lines of his face tense as he waited.

I took a bite of my croissant to buy more time. I really wasn't ready for this, but it was here. I could stay with him and deal with the fallout of the attention, or I could be left behind.

I already knew which choice I would make. But before I could relent, Brandon spoke again.

"Will you marry me, Red?"

The question floated on the wind, so low I almost thought I'd imagined it. It wasn't until I caught his gaze, shyly and carefully watching for my reaction, that I realized it was real.

I immediately choked on my croissant and started to cough.

"Jesus!" Brandon moved quickly to pound me on the back.

The tiny piece of pastry flew over the edge of the castle wall and into the dry grass piled below. I grabbed the edge to regain my balance, heaving breaths. In, out, in, out. It wasn't until I felt like I wasn't going to collapse that I looked back at Brandon.

"Are you okay?" he asked warily.

"Did you," I heaved another breath between my words, "just ask me...to *marry*...you?"

Brandon quirked his mouth in a shy half-smile. "Yes...?"

My jaw dropped, and I blinked. "You asked me to marry you. Like you were...asking for a Coke. Or if we should go get brunch."

Brandon bit his lip, the amusement in his expression quickly giving way more to fear.

"Well, I can do it again if you like," he said. "I could probably manage to kneel. Maybe rustle up some flowers. One of these vendors has to have something."

I couldn't tell if it was a joke.

"Seriously, though." He rushed in to stand closer, taking my hand in his and thumbing over my knuckles. His tall form blocked out the sun. His earnest face was all I could see. "Will you? Would you? Marry me, I mean."

All of the blood must have completely drained from my face, because his hand dropped to my waist, and he steered me to the nearest bench.

"Skylar, are you okay?" he asked me again as I sat down next to him. "Do you need to put your head between your legs or something?"

I took another deep breath, then exhaled slowly. I did it again. And again. Finally, when things seemed to be running normally again, I was able to look at Brandon. He still hadn't let go of my hand, and gripped it even tighter.

"This is..." I started, "really...unexpected." I tugged at my hand, and had to pull it away a bit more violently to get it free.

"So I guess that's a no, then," Brandon said dryly, unable to keep the bitterness out of his voice.

"Don't do that," I said quietly. "Please. This is a lot, you have to admit. On top of everything else."

"Do I?" he asked petulantly.

I bristled. "*Yes.* You *do!*" I took a deep breath. I didn't want to lose my temper, but it was incredibly frustrating that he couldn't seem to see what he was piling on me. "Brandon," I tried again. "Please listen."

As if unable to bear the short distance between us, he pulled me onto his lap, securing me against his chest while he played with my left hand, weaving his large fingers in between mine.

"I didn't plan it," he said as he toyed with my bare ring finger. His blue eyes blazed, more vibrant than the sky. "This moment. These last two weeks," he continued. "Skylar, it's been perfect, hasn't it?"

I softened. "Of course it has. It's been a dream. But Brandon—"

"I just want that to continue," he said, staring down at my fingers like they might combust in his hands. Like everything around us might evaporate.

When he looked at me again, his eyes were almost pained with naked yearning.

"I love you so fucking much, Skylar," he said. "You have no idea how much this time has meant to me. To wake up in the mornings with you in my arms. To know that even when I'm stuck on a conference call, I can hold you in my lap."

"Brandon, I'm not a lap dog," I said. "Even if we get married, I'm not going to follow you around like a puppy. I'm starting my own career in literally three days." I stroked his cheek, reveling in the feel of his soft hair.

His blue eyes cast downward. "I know. And I want you to have that, Red. I want you to pursue whatever dreams you want." He looked at me again, eyes full of love. "I just want to be there with you. I want to be your center, where you come back to. Because you're mine, babe."

I frowned and shook my head. "I'm not yours. I don't belong to you, like all your fancy things. I'm a person, Brandon, not something to collect."

Brandon chewed on his bottom lip for a moment, then pressed his forehead to mine, so that we shared the same breath.

"You're right," he said finally. "I had it the wrong way around. You're not mine. I'm yours. *I* belong to *you*. You're like the sun to me, Skylar. I can't see without you."

All my reserve broke at his words, and I wished more than anything we were not sitting on a very public bench, surrounded by groups of tourists. I kissed him tenderly on the mouth. His hand slipped around my head as he held me there, reveling in my lips in the soft morning light. When he let me go, he smiled, but his smile dropped when he caught the look on my face. He must have seen the words I was going to say next.

"If I'm the sun," I said carefully, "and you're mine—because you *are*, Brandon, you really are—then I'm not going anywhere. And that's the truth. I promise."

I cupped his face and nuzzled my nose against his, delighting in the unique scent of him. The strong, lean arm around my waist tightened, but Brandon sighed.

"So that's a 'no'," he murmured. He said it lightly, but couldn't quite mask the regret.

"That's a 'not right now'," I corrected him gently with another kiss, as sweet as I could muster.

He caught my lower lip between his teeth, and pulled me in for something much more potent that took my breath away. When he released me, his eyes were bright blue fire.

"I'm going to hold you to that, Red," he said. His tone joked, but his face said otherwise. My stomach tightened in response, but with fear or anticipation, I couldn't tell.

"Okay," I said. "Okay."

~

Chapter 35

In Boston, we returned to chaos.

"Jesus," I said as we looked out from the tinted windows of the private airfield's reception area.

Behind us, the staff of the airfield watched curiously while they manned the nearly empty area. To their credit, they probably weren't totally unused to seeing paparazzi at an airfield that regularly serviced semi-famous clients. The agent had seemed more annoyed than anything else when she'd informed Brandon of their presence. They had at least tripled in numbers since we left.

Brandon pushed a hand through his hair and sighed. Still in his vacation clothes— gray joggers, a red hoodie that hugged the contours of his arms, and his favorite frayed Red Sox hat—he looked a far sight from the CEO that most of Boston knew. His cheeks were still covered with dark blond shag I knew would be gone in the morning. Even after seven hours of flying and dealing with some serious jet lag, I wanted to devour him.

"Goddamn it," he muttered as he pulled his phone out of his pocket to check a message. He grimaced. "I should have requested security. I'm sorry about this, Red."

"Well, we knew this might be waiting for us."

I spoke casually, although the reality was actually kind of terrifying. The plane ride home had been spoiled with the news that Miranda had broken her story early. Apparently, Page Six had received a tip that we were in France together, so Miranda had decided to give an exclusive interview to *People*. It was a sympathetic puff piece in which she portrayed herself as the poor, blindsided wife who had only tried to make her marriage work. I, on the other hand, was a young, gold-digging homewrecker, but still anonymous, thank God.

"Maybe I should hang back," I said cautiously. "You don't need to be seen with me."

Brandon glanced at me with a frown. "Goddamn it," he said again. "*No*. We have nothing to hide, Skylar."

I clenched my teeth as I looked out at the mob behind the chain-linked fence. "If you say so."

I sighed and looked down at my clothes. After catching my reflection in the window, the idea of parading in front of paparazzi sounded really bad. Like Brandon, I was also dressed for comfort in black leggings, ballet flats, and a summer jacket. My hair was still in its braid over my shoulder, but looked a bit worse for wear, and I had foregone contacts in favor of my glasses.

"Should I at least change or something?"

Brandon snorted. "Don't give these leeches the satisfaction." He tugged me close for a brief kiss, ignoring the even more curious looks of the other few people in the small terminal. "Stop that," he said as I reached up to pat at my hair. "You look fucking adorable. Don't change a hair on your head." He spotted David waving at us from the street. "Come on, Red," he said as he pulled the bill of his cap low over his face. He glanced down at me as we walked toward the door. "You might want to put on your sunglasses instead."

As we walked out to the curb beyond the fence, Brandon worked to shield me from the wall of paparazzi, pushing back their eager bodies so that we could get down the sidewalk, although the clench of his jaw and the visible vein in his neck didn't go unnoticed, especially when one of them reached out to tug on my jacket.

"What's your name, miss? Are you Brandon's new girlfriend?" he asked.

"Hey! Step off, man!" Brandon pulled me more securely behind his large frame.

With a glare that should have turned the photographer to ash, he tucked me into the backseat of the car, safely behind its tinted windows. The photographers crowded the car, their bodies pushing against the glass so hard I thought it might break.

"Drive," Brandon commanded.

The Mercedes took off. Brandon looked at the smudge marks left on the windows with disgust.

"Fucking animals," he said, but his scowl morphed to sympathy when he got a look at me in the opposite corner.

I pulled off my sunglasses and took a shaky breath.

"Come here," Brandon said and pulled me into the crook of his shoulder

I sighed, letting my racing heart calm against his warmth, although I could hear his heart beating almost as fast. If I closed my eyes, I could pretend we weren't back in Boston. Brandon's hoodie still smelled like Marseille: of sunlight and grapevines and salty air. I inhaled deeply.

"I'm sorry," Brandon murmured, although he didn't loosen his grip around my shoulders.

I shook my head into his chest. "Not your fault."

"Well, it's my crazy ex that's doing it. It's partly my fault."

I wriggled out of his vise-hold to kiss him. The gesture seemed to soothe at least some of his guilt, and the tension in his shoulders fell slightly.

"We knew it was coming," I said. "I'll deal with it."

Brandon dipped his head for another kiss, this one a bit more intense than the last, and nuzzled my nose.

"Where did you come from?" he wondered with a sigh, and then pulled out his phone and started a text to Margie. "I'm going to hire us some extra security. It won't be like this for long, but I'm not a very good bodyguard."

I shrugged. I wasn't sure that was necessary, but then again, the wall of photographers had been pretty damn scary. I'd hate to be crowded like that if someone ended up getting violent. I fingered the edge of my jacket, still crinkled in the spot where the photographer had grabbed me. It was way too easy to see it getting worse.

I was surprised when the car merged onto the 26 toward Copley instead of getting off in the North End.

"Brandon," I said as I glanced toward the jagged buildings of my neighborhood, "I need to go home. I'm supposed to start work in three days, and I have stuff to do."

"I know," he said as he thumbed through his phone. "But I need to grab a few things at my place." He looked up, as if suddenly confused. "Did you *want* to stay apart tonight?"

I softened at his obvious desire to be close. "Well, I just thought...maybe you'd want some space. Watching me do laundry and clean my room isn't exactly exciting stuff."

Brandon perked a blond brow at me. "I don't know. You could probably make it pretty interesting. Especially if you do it naked."

I rolled my eyes, but still flushed at his wolfish expression. "Seriously, though. Don't you want a break from me?"

He sighed and absently kissed the back of my hand. "Um, no. I like the doldrums with you, Red. Did you forget that I asked you to move in with me just a few months ago?"

The lamps outside flashed across his face, which was warm, but inquisitive. I hadn't forgotten about that night, of course. A night when Brandon had made love to me on the giant (and ridiculous) piano he'd bought me, when he'd said he loved me, over and over again. When he'd asked me to live with him, I'd accepted. He showed me just how happy he *really* was about that, and then we'd promptly been discovered by his ex-wife.

It all seemed like a very long time ago.

I looked at his face for any kind of joke, but Brandon appeared to be completely earnest.

I cracked a small smile. "You want to play house with me."

With a grin that lit up the car, Brandon tugged at the braid on my shoulder. "Baby, I am *dying* to play house with you."

The sudden intensity of his blue eyes, somehow unfathomably bright even in the shadowy car interior, made me lose my breath. After a beat, Brandon finally dropped my hair.

"Besides," he said, "you don't know this yet, but you are barely going to have time to see me for the next, oh, five years or so. It will be everything I can do to convince Kieran to give you one night off a month."

I snorted. "It's not going to be that bad."

In return, all I got was a skeptical look that made the lines across his forehead wrinkle hilariously.

"You'll see," was all he said.

The car pulled into the garage in the back of Brandon's building, but there was another horde of paparazzi huddled outside the main entrance as we drove by. I shuddered.

"They really are vultures, aren't they?" I remarked.

Brandon just hugged me closer and kissed the top of my head. "Don't worry. They'll lose interest, and then we can figure the rest of this shit out together."

Once in the elevator, the fatigue of travel hit us both. It felt like it was five in the morning instead of eleven o'clock at night. By the time the elevator doors opened, I didn't care anymore about how much I disliked this apartment. I was ready to pull Brandon into his bedroom, and tire us both out to the point where we wouldn't wake up at four in the morning because of jet lag.

Unfortunately, we were going to have to wait. Cory Stewart was sitting comfortably on Brandon's couch when we walked in. His sharp glare found our clasped hands, flickered coldly to me, then looked to Brandon.

"Cory," Brandon said evenly. "It couldn't keep until the morning?"

"'Fraid not, boss. Miranda gave another interview that's going to be on the front page of the *Globe* tomorrow morning. Here, this is from a friend there."

He held out his phone to both Brandon and me to show us a proof of the story. An old picture of Miranda and Brandon, looking impossibly young and gorgeous together, was just under a headline that read "**Local Boy Does Good or Does Dirty?**" I took the phone and scrolled through the article. There was my name, printed loud and clear:

His new paramour appears to be a new Harvard Law graduate and former intern from Sterling Grove, Skylar Crosby. Their relationship raises several concerns about Sterling's ethics in the context of his rumored run for mayor.

The blood drained from my head all at once, and I was glad there was a sofa under my legs to catch me.

"Oh," I said as I leaned forward to put my head between my knees "Oh, God. Oh, *fucking* God!"

Brandon didn't say anything, just stared at the screen for a few seconds while his face turned bright red and looked like smoke was about to come whistling from his ear and nose. Then, all at once with an explosive movement, he picked up Cory's empty coffee cup off the table and hurled it the wall, where it shattered with a resounding crash.

"Fuck!" he yelled, tugging his hat off his head and sending it in the same direction as the mug.

He turned to Cory, who had the decency to cower a little bit, his eyes darting at the broken ceramic and coffee staining the white walls. I couldn't have cared less about the mess; I was struggling just to breathe.

"You couldn't have stopped this?" Brandon demanded. "What the fuck do I pay you for, Cory?"

Cory crossed his thin arms and frowned. "I'm not Miranda's keeper, boss. I did my best to hold off the *Globe*, but no amount of campaign access was going to stop them from running this story."

"They didn't need to bring Skylar into it. You couldn't have kept her name out of it?" Brandon growled, gesturing toward me. "Fuck!"

He sat on the couch next to me and reached a hand to my leg, but I curled inward, pulling my knees up against my chest and resting my forehead on the thin fabric of my leggings. I felt like I was going to throw up. Brandon looked like he wanted to tear apart the entire room. I just focused on breathing.

"I don't think I should go tomorrow night," I mumbled into my kneecaps.

"I agree," Cory said curtly above me.

When I looked up, he was watching me with a hard expression. I couldn't blame him. He was an asshole, but my presence in Brandon's life was making his job incredibly difficult.

"*No*," Brandon said even more emphatically beside me.

I looked at him. "Brandon. Let's be practical here. Tomorrow's announcement could be a way for you to deflect. You show up, look like your Camelot-looking self, and the whole city will think Miranda is just being desperate. But if I show up with you, *I'll* be the narrative, and you'll lose your momentum. Bad for you, and I *really* don't want this kind of attention."

Brandon stared at me with a pained expression, then shook his head. "Skylar, I told you, baby, I'm not doing this without you. If you don't come, Miranda wins. That's exactly what she wants!"

"No, she wins if I show up and pull the focus away from you," I replied. "All the more reason that I should stay away."

"I agree," Cory said again, although he seemed as surprised as I was that we were on the same page. "You have a chance to change the narrative here, boss. You make your announcement tomorrow night, and nobody's going to give a shit that your jealous, soon-to-be ex is throwing around her sob story. She'll just look like a desperate woman trying to hang onto the spotlight."

Then Cory sighed. "Look, I'll be straight. It honestly won't matter that much to *you* if she goes. You might look a bit like a ladies' man, but that's never stopped voters before." He bit his lip and nodded at me. "But it will matter for her. She'll look like the other woman in a town where half the people here don't believe in divorce. They'll say she's wrecking your marriage. That she only wants you for your money. You want me to go on?"

Brandon pressed his lips together so hard they turned white. I knew what he was thinking. For some reason, any mention of me as an extramarital affair, even though that's technically what I was, really, *really* pissed him off. He squeezed my hand hard enough that I had to pull it away and shake it out to make the blood return.

"I want to know where the fuck the *Globe* got a second source to confirm your name," he bit out.

"What the fuck does that matter?" Cory exploded. "The whole fucking world saw you holding her hand at the NECA benefit. This is what I've been telling you from the beginning!"

Brandon's eyes flashed at me. "You don't think Eric or Jane..."

I shook my head vehemently. "Absolutely not. And before you ask, neither would Bubbe or my dad."

Cory snorted, but quieted when I shot him a quick glare.

Finally, Brandon shook his head, and looked back at me, blue eyes pleading. "I still want you there."

"Brandon—" I started.

"Please," he said. "We can go separately, if it makes the two of you feel better. You can come with Cory, and he can bring you around the back of the hotel. There's no pictures of you anywhere yet; no one will know who you are. But I need to know you're there, Red. My family will be there—Ray and Susan are coming. And you're my family now too."

I realized then just how nervous he was about all of this. Brandon, a man who, beneath his confident exterior and many accomplishments, was someone who desperately sought the approval of those he loved. And now he was about to announce his entry into politics, a notoriously loveless industry. He wouldn't admit it in front of Cory, but I could see the truth in his deep blue eyes: he was terrified. He needed to have people who loved him in his corner while he took this huge leap of faith, and I was at the top of that list.

So I ignored what my instincts were telling me. I squeezed his hand. "Okay," I said. "I'll be there."

Brandon's shoulders relaxed noticeably, and he dropped his head onto my shoulder. "Thank you."

I wove my fingers into his hair while he buried his face in my neck. Cory threw his hands up in the air and swore profusely.

"Stop," Brandon said without taking his head off my shoulder. He pulled me closer, enveloping me in his strong arms. "I pay you enough, you big fuckin' baby. Find out how to get her in without anyone seeing her. Do whatever you need to do. But she's coming."

He gripped me tighter, so that the warmth of his body seeped through my clothes. I inhaled his scent, that familiar combination of almonds and soap, now laced with just a bit of salty sea air that was fading fast. It helped lessen the tension in my stomach, but not by much.

Brandon leaned in next to my ear. "And wear a skirt, will you? I want to see your legs."

I rolled my eyes and shoved his shoulder, but he just leered at my legging-covered thighs and waggled his eyebrows. I couldn't help but giggle. Even with the world heaped on his shoulders, the man really was a hopeless flirt.

~

Chapter 36

I left Brandon's apartment early in the morning despite his multiple attempts to keep me in bed, even though he had more on his plate than I did. Before leaving last night, Cory had said he would be there by seven to work on his announcement speech and plan a strategy for the fallout of the *Globe* article. I awoke just before six with a massive ball of dread lodged in my gut, and much to Brandon's chagrin, escaped soon after in the back of an Uber.

Even at that early hour, photographers were already parked outside of Brandon's building. No doubt more would arrive by the time the newspapers hit the sidewalks, and I was very, very glad that my name wasn't on the lease of Eric's apartment or anywhere else anyone could find my address. The front of my building was thankfully pap-free. For now.

I spent the morning unpacking, trying to be quiet so as not to wake up Eric. I wasn't sure if Jane was still here too. I hoped she was. Although I had doubts she and Eric could last an entire two weeks together, she had been sending me goofy selfies from the apartment up until two nights ago. I desperately needed Jane's advice right now.

I got a text from Brandon informing me that Margie was sending over a stylist around three. Cory had suggested the idea, which I'd fought bitterly at first. But Cory had insisted that if I *had* to be there, then I needed to look the part.

"You don't want to be a sidepiece, sweetheart, then you need to dress like his wife," he'd said just before he left, narrowly avoiding Brandon's lunge as the elevator doors closed.

As much as I hated to admit it, Cory had a point. My flaming hair was a dead giveaway, so between the paparazzi and my name in the *Globe* article, someone was going to put two and two together. I didn't want to look like a poor student when they did.

My phone rang, jerking me out of my thoughts. It was a New York number, although one I didn't recognize.

"Hello?" I answered, with the ball in my stomach tightened into a knot.

"Skylar, darling, it's Janette. How are you, my love? We heard you returned from France last night. Was it exquisite?"

I blew out a breath of relief, although Janette's banter wasn't really high on my list of priorities at the moment.

"Hi, yeah, we got back late. It was great. Marseille is beautiful, as I'm sure you know."

"Divine, darling, just divine. Although to be honest, we prefer Cassis."

Janette launched on a long, melodramatic comparison of Marseille and Cassis, the city that bookended the other side of the Calanques National Park. I separated my clean from dirty clothes as she yammered on about what she and her family had been doing since the Fourth. They were staying with her parents in New York, and they'd all been enjoying a reunion with family there. I waited for her to mention that she'd seen Dad, but luckily, no mention came. Good, I thought. The last thing my fragile father needed right now was a run-in with his ex.

"So, darling, I have to ask: has Brandon said anything about Maurice's offer?"

I paused, a black shirt in hand. "What?"

"I thought he might have said something. Maurice gave him such a wonderful presentation at the Cape, but he hasn't heard a thing from him or his associates. I know the two of you have been having a lovely time together, but really, don't you think it's a bit unprofessional to let things go for almost a month?"

"No more unprofessional than Maurice sending his wife to get at Brandon through his girlfriend," I retorted as I sat down on top of a mound of clean tank tops. "What the hell is going on, Janette?"

There was a sigh over the phone, then a brief bark at the kids: "Annabelle! Christoph! Really, can't you *please* take the incessant clamoring to the nursery!" Then, back to me: "I apologize for that, and for asking about Brandon. It's just that, dear Maurice really *is* a bit rumpled about the whole thing. He was so excited about the prospect of working with your beau, and he's just been a beast about it since. Perhaps you could mention it to Brandon. Would you, darling?"

I frowned at a shirt that was perfectly clean, but now crumpled in my hands. "Sure. I'll mention it."

"Wonderful, wonderful. That's all I can ask. Now, your brother and sister are simply dying to see you. We were thinking about coming to Boston tonight. What say you to dinner?"

I chucked the black shirt into the clothes hamper next to my closet. Why did she always have to talk like a character from *The Great Gatsby*?

"I can't, unfortunately. I have to go to a dinner thing with Brandon. Maybe later this week, depending on how work goes."

"Oh!" Janette said brightly. Then, after a brief pause: "Of course. Absolutely. You let us know what works, darling."

She quickly said her goodbyes, leaving me with the familiar feeling that I had just been involved in only a fraction of the conversation that my mother had been having. It was always like that with her; her head was always in the clouds or somewhere else besides with me.

My bedroom door creaked open, pulling me from my irritation. A long white leg, followed by Jane's black-spiked head, poked through.

I grinned. "Hey there, lover."

Jane snorted, then came in my and flopped onto the bed next to me, wearing a pair of men's boxer shorts and a T-shirt that looked a lot like Eric's favorite Yankees shirt. Her long legs splayed down the comforter as she collapsed into the pillows.

"Still!" she cried toward the ceiling. "Still your bed is more comfortable than mine. What *is* your secret, woman?"

I shrugged and continued unpacking. "Discount sheets? Lumpy pillows? I only ever spring for the cheap stuff, you know."

Inwardly, I had to chuckle. Brandon was always complaining about my scratchy sheets, but I wouldn't let him buy anything to spruce the place up. I had done just fine with my meager budget, and even with the coarse bedding, we both still preferred my homey little room to the cold majesty of his high-rise.

"So...two weeks, huh? Whatcha been...doing?" I did my best to leer at her, making sure the emphasis on "doing" was clear.

Jane just shook her head.

"First of all, you should never, ever do that with your face again," she said. "It makes you look like you're having a stroke. Second of all—" she parried the sweater I threw— "the fuck if I know."

She fell back into my pillows and pulled one across her chest. I stopped sorting clothes. It wasn't like Jane to get so...caught up in things. Especially to the point where her filterless wit wasn't readily available.

She sighed and buried her head in her hands, then gave a loud and extremely un-ladylike groan through her fingers.

"Fuck!" she griped. "It's...complicated. Eric is so..."

"Dreamy?" I teased.

"Annoying!" she shouted, just before apparently realizing that we were still in the same apartment as Eric and clapping her hands over her mouth.

I frowned. "If it's been that bad, why didn't you just go back to Chicago?"

"No, no, it *hasn't* been bad," she stated, this time in a much lower voice. "That's the annoying thing. See, that was supposed to be the point of this little two-week rendezvous. We were supposed to boink it out of our systems and remember by the end just how much we hate each other."

I pursed my lips sympathetically and rubbed my friend on the shoulder. She shuddered, as if the thought of actually liking Eric was too much to bear.

"He's really not so bad, Jane," I said. "I mean, I live with him. He's clean and usually pretty nice to me. Plus, if we're being real here, I don't think he ever hated you. Tell me again, why is dating him such a terrible thing?"

"Okay, how about, he's such a man whore, the guy keeps a thousand condoms in his closet." Jane looked up, her hands spread over her legs like she was going to catch said condoms from the sky. "I am not exaggerating, Sky. He buys them wholesale. There is seriously a cardboard box full of them. Right next to where he stacks his shoes in their boxes too, like a freak."

I chuckled. Neither fact was really that surprising. Eric was a sexually active neat freak. It made complete sense that he would be as conscientious about contraceptives as with his organization.

"Correct me if I'm wrong," I said gently. "But didn't you make, oh, weekly stops at the student health center all last year for free condoms?"

Jane gave me a look that would have frozen a lake. "Your point?"

I shrugged. "I'm just saying, you're kind of a match that way. I think you finally found a guy that can keep up with you."

"Yeah, and up with every other girl in the city when I'm not here." She buried her face in the pillow next to my shoulder.

"Why?" she moaned dramatically. "Why did I have to fall for a guy that has the nicest dick in Boston? I swear to God, it's like he laces that thing with coke."

If I'd been drinking anything, I'd have choked. "Jesus. I really don't need to hear about my roommate's junk."

Jane just groaned again and then hiccupped a fake sob.

"Well, if it's any consolation, I can also tell you that since you guys started hooking up, Eric has been spending every night in his own bed," I said. "And he does not bring girls home, if you catch my drift."

"You're about as subtle as a waterfall," Jane said dryly.

I shrugged and continued sorting. "I just think maybe you guys have a good thing going, despite the distance. Maybe you should give it a real chance."

Jane bit her lip. I tried not to smile. My friend was really and truly smitten, and a part of me was satisfied to see her meet her match. Maybe Eric, with his stolid, unflappable personality, was exactly what Jane needed.

"And you?" she asked as she sat up again. "Are *you* finally giving it a real chance? Please tell me that in two weeks alone with Brandon, you finally found time to tell him about the abortion."

The answer must have been clear on my face.

"You have got to be kidding me," Jane said. "Seriously? Skylar, what the fuck is going on?"

"I tried," I said weakly as I refolded a shirt and placed it on the bed. Then I picked it up and refolded it three more times before looking up. "I really did, Jane. But every time...I don't know...you don't know Brandon. The shit he's been through. The shit he's *still* going through." I sniffed, and pushed away a few tears that suddenly welled around my eyes. "The divorce, his company, and now he's supposed to be announcing his candidacy for mayor. But on top of all of that, here's this guy, this great, amazing man who has never really felt what it's like to have someone love him unconditionally. Not his parents, not his wife, not his foster parents, not his in-laws. No one."

I paused. The thought of all of this was making it hard to speak. Jane, for once, was devoid of pithy comments. I took a deep breath and continued.

"He wanted a family so badly with Miranda, but they couldn't have kids for some reason. And now, just when things are finally getting back to normal between us, you want me to tell him that I took away his next chance to be a father? Jane, I can't do that to him!"

I sniffed the tears away that were starting to fall in earnest, listening as my voice cracked painfully over the words.

"I love him too much," I said finally. "I love him too much to break his heart like that. He'd...he'd never forgive me."

"I don't think that's true," Jane said as she sat up. "I've seen the way he looks at you, Skylar. You could grow green moles all over your face and that man would be on his knees for you."

"Ew," I said.

Jane rolled her eyes. "You could be a secret government assassin. You could develop sudden alopecia and become completely bald. Hell, you could lose your memory tomorrow and that dude would go full-on *Notebook*."

I couldn't help but grin. She was being ridiculous, but in my heart, I knew that Brandon did love me like that.

"Seriously, though," Jane said as she gripped my hand to pull my attention back. "Sky, you have to tell him. Aside from the fact that it just might get out anyway now that he, and by default you, are in the public eye, you owe it to him. Not because he's done all of these amazing things for you and your family. You owe it to him because you love him. And when you love someone, you have to be honest."

I hung my head, playing with the folds in the duvet while Jane's words sank in.

"I know," I mumbled, more to myself than to her. "I know." I looked up with sudden resolve. "I'll tell him tonight. After the announcement. I'll tell him tonight, and if he doesn't want to be with me anymore, then I'll just have to accept it."

My voice wavered considerably on the last statement, prompting Jane to scoot next to me and wrap her skinny arms around me in a tight hug.

"He won't," she promised. "He won't."

"And you?" I asked. I swiped at the tears under my eyes, and Jane laughed.

"What about me?" she asked.

"How about you try a little honesty too?" I looked in the direction of Eric's room. "I think you'll find our young Dutch friend in there cares about you more than you think."

Jane sighed. "Maybe," she said. "We'll see."

Before I could say another thing, the buzzer rang, loud and obnoxious, through the apartment. I heard Eric shuffling across the floor as it continued, mumbling under his breath something about it being a "freaking Sunday" before he answered the call.

"Who is it?" he drawled. There was a muffled answer. Then, "Hold on."

Jane and I listened to the sound of feet shuffling across the apartment, followed by a swift knock on my door.

"Skylar, you in there?"

"Yeah, come in," I called.

Eric popped his head in, much like Jane had a few minutes earlier. His normally straight blond hair was standing on end, and he took in the scene of Jane and me with obvious, yet calm interest.

"Oh, hey," he said, nodding at Jane as if she has just stopped by for coffee and hadn't spent the last two weeks alone with him in our apartment. Then he looked to me. "Welcome back. Are you expecting a stylist?"

I nodded. "Yeah. Brandon's announcing his run tonight."

Eric's eyes widened at the news. "Okay then. She's on her way up." He then turned briefly to Jane, then flickered a look up and down her bare-legged body that would have turned me bright red in about three seconds. "I'm going back to bed," he said, and shuffled back out.

Jane rose to follow, almost as if pulled by an imaginary string. She backed out of the room with a look of faux-terror, though underneath it I could see clear joy.

"I'm so fucked," she said with a shrug. "Completely and totally fucked."

~

As it happened, the stylist that Margie had sent came with a bounty of dresses that we laid out on the bed, and when Jane reemerged from

Eric's room about an hour later, she was ready to drool with me over the sheer volume of couture I suddenly had hanging off a portable rack in my tiny bedroom.

"Feel this!" she said, fingering a long silk tunic. "Like butter."

The stylist, Mary, a middle-aged woman in all black who was probably the chicest person I had ever met in real life, just smiled.

"That's the latest Cavalli," she said. "Although to be honest, I wouldn't go with black for an event like this."

Jane and I both looked up from where we sat. We were both fans of the color.

"It's just that if you're going to be looked at like a political candidate's wife—"

"Which I'm not," I interrupted her.

Mary smirked. "Right. Well, I was given a specific brief. Let's just say black doesn't exactly scream out 'First Lady.' This was more something I brought for your friend here."

Jane and I both frowned at each other. I turned back to Mary. "What are you talking about?"

She pulled three papers out of her bright red purse and handed them to me. They were tickets for the dinner.

"I'm just a messenger," she said. "But apparently, Mr. Sterling thought you'd want your friends there tonight."

She looked at me sympathetically. Clearly, she had read the *Globe* article.

"Look, I've styled a lot of politicians and their, um, special guests," she said. "It will be nice for you to have your friends there if they can go."

I turned to Jane. "What do you think?" I asked. "Can you bear to spend your last night in Boston at this stuffy event?"

Jane squeezed my hand. "We'll be there."

I gulped and turned back to the clothes.

"Okay, Mary," I said. "You'd better show me just what *does* say 'First Lady.' Or, at the very least, what doesn't say 'sidepiece.'"

~

With Mary and Jane's help throughout the day, I found a dress that made me feel like a million dollars. Or, in Brandon's case, a billion. It was a floor-length, sky-blue column dress with off-the-shoulder straps and a boat neckline. A modest slit up to one knee would likely appease Brandon's request that I show off his favorite part of my anatomy without making me look too much like his mistress. It fit me like a glove, thanks to the last-minute alterations that Mary was able to pull off.

I stood in front of the full-length mirror in my room, going over my elegant transformation. Mary had also styled my hair, pulling it half up in a small bouffant with a French twist. I wore Brandon's cuff and a pair of diamond studs that were my college graduation gift from Bubbe, but otherwise kept the rest of my look simple, with natural make up and a bit of lip gloss.

"You look amazing, chick," Jane said as she came to stand next to me.

"You don't look so bad yourself," I said.

Jane patted her hands over her dress, which was a midi-length tea dress in a blocked red, white, and black pattern. Even though it was much more conservative than her usual Goth-punk style, she had still managed to maintain her edge with at least six different chunky silver rings and a pair of black Mary Janes that looked right out of a steampunk novel. She grinned and touched her bob, which had been tamed straight.

"Don't mind if I do," she said.

From where she was finishing packing up the rest of the clothes, Mary nodded satisfactorily. "I think my work here is done," she said.

"Thank you so much, Mary," I said, walking over to give her a brief hug. "We look amazing, and it's all thanks to you."

"Thank your man," she said with a grin. "Oh! That reminds me—I almost forgot. He told me to give you this and make sure you put it on."

She pulled a square velvet box out of her purse and opened it up for me.

"Holy shit," Jane breathed over my shoulder.

I couldn't even speak. Inside was a wreath of diamonds so bright I was practically blinded. The low lighting in my room flickered off the many facets, casting tiny rainbows all around the walls.

I blinked. "There must be some mistake."

"Oh, I would never make a mistake with Harry Winston," Mary replied haughtily.

She set the box on my bed, then gestured that I should face the mirror while she clasped the necklace around my neck. It fell just to my collar bone, perfectly complementing the fifties-style neckline.

"Now, this is just a loan," she said with a cheeky grin. "Mr. Sterling was adamant that I tell you explicitly. He thought for some reason you'd be upset if it was an actual present, though why you wouldn't want a gift like this, I'll never know."

"It's beautiful," I whispered as I drifted my fingers over the necklace, then down the silk fabric of my dress.

I looked like a completely different person. But I also looked like someone who could stand next to Brandon and look like she belonged. Gone was the tired, bedraggled almost-attorney with the holey jeans and the braid that was constantly falling out. Gone was the girl who couldn't deal with a man even paying for her dinner, let alone jewelry. I was glad to see her go if it meant I could be proud to stand next to Brandon.

"Hey, you guys almost ready?" Eric popped into the room, still fixing a cufflink. He caught a look at me and smiled appreciatively. "Damn, Crosby. You clean up nice."

"What am I, wilted spinach?"

Eric glanced at Jane next to me, then did a double-take. Almost immediately, his face turned the color of my hair. He tugged at the collar of his shirt and licked his lips. He took three massive strides to Jane before seeming to realize that they weren't alone in the room, then stopped to adjust his cufflink again. The movement reminded me of a cat who'd been sneaking around and suddenly started licking itself as soon as it was caught.

"I think," he said to Jane with another look that would have burned through metal, "I'll have to tell you exactly what I think of that dress later."

Jane opened her mouth, then closed it with a smirk. "I guess you will."

With a curt nod, Eric looked back to me. "It's time. There's a car downstairs."

I picked up the matching clutch and shawl that Mary had provided and took a deep breath.

"Into the lion's den we go," I said.

"Don't worry, Sky," Jane said as she shepherded us all out of the apartment. "Brandon made sure you had armor for this battle."

I could only hope she was right.

~

Chapter 37

This wasn't like the quiet, yet extravagant fundraiser I'd attended with Brandon a month ago. That event had been designed to be explicitly under wraps, held in a place where the rich and powerful in New England could gather without the press hanging over them.

The Burnside Hotel, however, was chosen for the exact opposite reason. A press horde clamored around the main entrance, where posh Bostonians were walking up a short red carpet to attend the gala. I didn't see Brandon, but we had already discussed that he would arrive on his own. His rumored announcement was the big news of the evening, coming on top of Miranda's *Globe* and *People* features.

Cory was holding a service elevator when we pulled up in the underground parking lot. His eyes bugged considerably when he caught a load of my necklace.

"Jesus!" he exclaimed. "When I said First Lady, I meant Nancy Reagan, not Marie Antoinette."

I touched the jagged edges of the wreath self-consciously. "Is it too much?"

"Abso-fucking-lutely *not*," Jane said adamantly as she looped an arm through mine. "Captain Manners here clearly doesn't know shit about fashion. Mary would have told Brandon if it were too much, Sky." She glared at Cory. "Would your boss like being compared to an eighteenth-century boy-king? Just wondering."

Just another reason why I was so glad to have Jane in my corner tonight. Cory's face turned the color of a tomato as he punched the button of the elevator with a little too much vigor.

"Sorry," he bit out as the doors closed.

Jane relaxed. "That's more like it."

Eric just snorted, bemused, and gave Cory a "what did you expect?" kind of look.

Cory escorted us to a ballroom set aside for the event. Although my name was in the *Globe*, no one as of yet had published any pictures of me, so Cory had arranged for my name card to read "Ellen Chambers," using my middle name and my mother's maiden name as a decoy.

The room was mostly full already, swirling with black-tie attendees dressed for one of biggest political fundraisers in Boston. I had already recognized several people, including local celebrities, senators, and the governor. I was grateful that Brandon had made sure there would be a few friendly faces in the crowd for me too; it couldn't have been easy to procure tickets for Eric and Jane last minute. Margie must have been on the phone all day.

Across the room, I caught the notice of Kieran, who stood talking to a few men, dressed similarly to them in a sleek black tuxedo of her own. She gave a brief wave and a smile—well, as much of a smile as Kieran was ever really capable of—and returned to her conversation.

"Come on, Ellie," Jane joked as we wove our way to one of the octagonal tables set up near the dance floor.

It wasn't quite the table of honor, which was in the center of the room, but it was close. Brandon's name was on a card at that table, right next to another one I recognized as we passed it: Miranda Sterling.

"Oh, *fuck*" I breathed as I caught sight of the elegant cursive writing.

Jane leaned over my shoulder, and her eyes widened.

"What the hell?" she asked in disbelief. "Do you think he knows?"

I shook my head. "No. He never would have demanded I come. He probably wouldn't have come himself." I pressed a hand to my cheek. "Jesus, like Groundhog Day, but a really awful night instead."

The tall, willowy form of Brandon's estranged wife was nowhere to be seen, but as soon as my eyes landed on the ballroom entrance, the entire frame was occupied by Brandon's broad shoulders. He raised a hand with a smile that was immediately clouded when he caught the look on my face.

Jane murmured something about her and Eric getting drinks and skirted away.

"Hey," Brandon said as he approached. "What's wrong?"

He looked camera-ready in a gorgeously slim-cut tuxedo. It was the same basic uniform worn by every other man in the room, but Brandon made them all look like shadows. Cory had turned a stylist on him too; he'd clearly had a haircut and a shave in the last twenty-four hours, so his usually tousled blond waves were shortened and tamed into something approximating a respectable politician's. Which, of course, was exactly what he was trying to be.

351

But nothing could tame the color of his eyes, the way they popped in a sea of black. I realized at that moment that Mary had chosen my dress precisely because it was the same color: the color of the Mediterranean, of a lake on a summer day. The color of the sky. It created a link between us that would be there no matter what. The woman really knew her business.

Wordlessly, I pointed to the small card sitting on the table. Brandon's eyes followed. His jaw dropped.

"What the fuck..." he wondered under his breath as he picked up the card and examined it as if it were a figment of his imagination. He looked at me. "I had no clue about this, Skylar. I *never* would have come if I'd known she would be here."

I believed him, but his obvious concern was reassuring.

"I know," I said. "And it's Ellen, by the way." I nodded at a few of the cameramen setting up in one corner of room.

Brandon's worry, however, dissipated a bit as he took in an eyeful of my outfit. Despite the obvious stress he was under, his mouth quirked with a sly smile.

"You look...wow." He reached out and touched the wreath of diamonds around my neck lightly, then traced his fingers over my collarbone. "I'm glad you wore this."

I touched the same spot. "It's beautiful. Too much, but beautiful."

Brandon shrugged with another shy half-smile. "I'd like to get you one of your own one day. When I know you'll actually take it."

He cocked his head, looking at me like I was a painting in a museum, a work of art. Slowly, however, his gaze started to heat up with a fire that quickly had me flushed.

"You need to stop looking at me like that," I whispered, even as he picked up my hand and started to run his thumb over my knuckles. From far away, his touch would have looked innocent, but up close, it was anything but.

"Like what?" he asked, making absolutely no movement to stop, neither the touch nor the heated look.

"Like I'm your dinner."

He bit his bottom lip, as if trying to process the comment. Then he released my hand, but leaned in. A bystander might have thought Brandon was telling me a quick secret, but they wouldn't know how his freshly shaved jaw felt against my cheek or the effect of his feather-light touch over my shoulder. It didn't matter that I had just spent the last two weeks straight with the man. Instead of quenching that thirst, time had only made it stronger.

"More like dessert," he rumbled into my ear, which he nipped lightly. "Your pussy's too sweet for anything else."

He stood up straight with a shit-eating grin that popped his dimples out in full force. I stared at him, my jaw dropped practically to the floor.

Brandon smirked as he dropped my hand, which fell against the silk of my dress like a limp fish. "You want me to reach up your skirt and prove it to you, Red? I could make you lick it off my fingers."

My eyes bugged out even further. "You did not just say that to me in a building full of politicians and donors! There are literally two congressional representatives and an attorney general in this room right now."

"Please. They're probably the biggest perverts of them all. You don't even want me to start on all the dirty things that dress is putting in my head," Brandon said with another sharkish leer. "But now you're not thinking about this anymore, are you?" He held up the card bearing Miranda's name and took a few backward steps toward the ballroom entrance. "I'll be back after I take care of this mix-up. You just keep thinking dirty thoughts about what I'm going to do to you later. With nothing on but that necklace."

With a wink, he spun on his heel and left me clutching the back of the chair. Suddenly unable to stand properly, I decided now was as good a time as any to take a seat at my table when Eric and Jane returned with drinks for all of us.

"Everything okay?" Jane asked, glancing back to where Brandon had gone. She handed me a glass of white wine, which I took gratefully.

"I think so," I said. "He's...taking care of it."

It felt strange to say that when I didn't know exactly what he was going to do. But I was ready to trust Brandon.

"Well, hello there!"

I turned to find Ray and Susan Petersen approaching. I stood up to give Susan a quick, but tight embrace, and she held out my arms to look me over.

"My, my," she said as she looked me over. "Aren't you a vision, Skylar."

"Thank you, Susan," I said. "You look great too."

She smiled, clearly happy with the flowy floral dress that draped over her small, squat form. I gave Ray an awkward kiss on the cheek. He looked as much a grumpy professor as ever in a stolid, if somewhat faded navy suit.

"Brandon is taking care of a mix-up with the guest list," I said as we took our seats. "He has to sit at a major donor table tonight, but I'll be here to keep you guys company."

Ray snorted. "Of course."

"These are my friends from Harvard, Jane and Eric," I said, ignoring the comment. I gestured at Jane and Eric, who both stood up briefly to shake the Petersens' hands.

"All lawyers?" Susan asked kindly as she accepted a glass of champagne from one of the roving waiters while Ray muttered something about a beer.

Jane nodded. "Yes, ma'am," she said. "Just graduated with Skylar. Now we're just waiting on our bar exam results."

"Oh, that's exciting!" Susan replied, clasping her hands together. "I thought about becoming a lawyer at one time. Until I met this old curmudgeon, anyway."

Ray just looked dourly at his wife, but I thought I saw a fond twinkle through his smudged glasses. Jane bit her lip, while Eric stretched an arm back behind her chair.

"Hey there!"

Brandon reappeared at the table and leaned down to kiss his foster parents hello before coming to stand behind me.

"Are you ready for your big night?" Susan asked excitedly. "Do you have a speech prepared?"

Brandon patted his breast pocket. "Right here. Cory and I were up all night finishing it."

He rubbed his forehead, the only sign I'd seen yet that he was nervous. But when he put his hand on the back of my chair, I could see the whites of his knuckles.

"You're going to be amazing," I said, giving him what I hoped looked like a friendly pat on the hand.

He looked down at me with gratitude, and captured my hand briefly with a tight squeeze before anyone in the room could see. Soon the waiters would start to serve dinner, after which would be a few speeches before some dancing. That was when Brandon would be making his announcement. He downed the rest of his drink, which looked and smelled like bourbon.

"Careful there, slugger," I said. "You should probably eat something."

"Red," Brandon said quietly, "I love you. But I swear to God, baby, you need to let me drink tonight."

Before I could reply, there was a kerfuffle at the ballroom entrance that caught our attention.

"What do you mean, I'm not on the list?"

A woman's voice rang out, clear and sharp, even over the din. Just past the doormen and the woman holding a clipboard, I could see dark hair, porcelain skin, bright pink lips.

My stomach dropped. Miranda.

Brandon sighed and set his glass on the table a little too hard. "I'd better go deal with this," he said, and stalked off without another word.

Our entire table watched as he entered the fray, and I saw Miranda's eyes, dark and sharp, perfectly lined and mascaraed, as they caught sight of Brandon's tall form. They brightened. Then they found me and turned venomous.

"Jesus," Jane breathed beside me. "If she were Medusa, you'd be stone right now."

I shuddered. Right now, Miranda was scarier than a mythical monster with snake hair.

I grabbed my clutch. "I should probably go."

"Oh, please don't," Susan piped up across the table.

Jane and I turned to find Susan staring at the entrance with obvious disgust.

Susan looked back at me and smiled. "She's just so...so..."

"Horrendous," Ray supplied dryly.

He raised a faint, white brow at me. It was probably the most positive reinforcement I'd ever receive from the man.

"Exactly," Susan chimed in. "Petty and vicious, and she's had Bran practically locked up in that big empty house for years. She's just mad now that he's finally moving on, whether she wants him to or not. And with someone as lovely as you, no less."

"Susan—" I started. I appreciated the votes of confidence, but that didn't mean me being here was a good idea.

"No, no, no," Susan continued. "Truly. He wouldn't be here tonight if not for you. He always hated the spotlight. You've got to know how you brought him out of his shell."

"She's leaving," murmured Jane, who hadn't stopped watching the scene over my shoulder.

When I looked back, Miranda had disappeared, and Brandon was making his way back toward our table.

"That's done," he said when he arrived, although he still didn't sit down.

I gulped. "Really?"

I hated the fact that I couldn't give him the hug and kiss he clearly needed, but there were already a few members of the press being escorted to a designated area by the ballroom's podium, not far from our table. Brandon nodded with a sweet smile my way, but made no move to touch me. It looked like it caused him physical pain.

"She's on her way home. But just to be safe, you should probably leave after the speech, Red. No doubt she'll tip off the paps that you're here."

I blanched. "Okay."

He looked across the room and waved to someone who was apparently beckoning at him. Cory was standing next to a group of other men in tuxedos, some of whom I recognized from the last, disastrous benefit.

"Time to kiss some donors' asses," Brandon said. "I'll be back when I can."

I watched him leave, and the ball of dread in my stomach grew. When I looked back to the table, I found Susan watching sympathetically while Ray stared with obvious disapproval.

"You don't look like you're very happy about tonight," Susan said lightly. "You must be upset about that feature in the paper today."

I sighed. "I'm here for Brandon, not myself. Not the *Globe* either."

"This isn't Brandon," Ray said abruptly. "Susan's right. He's never been one for this kind of attention, and now all of a sudden he wants to run for office?" The older man shook his head. He turned to me. "You did this?"

Confused, I shook my head. "He loves Boston," I said weakly. "Maybe he just wants to help make his city better."

It was hard to argue with what Ray was saying. I hadn't actually known Brandon that long, but in all that time, he had always seemed a supremely private person, never one for crowds or a lot of extra attention. This new venture was the complete polar opposite of everything I knew about him.

Ray just harrumphed. "There are a lot of ways to do that without being a damn politician, like Miranda always wanted him to be," he said. "He's too smart for this."

Susan didn't say anything, but concern was written all over her kind face. Eventually, she gave a small shrug. Before I could reply, my name was called out by not one, but two people.

"Skylar!"

Jane, Eric, and I all twisted in our seats to check for the competing voices.

"What in fresh hell?" Jane mumbled as she caught sight of Jared weaving his way through the crowd.

I frowned. "Jesus, this really is like Groundhog Day. Jared's family is Republican. Why would he be at a DNC event?" I rubbed a hand over my forehead. "When it rains, it pours, doesn't it?"

"Don't worry, chick," Jane said as she pushed back from her seat, yanking at Eric's suit jacket to stand him up with her. "We got this."

They quickly left to block Jared several tables away, but my attention was reclaimed again when the owner of the other voice touched my shoulder. I looked up to find my mother smiling down at me, dressed to the nines in an elegant, royal blue gown.

"Darling!" she cried, leaning in to air-kiss my cheeks. "Look at us. Practically twins, aren't we?"

I just stared, utterly confused. "Janette, what are you doing here?"

"Oh, we were invited last minute. We wouldn't have missed dear Brandon's big night, since we are practically family!"

She turned to the remaining two people at the table. "You must be the Petersens! Brandon has told me so much about you. I'm Janette Jadot, Skylar's mother."

Susan and Ray both accepted Janette's light handshake, both of them too stunned by her sudden presence as their eyes flickered between us. I couldn't move; this certainly wasn't the first meeting of the families I wanted to have with Brandon's foster parents. Not to mention, *when* had she had this supposed discussion with Brandon about them?

"Janette lives in France," was all I could say. "She's here visiting."

Janette turned to me. "I'm so glad you decided to come tonight," she said. "I wondered if we might sneak away for a quick chat."

I looked around the room, which was now full to capacity. Almost everyone had taken their seats, and the band had started playing some swing music.

"I don't really think right now is the best time," I said. "Maybe we can get coffee tomorrow."

"I'd really like to talk now," Janette prodded, even as she beamed at someone across the room and gave a cheerful wave. "It's rather urgent."

I frowned openly. "Janette," I said, calling her attention back to me. She looked down brightly, and her smile quickly faded.

"Not now," I said. "It's a big night. Tomorrow. Okay?"

Her jaw clenched for a moment, but then she nodded curtly. "Brunch at our hotel. I'll make a reservation for ten, shall I?"

I murmured my assent, and Janette disappeared to mingle. I didn't see Maurice, but no doubt he was also taking full advantage of the networking opportunities.

Jane and Eric came back just as the food arrived. The chicken marsala tasted like cardboard, and it suddenly felt like, even with my attempt to go undercover, all the eyes in the room were on me. The bodice of my dress felt very tight. I needed to breathe. I needed a break.

"I'm going to the restroom," I said to Jane, who looked at me with obvious concern.

"You need company?" she asked.

I shook my head. "No. I'll be right back."

I pushed back from the table, clutch in hand as I weaved my way toward the bathroom. Brandon was still mired by all the people vying for his attention, with Cory standing beside him like a loyal lapdog. He didn't notice when I left, and I was glad for it.

~

Chapter 38

Cupped in my palms, the water drained through my fingers in long, cool streams. I wanted so badly to splash it on my face, but I didn't want to ruin Mary's careful makeup job or get water on my dress. Reluctantly, I let the water go, then grabbed a napkin from the stack beside the sink and dampened it before pressing the cool cloth to my forehead. There. That was a little better.

Everything about this night felt like a mistake. Jared's unnerving presence, Janette's pressured hints, Miranda's surprise appearance... Ray was right; even Brandon's pending announcement just seemed wrong. The anxiety already lodged in my stomach was blooming into full-on frenzy, making me feel lightheaded. All eyes were on my beautiful man, and soon they would be on me too. I gasped into the mirror and focused on inhaling, exhaling, inhaling, exhaling. With both hands braced on the countertop, I stared at my reflection: the reflection of panic.

This wasn't me, this primped princess. I looked like an alien version of myself, preserved in a mask of diamonds and couture. I *did* look like Janette's twin. I was playing dress up in silk armor, but all the pretenses of wealth in the world couldn't protect me from the inevitable avalanche of press coverage and scrutiny that would, in all likelihood, expose every secret I had.

Green eyes or blue?

God, I was so stupid. I should have told him when I had the chance, when it was just the two of us. I took another deep breath, but it stuck in my throat. Everything made me feel like I was choking.

The door to the bathroom swung open, and Janette swept in like a queen. When she found me, it was clear by the look on her face that she hadn't come to use any of the stalls.

"Darling," she said frankly as she quickly crossed to where I stood. "You look like death. Do you have some concealer for those under-eye circles? Whatever is wrong?"

I maintained my grip on the counter.

"I'm just..." I started, finding it difficult to get any words out at all.

"Terrified?" Janette asked with a knowingly look. She reached up and patted a nonexistent hair back into place. "Well, of course you are, my love, and for good reason. In about thirty minutes, your life is going to change forever."

I clenched my teeth and inhaled again deeply through my nose, holding the counter even harder so I wouldn't fall over. "That's not really helping, Janette."

"Oh darling, please don't worry. It's nothing you can't handle. Especially once that man does what he's planning and finally pops the question, if he hasn't already. Things will get easier then."

I reared my head up, eyes wide. "*What* are you talking about?"

Janette leaned her slim hips against the counter so she could look at me in the face instead of through the mirror. She examined the tips of her French manicure as if we were discussing the weather.

"I hope you're giving him a run for his money with the prenup," she continued. "He's a catch, but in my experience, quickie weddings almost always end in divorce. Be smarter than that other woman. Get pregnant, and make sure the contract compensates for it."

As an ice-cold chill spread through my entire body as I wondered what the hell had just gotten into my mother. Granted, Janette often thought it was appropriate to give me advice that assumed far more intimacy than we actually had. But this was eerily close to the truth.

I stared stonily at the gold-flecked granite of the counter. "I don't know what you mean."

Janette tapped a long finger on the side of her nose. "That's it, darling. Keep your cards close. But I've seen the way he looks at you. You'll be married by the end of the summer."

"What the hell are you doing right now?" I demanded, feeling increasingly uneasy as I faced her directly. "What is this, some kind of demented pep talk?"

Janette shrugged, although she had the grace to look uneasy. "I'm just trying to help. I know how to play this game well, my love."

I might have believed her, except the kind look in her eyes turned to something colder.

"For instance," she continued as she drew a graceful finger up and down the edge of the sink, "I know that secrets in this world are capital. And since I've done you a little favor by protecting your secret, I'm hoping you'll do me one too."

"What are you talking about?" I asked shakily as my stomach dropped to my toes. "What *secret?*"

"You see, my love," Janette said, "we're a bit at the end of our ropes here, your stepfather and I."

I stared at my mother, suddenly finding her unrecognizable. Janette was a lot of things: a flake, a dilettante, a tease, a doll. But never this...Machiavellian. Who was this? She looked up, her wide green eyes, the same green eyes I had, suddenly as sharp as a knife.

"Goodness, this is awkward, isn't it?" Janette asked. "If you'd taken any of my calls, we wouldn't be here. We could have determined a path privately. But, as it happens, Maurice just can't wait any longer, and neither can I. I need my life back, Skylar."

"Your life back? What does that mean?" I asked, although I wasn't sure I really wanted to know.

Janette blinked. "Don't play stupid, darling. It *really* doesn't suit you."

"Janette, I don't know what you think I know about Brandon's business," I sputtered "but we don't really talk about the deals he's making. Mostly because it would be illegal."

"Skylar, I'm sorry, but you can*not* expect me to believe that you are so impossibly clueless!" Janette finally broke completely through her polished façade. "You must know what dire straits Maurice and I are in. Everything we had in France is gone. The house, the cars, all of it. We're living with my family right now, and it's horrendous! My mother—no, don't give me that look. You should be grateful I never subjected you to her."

"Janette, what in the hell are you talking about?" I asked, my voice rising with every word. "*What* happened in France? What did Maurice do?"

She turned a little green at the question, but to her credit, didn't completely turn away.

"My dear husband," she said in a voice that sounded anything but fond, "led some of his investors on a scheme that went...awry, shall we say." She gulped. "I refuse to go into the sordid details. But needless to say, all of *our* personal assets went to paying back some of that debt, and Maurice was sent here to procure new accounts. Otherwise, he'll be out and will likely go to prison." She laughed, a sharp sound that cut through

361

the air. "Hilarious, isn't it? I ended up marrying the French version of Bernie Madoff."

"So he thinks that Brandon is the golden goose that will get him back in the game," I finished, more to myself than to Janette.

When Janette looked up, her green eyes were wide with pure terror, set off further by the fringe of threaded eyelashes.

"Don't you see? We can help each other this way!" Her voice began to sound manic. "I'm from this world, Skylar, in a way you will never be. You help me stay in it, and I can help you navigate it. Teach you how to talk, how to dress, how to interact with these ridiculous people. Keep you from being a laughing stock! Help you keep your deepest, darkest secrets, even the baby!"

At the end of her final sentence, I froze completely, my hands utterly and completely glued to the counter. The rest of my body suddenly felt like cracked glass. Like someone could push me with a single finger and watch me shatter across the posh marble floor.

"What-*what* did you say?" I managed to get out.

Janette had the decency to look contrite. She closed her eyes for a moment and reached up to touch her hair again. It was her nervous tic, fixing imperfections that didn't exist. Checking her armor for chinks.

"I don't judge you for it, darling." She reached out a hand to touch mine gently. "Don't be like that. I understand, really. I've...been there myself once."

I blinked, confused. "With...Dad?"

Janette shook her head. "No, no, no. Later. One of...the others."

Her other husbands. I had always wondered, really, why she'd only ever had children with Maurice. Maybe in her odd way, she actually loved the man. But that didn't answer the question that was circling my head. How in the hell did she know about this in the first place?

Then, all at once, everything fell into place. I snatched my hand back and stepped away.

"So it was you," I muttered. "You were having me and Brandon followed, weren't you? It wasn't Miranda at all. It was you and Maurice."

Once again, Janette managed to look a bit contrite. "It was Maury's idea," she said. "I *told* him we didn't need to, that you'd help us out of the goodness of your heart if we just made the effort. But he was

362

convinced we would need leverage. Awful, I know, though it turns out he was right."

"So that's what this was all about?" I asked, more to myself than to her. "Spending the weekend in Cape Cod? Gallivanting to all of these stupid events? Carting your kids around like sideshow spectacles to lure me in?" My face felt like it was on fire, and I pressed my palms into my temples. "How long were you planning this? When I was in New York, Brandon and I were broken up. When did you start this...this...spying?!"

The words fell off my tongue like pieces of raw meat. I was disgusted by this. By everything. My own mother had had someone follow me, had paid someone to pry and uncover my deepest secrets so that she could blackmail me into helping her regain her fortune.

"That's not important." Janette looked uneasy as she wrapped her slim arms around her waist.

I furrowed my brow. "So how did you know about..."

"You were awfully loud at that bar after your exam," she said. She sighed. "I heard the tapes, and the boy you were talking to was more than happy to corroborate after you jilted him."

I gulped. Jared had ratted me out. And, I realized, was mostly likely the person who had corroborated Miranda's story to the *Globe* as well. What the fuck?

"One of the things I can teach you is how to put off potential suitors, or at least how to entertain them discreetly if you want," Janette said, almost as if she read my mind. "It's something I've learned well over the years. With looks like ours, they never stop. Certainly not after you're married." She patted her hair in the mirror, looking herself over appreciatively.

Suddenly I had absolutely no patience for her self-aggrandizing bullshit. "Did you tell anyone?" I demanded. "Anyone at all?"

Her green eyes widened, and she shook her head. "No, Skylar. I swear it, no one knows. And no one has to, if you'll just—"

Before she could finish her contemptible sentence, the door to one of the bathroom stalls opened, squealing on its hinges. Janette and I both froze, staring at each other in twin looks of horror as, on impossibly sharp heels that clipped across the marble floor, Miranda Sterling strode out in all her perfection.

Swathed in a sleek silver gown, she walked to the sink, and without looking at me, calmly washed her hands and dried them. I wondered if she did it that slowly to emphasize the fact that she still wore her rings: an impossibly large, square-cut diamond and an equally brilliant eternity band.

My left hand drifted up to my neck to touch the necklace. Miranda caught the movement, but her eyes dropped to my hand with its bare ring finger and down to my flat stomach. Then her gaze—cold, haughty, and blood-curdlingly knowing—swept up to my face. She smiled, and her slow, seeping grin turned my blood to ice.

She finished drying her hands, then turned on her heel.

"You ladies have a nice night," she said, and pushed the door open in front of her.

Janette brought a hand to her mouth. "Oh my. Was that..."

The terror that had been lodged firmly in my stomach since last night, when I'd seen the first evidence of Miranda's vendetta, blossomed throughout my entire body. Previously frozen in place, suddenly I couldn't move fast enough.

"I have to find Brandon," I said, moving quickly to leave. "I have to find him *right now.*"

"I'll help you!" Janette said with sudden determination. I whirled around to face her, with a finger in her face.

"You!" My voice was shaking while tears started to stream unbidden down my cheeks. I had fury, fear, frustration, all of it bubbling to the surface like I was a teakettle about to burst. "*You* have done quite e-*fucking*-nough! Stay the fuck out of my life! Stay out of my family's life! And tell Maurice he can take his fucking surveillance tapes and shove them up his tight French ass. If I ever feel even a whiff of a PI on my tail again, you two will be the first to enjoy a restraining order!"

"Skylar, wait!" Janette called out as I stormed out of the bathroom.

I didn't wait to listen to my mother. I should have listened to my own gut when it had told me not to let her close. But it was too late for that now.

I stormed down the hall, barely able to walk properly in the tubed shape of my dress, much less the heels that Mary had paired with it. I almost ran into Jared on my way back to the ballroom.

"Wow!" he yelped as I shouldered past him. "Skylar, what's up? Are you okay?"

Two seconds from losing it, I spun around.

"Am I okay?" I asked. "Am I *okay*? Well, I don't know, Jared. Would you be okay if you found out that your friend was a two-faced, shit-eating bastard who told your most personal stories to a perfect fucking stranger? Would *you* be okay, *Jared*?"

Jared held his hands up in defense, but when he caught the look on my face, they dropped. And then, to my surprise, he sneered.

"Well, what did you expect?" he said plainly. "You think you can get away with how you treated me? Do you know who my family is? People like us don't get turned down by a garbage collector's daughter."

He spat out the last words like they were some kind of disease. I shook violently.

"But I'll be honest," Jared continued. "Once you told me about your little secret, I was glad I'd dodged that bullet. I don't want used goods, especially a baby killer."

His words echoed down the tiled corridor, each one stabbing through my chest like a dagger. Jared just folded his arms over his chest and watched with something approximating glee while I crumpled.

"Who *are* you?" I asked, unable to think about anything else. Tonight was just one betrayal after another, to the point where I felt like I was living in an alternate universe.

Jared smarted. "I'm the same person I've always been, Skylar. You were just too dumb to see it."

He didn't even need to say anything else as the pieces clicked together. The number of times he'd mentioned that Miranda wasn't as bad as Brandon said. The fact that the Rounsavilles and the Keiths were old family friends. The way she never seemed to show up except when he was around.

"Oh my God," I gasped, my breath ragged as realization hit me. "You're the reason Miranda keeps showing up, aren't you? You were at the gala that that night, and now here again. You called her, didn't you? *Didn't you?*"

Jared didn't have to reply. His smug expression was answer enough.

"And the *Globe* article?" I continued. "It was you that confirmed that story? Who *gave them my name?*"

Jared shrugged. "They called. *I* don't have anything to hide, Skylar."

"You're a fucking sociopath," I spat back.

"Skylar?"

I turned around to find Kieran standing behind me, watching Jared with a curious, concerned look. How fitting, really. It was under Kieran's mentorship that I'd first learned about these kinds of people—consummate liars, pathological narcissists, people with no functioning sense of empathy. People who were excellent at posing as friends or lovers. A prince, she'd said, could turn out to be the devil in disguise.

I'd been so overwhelmed by Brandon's wealth at first, so worried that he would end up being that devil, that I'd forgotten to watch out for the other people in my life who fit the bill to a tee: My mother. My friend.

"What's going on?" Kieran asked, darting a sharp look at Jared. "Are you okay?"

I grasped her thin arm, an anchor in this crazy storm.

"I need to talk to Brandon," I said in a steadily cracking voice. "Before he gives his speech."

Kieran watched me for a half-second, then guided me to a small, empty conference room that stood off the side of the hallway. Jared strode away, hopefully back to the hole where he came from.

"Stay here," Kieran said as she guided me to a chair at a long conference table. "I'll get him."

So I buried my face in my hands and waited.

~

Chapter 39

Have you ever been trapped in an elevator? Had someone hug you so hard you couldn't breathe anymore? Had the wind knocked completely out of your belly?

That's what it felt like while I waited in the conference room, arms around my midsection, slowly rocking back and forth in the rolling chair while Kieran left to find Brandon. I prayed she would be able to bring him before his speech was supposed to start. I didn't think that he would announce his run before I returned. I hoped.

So I sat there, rocking, while the nondescript gray walls of the room closed in. I had played this scene over and over again in my mind over the last two months, rehearsing how exactly I would tell Brandon the news that I feared deep down would truly break us. That fear had stopped me so many times, but I couldn't let it now. He had to learn this from me—it was the only way he might forgive me for what I had done.

"She's just in here."

Kieran's voice was muffled through the oak door before it was pushed open, and she led a very worried-looking Brandon into the conference room. His ocean-blue eyes found me, and less than a second later, he was crouched by my side, large arms wrapped around my shaking form.

"Hey," he hummed against the crown of my head. "Shh, I'm here. I got you."

His kindness only made me shake more violently.

"Baby, what is it? What's wrong?" Brandon asked, as he cupped one side of my face with a big palm and stroked the edge of my cheekbone with his thumb.

The tenderness of the gesture choked up my throat, and almost immediately, tears started to flow again. I was so unworthy of his love—I could see that now. Maybe on some level, I always saw it. Even now, when Brandon had the world on his shoulders, when he was on the precipice of taking on even greater burdens and notoriety, he was still putting me first. I didn't deserve him.

"I-I have to tell you something," I managed to get out. "Before you...before you announce. There is something you need to know."

Brandon's normally smooth forehead crinkled in confusion. His hand rubbed my shoulder, and I fought the urge to lean in and let him hold me again. But that would be cruel and manipulative.

God, how was I going to get through it when I told him? When he inevitably left me?

"Hey," Brandon said kindly as he tried to pull me close again. "It's going to be okay. You can tell me anything, Red."

I resisted, but he wouldn't let me pull away. I relished his touch, knowing there was a decent chance I wouldn't get to feel it again after this.

"It's the campaign, isn't it?" Brandon asked as he pushed a hand through his hair. "It's too much, right? With Miranda here, it's too much. I can call it off, Skylar. Like I said, I won't do this without you."

"It-it's not that," I managed to croak.

Brandon blinked, his handsome face so thoroughly confused. "Then what is it?"

"It's probably this."

We both jerked our heads up as Miranda burst through the doors, holding a piece of paper and followed by Jared and Cory. She thrust it in front of Brandon. It appeared to be a black and white photograph of me leaving the free clinic in New York. Pictures I now knew had been taken by someone hired by my own family.

"What the fuck!" Jane's voice rang out as she and Eric tumbled in after everyone else. "She looks refined, but this chick just gouged half my arm."

She found me sitting in Brandon's embrace and gave me a look that said one thing loud and clear: I tried. I surveyed with horror at the crowd suddenly amassed in the room: three people eager to ruin me, the others there to help. So this was what it felt like to meet your executioners.

Slowly, Brandon picked up the photo. He looked to me, back to the photo, and back to me again, confusion riddled in thin lines across his forehead.

"What is this?" he asked. "Why were you...is everything okay?"

"It's what I'm trying to tell you," I said, my voice small and creaky as I looked at the damning picture. I could tell exactly when it was taken by the clothes and the way I was still walking with a protective hand over my midsection. I looked sick and underfed. I looked terrified.

Jane and Eric both came to sit at the table behind me, both of them looking curiously over my shoulder while they sat. Jane would obviously know what was going on. Eric, however, didn't have a clue.

"Maybe this will enlighten you, boss."

Cory set another piece of paper on the table, and looked at me with a satisfied smirk. My insides grew cold. Brandon immediately traded it for the first. I wanted to snatch them both away, but my body felt like it had lost all nerve endings.

"My sources in New York just delivered it," Cory said with a satisfied smirk at me. "Last of the vetting process."

"What is this?" Brandon asked again as he scanned the document.

He held out the simple white paper. I took it, although I already knew what it was. I didn't know how Cory had gotten it—a well-placed bribe, perhaps, even though whoever had leaked the information was breaking major privacy laws. He could write it off as part of the process of vetting Brandon's campaign run, but also, no doubt, it was something that allowed Cory to get rid of me. Because when I looked down at the paper, I saw the short record of my last free clinic visit, including the prognosis, with the words "mifepristone" and "misoprostol" written clearly under treatment.

"It's...it's the record of..." I trailed off, my voice hiccupping over itself. The words were literally so painful to get out. My throat ached with each one.

"It's a record of the abortion she had two months ago." Miranda's voice was clear and strong from where she stood at Brandon's shoulder. It rang through the room like a church bell. "It's simple, Bran."

Her long fingers stroked Brandon's thick hair. My tongue continued to lodge itself in the back of my throat, but I wanted to rip her fingers off. She was petting him like he was her dog, and the large diamond ring she still wore glinted under the fluorescent lights.

She set a proprietary hand on his shoulder before glaring at me. "She killed your baby."

Behind Brandon, Kieran covered her mouth with one hand and pulled her cell phone out of her pocket with the other. I closed my eyes again and cradled my forehead in my palms. I would have sold my soul to have been in any other room but this one. But, as Bubbe would say, I'd made my bed. It was far past time to lie in it.

"Oh, Christ on a fucking *cracker*," Jane retorted behind me. "That's a little melodramatic, don't you think? I mean, it was a cluster of cells at that point, not the divine infant."

"Jane," Eric said in a tone that said to shut the hell up.

"Well, it's true," she mumbled, but even I could hear the bitterness in my best friend's voice. She had thought my decision was a bad one from the beginning, particularly since it hadn't included Brandon. And she was right, of course. So very, very right.

Miranda was silent, but she continued to rub Brandon's shoulder, play with the curls at the base of his neck. Like she had a right to touch him that way. Like he was hers. My throat felt like it was being squeezed through; every bone in my body suddenly ached. But I knew I couldn't keep silent forever.

"Where did you get this?" I asked, finally finding the courage to look directly at Miranda. "This photograph? Were you having me followed too?"

She just arched a delicately shaped brow. "Turns out I didn't have to. Money will do a lot very quickly, sweetie," she said. "Especially with someone as desperate as your stepfather."

Beside her, Brandon blinked. Stun was written all over his features, rendering him utterly motionless while he stared at the papers in front of him. Then he finally looked at me. The utter horror in his clear blue eyes put an arrow straight through my heart.

"Skylar?" he asked in a voice that shook. "Is-is this true?"

Miranda's perfect, pink lips twisted into an ugly smirk. I gulped, begging my heart, beating so hard I could feel the vibrations through my chest, to slow down. It only beat faster.

My glass face obviously said it all. And for once, I wasn't sorry that I couldn't hide anything on it, because even if it cost me everything, the truth was out there. There would be nothing between us, even if the revelation blew us miles apart.

Brandon's face fell about three stories, and he literally fell backward in his crouch, as if his bones buckled under the pressure of his tall frame. He grabbed the edge of the table and squeezed so hard I thought his fingers might pop off as he moved to sit in one of the chairs.

"This is true?" he asked again. "You were—" his voice choked "—pregnant?"

I swallowed hard, trying and failing not to let my glance flutter around the room, to where Jane and Eric sat behind me, silently witnessing the proceedings, to where Miranda, Jared, and Cory watched with naked satisfaction, to where Kieran still stood quietly to the side, recording everything on her phone. She caught my gaze, but made no move to put her phone away. Good, I thought. Someone was doing what needed to be done to keep Brandon safe.

The paper in my hand crackled, and Brandon's eyes zeroed on it. He plucked it from my grasp and examined it again.

"And it was mine?" he asked once he'd determined he wouldn't learn any more from the paper, which he crumpled up and shoved into his jacket pocket.

My cheeks flamed. "Of course it was yours."

"And you never thought to say?" Brandon demanded in a low voice that was raising with every syllable. His eyes were suddenly very red around the rims, and his whole body vibrated. "You didn't think to tell me I was going to be a father?"

He swiped angrily at a few stray tears that escaped on the last word. The sight of them caused mine to flow freely all over again.

"I-I didn't mean to—" I started weakly.

"Didn't mean to what? Tell me about my own *kid*?" Brandon demanded in fractured, painful words. He snatched the paper out of his pocket and scanned it again. "Is this what you used? This mis-to-pro-stol? Is that what kill—what did it?"

I wiped at my tears, which just kept coming. Jane tried to pass a handkerchief over my shoulder, but I pushed it off. I didn't deserve pity right now. I didn't deserve anything but what I was getting.

"I...yes," I said in a splintered voice that didn't feel like my own. "Yes."

The room crackled. Miranda laid her hand back on Brandon's shoulder. I snarled at it this time, but Brandon flung it away when he stood up so quickly that his chair knocked clean over.

"'You can't hide things from me,'" he intoned nastily. "Isn't that what you said? 'We have to be honest with each other no matter what, Brandon.' Did I get that right?"

My face burned at his words—my words, which I'd used so sanctimoniously. "Yes," I whispered. "But, Brandon—"

371

"But *nothing*!" he roared.

He turned to leave, but stopped in the doorframe. His blue eyes were bright and full of pain. My tears continued down my cheeks in oceans, but he just watched impassively.

"It's not your fault, Bran." Miranda's voice rang out, snide and condescending through the room. "Lies, thievery. You can't expect much more from people who don't understand people like us. Who can't ever imagine what we have."

Kieran and I both stared at the woman who was so impossibly tone-deaf. Had she forgotten where her husband came from? That at one point in his life, he had had less than every single person in this room by a long shot?

Miranda just glared back with a thin eyebrow torqued up her high, glossy forehead. "For all you know," she said to Brandon, "she was just in it for the jewelry. Come to play dress up once the Bank of Sterling was open for business. Trying to pretend she's Cinderella."

Behind her, Jared snorted. "Pretend is right."

Miranda laughed.

Cory, of course, had to add in his two hateful cents: "No one in Boston will forgive an abortion, boss. Not in a city that's half Catholic."

In a sudden frenzy, I unclipped the necklace from around my neck as I finally found the strength to stand up. This was why I had always been so reluctant to accept gifts from him at all. There was always going to be someone saying things like this, accusing me of being in it just for his money.

"Here," I said as I held out the sparkling rope.

Brandon stared at the necklace like it was some kind of alien. He looked like he was trying to stop from crying.

"Take it," I said. "You know I never wanted this. I...I only ever wanted you."

Brandon's eyes flickered up from the necklace. For a moment, even with all of the sadness I saw there, I thought he might pull me to him, whisper it was going to be okay. There was still love shining through his grief. I could see it; it drew me to him, a moth to his sparkling blue flame.

He took the necklace from my hand, fingered it for a moment. Then his eyes shuttered. He dropped the necklace into his pocket.

"Then you shouldn't have broken my heart," he said, so quiet and forlorn that my heart practically wrenched out of my chest.

"Brandon," I begged. "Brandon, *please!*"

I tripped over myself trying to cross the short space between us, finally collapsing in front of him on my knees. Gently, he pulled me up to stand, and I gripped his hands, thirsty for his warm touch, luxuriating in it. And for a minute, I thought things might be okay again. I thought he might forgive me.

"You promised," I whispered as tears fell freely down my face, streaming rivers over my painted cheeks. "You said you'd never stop chasing. You said I had to stop running. Well, I'm *here*. I'm here for you now, and I know it's hard, but I'm not going anywhere!"

Brandon stared down at our clasped hands. His big fingers were motionless and wooden under mine, which clenched his palms so hard I knew he'd later see moon-shaped crescent marks from my fingernails. His thumb crept over my wrist and toyed with the edge of my bracelet: the silver cuff he'd given me, engraved with the immortal words of Yeats, written for a lover he'd chased his whole life.

One man loved the pilgrim soul in you.

And then, in one small, heartbreaking movement, Brandon pressed my fists back to my chest and let go.

"I can't."

The words were so low I barely heard them, but they had the power of a wrecking ball. My hands, as if by reflex, rose to the bared skin at my sternum and pressed at the spot that threatened to crack open.

"Brandon," I tried again, my voice unnaturally weak and pathetic. "Please!"

I saw then in his eyes, glossy, red-rimmed sapphire depths that were barely hanging on to his composure, a depth of pain I never thought possible. The rest of him was as immaculate as ever, but in his eyes, there were layers upon layers of hurt that arrowed through me in a second. And I had put it all there.

"I don't want you here," Brandon said finally, each word landing like a hammer. "Go."

He left. Miranda cast one last dagger-laced glance at me before exiting, Jared and Cory close behind.

"Don't think you're getting away with this," I heard Kieran say as Miranda passed. Then she looked at me with open pity. "I'll have a car come around to the garage," she said before she too walked out.

"Sky."

I turned and fell into the thin arms of my best friend, allowing her to soothe and stroke my hair while Eric looked on sympathetically. My whole body shook, wracked with the pain of what I'd just lost, the pain of my own mistakes.

"Come on," Jane said as she stroked my hair like I was a child. "Let's get you out of here."

I pushed away the strands of damp hair pasted to the side of my face. This time I accepted Eric's handkerchief, which I used to dab at the mess.

"We'll come with you," Jane said, turning to leave. "We were only here for you to begin with."

"No," I said as I handed Eric back his hankie. "You guys should enjoy your last night together. I...I just need to be alone."

"Sky," Jane started, obviously disagreeing with my plans. "It's fine. We can just—"

"No," I said with a vigorous shake of my head, causing what remained of my twist to come tumbling down over my shoulders. "I just want to be alone."

I didn't deserve anything else.

~

Chapter 40

I snuck out a service entrance in the garage instead of taking the Uber that Kieran had called, ignoring the Honda that was clearly waiting at the curb. Instead I walked home, ignoring the pain of the straps of my designer sandals dug into my swollen feet, ignoring the blisters that blossomed on the sides of my heels.

It took me five blocks to be able to walk and see at the same time, and five more to stop ugly-crying completely. I didn't know where exactly I was going, but eventually I found my way back to my apartment, where I tore off the beautiful blue dress and threw on clothes that felt more like me, less like I was playing dress-up and more like I was just Skylar, in all my horrible, imperfect glory.

In my favorite old jeans and a faded Harvard Law T-shirt, I pulled the remaining pins out of the hair and tossed them on my bureau before I twisted my carefully curled locks into a braid. With painful swipes across my cheeks, I removed all of the makeup, scrubbing my freckled skin clear so that it shined, ruddy from the crying and violence of my ministrations.

My eyes were puffy, my skin mottled between red and gray. I looked awful. I looked exactly how I felt.

My eyes caught the mass of shiny mahogany in the corner of my room: the piano from Janette. Its sheen mocked me—such a beautiful gift with such ugly intentions. Since Cape Cod, I'd actually started to play it, started to polish its surface, which was now stacked with sheet music. How could I have been taken in by her again? I was no better than my father.

With a strangled shout, I hurled the nearest, heaviest thing at the piano—a stone paperweight on my desk made of a blue agate geode. In certain lights, it sparkled just like Brandon's eyes when he was happy. When he looked at me with love. But the piano was a stalwart beast that barely retained a scratch; the geode cracked in half and fell to the floor in pieces.

I screamed into my pillow. I gazed around my bedroom, with its bright blue walls exactly the color of Brandon's eyes, the rumpled sheets that would probably still smell of his soap-and-almond scent, the stray pieces of men's extra-large clothing in my closet and in the dresser drawer I'd given him. I couldn't stay in a room I'd designed unwittingly to remind me of the man I'd just betrayed, the man whose heart I'd torn out and, in the process, torn out my own.

Just the thought caused another avalanche of tears. *You shouldn't have broken my heart*, he'd said, and God, I knew it. My own heart was like the geode, smashed completely, scattered all over Boston.

And worst of all, I'd done it to myself.

I yanked my purse off the back of my desk chair and pulled the leather strap over my chest. I stuffed my wallet into the bag, but decided to leave my phone, already full of messages from Jane, Eric, and Kieran, on my desk. I had to get out of here, yesterday, and I wasn't interested in anyone being able to find me.

I wandered around the streets of the North End for what felt like hours until I came to a nearly deserted diner near the highway, the kind of place that only old-time locals still went to because it was so far off the main streets. Gray and tube-shaped, it was grimy and empty—the only kind of place I deserved to be.

I grabbed a seat on one of the torn vinyl stools at the bar and ordered a coffee from the tired-looking waitress named Faye who had one of the thickest Boston accents I'd ever heard. When I took a drink, I scowled. It was weak and tasted like an ashtray, and I didn't even like coffee in the first place. So I took another sip, and then another.

The small TV above the counter had been turned to a local news station. A clip of Brandon popped onto the screen, and my heart twisted.

A low whistle came from Faye. She was older, with lines down her weathered skin and limp, graying roots of her bottle-blonde hair showing at the scalp. She watched the footage of Brandon on the red carpet with obvious appreciation.

"Could...could you turn it up?" I requested in a voice that still croaked a bit.

The waitress turned to me with a knowing smile. "Gorgeous, ain't he? Local boy too. I'd vote for that smile in a hot second."

She turned up the television to an audible level, and we listened together as the anchor narrated the events of the night:

"In a move that has been rumored for months, Brandon Sterling, CEO of Sterling Ventures and name partner of Sterling Grove law firm, has formally announced his bid for mayor of Boston. The DNC is expected to endorse the local entrepreneur and philanthropist."

The screen cut to a brief clip of Brandon announcing his run to the roomful of reporters at the event I had just fled. My chest contracted. You couldn't tell he had just walked out of the room where I'd broken his heart, where I'd broken *us*. Every hair was perfectly in place, not a wrinkle, not even a crooked shirt cuff.

But I could see the slip of white paper barely sticking out of his jacket pocket. I could see the distance in his eyes as he made his announcement, and the dulled expression made my heartache even worse. I had done that. I had snuffed out that light in him that shined so brightly.

The anchor droned on.

"Despite an interview yesterday from Miranda Sterling detailing some of the recent troubles in their marriage, Sterling's relationship with his wife seemed to be as affectionate as ever as they appeared together after the announcement."

My face turned hot with fury as the screen cut to another clip of Brandon shaking hands with people in the room while Miranda stood by his side, her arm tucked easily into the crook of his. They looked so natural together, like they had done this time and time again. She was much taller than me, with movie star looks, likely perfected over the years with gentle nudges from a dermatologist, that matched her husband's. Together they glowed.

I wanted to vomit.

"Lucky bitch," the waitress murmured to herself as she watched the clip. She looked to me over her shoulder with a wry, raised eyebrow. "Am I right, or am I right?"

I couldn't speak, so I just nodded and took another sip of the ashy coffee. Lucky bitch indeed.

The anchor continued: "The announcement preceded an additional, surprising twist that Sterling intends to divest fully from both of his businesses in order to avoid any conflicts of interest."

Surprising to them, maybe, but not to me or anyone else close to his life. The clip cut away to pictures of Ray and Susan, who stood next to him with bewildered expressions. I wasn't the only one who was overwhelmed. I wondered how many times Brandon's tendency toward largesse made them feel like this.

The coverage cut to another clip from Brandon's speech, in which he spoke carefully and clearly, his voice radiating confidence and poise:

"If I'm going to do this, I'm going to do it right. I must remove all ethical obstacles in my path, anything that might call into question my dedication to making Boston a better place for everyone. As anyone who knows me will say, when I do something, I give it everything I have. So from this moment forward, I serve the people of Boston, and no one else."

There was a smattering of loud applause, although I didn't miss the look of utter and complete shock on Miranda's face before Brandon flashed the crowd his trademark smile and the clip cut back to the anchor. She pivoted to another news story, and I turned back to my coffee, my chest hollow and numb.

"You okay, hon? You look like you're having a rough night."

Faye tapped her scraggly fingernails on the stained countertop. There were only a few other people in the diner: an obviously inebriated couple crowding one side of a booth and an off-duty construction worker who looked even more tired than I did.

I sighed and nodded. "I'm fine."

Faye looked like she didn't believe me, but just refilled my coffee cup. "Can I get you somethin' to eat? You look like you could use a bite or two."

In fact, my stomach was growling again, but I couldn't have eaten a thing. I just shook my head and drank my coffee, relishing the bitter, stale taste. I toyed with the silver cuff still hanging around my wrist, more solid than the rest of me felt. I pulled it off and ran my thumb over the gold-embossed inscription.

One man loved the pilgrim soul in you

It was fitting really. I'd looked up the poem it came from so many times that I had it memorized. It was one of the many beautiful pieces of poetry that Yeats had written for Maud Gonne, his decades-long unrequited love. He chased her for almost twenty years, during her marriage to another man, even to the point where eventually he proposed to her daughter just to get to her. It was a mad love, the kind of love that lasted a lifetime.

I'll never stop chasing you, Brandon had once told me. He had given me this bracelet after I'd put him off again and again. The quote, a bit from a poem where Yeats warns Gonne of the regrets she'll have, referred to the uniqueness of his adoration for her. That he saw her as no one else. And that one day, she'd realize it and wish she had acted differently.

I didn't need to wait until I was old to have those regrets. I was completely and utterly filled with them. Now it seemed that the tables had turned. I'd be the one loving Brandon's pilgrim soul. I'd be the one pining for someone else my whole life while he moved on to bigger and better things.

~

The night sky was completely black when I finally shuffled up the stairs of my apartment, well past midnight. I took comfort in the fact that I could continue my wallowing alone. Eric and Jane would be gone, off to bid their farewells at the airport before Jane left for Chicago.

But as my head peeked over the landing of the third floor, I caught sight of a pair of men's black leather shoes and black pants through the weathered wood railing. Momentarily, my heart surged. Brandon.

"There she is. How you doin', Red? Thought you'd never get here."

And just like that, my heart fell to the bottom of my stomach. There was another person who called me that sometimes. The voice, thick with Brooklyn twang, raunchy in its slow, thick-lipped drawl, made my skin crawl.

Three more pairs of feet appeared next to the originals. I looked up. The round, sweaty face of Victor Messina leered over the railing, his half-smile pushing into the layers of fat that surrounded a set of tobacco-stained teeth.

"We been waitin' around here for a while, sweetheart," he greeted me. "Now, now, don't run off, baby girl," he said as I took a few steps back.

He pulled aside his jacket to reveal a paunch that piled over the edge of a handgun tucked into his waistband: a nine-millimeter Glock, the kind I'd seen before, toted by neighborhood gangsters and on homicide specials.

"How-how did you find me?" I asked, my voice unsteady as I gripped the edge of the railing, tensed like a rabbit. *Run*, a voice inside my head screamed. But the gun was big and black, and I was stuck.

379

"Oh, it wasn't so hard," Messina said, smacking his thick lips. "You made a mistake, see, challenging Katie like that. She don't like bein' challenged so much. She'll get even with you later."

He chuckled with his henchman, as if they were both sharing some recalled memory of Katie Corleone, one that was almost certainly not appropriate for most people to know about. Every muscle in my body pulled taut.

"She mentioned your man, and imagine my surprise when she told me he'd been on the cover of a magazine last month. And now he's runnin' for mayor?" The gangster clicked his tongue, causing the collection of skin under his jaw to wobble. "Now that's power."

"I'll—I'll call him," I volunteered, my voice tripping over itself. "He'll give you whatever you want, I know he will."

Victor nodded in agreement, and his friends nodded as well, their fat heads bobbing in terrifying unison.

"Oh, I'm sure he will, honey." But his eyes glinted like steel. "Which is why you're gonna come with us, Red."

Maybe it was the look in his beady eyes. Maybe it was the thought of having his ham-shaped fingers on me. Maybe it was the basic realization that if I did go with Victor Messina, I might not ever come back. But my fight-or-flight instinct switched on.

"No," I said.

My feet started to work before my brain did. Moving on pure instinct and adrenaline, I fled down the stairs, ignoring the gunshots that slammed the plaster behind my back. Messina's and his thug's heavy footsteps slammed on the cracked marble stairs, but not as quickly as mine. GET OUT, my brain shouted at me, over and over again.

There it was: the heavy brass door that would lead to my cobbled street, and then to Hanover, to crowds, to police officers, to safety. I sprinted towards it while Messina and his thugs hammered down the last flight of stairs behind me.

Hand outstretched, I almost reached the door.

And then I tripped on a broken tile. And I fell.

"Get her."

Before I could even start to struggle, the last thing I saw was Messina's angry, bloated face stretched into a vengeful smile.

"Got ya, sweetheart," he stated clearly, before slammed the butt of his gun to the back of my head.

Then I saw nothing at all.

~

Epilogue

David pulls the Mercedes in front of Skylar's brick building, a black SUV of security right behind us. It's not a building I like much. The dilapidated outside, with its crumbling mortar and casual graffiti on the corners, reminds me too much of the kinds of places where I grew up before finding some peace and stability at the Petersens' house. Places where I was crammed into bunkbeds a foot too short for my legs. Places where sometimes I'd get the harsh end of a belt if I cried too hard or chewed too loud. Places where sometimes the older kids would try to touch me in ways I knew, even as a little kid, were wrong. Places where I learned to defend myself against just about anything.

I'm not sure what I'm doing here. I take out the white paper, creased again and again, first from being kept inside her stepfather's pockets, then Miranda's hands, then stuck in my jacket for the last several hours. It looks so harmless, but it's basically a hand grenade, considering what it just did to my life. To my heart.

I stare at the building while I pull my tie loose and unbutton my shirt collar. My jacket is on the seat beside me. It's hot, even for Boston in July, even for one in the morning. Fifteen years ago, in this mood? I'd have been picking a fight in a bar, maybe already been kicked out. But right now, I'd like to be back at my apartment, go for a dive in the rooftop pool for the penthouse residents. I'd like to turn on SportsCenter and watch Red Sox highlights until I pass out on that ungodly uncomfortable couch. I'd like to throw back a bottle of bourbon and pretend this night never happened.

But instead I'm here, and I couldn't tell you why. I should be done for the night. I made my announcement to a roomful of onlookers, satisfying Kieran and Ray and Susan and everyone else who expects me to do great things. Scariest fucking thing I ever did. And I did it without the one person who doesn't expect me to be anything but myself, the one person who has only ever wanted me for just me. I thought of her warm green eyes, her kissable smile the entire fucking time. I felt like my insides were turning to dust.

Then I walked back to that same conference room where my heart had just been pulverized and informed my soon-to-be ex-wife that she'll be signing our divorce papers tomorrow, or else I'll file the charges myself against her, Maurice, and Jared for conspiracy and extortion. Thank God for Kieran and her phone, is all I can say about that.

And now I'm here. To do what, I don't know. But Skylar's my magnet, my True North. Every time I close my eyes, all I can see is her face, the pain etched across her delicate skin that shows so beautifully every emotion she has. I don't know if I can forgive her for what she's done-—every time I think of it, my chest practically caves in. But I can't just walk away. I don't know if I ever could.

"Getting out, sir?"

David has opened my door and smiles at me with a kind face—the kind of expression I've always hoped to see from Ray, and once upon a time, my own father, who is still rotting in prison.

I shove the paper back in my pocket and get out.

The door to the building is hanging ajar again. It's something I've been wanting Skylar to take up with her landlord for a while. I don't like the idea of her staying in an unsecured building, especially with everything up in the air about her dad's issues.

I push open the door and enter the building, but I hesitate. Maybe I should wait. Tensions are high, and my chest still feels like I can't breathe. It might be better if I wait until tomorrow, until I've taken out my pain and frustration on my trainer, until I can approach the situation with a clearer head. Things are always better in the morning.

But then I see it: the small leather pouch that looks completely familiar, lying at the bottom of the big, cracked stairwell. The hair on the back of my neck stands up as I realize who it belongs to. *Skylar.*

Slowly, I crouch down to pick it up. It's missing its wallet, and one side of the strap has been torn from its stitching. I turn toward the glass entrance and beckon my security manager, Craig. Craig is former military and also a former cop. He knows his shit, which is why I hired him. He also has about as much warmth as a refrigerator.

"Sir?" he asks as he strides into the lobby. He takes one look at the purse in my hands and starts scanning the area for the same things I am: signs of struggle.

My whole body turns cold as I find what I'm looking for: a streak of blood on one of the stained white tiles. Craig sees it too. Immediately, he presses the button on his earpiece.

"We've got a two-oh-seven Adam with signs of struggle."

I'm already bounding up the stairs, stumbling as I see the clear blasts in the plaster walls, a few empty shells lying on the floor.

Her apartment door is open, its lock clearly broken. Skylar's phone is sitting on her desk, which tells me one thing: she never actually made it inside.

"Cardinal's absent from the scene," Craig says behind me. "Clear two-oh-seven."

But I can barely hear him. Now I can't think of anything else. Not a baby that never was. Not the fact that I just became a politician.

All I can think is: I gotta find my girl.

To Be Continued...

Thank you so, so much for reading the second part of the Spitfire Trilogy. If you enjoyed this book, please take a few moments to review it. Your feedback means everything to indie authors like me.

For updates and excerpts for upcoming works, follow me on Facebook at www.facebook.com/authornicolefrench
or sign up for my mailing list at www.nicolefrenchromance.com.

XO,
Nic

Acknowledgments

To start, I have to once again thank my family, especially my husband, dude of all dudes, for giving me the time and space to write this story. I know it's hard when I get lost in a story for sometimes days at a time, so thank you, babe, for letting my imagination take over our life every now and then. I love you.

I'd also like to thank the usual suspects who are essential to writing this story. Burton, my legal translator, who gave me especially juicy details about the terrible behavior of new law grads after taking the bar exam. Sarah, again, for her Yiddish consultations. Michaela and Talia, for your fantastic beta reading. And Ava, Lacie, and Jessica for all the help and support in these final editing and design stages. I'm so lucky to have tapped into such a fantastic community of indie writers. I am in your debt.

And of course, **I want to thank YOU, the reader.** For every one of you who has told me you're in love with Brandon, I say: ME TOO! For each of you who has sent me a note, a review, a kind word encouraging this story along, you make my heart sing. Skylar and Brandon's journey can't continue without your support and investment: this next book, their Happily Ever After (and yes, it IS coming) is for YOU.

xo,
Nic

About the Author

Nicole French is a lifelong dreamer, hopeless romantic, Springsteen fanatic, and complete and total bookworm. When not writing fiction or teaching composition classes, she is hanging out with her family, playing soccer with the rest of the thirty-plus crowd in Seattle, or going on dates with her husband. In her spare time, she likes to go running with her dog, Greta, or practice the piano, but never seems to do either one of these things as much as she should.

Connect with Nicole French

For more information about Nicole French and to keep informed about upcoming releases, please visit her website at www.nicolefrenchromance.com.

Like on Facebook at www.facebook.com/authornicolefrench
Follow on Twitter at www.twitter.com/nfrenchauthor
Follow on Instagram www.instagram.com/authornicolefrench
Follow on Pinterest www.pinterest.com/nfrenchauthor

Acknowledgments

First and foremost, I'd like to thank my mom for her sense of romance and whimsy. If it hadn't been for the years and years of watching chick flicks and reading romance novels together, I probably wouldn't have the sense of optimism needed to write romance in a world like today's.

Secondly, I'd like to thank my husband and my family for giving me the support I need to write, even if it's just for twenty minutes a day while the kid is taking a bath. Writing kept me sane in these first crazy years of our life together, and it keeps me present moving forward too. I love you, always.

There are a lot of people who also took the time to help with the production of my first novel. Sarah, for her lovely advice on plot development and Yiddish. Don, for his exclamations when I told him I was attempting my first novel, and that it was actually genre fiction to boot. And more than anyone else, Burton, who was my final beta reader and legalese extraordinaire. Couldn't have written half the book without you. Thank you, friend!

And most importantly, **I want to thank you, the reader.** Skylar and Brandon's journey can't continue without your support and investment. If you enjoyed their story, **I would so, so, so appreciate your review on any of the online retailers through which you purchased this book.** I can't do this without you, lovely readers, who are the real muse of these stories.

About the Author

Nicole French is a lifelong dreamer, hopeless romantic, and complete and total bookworm. When not writing fiction or teaching composition classes, she is hanging out with her family, playing soccer with the rest of the thirty-plus crowd in Seattle, or going on dates with her husband. In her spare time, she likes to go running with her dog, Greta, or practice the piano, but never seems to do either one of these things as much as she should.

Connect with Nicole French

For more information about Nicole French and to keep informed about upcoming releases, please visit her website at www.nicolefrenchromance.com.

Like on Facebook at www.facebook.com/authornicolefrench
Follow on Twitter at www.twitter.com/nfrenchauthor
Follow on Instagram www.instagram.com/authornicolefrench
Follow on Pinterest www.pinterest.com/nfrenchauthor
Check out my Goodreads Page!

Made in the USA
San Bernardino, CA
11 September 2018